EVIE GRACE

The *Golden Maid*

arrow books

1 3 5 7 9 10 8 6 4 2

Arrow Books
20 Vauxhall Bridge Road
London SW1V 2SA

Arrow Books is part of the Penguin Random House group
of companies whose addresses can be found at
global.penguinrandomhouse.com.

Penguin
Random House
UK

First published in Great Britain by Arrow Books in 2020

www.penguin.co.uk

A CIP catalogue record for this book is available from
the British Library.

ISBN 9781787464414

Typeset in 10.75/13.5 pt Palatino
by Integra Software Services Pvt. Ltd, Pondicherry

Printed and bound in Great Britain by Clays Ltd, Elcograf S.p.A.

Penguin Random House is committed to a
sustainable future for our business, our readers
and our planet. This book is made from Forest
Stewardship Council® certified paper.

To my family and friends

Acknowledgements

I should like to thank Laura and everyone at MBA Literary Agents, and Jennie and the team at Penguin Random House UK for their enthusiasm and support for 'The Smuggler's Daughters' series.

Chapter One

Every Herring Must Hang by its Own Gill

Deal, December 1812

'Miss Winifred Lennicker of Compass Cottage, Cockle Swamp Alley, Deal. You are charged that on the eighth day of December 1812, you were found in possession of goods illegally imported from France, namely a half-anker of cognac hidden in a handcart. Furthermore, you obstructed a Riding officer whilst he was carrying out his duties in accordance with the law.'

Trembling, Winnie stood listening from the dock as Reverend North, a well-fed gentleman in his fifties, wearing a cassock and Canterbury cap from which dangled strands of powdered grey hair, gazed at her from the Bench in the crowded courtroom. She glanced from the vicar to his fellow magistrates, Mr Norris, a portly figure with a florid complexion who had placed his whip and gold watch on the table in front of him, and Mr Causton, landlord of the Waterman's Arms. Standing to their left was Officer Chase who was bringing the case against her on behalf of the Revenue, watched by an audience of Winnie's family, and many of the townspeople of Deal, both friends and strangers.

The stench of sweat and filthy clothes cut through the perfume of rosewater and the herbs that had been scattered across the floor, making her retch. She was in deep water and it wasn't her fault.

'How do you plead?' the vicar went on.

'Stop!' interrupted Officer Chase. 'There is another charge to be included.'

Reverend North gave a weary sigh. 'I understand that you are keen to obtain a conviction and hold this young woman up as an example to those who are involved in the free trade, sir, but may I suggest that your enthusiasm has as much to do with your desire for pecuniary reward as it does for your wish to see justice carried out.'

'You may suggest no such thing,' Officer Chase protested as a ripple of laughter spread through the courtroom. Everybody knew that he would receive a bonus if the case that he'd brought against Winnie was proven.

'These are summary offences that can be dealt with quickly and quietly by the Bench here,' Reverend North said haughtily.

'The prisoner –' Winnie didn't like the way the officer lingered on the word '– tried to deceive me by pretending to be someone else. Impersonation is a capital offence. Miss Lennicker must go to trial at the Assizes in front of a judge and jury. I am determined on this course – I will not be gammoned by the villains of Deal any longer. They have led the Revenue a merry dance for long enough.' Officer Chase was a young man, of not more than five and twenty, who stood tall and straight-backed in his riding clothes, his spurs flashing at his ankles. 'Of course, we all know why you won't consider this latter charge, Reverend ...'

'Are you questioning my impartiality?'

"E's a man of the cloth, and as honest as the day is long,' someone shouted.

'What am I to think when it's always the same? My orders are to arrest those responsible for importing contraband, yet no matter how many times I bring prisoners in front of the magistrates in this godforsaken town, they get away with their crimes. I've been a Riding officer for over a year now, employed along the coast to intercept the free traders as they carry goods inland, having dodged the Revenue cruisers looking out for them at sea. I'm no longer wet behind the ears. I've seen how this works.'

'What do you expect? You'll catch anybody who's goin' around mindin' their own business, then plant evidence on 'em,' called another heckler.

'You have no proof,' Officer Chase said, his face scarlet with annoyance.

'Quiet, please.' The vicar raised an eyebrow. 'Let the officer speak. We haven't got all day.'

'I object to Mr Norris being present on the Bench.'

'On what grounds?'

'The accused is known to him. He is married to the prisoner's cousin.'

'I see. Why did you not mention this, George?'

Mr Norris leaned forward, squinting in Winnie's direction.

'I apologise for not making the connection. I am barely acquainted with my wife's cousin,' he said awkwardly. 'I hardly recognise her – she has grown quite paunchy, like a bitch in whelp.'

'She *is* in whelp, I reckon,' Winnie heard Mrs Roper muttering to one of the other boatmen's wives as Officer Chase asked Reverend North what he was intending to do about Mr Norris. The crowd, impatient with the delay for a point of order, began to talk amongst themselves.

Winnie noticed her brother-in-law, Jason Witherall, a Deal boatman, standing shoulder to shoulder with his crew, having decided to attend the hearing rather than launch their giant three-masted lugger, the *Whimbrel*, that day. Usually they would be out cruising, delivering pilots, anchors and letters for the merchant ships and men-o'-war that were anchored in the Downs, the stretch of deep water that lay between Deal beach and the Goodwin Sands about a league distant. Or they would be rescuing sailors and cargoes from vessels in distress for salvage money, cover for their more profitable activities.

She was touched by their support. The free traders often fought each other, but when they were running prohibited goods – gin, silk and lace – from Gravelines, unloading them and carrying them inland to hide or sell, they worked together in harmony against the Revenue. However, Winnie couldn't help wondering if their presence, along with that of the other families who were involved in the free trade – men, women and children – all staring at her when she hated attention of any sort even at the best of times, was more of a hindrance than a help.

The vicar brought his gavel down thrice, calling everyone to silence.

'Mr Causton and I have come to a decision. Mr Norris will remain in his place, but he will not make a judgement on this particular case. Contrary to your opinion that we are biased against the Revenue, Officer Chase, we have also decided to hear your charge that the prisoner took on another person's identity with intent to deceive.' The vicar's words turned the blood in Winnie's veins to ice.

Gasps of shock and cries of horror echoed around the courtroom and some of the onlookers started to argue that it wasn't right or fair.

Winnie searched the crowd for her sisters, catching sight of them as they pushed their way to the front. Louisa who was twenty, two years older than Winnie, and married, was leading their younger sister, sixteen-year-old Grace, by the hand. Both were dressed modestly in their Sunday best, Louisa in a navy gown and redingcote, and Grace in one of Louisa's hand-me-downs, a dark brown dress adorned with black ribbon.

'My sister has done nothing wrong,' Louisa said, addressing the magistrates. 'It's me who should be on trial, not her. We were out all day yesterday, selling provisions to the ships in the Downs. When we returned, I left the handcart unattended outside the house for a while. Someone must have placed the cask inside it then.'

Winnie was grateful to her for trying. In fact, she rather expected it because Winnie's presence had distracted Officer Chase, meaning Louisa had got away. However, her sister's intervention would make no difference. Nothing would. She didn't care about the minor charges – the Deal magistrates were notorious for making sure that the punishment fitted the crime. For being found in possession of some cognac and obstructing a Riding officer, she might get a fine and a spell in gaol, but if indicted on the charge of lying about her identity, she would be on her way to the Assizes.

Her throat contracted as though the noose was already tightening around her neck.

She squeezed her eyes shut and pressed her hands to her ears as the courtroom descended into uproar. If asked to describe herself, she would say she was a humble and ordinary young woman who loved cooking and cleaning. Only a few days ago on Stir Up Sunday, she had been making plum pudding for the Christmas festivities, stirring currants and raisins with eggs and flour until her arms ached. How had she come to this?

The previous morning, she'd woken with a sense of unease which intensified when she noticed the pennants of grey cloud streaming across a fiery sky as she swept the pavement outside the cottage with its tall chimney stacks and tiled roof. Blowing on her fingers, she'd returned inside to find Louisa and Grace lining up baskets of pies and apples, and packets of salted pork in the hallway.

'Red sky in the morning, sailors' warning,' she said.

'That won't stop us,' Louisa scolded lightly. 'The weather's set fair, according to Jason. He left hours ago. Apparently, the herring are swimming up in walms – I thought we'd do a little fishing at the same time. Oh, Winnie, don't be such a mouse.' She smiled. 'Jason will rush to our rescue if anything should go wrong, which it won't. He's out with the *Whimbrel*, taking a pilot out to one of His Majesty's ships.'

Grace disappeared into the kitchen to fetch the net that Winnie had repaired using fresh twine and wooden shuttles the evening before, straining her eyes in the flickering flame of a tallow candle. Grace had rinsed and dried the pigs' bladders that their uncle had sent from Limepit Acres. Louisa had sewn up the holes and filled them with cognac. It always arrived from France concentrated to seventy per cent proof, but they watered it down and caramelised it to suit the English preference.

The bladders were sitting in string bags in a bucket. Winnie eyed them with distaste.

'There are two each,' Louisa said. 'Two for you, two for me.'

'What about Grace?' Winnie asked.

'Louisa says I'm too much of a clumsy clodpole to carry cognac – I've burst one too many bladders in the past.'

6

Grace chuckled. 'I'm going to bring some lace in case I can persuade a jolly Jack Tar to buy a piece for his sweet-heart.'

'Take this.' Louisa handed Grace a length of white galloon. 'It isn't the best and it's a little grubby, so I can't sell it to our more discerning customers.'

She meant the ladies of the ton with their snowy faces and dark eyebrows, Winnie thought as Grace wrapped it around her middle over her dress, then fastened her cloak over the top.

'I wish I had a figure like yours.' Winnie envied her younger sister's elegance and narrow waist. A head taller than Winnie and almost the same height as Louisa, Grace had recently shot up like a runner bean.

'Some ladies can't help being stout,' she said gently.

She was being kind, refraining from giving Winnie the truth. She wasn't merely stout – she freely admitted that she was beginning to look like one of their uncle's fat pigs.

'We are both jealous of your hair,' Louisa joined in. 'God blessed you with golden locks while we take after Ma, God rest her soul.'

Winnie felt slightly mollified – Louisa's hair was dark brown, and Grace had thick ebony tresses – although her sisters' attempts to cheer her up couldn't pull her out of the megrims. Louisa considered herself the luckiest woman alive, being married to Jason Witherall, or Marlin – short for marlinspike – as he was known among the men, while Grace was always happy and smiling, with hardly a care in the world.

Winnie helped load the handcart, a painful reminder of Billy who was supposed to have oiled its squeaky wheels but had never got around to it. She didn't enjoy feeling sorry for herself, but she considered that she'd been hard done by. Since her beloved Billy had been taken by the

7

gangers back in August and 'volunteered' for service in the King's Navy, threads of sorrow and anxiety had woven themselves inextricably into the fabric of her daily life. She thought of him every day, missing his warmth and cheeky smile, and each night, she lit a candle for him to light his way in case he should arrive back home.

As she walked with her sisters along Cockle Swamp Alley and crossed Beach Street to the shore, two bladders of cognac hidden under her skirts, Winnie refused to consider that Billy might not be alive. They passed the sheds and boats that lined the steep shelving beach where some of the older boatmen were looking out to sea. Old Mr Witherall, who stood with a blanket around his shoulders, was chatting to Smoker Edwards, who was perched on a tub. Terrier Roper was leaning against a capstan, cutting baccy for his pipe.

Master Appleton was waiting for them, his nose dripping congbells in the cold air. He was twelve years old and small for his age.

'Mornin' ladies,' he grinned, revealing the gap in his upper jaw where he had lost his two front teeth after an incident with a mast. Having relieved Grace of the handcart, he shoved it across the shingle to their boat, the *Curlew*, one of a handful left at the top of the slope between the huts and piles of lobster pots.

'Good morning, Cromwell,' Grace said.

Shivering despite wearing two flannel petticoats, two pairs of stockings, a felt hat and gloves, Winnie gazed from the small fishing boat and her single mast to the three hundred or so merchant ships, men-o'-war and Revenue cruisers assembled in the Downs beneath a flat grey sky. An East Indiaman, an armed merchantman in her characteristic black livery with a cream and yellow trim, and copper below the waterline, stood nearby. There

8

was barely a ripple to be seen across the surface of the sea. Where was Billy? Was he out there somewhere?

She winced as Louisa pinched her arm.

'What was that for?' she said, affronted.

'You're supposed to be helping us.'

'I'm sorry,' she muttered.

'I'm sorry too. We're all thinking of him,' Louisa said gently, her eyes filled with compassion.

'Thank you.' Overwhelmed, Winnie turned away, hiding fresh tears as she picked up a basket.

It wasn't long before they had loaded the *Curlew* and were ready to launch, Winnie and her sisters sitting in the boat with Cromwell, holding tight to the gunwales and looking down at the sea thirty yards below, while another of the shore boys prepared to release the rope attached to the *Curlew*'s bow.

'Let her go,' Louisa shouted, and the shore boy let go of the rope.

The *Curlew* began to move stern-first, accelerating over the rollers that were laid in a row down the beach, until she flew into the water, hitting it with an enormous bang. As she settled, Cromwell used an oar to push them clear of the beach. Winnie took the helm while Louisa and Grace rigged the lugsail and Cromwell bailed out a couple of buckets of water from the *Curlew*'s hull, and they set out across the water, joining the other small boats competing to provision the large vessels that stood in the roadstead.

Later, they cast out the net and fished for a while at a mark to the south. Looking behind her, Winnie could see the white cliffs of Dover and to the north, the town of Deal with its muddle of houses – some with red Dutch roofs, some tiled, some thatched – built along the beach. There were tents as well, thrown up on the spit by the wives of the soldiers who had been called to war. Having nowhere

9

else to go, they had followed their men as far as they could and settled down to wait for them to come back.

'Winnie, you are in a world of your own,' she heard Louisa say. 'I said, it's time we were going home.'

'It's turned out to be a good day, despite your doubts to the contrary,' Grace said cheerfully, looking at their empty baskets and the leather buckets spilling over with herring. 'We've sold everything except the lace, and the Revenue didn't bother us.'

Winnie had to admit that it had been better than she'd expected.

Having left the herring to rouse in salt for a few hours the same evening, it was after dark by the time Winnie went back into the hang, a small extension attached to the rear of the cottage. Using sticks as spits, she hooked the silver fish by the gills along their length, then clambered up the ladder to hang them in the dark chamber above her head where the timbers were tarred with oil and smoke from years of use. After climbing down again, she fetched a candle and touched its flame to the pile of oak shavings, coaxing them into a quiet smoulder.

She watched a curl of smoke rise into the air and snake its way around the deeply forked tails of the row of fish, transforming them into bloaters. By morning, the skins would have turned to gold and their flesh grown soft, gamey and ready to eat – just as Billy liked them.

Winnie dashed a hot tear from her cheek as she remembered their neighbour's son, a boy with dirty knees and a twinkle in his eye, whose father had gone to sea a few weeks after he was born and was never heard of again. They'd called him 'carrot top' and 'big ears' and teased him mercilessly about his freckles and the holes in his shoes until Ma had given them a stern telling-off. Mrs

Fleet, his mother, struggled to get by, and Ma used to give her their broken bloaters while Pa took Billy out fishing.

She recalled one occasion when they had returned from a fishing trip. Billy, who could only have been about nine or ten, had dragged a bucket of fish into the house.

'It's the best catch I've ever seen,' he'd grinned, his eyes lit up with joy. 'Mr Lennicker says I can take some 'ome to Ma to sell them fresh from the barrer.'

''Ow many 'errin' did we bring back?' Pa said, bewildering him.

Winnie, who was eight at the time, had known that he couldn't count to more than the sum of his fingers and toes. She'd watched him put the basket down, put his finger to his mouth and stare towards the ceiling, thinking.

'Well, lad?' Pa had said.

'There's one missin',' he'd said, and Pa had roared with laughter.

Winnie had thought that Billy might burst into tears, but he hadn't.

'You're a smart one,' Pa had chuckled, and Billy had started laughing too. 'Mrs Lennicker will l'arn you some 'rithmetic. I'll tell you 'ow to count 'errin' into warps, long hundreds, cran baskets and lasts.'

Billy hadn't been entirely attentive to his studies, preferring to be down on the beach with the other shore boys than in the parlour with Ma, but he had learned his numbers and a little reading and writing.

Mr and Mrs Lennicker had taken him in when he was orphaned at fourteen by his mother's untimely death. He had become a good companion to their father, the son he'd never had. At first Winnie had been jealous of the time he spent with Pa, but her feelings had altered, and she had fallen for him.

'Winnie! Are you avoiding us?' On hearing Louisa's voice, she checked that the shavings were still burning, and reluctantly left the hang.

'Oh, there you are,' Grace said, as Winnie entered the kitchen where the flames of the fire in the inglenook gave the whitewashed walls and rush mats a golden glow. It was her favourite part of the house, the heart of their home.

There was a table and several chairs in the centre of the stone floor, a dresser that held their crockery and cutlery, and a slab of seasoned driftwood that served as a mantel over the fireplace. The brass candlesticks on the mantel glinted beside the pot of gauges and needles for mending nets.

'What is it you want?' Winnie addressed Louisa who was tucking a small packet inside her bodice.

'A stranger called,' Grace said.

'I didn't hear anyone.'

'That's because you were hiding like Pa used to.' Louisa smiled wryly and Winnie smiled back, recalling how their father would disappear into the hang with his pipe when their aunt and cousin used to call.

'Who was it?'

'A stranger – I told you. There's no need for us to know his identity. In fact, the less we know, the better. Suffice to say, I have some papers and cognac to deliver to a gentleman who's waiting at the Five Bells at Ringwould and you're both coming with me.' Louisa looked from Winnie to Grace and back. 'I would ask Jason, but he isn't home yet.'

'I'm not going,' Winnie said quickly. 'It's terribly cold and dark and the only people about are those who are up to no good.'

'You can't mean Old Boneyparte and his Grande Armée,' Louisa said. 'The news is that he's in retreat from Russia.'

'How do you know that's true? It could be a rumour to put us off our guard.' Winnie could hardly remember a time when they hadn't been at war with Napoleon. Since she was a child, she'd seen him as the bogeyman, waiting on the other side of the Channel for his chance to invade England.

'I'm not worried about the Frenchies,' Louisa went on. 'It's the drunkards and thieves, and men who would take advantage of a lone woman.'

They were living in dangerous times. The Great War against the self-appointed Emperor of France, and Mr Madison's War, the conflict against America, had brought an influx of foreigners to Deal. People came to work in trades such as ship's chandlery and ropemaking, while the wives of the men sent to reinforce the Marquess of Wellington's army on the Peninsula, brought their children to wait for their return. There were soldiers, sailors, naval officers, builders, provisioners and sailmakers. And then there were the rest: the pickpockets, robbers and ruffians.

Winnie's reflection scowled from the polished copper pan that hung from a hook beside the fire. She was tired out, having been on her feet all day. Where would she find the strength to walk the three miles or more to Ringwould?

'I can't afford to turn work away. I'm doing this for us, our family.'

Winnie felt a little uncomfortable because Louisa had always done her best for her and Grace, and she was too kind to remind them that they depended on her husband's goodwill for their keep and the roof over their heads. Jason had bought Compass Cottage when it was auctioned off to pay some of their father's debts after he died.

'The three of us will keep each other company,' Louisa added in a tone that brooked no argument.

Why did she always let her sister twist her arm? Winnie grumbled to herself when they were walking along the alley, wrapped up against the cold. Following Grace and Louisa, she pushed the handcart along towards the High Street, its wheels squeaking with every turn, and the contents of the cask that was hidden beneath a sheet inside it, sloshing about.

As they travelled further, making the most of the light from the crescent moon and stars, the great stone walls of Deal Castle loomed from the shadows.

'Listen,' Grace whispered, slowing down. 'There are men on horseback … they're coming this way.'

'It's the gobblers, Riding officers. Hide,' Louisa muttered.

'Who goes there?' a voice rang out.

'There's no answer – perhaps it is a very large mouse.'

There was laughter as Louisa and Grace's figures melted into the gloom, leaving Winnie stuck with the handcart. As the two mounted officers approached her, her heart missed a beat, and then another, slowing down so much that she was afraid it was going to stop altogether.

'Show yourself, missus.'

Almost blinded by lanternlight and scared witless, Winnie had no choice but to step forward when she recognised the men from past confrontations: Officer Chase and his superior, Tom Lawrence.

'Your name?' Officer Chase asked, apparently not realising who she was in the darkness.

'Mrs Fleet,' she replied after a moment's hesitation.

'I didn't know Billy had got wed before he left. Tell me your name truthfully.'

'I've told you – I'm Mrs Fleet.' She went on to fill the silence, remembering to speak roughly like a peasant woman, not a lady as her mother had always insisted upon.

'I've been nursin' my sister-in-law since she fell bodily ill last week,' she elaborated. 'We buried 'er yesterday.'

'Then I'm sorry for your loss,' he said with mock gravity. 'Do convey my commiserations to this imaginary sister-in-law of yours. Billy doesn't have a brother.'

He had caught her in a lie, and she had got herself into a tangle. She tried to think of an explanation, her mind frozen like her fingers and toes. Louisa would have known what to say and how to put it in the best light, but she'd gone and left her in the lurch.

'Don't treat me like a fool, Miss Winnie Lennicker. I'm not going to let you or your sisters pull the wool over my eyes again.'

'You cannot rummage me,' she said, alarmed at the thought of anyone except her Billy touching her.

'That's true as you are a member of the fairer sex, but there's nothing to stop us examining the handcart for contraband.' Officer Chase jumped down from his horse, looped the ribbons over his arm and stepped closer.

Winnie couldn't bear it, knowing that her part in a crime was about to be discovered.

She shoved herself between the officer and the handcart, planted her palms on his chest and pushed him away.

'Oh dear,' he smirked. 'You aren't helping yourself, are you? I'm going to have to arrest you for obstructing a Riding officer in the course of his duty.'

In her panic, she made to run, but he grabbed her by the arm and hissed in her ear, 'You would be wise not to add to your tally of misdemeanours. Understood?'

'Yes, sir,' she stammered.

'Good.' He drew a cutlass and used the tip of the blade to lift the corner of the sheet, revealing the cask. 'Aha, it's as I suspected.'

'Something to keep up our spirits on a long cold night?' Tom Lawrence suggested.

'We will take it to the Customs House in the morning—'

'After we have tested the contents,' Tom guffawed. 'Let me take the seized goods and your horse while you see this young woman to gaol.'

'No,' Winnie gasped, looking around wildly for her sisters. 'It queers me as to how that got there.'

'You know very well – either you or one of your sisters put it there.'

'But I want to go home.'

'The magistrates will decide in the morning what will happen to you,' Officer Chase said. 'I anticipate that justice will be served.'

She cried as he led her along the streets to the gaol where a miserable old hag with no teeth locked her in a room with three other women, who had been arrested for whoring and theft. The privations of the gaol – the cold, hard floor, the thin blanket crawling with bugs, and the congealing mass of cold porridge – were sickening, but she barely noticed, being consumed by fear and regret, and resentment that her sisters had abandoned her to this fate.

The vicar's voice and the rat-a-tat-tat of his gavel brought her back to the present.

'Pray silence, ladies and gentlemen.' The audience settled and Reverend North turned to address Officer Chase. 'Did you see the prisoner place the cask in the handcart?'

The officer frowned. 'No, I can't say that I did.'

'Then you cannot confirm that Miss Lennicker was aware that she was transporting illegally imported goods?'

'No. But her unwomanly behaviour in trying to prevent my search added weight to my view that she is guilty of the charge.'

16

'The law relies on evidence, supported by witness statements, not your perceptions,' Reverend North said. 'The allegation of possession cannot be proved beyond reasonable doubt. However, I find the prisoner guilty of obstruction.'

Winnie struggled to breathe as she awaited the decision on the third and final charge.

'I have read your superior officer's statement regarding your charge that the prisoner attempted to mislead you by taking on another person's identity. Miss Lennicker was pretending to be married, that's all. She was, in effect, impersonating herself. That is not a capital offence.'

'What you are saying is fustian nonsense,' Officer Chase exploded, losing his temper as well he might, Winnie thought, knowing he had come within ames-ace of sending one of his adversaries to the Assizes. 'It's a bag of moonshine.'

'How do you respond, Miss Lennicker?' the vicar asked her directly. 'Why did you tell the officer that you were Mrs Fleet?'

How should she answer? Winnie was torn. Reverend North was giving her a way out. In truth, she had pretended to be someone else, hoping that the Riding officers wouldn't recognise her as one of the Lennickers, but it appeared that if she gave her secret away, she would avoid the gallows.

Suddenly, she found her voice. Burning with shame, she confessed.

'I am with child,' she said. 'I didn't want anyone to think badly of me.'

'She gave a false name to protect her reputation, not to evade justice. The charge is dismissed.' The vicar raised his hand as the officer opened his mouth to argue, then closed it again. 'Officer Chase, have no fear – you will

17

receive your bonus. I sentence the prisoner to one hour in the stocks as an example to others. That is all.' He turned to the guard. 'Mr Stripe, take her down and bring the next prisoner in front of the Bench.'

As Winnie was being led away, she looked for her sisters. Louisa was smiling with relief while Grace appeared dumbfounded – understandably, having found out that the sister she looked up to was carrying a child out of wedlock. She had made a fine mess of things. Not only had she been humiliated in the courtroom, she was about to be disgraced in the stocks.

It was her own fault – she had set out on the wrong course, bringing her misfortunes upon herself: lying with Billy before they were married; failing to stand up to Louisa. She recalled a saying their Ma used to use: every herring must hang by its own gill. From now on, she vowed to stand up for herself and – she stroked her belly – her unborn child.

Chapter Two

Taking Stock

Winnie had to wait in a side room for the magistrates to deal with the second prisoner who was let off a charge of smashing – passing off bad money as change – before she was taken into town. Exhaling beery fumes, Constable Pocket led her through the crowd on the way to the market. Winnie stared at the ground as she was jostled and shoved along the streets. They were jeering at her, pointing fingers, mocking. Now she knew how Billy must have felt when One Eye had had him tarred and feathered and led through the town.

''Ave a care,' she heard someone say – Mrs Roper, she guessed. 'Who in their right mind drags a woman 'eavy with child to the stocks to be gawped at?'

'She kept that under 'er 'at, didn't she?' Mrs Edwards, who was in her mid to late thirties and wearing a cap and grubby apron over a dark dress, wagged her finger.

'Under 'er skirts, I think you mean, Mrs Edwards.' Another voice had joined in, that of Louisa's mother-in-law, Mrs Witherall.

''Tis a shame young Master Fleet didn't think to keep it inside 'is—'

'Mrs Witherall, wash your mouth out with soap and water. There are young lads with impressionable minds present.' Winnie caught sight of Louisa's father-in-law whose hair, once blond, was now lightened through with grey. His eyes were blue, like his son's, but deeply creased at the corners and his complexion was weathered by the elements.

'We don't know for sure that it's Billy's whelp.' Mrs Roper carried a wailing toddler on her hip, one of her twelve sons and daughters. There had been one more, a boy who'd died from drowning, falling from his father's boat, when Winnie was five or six.

'We don't know that much about 'er, not really,' Mrs Edwards observed. 'She's one of the quiet ones – she 'ides that golden 'air of 'ers, and keeps 'erself to 'erself, always in the shadow of 'er sisters.'

'She always gives the impression that butter wouldn't melt in 'er mouth,' Mrs Roper added gleefully. 'Oh, what a delightful scandal.'

'Winnie, don't listen to the old fishwives,' she heard Grace say from nearby.

'Grace, mind your tongue,' Louisa joined in. 'But you're right in your sentiment. It's a lie. Our Winnie is not with child – I know it for a fact. She is stout, that is true. But she has an excellent appetite, so it isn't surprising that she has lost her waist.'

Winnie wished that Louisa would keep silent on the matter. It was only making things worse.

'You're tryin' to tell us that she's all belly because she partakes of an excess of belly timber?' Mrs Edwards grinned, and the other wives laughed.

Burning with shame, Winnie shuffled along with her hands bound behind her back. The ropes dug into her flesh, but she felt that she deserved the pain as penance for her folly. It wouldn't happen again, she would make sure of it.

20

As she passed the stalls in the market, the traders pressed in towards her – she could see their shadows but couldn't bring herself to meet their eyes.

What was it about their run of bad luck? First, they had lost Pa, murdered by One Eye, leader of the Rattlers, a rival gang. Then she had lost Billy. And now this.

Pa had used to say that they couldn't go to church when there were nets to mend, and Louisa maintained that praying when you were going about your usual business was just as good as attending a service, but perhaps they'd been wrong. Winnie vowed to make up for their ungodly way of life as she stumbled along.

''Ey, miss, you can stop now. We're 'ere,' she heard the constable say gently, his hand on her arm.

She looked up at the dark wooden boards of the stocks rearing up in front of her from the corner where Market Street joined Lower Street.

Dignity, she thought as Constable Pocket untied the ropes and let them fall from her wrists. I will be dignified.

'This way,' he said, and she walked to the bench behind the stocks that were bolted to the ground because someone had stolen the previous set, using them as firewood for signalling to the luggers from the beach during a run on a dark night.

'Stop. Stop! She must be made comfortable.' Mrs Edwards thrust a cushion into the constable's arms. With great ceremony, he placed it on the bench.

'Take a seat, miss,' he said, a small smile on his face, as one of Mrs Roper's children gave him a blanket.

As Winnie sat down, he draped it around her shoulders. Although it reeked of lanolin and sheep's treddles, she was grateful for its warmth as she rested her ankles in the cut-outs in the lower board, and the constable lowered the first hinged panel to trap her legs. Meekly, she extended

21

her wrists, allowing him to trap them with the second stock-board.

''Ow is that?' he said in her ear.

She didn't have a chance to respond because of the egg that came splattering against the stocks, sending its stinking contents splashing across her chin. Looking straight ahead, she spotted one of the Rattlers' wives with a young lad holding a bucket.

'You throw it, Ma,' he was shouting.

'No, you do it,' the woman said. 'You 'ave a better aim than me.'

He threw another missile. This time a rotten cabbage hit Winnie on the head, then fell to the ground, leaving drops of brown liquid trickling past her eyes. As her tormentors cheered and the lad came forward to throw the potato peelings and slime that were left in the bucket at her, she retched in disgust.

How much more would she have to endure? she wondered, closing her eyes to await the next onslaught of projectiles.

'I'll go and fetch some more,' she heard the lad say.

'Oh no, you won't,' Constable Pocket shouted. 'Look what you've done to my coat. I'll 'ave your guts for garters.'

''E's very sorry, sir, but you shouldn't 'ave been standin' in the way,' the woman replied.

'I wasn't,' Constable Pocket argued. 'Go 'ome.'

The woman and her son retreated as a shrill voice called, ''Ot pies. 'Ot pies!'

'Oh, it's the comely fat cook,' murmured one of the men as Mrs Stickles, proprietor of Molly's Pot House, rounded the corner. A figure dressed in white with a veil over her face followed with a handcart laden with pies.

'You keep your 'ands off that woman, Mr Kesby,' one of the wives said.

22

'I only 'ave eyes for 'er pies, Mrs Kesby. And a rumblin' belly for 'em.'

'It's all right, miss. They aren't goin' to throw 'em at you,' Constable Pocket said. 'Them pies are too good to waste.'

The woman in white pushed the handcart over to the stocks.

'Ma says there's one for you – on the 'ouse.' She gave the constable a pie. 'There's one for you too, dear Winnie,' she added. 'I'll 'elp you …'

'Thank you, Nancy, but I'm not hungry.'

'You should 'ave somethin' – you're eatin' for two.' Nancy broke off a morsel of pie and fed it to Winnie who couldn't deny that it tasted divine: beef that melted in the mouth, softly cooked onions, crispy pastry. 'Oi, leave 'er alone,' Nancy snapped at a pair of urchins who were having a go at pulling off one of Winnie's boots.

'Why is everyone being so kind?' Tears sprang to Winnie's eyes.

'It's wrong to treat a woman in your condition like this. I want you to know that I'll 'elp you in any way I can.' Nancy had been born on the wrong side of the blanket too, the product of a brief union between Mr Lennicker and Mrs Stickles, a woman of ill-repute who had managed to restore her reputation in part by virtue of her hot pies.

Pa had been married at the time. It had been a terrible shock when Winnie and her sisters had found out only this year – after his death – that they had a half-sister, one who had led a hidden life at the Rattling Cat, thanks to her scars from the pox and the wounds inflicted by One Eye. Their landlord had employed Mrs Stickles as a barmaid and cook, keeping mother and daughter like prisoners, using violence and threats. He had forced Nancy to support the Rattlers' cause, sending her out dressed in

23

white as the ghost known as the Fey Lady to haunt the maze of passageways and cellars beneath the houses in Deal where they had stashed the goods.

Winnie couldn't condemn their father for his indiscretion, not the way she'd been carrying on with Billy. Grace had been critical of him, but she hadn't experienced the overwhelming power of love and desire, Winnie thought. Not yet.

At least Nancy's life had changed for the better since Winnie, Louisa and Grace had helped her and her mother escape from the inn.

Winnie thanked her, knowing that Nancy didn't care much for being out and about. Chewing on another piece of pie, she looked across the street to find her sisters approaching with a tankard of steaming liquid.

'Here's some milk and brandy to warm your cockles,' Grace said.

Nancy took it from her, lifted her veil and took a long draught.

'Just checkin' it isn't too 'ot,' she said cheerfully before letting Winnie have a drink.

'I'm sorry for what happened, Winnie,' Louisa said. 'We'll talk later.'

'I'm not sure that I can bring myself to speak to you. It was your actions that brought me to this,' Winnie responded as Grace wiped the dirt from her chin.

'I'm offering you an olive branch – you don't have to snap it back in my face.' Louisa turned and stalked away. Winnie leaned forward and rested her chin on the top plank.

'She's taken it badly, you know,' Grace said. 'She's finding it hard to forgive herself.'

'She will though,' Winnie said. 'Her hide is like an elephant's.'

'That isn't true. Oh, I hope you two aren't going to fall out over it. Promise me you'll listen to what she has to say ...' Winnie noticed how Grace's gaze drifted towards a young man who was approaching, skirting the crowd with a rough-coated black longdog at his heels. A fine silk bandanna was wrapped around his neck and he wore a shabby overcoat, long pantaloons and sea boots. He came up and stood directly in front of the stocks.

'Good day, ladies,' he mocked. 'What a turn-up, a Lennicker snared like a hare and thrown in the stocks – I should 'ave brought somethin' to pelt you with. I'd advise you to be more careful in future. Who knows where you'll end up next time?'

One Eye Feasey's son was about four years older than Winnie. Everyone acknowledged that he was handsome in a rugged kind of way, with curly hair the colour of jet, and dark brown eyes, but his unkempt appearance didn't please her in the slightest.

'Leave her alone, Isaiah,' Grace said.

His voice softened. 'I didn't mean to upset you.'

'When you hurt one of my sisters, you hurt me as well,' Grace said fiercely. 'Leave off gloating and go away!'

He bowed his head briefly and walked off, disappearing in the direction of the beach.

'That's him been told,' Grace smiled.

'Why does he humour you?' Winnie looked up and stared at her sister. Her cheeks were pink and there was a sparkle in her eye. 'You don't ...?'

'Oh no. I don't have a fancy for him. He's dirty and old, and goes around looking like a beggar. And he's a Rattler. Do you really think I'd associate with the son of the man who murdered our father?'

'No, of course I don't, but you do seem to be on very good terms with him.'

'Listen.' Grace changed the subject. 'I can hear music.'

A band of fiddlers and pipers were marching down the street, playing a merry tune. They stopped a few yards away and set themselves up in front of a shop window where the leader scraped his bow across his strings to start the ballad of Henry Martin. The crowd joined in to sing of how he went to rob a lofty merchant ship.

'I will take from you your flowing gold, flowing gold.'

As the story took a gruesome turn, with the sailors' fair bodies turned to the sea, Winnie tried to close her ears, reminded again of Billy. Was he out on the water fighting for King and Country, or was he dead, perished by drowning, sickness or musket ball?

When the chapel bell rang at the top of the hour, the constable released her from the stocks.

'That wasn't so bad, was it, miss?' he said as she rubbed her hands together to encourage the blood back into her fingers. 'You're a lucky one, 'avin' so many friends.'

She smiled wryly – she was under no illusion. They had turned up out of respect for Louisa, the Lace Maiden as she was known among the free traders, not her, plain Winnie. She handed back the blanket and, with Grace holding her hand, and Louisa and the wives walking along behind them, she made her way home.

Grace unlocked their green front door and let her sisters in. Winnie went straight to the kitchen to warm herself in front of the embers that glowed feebly in the fireplace.

'I'll make some tea.' Grace poured water into the copper kettle while Louisa stoked the fire and added a few sticks. As the flames rose, Winnie felt the ire that had been simmering in her breast, start to boil over.

'Why did you leave me to face the gobblers alone?' she exclaimed. 'What on earth possessed you, Louisa? I told you I didn't want to do it! It's all right for you two. I can't lie to save my life.'

Louisa's forehead creased. 'You convinced Reverend North that you were telling the truth. You barely blinked as the words flowed like quicksilver from your mouth.'

'I wasn't lying about that.' She hesitated before going on, 'I am with child. So there, now you know.'

'Oh dear, you have sprained an ankle.' Grace bit her lip.

'It's impossible,' Louisa said. 'I thought you'd lost the baby.'

'So did I.' Winnie stroked her belly, squirming in the face of her sisters' interrogation. She hadn't convinced Officer Chase with her lies, but she had been lying to Louisa and Grace for months.

'It is Billy's?'

'What do you take me for?'

'I'm sorry. I didn't mean ...'

'Billy and I ...' Winnie cleared her throat. 'We were planning to get married, before he was taken away from me. I know I shouldn't have gone along with it, that we should have waited, but I wasn't to know how things would turn out. Anyway, I was sick and my courses stopped, and I was scared witless, thinking that I was with child, but then the sickness wore off and my courses returned. I told you so, Louisa.'

'I remember – it wasn't long after Billy was taken.' Louisa was still frowning. 'Are you sure you aren't just a little corpulent?'

'The child has quickened.' Winnie burst into tears. 'I couldn't tell you – I was too ashamed.'

'We'll speak to Mrs Witherall to see if she's heard of this before.'

'Please don't. I'll go away. I'll leave Deal to spare you the mortification. I've let you down, both of you.'

27

'We can't allow you to do that,' Grace said quickly. 'Can we, Louisa?' Her tone turned to one of doubt.

'I'll go,' Winnie repeated. 'Louisa, you and Jason are moving up in the world, associating with the likes of Sir Flinders. You've dined with him and his wife at Mundel Manor, and you're well acquainted with their daughter, Mrs Tempest. They won't give you the time of day if they find out that your sister is the subject of a scandal.'

'You're making too much of it,' Louisa said. 'The Flinders have no interest in what we do. Jason and I were invited in honour of us having saved Mrs Tempest from the *White Hind* when she foundered on the Sands.'

Winnie remembered how Jason and his men had gone out with the lugger on the night of one of the worst storms in living memory, taking Louisa with them. Grace had begged her not to go, saying that she and Winnie needed her as well, but Louisa had insisted on risking her life to rescue others.

'Lady Flinders was insufferably condescending and her guests nothing special. It was supposed to be a party, but apart from Mrs Tempest's company, which was most agreeable, it was quite dull, nothing like our celebrations on the beach. I know which I prefer, so I'm not going to pay any consideration to the Flinders' feelings on a matter that is our family's alone.'

'What about Jason? What will he think? He won't want me here with a squalling babe.'

'I'll talk to him,' Louisa said. 'Just promise me you won't do anything rash ...'

Winnie knew that her sister was referring to the attempt she'd made to end her life with an excessive dose of laudanum when she'd first thought she might be with child, and Billy had gone.

'I promise,' she said.

'Good. Then we will carry on as normal.'

'You have us, Winnie,' Grace said. 'Remember that nothing is ever as dark as it seems.'

Lying in bed that night in the room she used to share with Louisa, Winnie listened to the rumble of barrels overhead. The Rattlers were rolling them along the valley formed by the intersections of the roofs of the houses in Cockle Swamp Alley, part of a hidden pathway leading from the Rattling Cat to an attic that belonged to a member of Isaiah's gang.

'Oh Billy,' she murmured, remembering how she would rail at him for leaving piles of sand on the floor when he took off his boots, and tease him about his cowlick of red hair that sprang up despite everything he used to try to defy it, until the day came when she realised that what she felt for him was something more complicated and delicious than annoyance.

He had fallen out with Louisa when she'd confronted One Eye Feasey at the Rattling Cat over Billy's revelation that the injury which caused dear Pa's death was not the result of an accident as they'd been led to believe. Billy had been present at the time and Winnie knew out of the whole lot of them – the gamblers and drinkers who frequented One Eye's tavern – whose word she trusted. Mr Lennicker had arrived with his pistol in his hand and a grievance on his lips. One Eye, having taken offence at what he'd said, took his piece from under the counter and shot him in the arm. He might have lived, had gangrene not set in, but Winnie couldn't think about that. Just as Reverend North often preached – the Lord above moved in mysterious ways.

When One Eye realised that Billy had blabbed, he had sent a couple of the Rattlers, Awful Doins and Lawless, after him.

Winnie recalled Billy's howls of 'No! Get your 'ands off me!' when they grabbed him off the street, and how she'd run after them, ignoring Louisa's orders not to.

A crowd had surrounded the men, egging them on as they stripped the shirt from Billy's back. He almost got away, only to be tripped up in front of One Eye who ordered them to brush warm pine tar across his skin. As Billy groaned in anguish and Louisa confessed to what she had done, Winnie began to cry. The crowd threw feathers at him which stuck to his face, torso and bony arms, making him look like a scrawny seagull, but they weren't done with him yet. They paraded him from one end of Deal to the other before they let him go, stumbling into Winnie's arms.

'Come home,' she begged, holding him tight.

'I can't,' he said, his hands on her waist. 'I've never been so 'oomiliated in my life. I'll never show my face 'ere again.'

'Winnie, this is most unbecoming of you,' she heard Louisa say, and she let go of him quickly, like a hot chestnut.

'Come,' she'd repeated. 'Come home with us.'

Back at the cottage, he had sat down in the kitchen, his elbows on the table, the feathers quivering across his arms and back. Grace had removed as many of them as possible while Billy winced and complained, and then Winnie had scrubbed his face and arms with warm water, soap and sand, while Louisa looked on.

'I hate that we have to earn money this way – it's asking for trouble, bringing us into conflict with the likes of the Rattlers,' Winnie said. 'I hate how we have to creep about in the dark, looking over our shoulders.'

''Ave a care!' Billy yelped. 'You're pullin' my 'air out.'

'I'm trying to be careful, but ...' Winnie returned to the subject of the gangs and the honourable trade. 'We have to stop before we come to grief, and this is as good a time as any. We can make our living out of fishing and taking in a little sewing. I don't want much – a happy home with you and my sisters.'

'With food to fill our bellies,' Billy added.

'And beautiful gowns like the ones that Miss Flinders wears,' Grace joined in.

'That might be a stretch too far,' Louisa smiled.

'So, we are all in agreement?' Winnie said.

'There's still some lace and cognac to sell,' Louisa insisted. 'And we still need to find the money for a new boat.' The Lennickers' old boat, Pa's beloved *Pamela*, named after his wife, had recently been stolen.

'After that, then?' Winnie insisted. 'Promise me that we'll stop.'

'I can't promise anything. Let's take one step at a time.'

When all the feathers and tar had gone, turned into a dusting of ash on the fire and a lingering scent of rotten eggs, Winnie stayed with Billy, serving up bread and minted cheese from which she'd cut out the worst of the mites, while Grace and Louisa ran an errand.

'Thank you,' Billy said. 'I'm sorry to 'ave been such a nuisance, but I couldn't 'ave got all those feathers off by myself, not without bein' a contortionist. Oh, I feel like a proper goose.'

'You looked like one too, and you did make rather a fuss. You're glowing.' Smiling, she reached out and touched his back, the contact sending a flare of heat through her fingertips that, like a spark from the end of a taper, set her senses aflame. Her cheeks alight, she apologised and moved aside, busying herself with putting away the knife and breadboard while he excused himself, saying he was going upstairs to find some clothes. When he'd gone, she felt bereft and confused.

Pa had treated Billy as a son, and her sisters had considered him a brother, but Winnie had seen him as something more, her future husband.

As she tried to sleep, her belly tightened until it was as hard as a keg, then softened again, reminding her of her predicament. Louisa was right that she had to continue in the free trade – how else could she remain at Compass Cottage with her sisters, and look after Billy's child?

Chapter Three

Making Hay while the Sun Shines

A sennight had passed since Winnie's humiliation in front of the magistrates and she was keeping busy, attempting to forget the way her disgrace had been revealed in front of her friends and neighbours. Having returned from a lucrative provisioning trip on the *Curlew*, selling flour, cheese, butter, vinegar and beans, she was in the kitchen with Grace, scrubbing and peeling carrots, and chopping them up with onions and the good parts of a turnip that was riddled with wireworms.

Louisa was down at the beach waiting for Jason and his crew to return with the *Whimbrel*. It wasn't unusual for them to stay away for a night or two, taking it in turns to sleep side by side, four at a time in the cabin on the forepeak of the lugger, but there had been rumours of a confrontation. A fisherman had brought news of an explosion at sea. Too afraid to investigate, he had hauled in his nets and made for shore.

Winnie melted some lard in a pot over the fire, then threw in the vegetables, letting them sizzle before adding stock that she'd made from fish heads and herbs. The aroma of cooking food reminded her of Ma and how she'd taught her to run a tight ship.

Mrs Lennicker had been born into a family of successful market gardeners who had strongly disapproved of her marriage, a union she had entered into for love. Afterwards, finding herself living in unexpected penury, she turned her husband's fortunes around by dint of hard work and household economy, and an enthusiasm for the free trade.

'Hark. Can you hear that?' Grace said, wiping her hands on her apron.

'Your ears are sharper than mine.' Winnie could only just hear the sound of shouting coming from the beach.

'Are you coming?' Like a sylph, Grace slipped out to the hall, and having checked that the stew wasn't about to boil over, Winnie followed. By the time she joined the crowd assembled at the top of the slope, she could barely catch her breath.

'What's happened?' she gasped, looking towards the sea where the men and boys were hauling the *Whimbrel* up the beach. At forty feet long and at least seven feet wide, she normally looked quite imposing, especially armed with her eleven three-pounders, but she appeared to have suffered some damage. Part of her hull was caved in, the wood splintered around a hole three foot in diameter, and one of her guns was missing. 'Where's Marlin? Where are the men?'

'Over there.' Grace pointed towards a group of the boatmen's wives and daughters who were gathered around a supine body.

'Jason?' Winnie's heart missed a beat. Taking Grace's hand, she hurried across, her feet slipping and sliding on the stones.

'No, it's Terrier.' She turned at the sound of Louisa's voice to find her sister standing at her husband's side, his hair glinting gold in the late afternoon sunshine. He had lost his hat and was wearing a cloth bound across his cheek with a bandanna, below which was a trickle of dried blood. His shirt was torn and stained, and his coat was hanging off him in tatters.

'We had a run-in with the Frenchies, a privateer, one of many ships now with letters of marque allowing them to carry out naval warfare.'

'That's terrible,' Winnie said, thinking how scared the crew must have been.

'One of our guns blew up when we fired back at them. Terrier's in a bad way ...' Jason swallowed hard and rubbed his eyes. 'We've given him brandy and bandaged the wounds. I've sent Cromwell to fetch Doctor Audley, but Winnie, is there anythin' you can do to help him? You have a gift for nursin' the sick and injured.'

'I'll do what I can.'

'Step aside. Let the young lady through,' Jason called, walking ahead. The crowd parted, allowing her to pass and kneel at Terrier's side where Mrs Roper was on her knees, wailing and rubbing his hands.

'Don't leave me,' she begged. ''Elp 'im. Do whatever you can.'

Winnie was afraid that he was beyond help. He had no external sign of injury, but his lips were blue and his breathing slow and shallow.

'What about more brandy? Or a dose of saltwater?' Mrs Roper sobbed, strands of long hair sticking to her face.

'Throw a bucket of cold water over 'im – that'll bring 'im back,' Smoker Edwards suggested. 'I've seen it work before.'

'I've seen it finish a man off,' said another of Jason's crew, squaring up to him, but before a riot could break out, Doctor Audley arrived on his grey mare. Winnie considered him to be the most learned gentleman of her acquaintance, but there was nothing he could do. As he brought his bag to the patient's side, Terrier took his last breath and expired.

Mrs Roper collapsed over her husband's body, crying her heart out, and Mrs Edwards, having handed her children over to Mrs Witherall, knelt to console her.

Choked with grief for the widow and her family, Winnie struggled to her feet. She slid her arm around Grace's waist as Doctor Audley explained what would happen next.

'There will be an inquest for the coroner and jury to view the body of the deceased, examine the witnesses and reach a conclusion about whether this was murder by foul play or misadventure. The constable will notify the coroner and Reverend North will no doubt be prevailed upon as officer of this parish to rent premises and summon witnesses.'

'We know very well what 'appened and there is no redress. It was the Frenchies who killed 'im,' Mrs Edwards said fiercely.

Winnie shuddered at the thought of Old Boney paying his countrymen to intercept foreign vessels, take their crew prisoner – or kill them – and steal their ships and cargoes. It was true to say that the British government did the same, enlisting British captains to act as privateers against the likes of the French, but Winnie could forgive them for that. Napoleon had started the war, proclaiming himself Emperor of France. As far as she was concerned, he had the blood of many on his hands, including Terrier.

'We'll take him to the Waterman's Arms,' Doctor Audley said. 'The curiosity-mongers can look on him there.'

Winnie and Grace followed the men who carried the body of the departed to the inn where Mrs Causton sent out for fresh supplies of ale, taking the opportunity to make a little extra from the stream of visitors who would turn up to attend the inquest.

The women cried and the men stood by, red-eyed and sniffing.

'It won't be the same, not seeing 'im on the beach, smokin' 'is pipe,' Old Mr Witherall commented. 'I've known 'im since 'e was a babe in arms.'

Mr Edwards nodded, his face grey with shock. 'It's been a long time since we lost one of our own.'

'I can't bear it any longer,' Winnie said. 'There's nothing more we can do here.'

She and Grace hurried back to Compass Cottage, and Winnie pushed the front door open.

'Can you smell burning?' Grace asked.

'The stew!' Winnie exclaimed, suddenly remembering. 'It will be ruined.'

Without taking off her boots, she ran into the kitchen.

'Do you think you can do something to retrieve it?' Grace looked over Winnie's shoulder into the pan as she scraped the blackened vegetables from the bottom with a wooden spoon.

'It would take a miracle, and although it's blasphemous to say so, I don't believe there is such a thing. Look at what's happened.' She stirred the remains of her cooking – not only was it unappetising, she didn't think she could eat anything anyway. 'I'm not starting again,' she sighed.

'Jason will be expecting his supper.'

'I'll go to Molly's and buy a pie.'

'I'll come with you.'

'No, it's all right. I won't be long.' Winnie needed some time to herself, Terrier's demise having triggered thoughts of Billy and whether or not he had met with a similar fate.

Having counted out a few coins from the box that they kept on a shelf in the hall for housekeeping money, she went out again, making her way to the pot house. Dusk was falling, painting the mackerel sky in the west with shades of indigo and pink.

As she was passing the Rattling Cat, a carpet bag came flying out through the door and landed with a thump in the gutter. A man – a higgler, she guessed from the state of his clothing – came stumbling out next, followed by Isaiah and his snarling longdog.

'You're makin' the place untidy, you ol' varmint. No money, no ale!' Isaiah ranted.

Frowning at the landlord's rough treatment, Winnie made to walk past, but when Isaiah aimed a kick at his victim's ankles, tripping him up, she stopped. The man grunted as Isaiah stamped on his hand. She couldn't stand by as she would have done in the past – her recent experiences had given her the courage to confront injustice.

'Leave him alone!' she shouted.

'It's nothin' to do with you. 'E's a criminal. Not much different from yourself, in fact.' Isaiah hawked and spat at Winnie's feet, but she refused to back down.

'I shall send for the constable,' she said, enraged.

Isaiah laughed grimly. ''E's been dragged off to notify the coroner of Terrier's passin' – not that anybody will be able to get any sense out of 'im. 'E's been crookin' 'is elbow in there –' he nodded towards the tavern '– since last night. Be off. Both of you!' He turned and strode back inside, the door swinging closed behind him.

'May I help you, mister?' Winnie turned to the man who was back on his feet, slinging his bag over his shoulder. His face was haggard, his eyes black pools of desperation set deep into their sockets. He looked to be about forty years old, but Winnie suspected he was younger.

'There's nothin' you can do for me, missus. I 'ave my pride.'

'I'm sure you do, but ... what brought you to the Rattling Cat?'

''Unger,' he said. 'I thought I'd stop for a drink and a bite to eat.'

'I can recommend Molly's Pot House instead – Mrs Stickles makes the best pies in Deal.'

'Ah, I thought I 'ad a couple of shillin's left, but when I searched my pockets, I found myself sadly cucumberish.'

'You are a sailor?' she asked, noticing the tattoo – a mermaid's tail curving across his forearm.

'Used to be. When I returned to England a few months ago, 'avin' served King and Country, I assumed I'd be welcomed with my fellow sailors as 'eroes, but, blinded in one eye and 'alf blind in the other, I 'ave been cast on the midden.'

'You must have a pension, at least?'

'Oh yes. An amount that I signed up for in Greenwich. It isn't enow to keep body and soul together. I can't work; my wife ... she took sick and died while I was away. My children – three of them – languish in the poor 'ouse.'

'I'm very sorry to hear it,' she said softly. 'How old are they?'

'Six, eight and nine. Two girls and a boy.'

Winnie could have cried for them. 'Come with me and I will buy you a pie.'

'I can't accept, missus.' His eyes glazed with tears. 'I 'ave nothin' to give you in return.'

'Have you ever heard of a volunteer called Billy Fleet?'

He frowned. 'I can't say that I 'ave.'

'He's my sweetheart – I haven't seen or heard from him since he was impressed last summer. I live in hope that one day I'll see him again – and in the meantime, if he's in any trouble, someone will take pity on him and treat

39

him with kindness and generosity. And if he's offered food, he will accept it. You understand?'

The ghost of a smile crossed the man's eyes. 'I think I will 'ave that pie, after all.'

Winnie showed him to the pot house where Mrs Stickles was serving.

'Two beef and onion pies, please,' she said. 'That's one for me to take home and one for the gentleman here. What is your name, sir?'

'Mr Jones. Bless you, my darlin'. I wish for your sake and that of your sweetheart, this fightin' will end and all men will live in peace and 'armony.'

'I share your sentiment.' Winnie had been born in 1794, a year after the execution of Louis XVI and Marie Antoinette. The French Revolution had come to an end in 1799, when she was five years old. Ma would talk of how French aristocrats had been smuggled into England to escape the guillotine and Isaiah would later regale them on the beach with gory stories of men and women having their heads cut off. 'Do you think there is any hope of an end to the wars?'

'I'm told that the news in the papers is positive, but the stories of the soldiers and sailors comin' 'ome are more truthful,' he said before thanking her and taking a seat at one of the tables.

'What's this about the *Whimbrel* comin' under fire?' Mrs Stickles said as she ladled gravy into a jug. 'I 'eard that Terrier came to grief, that 'e's dead and gorn.'

Winnie nodded.

'I shall send Nancy round with a meal for Mrs Roper and her children.'

'I'm sure it will be much appreciated.'

Mrs Stickles leaned in close, her breath stale as she spoke in a whisper.

'I 'ear things, Winnie.'

Winnie's forehead tightened. She was used to receiving confidences – people trusted her to keep her silence and not sit in judgement – but this revelation was most unexpected. 'You are having visions?'

'No, not that. There's an Englishman who's taken a shine to me. I don't know what it is about 'im, but 'e reminds me a little of your father, and I 'ave 'opes. 'Igh 'opes.'

Winnie didn't want to hear about Mrs Stickles's affairs of the heart. After all, she was the woman who had tempted their father into a brief liaison while he'd been married to their mother. Nancy had been the outcome of their union, and Pa had paid Mrs Stickles a contribution for her keep – and her silence – for many years. What made it worse was that Nancy's mother, with her stained frontage and dirty apron, had been a lady of the night, a whore, before she had been given the chance to turn her life around and run her own establishment. Not that Winnie could condemn her now after what she'd done, committing a sin with Billy, and not just once, but several times.

'Then I'm very happy for you,' Winnie said quietly.

''E says 'e'll be back – it's going to be a reg'lar arrangement. Anyway, 'e was askin' after the Lace Maiden, if I knew of 'er.'

'What did he want with Louisa?'

'I don't know. I didn't let on that she was almost family to me. I 'ope I did right.'

'Yes, you did. We don't want any snoopers.'

Mrs Stickles chuckled. 'You never know what secrets they might uncover.'

'What is his name?'

'Mr Gambril.'

41

'I don't recognise it. Did he give you any indication of what business or profession he follows? Could he be one of the Customs men?'

'I'll see what I can find out. 'E was most complimentary about my pies. And 'e promised 'e'd be back. There was one other thing – 'e was makin' notes in a book. I can't read – I 'ave bad eyes – but 'e was most protective over it. Whenever anyone passed 'is table, 'e gave 'em a shifty look and 'id the book away, as if 'e didn't want anybody to know what 'e was writin' down.'

'Perhaps he is composing his life story, or a novel,' Winnie said. 'Or poetry about love?'

'I've seen enough of 'uman behaviour to notice that 'e was up to somethin'. I'll winkle it out of 'im.' She changed the subject. 'You will remember to bring my dish back, won't you?'

'I'll return it tomorrow. How much do I owe you?' Winnie counted out the required amount in shillings and pence and slid the coins across the counter, leaving Mrs Stickles to serve Mr Jones while she carried the pie back to Compass Cottage.

She had just started to cross Beach Street when a yell and clattering of hooves pulled her up short. A carriage – a four-in-hand of black horses – was flying towards her.

'Look where you're going, miss!' the driver roared.

Clutching the pie dish, she threw herself back from the kerb, her heart pounding as the carriage carried on by.

It belonged to Sir Flinders – there weren't many in Deal and the surrounding area who could afford such an extravagant rig, and nobody else travelled about with such unseemly and dangerous haste. He claimed to care for the common man – and woman – but it was a sham when his careless order to his driver to hurry through town could have killed her. Having recently entered Parliament, he also held other privileged positions in society, thanks to his father's success in the business of insuring ships. According to Louisa, he had dined with General Wellesley and conferred with William Pitt the Younger on various financial matters in years gone by. Despite his being an Englishman, though, Winnie couldn't help lumping him together with Old Boney as a 'bad man'.

Once she'd recovered her wits, she carried on to the cottage and let herself in.

Jason had washed and changed, and was sitting beside Louisa at the kitchen table, holding her hand as he downed a tankard of ale.

'What took you so long?' Louisa asked, looking up.

'Mrs Stickles wanted to gossip,' she replied, deciding not to mention that she'd spent some of the housekeeping on feeding the sailor. 'How are you, Jason?'

'A little bruised, that's all. It's my pride that's been hurt more than anythin'.'

'It wasn't your fault. You mustn't blame yourself,' Louisa said.

'I don't know. I keep thinkin', if only we'd turned about sooner. We might have missed her—'

'The privateer?' Louisa interrupted. 'You said yourself it was bad luck – you were in the wrong place at the wrong time.'

'We'd transferred an anchor and cable to the *Elektra* then picked up a pilot from the *Sandpiper* before a man-o'-war – one of ours – reported that there was a brig takin' in water. Seein' that we were nearby, we went to her aid, but when we reached her, the captain had brought the situation under control and we weren't needed. It was then that the privateer had us in its sights.' He shook his head slowly, then winced. 'Ah, my head is poundin', but I'm grateful for small mercies. All I have is this shrapnel graze – another inch and I'd have lost an eye.'

Winnie dished up the pie and poured the gravy which spread slowly, glistening and sticky across the plates.

'I'll have to attend the inquest as a witness,' Jason continued. 'After that, I'll visit Mrs Roper to tell her that we'll pay for the funeral and talk about any other help we can give her.' The crew of the *Whimbrel* had created a fund from a percentage of the income they earned from their hovelling trips. Available to support bereaved families, it had lain untouched for many years. 'Louisa, you'll come with me?'

'Of course.'

'We go out almost every day, with barely a thought for our safety. An incident like this brings it home, doesn't it? It's a timely reminder to us to make every single day count.'

'I was nearly run down by Sir Flinders' carriage,' Winnie said. 'He was in a dreadful hurry.'

'He is always in a hurry – it's common knowledge that he's given up his position as magistrate here in Deal because he's too busy with the higher-ups in London,' Jason said. 'He has ambitions to become the next Prime Minister – that's why he's makin' friends in high places. He's the type who will associate with anybody who's willin' and able to give him a leg-up. I heard from Old Mick –' he was one of their tub carriers '– that he'd invited a Frenchman for a huntin' weekend at the manor.'

'Why would you associate with the enemy?' Louisa said.

'Because this gentleman, Monsieur Boule, is workin' against Napoleon. He represents a Jacobin committee that's out to overthrow the self-styled Emperor of France. He came to England because, as an ex-officer of the French

War Ministry, he was forced to flee his home country when his allegiance to the royalists was discovered. It's quite a story.'

'What does Sir Flinders seek to gain from him?' Winnie asked.

'He wants approval from his fellow Members of Parliament and those who elected him. I imagine that Monsieur Boule has provided intelligence, information about the French army that will be very useful to our side. By introducin' the Frenchman as his prize, Sir Flinders will be fêted for helpin' bring the war to an end. That's what I think.'

Grace came into the kitchen. She and Winnie sat down, and Jason said grace for the first time in many months.

'We pray for Mrs Roper and her children, and for the safety of those in peril on the sea, and for peace. And for Billy to come home. Amen.'

'Amen,' Winnie echoed.

They ate in silence until Jason put down his knife and fork and asked Louisa to cut him a slice of bread.

'I don't know how long it will take to repair the *Whimbrel*.' He wiped his plate clean. 'The damage is significant.'

'At least you have the *Spindrift*,' Grace said, joining the conversation.

'We need the lugger ready in time for the next run – she's much faster and easier to handle than the galley punt.'

'You are already planning the next run?' Winnie asked, shocked.

'We have to make hay when the sun shines,' Louisa said. 'The fighting won't last for ever. When peace returns, things are bound to change. If the ban on imports of French goods is ever overturned, what will we do for money?'

'We'll carry on fishing and provisioning,' Winnie responded. 'The naval provisioning yard will close, but we'll still have the merchant ships ...'

'They won't bring in much,' Louisa objected. 'Everyone will be competing for their custom.'

'I don't want to carry on. You will count me out this time – I won't have anything to do with it.'

Louisa's eyes flashed with annoyance.

'I am with child,' Winnie said emphatically.

'All the more reason for you to take part. You have your child's future to think of. There's a fortune to be made from the fine French lace and cognac that old Boneyparte lets the boatmen bring back from the merchants at Gravelines. I've said it before- we've done well out of the arrangement so far. You can't disagree with that, Winnie.'

'Last year, lace was our most profitable commodity,' Jason said, 'but there is another export that is increasin' in importance. I think we should make sure we have a piece of that pie, so to speak, so to that end, I've decided to buy another boat.'

Winnie noted Louisa raising an eyebrow. Although not in control of the purse-strings, having given up her right to own property on her marriage, she was still the keeper of the accounts.

'A galley with twelve oars each side,' Jason went on, 'clinker built with the planks overlappin'. She'll be very light and fast enough for a crew to row her across the Channel in less than six hours.'

'A guinea boat, you mean?' Winnie said, recalling the first time she saw one. Before Billy disappeared, they had been sailing the *Curlew* back from the fishing grounds, at the start of shot-fare, the mackerel season. Louisa had been steering a course through the shipping in the Downs – at least seven hundred vessels on that day – when Billy had spotted a galley with twelve oarsmen, skimming through the water faster than any cutter.

Ignoring Winnie's question, Jason continued, 'It's been illegal to export English gold for the past fifteen or sixteen years and the pound has fallen in value, which means that speculators have been buyin' gold in London with British banknotes.'

'Good for them,' Louisa interrupted him. 'Everybody knows that banknotes aren't worth the paper they're written on.'

'Anyway, I was goin' on to say that they sell the gold on the Continent for a fifteen to twenty per cent profit. Napoleon is encouragin' the flight of guineas to France with the intention of bankruptin' our country.'

'Why should he have England's gold?' Grace asked.

'It's complicated by the fact that our government sends gold to Wellin'ton to fund his army,' Jason explained. 'The venturers who finance the transfer don't have any scruples as to whose side they're on, as long as they're makin' a profit. I don't see why we can't do the same.' He smiled. 'Parliament's banned imports of French brandy because of the war, but we still do a good trade in it. It isn't hurtin' nobody.'

'I don't like the idea that the guineas are going over to France to fund the men who are fighting against our soldiers,' Winnie said.

'If we are sendin' gold of equal value to Old Boney and Wellington, I say that's fair and even-handed. I don't have any qualms about it. What do you say, Louisa?'

'It seems that you've already made your mind up,' she said, giving him a look that meant, *I'll be having a word with you in private*.

'I've already been in contact with Mr Cork. We'll work out how to hide the gold, perhaps within the structure of

47

the boat, and then we'll carry goods back from the merchants in Gravelines, along with any intelligence that we receive on the French side. He'll pay our fee for transporting the gold plus the usual percentage for moving the goods. But before that, we'll do another run as we've always done.'

'Whist, my dearest,' Louisa warned. 'Your voice carries.'

'And the walls of this house are very thin, I know.' Jason smiled wryly. 'We will keep this conversation to ourselves. What do you think, Grace? You'll be able to have a new dress every day,' he added, when she hesitated.

'I am not a flibbertigibbet who is easily impressed by a length of muslin,' she responded. Despite her trials, Winnie smiled as Grace went on, 'I should like a new gown, though, just one or two, or enough that I have one for every day of the week.'

Jason looked at Winnie. 'What do you say, bearing in mind that we're doing this for the family – and for Billy when he returns?'

'You have twisted my arm,' she said grudgingly. It seemed that, trapped by circumstance, she had no choice.

Chapter Four

Christmastide

It was Winnie's first Christmas without Billy. She and her sisters and Jason had dressed in their Sunday best and joined their neighbours walking to St George's chapel of ease where they paid their respects to Terrier, his grave not yet marked with a headstone, before passing the other monuments to master mariners and ordinary seamen who had gone aloft.

'You are late, but no matter,' Reverend North said, greeting them at the entrance to the building.

Winnie glanced at Grace who had insisted that she couldn't leave the house until she had trimmed her bonnet with a fresh ribbon and a snip of holly, but Grace's tardiness didn't appear to have upset the vicar on this occasion. His mood was mellow, his lips stained the colour of claret.

'I'm delighted that you could attend the service, Mr and Mrs Witherall, and the Misses Lennicker. This joyous day is turning out to be one of many miracles.'

'You have received our gift to the Church?' Jason enquired.

'Indeed, and I have found it to be more than satisfactory. The season's greetings to you all.'

The congregation settled in the pews and the service proceeded with readings, songs and prayers. They sang 'Come, Thou Long expected Jesus' and 'Hark, the Herald

Angels Sing', and then Winnie knelt to pray for Billy and for Mr Jones and his children, forced by poverty to live apart. There would be no joyful celebrations for them. As the child kicked inside her belly reminding her that it wouldn't be long before her confinement, she glanced at Louisa kneeling to her left, her head bowed, her lips moving silently. Perhaps it was unfair of her, but she speculated that Louisa was praying for the success of their next run and the completion of the guinea boat.

To her right, Grace, resting her elbows on the ledge of the pew in front, was staring heavenwards. Was she praying for the souls of their parents? Winnie wondered. Her mind began to wander, transporting her back to a time when Louisa had taken the family's troubles on her shoulders and kept them to herself.

It hadn't been long after they had buried their father when Winnie, having wrestled with her conscience, had joined her sisters at a dance being held at the Waterman's Arms. Billy had dragged his feet about going too, but eventually he had dressed up for the occasion in dark pantaloons and a black shirt with a high collar and what Winnie considered to be ridiculous ruffles down the front. It was an article of dress that had been top of the mode many years before.

As pipers and fiddlers played a riotous jig, Winnie and Grace tried to persuade Billy to dance with them.

'Mr Lennicker was a merry soul. He wouldn't have wanted us to be sad,' Winnie said.

'I can't 'elp grievin'. 'E was like a father to me.'

'I know, but you will feel better for a dance. I always do,' Grace said. 'Please, Billy.'

'I don't feel like it. No offence.'

The rejection was more painful than Winnie had expected, but she shrugged it off.

'We'll have to find someone else to dance with, Grace.'

'There are gentlemen queuing up to ask us,' Grace smiled.

'Ned and David can 'ardly be described as gen'lemen,' Billy said, following Winnie's gaze towards the edge of the room where a group of the boatmen's sons were staring eagerly at her and Grace. Winnie tossed her head in what she hoped was a haughty manner. She had no interest in them, but if Billy wouldn't dance ...

'I suppose it wouldn't do any 'arm to take a turn,' he went on. 'Mr Lennicker will be lookin' down on me, makin' sure I'm protectin' 'is daughters.'

Grace winked at Winnie as he followed them.

In the whirl of laughter and dancing, Billy put aside his sorrows, and later, he took Winnie's hand and pulled her aside. He stood in front of her and all she could see was his winning smile and the spark in his eyes, and it was as if the world had stopped and they were the only ones in it.

'I'm the luckiest lad alive,' he murmured. 'I've been dancin' with the prettiest girl in Deal.'

'Dear Billy,' she whispered, as his body stiffened, his eyes widened, and his mouth formed a questioning O.

Fearing she had overstepped the mark in assuming that he might have a fancy for her, she turned and slipped away, mumbling excuses. She had a headache and it felt wrong after all to be going out so soon after Pa's death ... Quietly, she made her way home.

She didn't see Billy the next morning, making her wonder if he was avoiding her, but later that day, he joined her in the kitchen, his hands behind his back.

'I've got somethin' for you.' He held out a punnet of strawberries. 'I didn't steal 'em or nothin'. I bought 'em for you from the market – I know 'ow much you like 'em.'

'I'm not cooking anything special for supper, if this is your way of trying to get around me, Billy Fleet.' There was stew – mutton and pearl barley – simmering over the fire.

'I'm not expectin' anythin' in return.' He flushed to the roots of his hair. 'Unless ... no, I can't say it. Take one. Go on.'

She took one and bit into it, dribbling juice down her chin and chuckling as she wiped it away with the corner of her apron.

'Oh dear, that stain will never come out, but it's so delicious that it was worth making a mess for.'

'Are they better than the ones your uncle grows? Mr Laxton 'as a reputation for growin' the best berries in the county.'

'I'll have to check.' The stew began to boil, bubbles rising to the surface, expelling gentle bursts of steam. 'May I?' She took a second strawberry then a third, aware that Billy was watching her, his gaze drifting from her mouth to the curve of her breast, and up to her eyes. 'What do *you* think?' she teased.

'Oh, they're lovely, very nice,' he said.

'I'm talking about the strawberries,' she giggled. 'You haven't tried one yet.'

'Then you've caught me out. Winnie, I'm mightily fond of you,' he said softly. 'I've flirted with other girls, but—'

'They aren't interested,' Winnie finished for him. She had heard stories of Billy's attempts at finding love: how he had asked Margaret Hibben's younger sister, Alice, to walk out with him. Margaret had a reputation, having broken off her engagement to Jason before he married Louisa. Alice had agreed to a clandestine meeting with Billy, but when he turned up, she was accompanied by her three best friends who joined her in mocking him for

52

ever thinking he stood a chance with her with his wayward hair and bat ears.

Billy looked at her, pained.

'I'm sorry,' she whispered. 'That didn't come out right. What I'd like to know is why you would look at other young ladies, if you have a fancy for me?'

'That's just it. I've been makin' myself look at them, but none of 'em match you in my affections.' He brightened. 'We've always been friends, 'aven't we? We 'aven't fallen out that many times in the past.'

Winnie couldn't disagree.

'I've tried to think of you as a sister, but when I'm with you, I feel like – well, I can't breathe. It's like I'm drownin'.' She felt her forehead tighten as he went on, 'I don't mean it in a bad way. When we're together, on the boat, on the beach, at 'ome 'ere in the kitchen, all I want to do is kiss you.'

Her heart thudded as the logs on the fire began to hiss and spit.

'I'd better deal with that,' she said, tearing herself away to grab the pan off the fire and leave it on the mat on the table. 'What are my sisters going to say when they find out?'

'They won't – I'll go to the butchers and pick up some meat.'

'The stew will be fine. What I mean is, when they find out about you being sweet on me.'

'I hope they'll be 'appy for us.'

'I'm not sure what Louisa will say.' She rather feared her older sister's reaction.

'Let's keep it to ourselves for now – it's nobody else's business anyway.' If she was being honest, Billy looked a little relieved. 'I'm not in a position to support a wife, not yet. Although I do 'ave plans, and dreams of being a success just like Marlin. One day our ship will come in and we'll marry and buy a cottage on the beach. In the meantime, let's take …' he took her hands and leaned in close '… one kiss at a time.'

With a jolt, Winnie found herself back in church with the scent of pine and incense swirling around her nostrils. There were wreaths of holly heavy with scarlet berries, and rows of beeswax candles, reminding her of past Christmases when Billy was with them, singing his heart out.

She and her sisters resumed their seats and prepared to listen to the vicar's Christmas sermon. In the distance, she heard the clanging of a bell being rung from the beach. The boatmen in the congregation stood up and swiftly made their way out through the door at the side of the chapel which had been made to allow them to arrive and leave without disrupting church proceedings. Jason glanced back towards Reverend North with a nod of apology.

'I shall continue,' the vicar said when they had gone, but the remaining congregation had other ideas.

'What do you think has happened?' Grace whispered.

'We'll find out soon enough,' Louisa muttered back.

'It's strange that they've 'ad to rush away. The weather's set fair and the sea's flat calm,' Mrs Witherall observed from the pew behind them.

'One of the shore boys 'as seen somethin' gone asprawl and raised the alarm,' Mrs Edwards contributed. 'We should go down and 'ave a look, show our support for our 'usbands and sons.'

'I beseech you, ladies, to wait until the end of the service in which we give thanks to God for the birth of His son, Jesus Christ. There is a special place that burns with fire and brimstone for those who would seem to be lacking in gratitude.' Reverend North brandished his book of sermons and dropped it back on the lectern where it expelled loose pages and dust. Mrs Witherall and Mrs Edwards, first on their feet, hesitated. Louisa, who had followed suit, sat down again. 'What good will watching from a distance do? You will serve your souls and those of your husbands far better by continuing with our Christian worship. I will add a short prayer in respect of the boatmen who risk their lives to save others ...'

The women, having sat down again, perched on the edge of their seats, ready to leave as soon as the vicar released them from the threat of eternal damnation, and within the hour, the congregation were on their way to the beach.

'The boats are still here,' Louisa exclaimed.

'Not a single one has gone out,' Winnie confirmed. 'Cromwell, you weren't in church,' she called, and he paused from skimming stones with some of the other boys, and strolled up the slope towards her.

'The vicar told us to keep away – 'e doesn't like us bein' boisterous in the pews.'

'I see. Where are the men? Have you seen Marlin? We heard the bell ...'

'Ah yes, they paid me a whole shillin' to ring it – and not to tell anyone where they are.'

'It's obvious, isn't it?' Louisa said.

'They've taken shelter in the Waterman's Arms,' Mrs Edwards shouted.

'Shelter from what?' Mrs Witherall said crossly.

'Reverend North and their lovin' wives ... I know who won't be 'avin' a slice of plum puddin' with his dinner ... or anythin' else,' Mrs Edwards said coarsely. 'This way, ladies. We'll drag 'em out by the 'air.'

Winnie and Grace waited for Louisa to fetch Jason who came quietly.

'What do you think you were doing, shamming us like that?' Louisa was trying but failing to keep a straight face. 'You could at least have taken us with you, but you left us there!'

'We thought it a great ruse,' he said, shamefaced. 'Oh, come on. Don't pretend you don't sit there in church, plannin' your escape. Am I forgiven?' He offered his arm to his wife. After a moment's hesitation, Louisa took it and the four of them walked back to the cottage.

Once indoors, Grace changed into her workaday clothes and went to fetch their goose which had been roasting in the oven at the pot house. By the time she returned, Winnie had laid the table with a white linen cloth, their best cutlery and a vase of holly, ribbons and silk roses, and Louisa had lit the candles around the parlour.

Jason carved the bird without snaggling it, while Winnie dished up the vegetables and gravy.

'I assume the extra place is for Billy,' Louisa observed.

'I hope you don't mind,' Winnie said.

'You can give the leftovers to one of your waifs and strays. Mrs Stickles mentioned it the other day, how you'd bought a pie for a starving sailor. I fear that you have been taken in by a briny vagabond – you know how these swearing rogues are. They make their money fly by the handful, then squander it when they are back ashore.'

Winnie flushed. 'I should have asked you first – I'm sorry.'

'It's all right – just don't make a habit of it,' Louisa said.

'He had a very sad tale to tell.'

'I'm sure he did – they all do.'

'My dear wife, you are a harsh judge of a man's situation,' Jason said. 'Many of these ex-naval seamen are in dire straits.'

'I know, but in my opinion, charity should be carried out in moderation and according to the donor's means.'

'We are comfortably off,' Jason countered. 'We can afford to give away a few pies.'

Winnie understood why her sister was precious about money. When Pa died, it was Louisa who had suffered most from the debts he left behind, being exposed to the threat of losing her virtue and the roof over their heads to the attorney, Mr Trice, if she didn't find the means of paying back the man they called the fusty weasel.

Grace cleared the plates whilst Winnie fetched the plum pudding. Louisa prepared warm milk and brandy to drink with it.

'Going back to the subject of being able to afford things, I have gifts for each of you to show my appreciation for everything you do,' Jason announced when he had finished off the dessert course with a little cheese. He stood up and opened the panel to the side of the fireplace, revealing a hiding hole, from which he pulled out a hessian sack. 'This is for my darling wife.' He took out the first gift and handed it to Louisa who was blushing with delight.

He watched her with a quizzical expression as she unwrapped it.

'It's a book,' she said, her voice filled with excitement. 'Oh?' Her tone hardened. 'It's a recipe book.'

'I thought you'd appreciate it,' Jason said, apparently unconcerned by Louisa's reaction.

'It's a wonderful gift,' Winnie said. *'The Art of Cookery Made Plain and Easy* by Hannah Glasse.'

'You have it, if you like it so much,' Louisa said quickly. 'Jason, I won't have you casting aspersions on my skills in the kitchen.'

Winnie glanced towards Grace who was rolling her eyes. Louisa didn't like anyone to think she was anything other than perfect. Jason had hurt her feelings and Winnie suspected that he wouldn't hear the end of it for a long while, but something was amiss. He gulped and his shoulders shook, and suddenly, he burst into great roars of laughter.

'Oh, I got you there,' he gasped.

'You were gammoning me again!' Mollified, Louisa went on, 'What am I going to do with you?'

'I have your gift here – the real one.' He took a small box from the sack and placed it on the table in front of her. 'Open it.'

Winnie felt a twinge of envy when Louisa opened the box and took out a gold chain with a sapphire pendant. Beaming, she held it to her neck.

'It's beautiful,' she breathed as Jason reached behind her to fasten the clasp and brush his lips against her cheek. 'How can I thank you?'

He answered her with a grin, and she turned away and slid the secret drawer in the table open. She palmed an object from inside and dropped it into his hand.

'A pocket watch!' said Grace as he picked up the gleaming gold timepiece, turned it over and opened the back to reveal its inner workings.

'It's marvellous.' He tipped his head to one side. 'How did you know?'

'You've mentioned it often enough – I had it engraved.'

He closed it and read the inscription on the back before clasping the watch in his hand. 'I shall treasure it for ever.'

58

Winnie saw how her sister's eyes sparkled with happiness, but the pleasure she felt in seeing Louisa's joy was tempered with regret that it wasn't her who was the contented wife.

The four of them exchanged further gifts: a bonnet for Winnie; a new gown for Grace; a shawl for Louisa and a cap for Jason. Afterwards, they played games and cards – All Fours – until dusk when Winnie and Grace washed the dishes and put them away.

Winnie placed Billy's untouched plate aside, telling Grace that she would give the food to Mr Jones the following morning, if she could find him.

She retired to bed early, cuddling up with one of Billy's shirts that he'd left behind, the black one with the silly ruffles. She recalled how she'd been asleep one night when he'd come back from one of the taverns, falling around outside on the street. There had been a crash and a yelp as one of the neighbours threw a bucket of water – bucket and all – from an upstairs window, followed by laughter. Winnie had picked up the candlestick and run downstairs to find Billy on the doorstep, his hair stuck to his forehead and water dripping from his nose.

'Is it water?' she asked.

'I think so.' He grinned. 'It could 'ave been worse.'

'What's going on? Who is that causing a commotion loud enough to wake the dead?' Winnie glanced towards the top of the stairs at the sound of Louisa's voice.

'It's nothing to worry about,' Winnie called back. 'The Rattlers' cats were scrapping in the street again.'

'I've never heard of cats wearing hobnailed boots,' Louisa shouted back. 'Is Billy home?'

'I've just tripped over his boots,' Winnie said quickly, flashing him a warning glance. 'He must be abed.' She had told Louisa an untruth, but she was unashamed because it was dark except for the candle that was dripping wax, and Billy was beside her, his hand creeping behind her back and settling on the curve of her waist.

'Goodnight then,' Louisa called.

'We can sit up together,' Winnie whispered.

'I think that's an excellent idea,' Billy murmured, his breath warm against her ear as he steered her to the parlour where they sat side by side in silence. Winnie extinguished the candle, listening for the tiny hiss of steam as the flame went out, and another, entirely different flame ignited in her breast. They stayed there, kissing, for as long as they dared, knowing it was wrong, even though it felt right.

Winnie's belly was tight and her heart sore. She pressed her face into Billy's shirt, but his scent was fading, and she was struggling to hold on to it.

Chapter Five

The Darkest Hour is Just Before Dawn

It was almost midnight on the day after Epiphany and Winnie was lurking in the sandhills to the north of Deal with her sisters and the ponies that they'd borrowed from Abel Brockman, Jason's cousin who was a horse dealer and son of the local mill owner. There were three of them: one black, the other two dark bay, their white markings painted out with blacking, their hooves wrapped in hessian.

Blowing on her gloved fingers, Winnie peered through the shadows of the marram grass from her vantage point just below the ridge of one of the dunes. Their spout lantern had gone out, but it made little difference, it being a clear, starry night.

The sea began to swarm with little boats that emerged from the nearby inlets, their rowlocks muffled with rags, their oars dropping into the water with barely a splash. Then she spotted the giant lugger – repaired just in time for the run – rocking gently on the water close to the shore, her black canvas sails furled, her name blacked out and her guns glinting in the moonlight. She still expected to catch a glimpse of Billy's silhouette among those of the *Whimbrel*'s crew as they unloaded their cargo of contraband on to the smaller boats waiting to ferry it to the beach.

'I'm so cold that I'm frozen to the spot,' Grace grumbled from beside her. 'Why don't they hurry up?'

'They're working as fast as they can,' Louisa said.

'I wish we were at home beside the fire,' Winnie lamented. 'We could be sitting with our feet up, drinking a glass of wassail.'

'Have patience, both of you. Good things come to those who wait.'

'We'll die from the chills or winter fever before then,' Grace observed.

'It won't be long before they give us the sign to join them,' Louisa said.

In the meantime, all they could do was watch and wait. Winnie's mind drifted, thinking back to the fateful August day when the press had taken Billy.

There had been rumours of a press officer going around Ramsgate with his gangers. It was no ordinary press, but a hot one which meant that they would take almost anyone, including men like Marlin despite their papers of exemption, because the navy was short of sailors to take part in the wars against France and America. Even though a seafaring man was worth two landlubbers, they took bootmakers, shopkeepers and chandlers, hoping that a spell at sea would knock them into some kind of shape.

As the evening shadows lengthened, Abel Brockman had ridden along the beach to warn them that the gangers were on their way to Deal. Immediately, Winnie had run across to the *Whimbrel* to check that Billy had heard the warning.

'We heard,' Jason confirmed as Billy turned pink, and she felt a little sorry that she had made him feel less of a man in front of the friend he idolised. 'I think that a fishin' trip is in order. We have more chance of gettin' away on the lugger than hidin' in town. If the Yellow Admiral's on the lookout, we'll disappear into the Sands and stay there for a while.'

Winnie had hesitated when Louisa had tugged at her arm. Yearning to kiss her beloved, she had to be content with telling him to take care, before she tore herself away from the beach and hastened up and down the alleyways with Louisa and Grace, hammering on doors and shouting that the gangers were on their way.

The warnings had come too late.

Back down on the beach, a throng of women and children were surging around the gangers who had clapped the men into cuffs and leg-irons and forced them into line. The women wailed and shouted, pushed and shoved, but the gangers shoved them back. The men were fighting against their bonds as their captors, armed with carbines and sticks, forced them to march along the shore in the direction of the barracks, where they stopped to wait for a jollyboat to take them to a naval tender in the Downs.

Feeling sick, her palms sweaty and her heartbeat erratic, Winnie tried to restrain herself from running after them, knowing that Louisa wouldn't like it, but as they pushed Billy roughly into the jollyboat, she could hold back no longer. She charged at one of the gangers, her fists raised in anger.

'Let him go. I need him. We need him ...'

'I'm sorry, missus.' The ganger caught her by the wrists as her sisters rushed across to drag her back.

'Winnie, stop it,' Louisa said, hauling her away by the waist.

'Whose side are you on?' Winnie spat, her ribs rising and falling with each breath. 'Let me go.'

'You're making a terrible scene – everybody's looking at you.'

'I'm going after them ...'

'How, when you can't swim?' Grace held on to Winnie's arm.

'I can't stand by and do nothing.'

'And we won't, I promise,' Louisa whispered into her ear as the gangers pushed the jollyboat into deeper water, and the guards picked up the oars and rowed the men towards the tender where they would be held for the night, or until they agreed to volunteer for the King's shilling. Billy sat with his head bowed, his shoulders slumped, and Winnie's heart broke.

'Why have they stopped?' The tension in Louisa's voice pulled her back to the present. The light in the small cabin at the *Whimbrel*'s forepeak went out and the figures of her crew stood immobile on the open deck beneath the boat's three towering masts.

'They must have heard something,' Winnie murmured.

'Where is the *Spindrift*?' Grace asked. 'I can't see her.'

Winnie couldn't see the galley punt either, but then she spotted her single mast, dark canvas and painted keel arriving alongside the lugger, and she could breathe again. On the signal from the shore – the blue flash and deadened report of a pistol – the *Spindrift*'s crew took in her sail and the *Whimbrel*'s men continued unloading the goods.

The sandhills came alive. The tub carriers, duffers and their womenfolk, guarded by the batsmen carrying staves of ash, started to walk towards the sea, moving across the sand like a column of emmets, preparing to collect the goods and run them into town where they would stash them away in the cellars, attics and passageways that they used as hiding holes, or carry them inland, dropping them off at various farms to be hidden in hayricks and turnip clamps. Others would transport goods to Canterbury and London to be sold directly to merchants and peddlers or be delivered to the financiers or 'venturers' who had paid for them.

'There's the *Curlew* alongside the *Whimbrel*.' Winnie was aware of Louisa linking her arm through hers, reassuring her that her sisters wouldn't abandon her this time.

'How can you tell?'

'There are two figures, one taller than the other – Mr Witherall and Cromwell,' Louisa explained. 'Let's go.'

Grace made a clicking sound in her throat, and the ponies shifted, their leather harnesses creaking as they followed Winnie and Louisa down through the dunes and on to the beach. The group stopped at the edge of the water where even the waves seemed to have been silenced for the occasion, the breakers rolling across the sand, their inrush and retreat barely audible.

Mr Witherall brought the *Curlew* in as close as possible, then Cromwell jumped out and carried the goods to the beach, splashing through the shallows.

'Whist!' the old man warned. He seemed unusually bulky about the legs, with six pounds of baccy in a pair of stays. 'We don't want to invite any trouble from the gobblers.'

'They've gone north to Sandwich, thinking that we're going to bring the goods in there.' Winnie couldn't miss the triumph in Louisa's voice as she continued, 'We arranged for Lawless to misdirect them. Not only have we fooled the Riding officers, but we've outwitted the Revenue at sea. Black Dog and his crew have taken their boat out to divert their attention from the *Whimbrel* and *Spindrift*. They'll be leading their cruiser a merry dance around the Sands, but we must make haste because it won't be long before they realise that they've been shammed.'

This was news to Winnie.

'Why have you roped Isaiah and the Rattlers in to helping us?' she asked as more of the smaller boats came in and the landside smugglers pounced – a good team could run five hundred tubs ashore in twenty minutes. 'They can't be trusted. We fell out with them because they did us wrong. Louisa, this is madness. Pa will be turning in his grave.'

'I haven't forgotten, or forgiven them, but we've had to agree a truce. The authorities have redoubled their efforts to stop the free traders pursuing a profit. Not only do they arrest everyone they catch breaking the law, but they impound their boats and cut them into three. Can you believe it? It's theft.'

'It is a waste,' Winnie agreed.

'I thought that they adopted some of the better boats into the navy for the service of Fat Prinny and Farmer George,' Grace added, wrinkling her nose at the mention of the Prince Regent and the King.

'My husband would be devastated if anything happened to his precious lugger. Sometimes it feels like there are three people in my marriage, one of whom is the *Whimbrel*.' Louisa was looking away, but Winnie knew she was smiling.

She and Louisa helped Cromwell carry the goods to safety, piling them up above the tideline that was marked by dark skeins of seaweed and gleaming shells. As Grace led the ponies down to the tidy stack of bales and bags, all wrapped in oilskins, Winnie noticed how Louisa tucked a small packet inside her cloak before wishing Cromwell farewell.

'Watch your backs, ladies,' Mr Witherall called as the boy scrambled back on to the *Curlew*.

The sisters loaded the contraband on to the ponies' backs, securing it to their harnesses. So far, so good, Winnie thought, as they headed back into the sandhills, leading one animal each. By dawn, having delivered the lace and silks to Mr Cork, and returned the ponies to the mill, they would be tucked up at home in the warm.

'Hurry. I don't want to keep Mr Cork waiting,' Louisa said.

Winnie understood why Louisa didn't want to upset him. She had been recommended to him by Sir Flinders of Mundel Manor in return for Louisa having risked her life to save his elder daughter and the other passengers when the *White Hind* had foundered on the Goodwin Sands. A shiver ran down Winnie's spine as she looked out to sea towards the giant ship gobbler that ran north to south beyond the Downs. Invisible now in the darkness and with the tide covering it, it lay in wait like a basking monster, hungry to swallow any vessel that drifted by.

Having been introduced, Louisa and Mr Cork had agreed a contract, and since then Louisa and her sisters had delivered run goods to him. He acted as agent to various of the clergy and gentry of East Kent who invested in the free trade, financing the purchase of vast quantities of lace, wine and other luxury items from France. As the intermediary for the foreign merchants in Gravelines, he made sure that they packed their goods as small units that were of a convenient size for the free traders to carry away. The boatmen collected the cargo and shipped it back to England for transport to Canterbury and London in return for a fee, a percentage of the profits made. When it had been sold, Mr Cork collected the money and forwarded it to the merchants, subtracting his commission first.

He allowed the sisters several months' credit, knowing that they'd always pay up in the end. On occasion, he asked Louisa to invest in contraband for his personal use, or on behalf of other contacts of his, a London draper for example, or a publican with space in his cellar, or sometimes ... there were other, respectable gentlemen who liked to be involved, people you would never imagine ... but it was perfectly safe for them. They handed over their money to Mr Cork and he did the rest.

As they walked, Winnie heard noises: muffled footsteps, the odd cough, the sharp bark of a fox and hoot of an owl, signals perhaps passing between groups of smugglers as they dispersed into the shadows. There were duffers carrying bags or dollops of tea, the tub carriers laden down with half-ankers containing wine and brandy, and the rest making away with what was left – a consignment of silk bandannas, a package of the finest French gloves, and a gold watch or two.

'I think someone is following us,' she whispered.

'You're worrying unnecessarily. We have the goods, the boats have stood to sea, and there are plenty of batsmen about to protect us.' Louisa's insistence began to persuade her that they were safe.

Making slow progress, they reached the ancient highway, a sandy track that ran between Deal to the south and Sandwich to the north. Turning away from home, they passed the looker's cottage and the Chequers Inn which was in darkness. As she trudged along, Winnie wondered how long it would be until her confinement and how she would feel when the infant arrived. Perhaps its presence would excuse her from joining in with future runs. Her spirits lifted briefly then sank again when she realised that Louisa would no doubt ask Mrs Witherall or Nancy to mind the child for her.

Moving away from the highway, they crossed a field, the moonlight making them more conspicuous than

Winnie would have wished. The grass was white with frost and the ground ringing underfoot. Something cracked. Louisa gasped and stopped, swaying slightly on one leg.

'What have you done?' Winnie dashed forward to help her.

'I've gone and twisted my ankle, that's all.'

'Can you walk on it?' Winnie asked as Louisa rested her arm on her shoulder. Holding up her skirt, she placed her foot on the ground, but as soon as she tried to put any weight on it, she cried out.

'I don't think I can.'

'Never mind,' Winnie said. 'You'll have to ride Gubbins.'

'Is he broken to ride?' Grace cut in.

'I imagine so – he's pretty well trained in other ways.' Winnie transferred the luggage from the black pony to one of the others, before helping Grace bundle Louisa on to his back.

'He hasn't taken offence yet,' Louisa grimaced, sitting up straight and looping her fingers through the harness. 'I thought he might buck me off.'

'Good boy,' Grace said, as Gubbins turned and nipped Winnie's arm.

She scolded him as they moved on, but they'd only taken a few steps before the pony decided that he'd had enough of their adventure and planted his feet. No amount of cajoling, whispering into his furry ear or poking him with a hazel twig would convince him to change his mind.

'Lead the others away and he'll follow,' Grace suggested. She had a way with animals, but Gubbins didn't take any notice of her either.

'I'll walk ...' Louisa's voice faded, and her body began to sag. Winnie darted to her side and half caught, half hauled her off the pony's back, and sat her on the ground, wondering what on earth they were going to do. The fact they had no smelling salts was the least of her concerns. They were in the middle of nowhere on the coldest night of winter so far. Louisa's husband was out with the *Whimbrel* and the landside smugglers had disappeared. How she wished Billy was here.

'Should we shout for assistance?' Grace whispered.

'It's too dangerous – who knows what villains are about? And we can't afford to attract the gobblers, if they should be on their way back from Sandwich.' Winnie patted Louisa's pale cheek. 'Wake up.' At the third time of asking, Louisa slowly opened her eyes.

'It's no use. I can't go any further,' she stuttered, her lips blue with cold.

'Then we'll take you straight home before you freeze to death,' Winnie said quickly, delighted for the excuse not to continue to their rendezvous with Mr Cork. 'We can take the goods with us or hide them nearby to collect another day.' There were plenty of hiding holes in the vicinity: a turnip clamp; a haystack; an abandoned boat.

'No, that's impossible. Mr Cork is expecting us – we can't let him down. It will do my reputation no good at all.'

'Let the dressmakers and ladies of London shed tears because they haven't received their lace,' Grace said. 'What does it matter?'

'Your health is of greater importance than the ladies' trivial cares,' Winnie said. 'If we can't take the goods to Mr Cork, he can't have them and that's all there is to it.'

'It isn't the lace I'm worried about.' The whites of Louisa's eyes gleamed in the moonlight. 'Mr Cork has entrusted me with another … matter. It cannot wait, so Winnie, you and Grace must carry on to the rondy as arranged. I'll find a stick to lean on and hobble home.'

'What is this other matter?' Winnie suspected that Louisa was concealing something from them, an unfortunate habit of hers.

'I can't say.'

'Then we will go straight home.' Winnie would give Louisa no quarter for keeping secrets.

'I really can't tell you – the less you know, the better it is for your health, if you get my meaning. Suffice to say, I have a package to deliver into Mr Cork's hands forthwith. It's urgent. The gentleman who requested his assistance is paying handsomely for it.' Winnie glowered at her and she continued, 'I agreed because it seemed like money for old rope – until I went and crocked my ankle.'

'If we are going to help you, we need to know everything,' Winnie said.

'Come close then. Both of you. If this gets out, I'll be in great danger. Promise me neither of you will breathe a word.'

'Promise,' Winnie and Grace murmured at the same time as they leaned towards Louisa, straining their ears to hear what she had to say.

'I'm carrying something of greater value than cognac and lace.'

'Gold?' Grace said.

'No, despatches, intelligence of national importance.'

'I don't understand.' Grace frowned.

'Remember how I carried papers to the gentleman at Ringwould?' Winnie nodded and Louisa continued, 'It's the same: information that our spies in France are sending to London to help our admirals and generals in the war against Napoleon. It could change the course of the fighting. There are lives depending on it.'

'Then these papers must reach Mr Cork tonight,' Winnie decided. 'Grace, take Louisa home. I'll go on to the rondy.'

'Why the sudden change of heart?' Grace asked.

'If it will help us against Old Boney, then I'll do anything. The sooner the fighting's over, the sooner our men can come home,' she said bravely.

'What about the rule, there's safety in numbers?' Grace said doubtfully. 'Look what happened the last time we met with the gobblers.'

'The gobblers aren't here.'

'There are other dangers,' Louisa said. 'Oh, I'm not sure. I'm torn. I'll never forgive myself if anything should go wrong. I don't think I said sorry properly, Winnie. I was so wrapped up in the idea that you had let yourself down with Billy that I didn't apologise for leaving you in the lurch when Officer Chase and Tom Lawrence turned up. I thought they'd come after me, not you, because they've always wanted to catch the Lace Maiden in possession of contraband and have her put away, or worse. You must have been petrified.'

Winnie didn't know how to respond. She certainly didn't feel like saying thank you. It's too little, too late, would have been closer to the mark.

'You should have waited with me – then we could all have swallowed the pill together.'

'But what would have been the purpose of that?'

There was no point in arguing with Louisa, she thought. They were wasting time.

'I'll go,' she said. The sooner she met with Mr Cork, the sooner her nightmare would be over.

'I'm very grateful,' Louisa said. 'I won't forget this, Winnie. Grace, take our commission, then we'll return home and wait for you. If you aren't back by dawn, we'll raise a hue and cry.'

Grace removed a few pieces of lace from a bale on one of the ponies' backs and wrapped them around her middle beneath her cloak. It wasn't strictly commission – it was Louisa's way of making a little extra on the side. She had an arrangement with some of the young ladies in the area and Mr Gigg, the draper.

'Take care, Winnie,' Grace said as she helped Louisa to her feet. Louisa handed Winnie the package, and Winnie tucked it inside the inner hem of her faded black velvet bonnet where she'd left a section open to form a pocket suitable for a bag of tea or a length of lace. Grace tied the lantern to the lead pony's saddlebag before turning to offer Louisa her shoulder to lean on.

'You must take the pistol.' Louisa held on to Grace's arm while she removed the firearm from her garter and the powder horn from the cord around her neck. 'It isn't loaded, but I suggest you keep it primed. You must have this as well.' She handed Winnie the gold watch that she'd given Jason for Christmas.

'I can't take this,' Winnie said, holding the watch.

'Jason lent it to me so I could keep an eye on the time. You can give it back in the morning. Oh dear, it doesn't feel right, letting you go alone.'

'Don't worry. I'm armed –' Winnie felt the weight of the pistol in her hand '– and I have three wilful companions. What can possibly go wrong?' she added with false bravado, her heart pounding against her breastbone.

Chapter Six

Small Mercies

Listening to her sisters' footsteps fade as they made their way back across the field, and unable to feel her fingers or toes for the cold, Winnie took hold of Gubbins's bridle and led him away. His companions followed one behind the other as she carried on, joining the track at the perimeter of the field.

A twig cracked underfoot. She almost leapt out of her skin.

'You're giving yourself the frights,' she scolded herself. *Keep going, Winnie. It isn't far now.*

Something came crashing out of the dunes, landing with a thump behind her, and the next thing she knew she was caught by the neck in the crook of a man's elbow with the cold metal muzzle of a pistol pressed to her temple.

'Let me go!' she cried, as the ponies cantered off into the distance.

'Don't waste your breath screaming and shouting, miss. There's no one here to hear it.'

'Sir, unhand me.' She had never been so scared.

'I can't do that, I'm afraid.'

His supercilious tone angered her.

'How dare you!' She twisted and sank her teeth through his greatcoat, pinching the flesh that clothed his forearm, but he barely flinched.

'One more move like that and I'll ...' he growled, tightening his grip on her neck.

Was he about to force himself on her? Would he leave her for dead like poor Mary Bax who had been murdered by a foreigner, a deserter from one of the ships who had slit her throat in the sandhills many years before? Or was he about to bury her alive as was the punishment for thieves in centuries past?

Dear God. She began to pray frantically for salvation.

'You are asking yourself, who is this gentleman and what does he want with the young woman known as the Lace Maiden?'

'You are mistaken,' she said, but he wasn't listening.

'You know very well what I seek,' he went on. 'As a woman reputedly of great intellect, I'm sure you comprehend the wisdom of bowing to my command so your ordeal can be over and done with. Do you understand?'

'Y-y-yes,' she stammered, her mouth dry and her body shaking, as she tried to make out the man's features, wondering if she recognised him. He spoke with a cutglass accent and his breath smelled of roast beef, and she had the impression that he was older than her by twenty or even thirty years.

Slowly, he released his grip and took half a step back before slipping the pistol into his belt and taking a knife from his pocket. She stood quivering as he began to rummage her.

'Ah, look at this,' he said, briefly examining Louisa's pistol before tucking it into his belt alongside his own. She wished she'd listened and kept it primed and ready, not that she could have brought herself to fire more than a warning shot to scare him away.

'Hand me your cloak.'

'It is very cold, sir,' she said, thinking of Jason's gold watch, but she couldn't save it. When she reluctantly divested herself of her cloak, he found it and slipped it into his greatcoat pocket. He ran his odious hands over her back and chest, patting her through her clothing, then squatted down and groped around underneath her heavy petticoats and skirt, moving his hands up her stockinged legs. Having reached the soft skin above her garters, he stopped. Winnie squeezed her eyes shut and waited with a hammering heart for the inevitable assault of his fingers …

Nothing happened.

Her attacker stood up and straightened. In the slanting rays of the moonlight, Winnie noticed that he had a Roman nose and a missing tooth.

'What do you know of a gentleman by the name of Monsieur Jean Boule?'

She thought she had heard of him but couldn't for the life of her remember when or why. She wanted to be helpful – she didn't want to die.

'I've h-h-heard of a Mr John Bull, the archetypal Englishman, a stout man in a tailcoat with a top hat and white breeches. I've s-s-seen him in the newspapers.'

'I shouldn't be too clever if I were you, miss. I would be much obliged if you would remove your boots.'

'You mean I have a choice?'

'None whatsoever.'

She could hardly unlace them for trembling, but eventually she managed to take them off. The stranger picked them up and studied them minutely before cutting the soles from the uppers with his knife and ripping the seams apart. Shaking his head, he tossed the boots aside.

'Your bonnet,' he said.

She took it off and held it out to him, feeling sure that all was lost and she would never bear her child, or lie in

Billy's arms, or spend time with her sisters again, but as her hair tumbled free, his manner changed. His self-assurance – arrogance, even – seemed to evaporate. He didn't take the bonnet – he merely asked her to turn it over so he could take a perfunctory look inside.

'I am sorry to have troubled you,' he said stiffly, before turning and leaving her, his figure melding into the shadows of the hedge. Her temple throbbed, and her mouth was filled with the metallic taste of blood. Her boots were lying ruined with her cloak at her frozen feet. She felt afraid, deeply shocked and confused.

He had taken the watch, but he hadn't been interested in the contraband or in taking her by force and having his way with her.

With a shudder of cold and revulsion, she picked up her cloak and wrapped it round her shoulders before taking off her glove and putting her finger and thumb between her lips. She blew sharply, three times over, at which the ponies reappeared, greeting her with a soft nicker of recognition. She tore open one of the bales, then another until she found a handful of silk bandannas which she used to bind her feet. Growing bored, the ponies wandered away to nibble at the grass. She whistled again and they returned.

Winnie had taught Billy to whistle, a skill that came in useful, not merely for their forays into the free trade.

She recalled his first inept attempts and how she'd mocked him.

'I can't do it,' he'd said. 'Mrs Fleet wasn't a whistler.'

'Cover your teeth with your lips.' Winnie had to gulp back tears of laughter because it made him look even more comical than before. 'Use your thumb and middle finger. Watch me. Like this. Push your tongue back and breathe

77

in, then out. Harder.' Billy's complexion turned a deep shade of beetroot as she cupped her ear, teasing him, until she heard the faintest whistle.

The following day, she'd been walking along the shore when she'd heard the song of a blackbird coming from inside Pa's old hut. Fearing that the poor creature was trapped, she had gone to investigate.

She'd pushed the creaking door open and found herself dragged inside. With a cry of alarm, she'd turned to find herself in Billy's arms.

'What do you think, Winnie? I've been practisin',' he'd said, grinning from ear to ear.

'You scared me out of my wits,' she'd scolded, giving him a gentle dig in the ribs.

'Let me make it up to you.'

'How do you think you're going to do that?' she'd said archly.

'Like this ...' he'd said, pulling her close and planting a kiss on her forehead. 'And this ...'

She sensed Billy's presence. No matter how far away he'd sailed, tonight he was at her side in spirit. Strangely comforted, she caught Gubbins and leaned on his withers, using him to take a little of the weight off her feet which felt like blocks of ice.

She didn't know the rendezvous well, having only passed the crumbling farmhouse at Nomansland Farm and the barns that surrounded it a couple of times in her life. The darkness disguised the dirt and neglect as she rounded the corner into the yard, the ponies snorting as they caught the stench of pigs in their flaring nostrils. Their unease made her nervous.

Was she walking into another trap?

Plucking up all her remaining courage, she followed the arc of light from a lantern hanging from a hook beside the back door of the house.

'Who goes there?' A woman emerged, a knife glinting in her hand. 'Show yourself.'

'I'm here on behalf of the Lace Maiden. Mr Cork's expecting me,' she said, trembling like brawn jelly from the cold and shock.

The woman moved closer and looked her up and down. She was middle-aged, tall and thin, and had a white streak in her dark hair, reminding Winnie of a badger.

'It appears that you aren't 'ere to murder us in our beds. I don't like this at all. Never again.' The woman slipped the knife into a belt that was tied around her waist over a frayed brown dress covered in stains.

'Tobias, Jack, wake the boy and ready the 'orses.' The woman's order brought the figures of two men hastening into the yard. 'This way, missus,' she went on as one of them caught the ponies and began to unload the goods. The other opened a door to one of the barns and disappeared inside.

Winnie stumbled after her – she couldn't feel her hands or feet – along a dark passageway that smelled of wet dog, until they reached another door. The woman pushed it open and waited for her.

'Hurry – you've kept 'em waitin' long enow.' She pushed Winnie into the farmhouse kitchen, a room three or four times the size of the kitchen at Compass Cottage, with a lofty ceiling and a few logs burning in the massive stone fireplace. There were two gentlemen sitting at an oak table in the centre, their faces lit by a branched brass candelabra.

The younger man, wearing a navy coat with a cape attached over his riding clothes, pushed an empty plate away from him and jumped to his feet. The older one stood up slowly, his hand on the small of his back as he slipped a silver snuffbox into his pocket. He was of short stature, dressed in a shirt with a high-collar and white cravat. Beneath his unbuttoned jacket, Winnie caught a glimpse of an elaborately embroidered waistcoat.

'You took your time,' the younger man said, wiping his mouth in what Winnie considered an uncouth manner. He turned to the older man. 'I have recommended various gentlemen to you, yet you prefer to employ common women to carry what is highly sensitive material.'

'Please desist in your reproof.' The older man peered at her closely. 'This young lady has clearly suffered some trauma.'

'You say you have your people fully checked and warranted—' The younger man stared at her feet with distaste. Ashamed, she tucked her toes beneath the muddied hem of her dress. 'You should have been here hours ago – I've had to sit here in this draughty hellhole instead of enjoying the delights of the city.'

'The latter admission lays you open to discovery and detection,' the older man said. All the while they were arguing, Winnie was gazing at the fireplace, wondering how close to the flames she dared creep without setting her clothes alight.

'You have the package?' the younger man said.

'I am in possession of an item that I am to deliver to Mr Cork,' she said, uncertain whom she was addressing. Her teeth were chattering uncontrollably.

'I am he,' the older man said. 'Allow me to introduce myself and my acquaintance, Mr Buckley. I am Mr Cork.'

She didn't care if this man with the sallow skin and eyes the colour of coffee was the Queen of Sheba. All she wanted was to lie down by the fire to let the heat seep back into her bones, and it seemed that Mr Cork had noticed her pain.

'Sit down, young lady,' he said, offering a chair.

'The papers,' Mr Buckley snapped, unable to disguise his impatience as she took the weight off her feet.

'Please, hand them over,' Mr Cork requested.

Her fingers trembled as she removed her bonnet, untying the ribbon at her throat. She took the package from the flap inside and made to hand it to Mr Buckley, but Mr Cork snatched it away from him.

'My clerk will make a copy before I release them to you.' He turned towards the corner of the room – Winnie hadn't noticed before, but there was a very young man, hardly more than a boy, dressed in dark clothing and mittens, sitting at a small card table. He brushed away some cobwebs from the top, then proceeded to copy the despatches, dipping a goose quill into a bottle of ink and screeving across a fresh piece of paper.

'Not the newspapers, Mr Todd. Just the letters,' Mr Cork said. 'He'll go far, this one. He's a clever boy, but his mother dropped him on his head when he was an infant, a mixed blessing as the accident endowed him with the prodigious ability to make accurate copies of documents such as these. Unfortunately, it also rendered him mute.'

'I don't know why you're wasting our time doing this,' Mr Buckley complained, his moustache bristling.

'It's part of the system that I've set up to maintain security and secrecy,' Mr Cork bragged. 'I apologise for your inconvenience. It is frustrating to add further delay when you have an urgent desire to return to London. Tell me, is there a special lady waiting to entertain you, sir? A Mrs Snow perhaps, whose husband is currently at home in the shires, confined by the terrible weather we've been experiencing?'

'I don't know this lady of whom you speak,' Mr Buckley said sharply.

Mr Cork smiled, not superciliously, Winnie thought, but affably.

The clerk blotted his papers, folded and sealed them with an anonymous blob of wax. Mr Cork thanked him and handed them to Mr Buckley, who grabbed his hat from the top of the dresser and rammed it on to his head before leaving without another word.

'I should apologise for my companion's ungentlemanly behaviour.'

'I think he should apologise himself,' Winnie said weakly.

A small smile crossed Mr Cork's face. 'Miss Winnie Lennicker – you see, I know who you are. Why are you not wearing shoes?'

'I was attacked and robbed, sir.' She told the truth to account for the fact that some of the beautiful silk bandannas she was supposed to have delivered were currently in tatters and covered in mud.

'By whom?'

'A stranger. He didn't touch the run goods ...' She refrained from mentioning Jason's gold watch.

'Did he express an interest in anything particular the despatches, for example?'

'Ah, I kept them from him—'

'Then you have done excellent work, my dear.'

It had been by accident, not design, she wanted to say, but sheer exhaustion stopped her.

'Can you describe this rogue for me?'

'It was dark ...' Her head began to swim. She leaned back and closed her eyes.

'Mrs Woods, may I prevail on you to give this young lady a cup of tea with a drop of something stronger. She is chilled to the bone.'

'It'll cost 'er a shillin',' Mrs Woods said.

'I will bear it,' he said rather sharply. 'Miss Lennicker, do you recall anything, no matter how insignificant, that would help identify this man?'

Mrs Woods slid a cup of steaming tea across the table, letting it slop into the saucer.

Winnie picked it up and took a sip. It was so hot it rattled her teeth and burned her tongue, but she didn't care. All she wanted was to be warm.

'I thought at first that he was—' She almost went on, a fellow free trader with whom she might intercede, but she bit her lip just in time, unsure exactly how much Mrs Woods knew about the smugglers' operations. 'Oh, I don't know. His boot tops weren't in good order, and there was no neatness about his rigging.'

'Was he a Frenchman?'

'No, English, and very well spoken. I remember he was wearing a dark greatcoat and gloves.'

'Did he hurt you?'

'I'm a little bruised where he caught hold of me, that's all.' Her body would mend. She wasn't so sure about her mind – she doubted she would ever traipse about in the dark alone in future.

'Then I conclude that we have been very fortunate on this occasion. Where is your sister?'

'She met with an accident on the way,' Winnie replied, not wanting to reveal too much. 'Knowing how important the papers were, I took it upon myself to deliver them in her place.'

'I'm impressed by your bravery and devotion to duty.' Mr Cork took several coins from his pocket and placed them on the table. 'Mrs Woods, this is to cover your expenses as agreed in advance and pay for the loan of a pair of boots for the young lady here. I will be on my way.

Miss Lennicker, please inform the Lace Maiden that I'll be in communication with her shortly.'

Winnie made to stand up, but he held out his hand to stay her.

'There's no need to hurry away. I implore you to regain your strength and wait until first light before you travel. You must take some consolation from your ordeal on this harsh winter's night, knowing that you have contributed in no small way to our campaign to win the war against Napoleon for King and Country – and have helped me to maintain my reputation among my contacts. I trust we shall meet again. Farewell, ladies.'

With that, he was gone. Winnie listened for the sound of horses and carriage wheels to fade, then sat back in her seat, watching the flames dancing in the grate while Mrs Woods retreated to another part of the house to fetch her a pair of boots, which she had to stuff with straw to make them the right size.

'They'll 'ave to do – they're all we've got. This is a farm, not a bootmaker's shop.'

'I'm very grateful,' Winnie said.

'You've 'ad the luck of the devil, I'd say,' Mrs Woods said in a kinder tone than before.

Either God, or Billy – or both – had been looking down on her. If she had lost her way or stayed outside any longer, the cold would have killed her.

She must have fallen asleep, because she woke with a jolt. Bleary-eyed and unsure at first where she was, Winnie struggled up, sore from sitting on the hard chair. Having laced up the loaned boots, she looked for Mrs Woods to thank her for her hospitality, but she had gone out. With the straw pricking her feet, she went out to the yard, walking straight into an eerie dawn that shrouded the buildings in fog.

As she stepped carefully between mounds of muck and stones, the shadows of the three ponies loomed out of the mist. She gathered them together and headed for home, allowing Gubbins to pick his way through the landscape, guiding her along the route.

Silver droplets of moisture formed on the ponies' forelocks and their breath turned into miniature clouds that swirled away into the great drifts of fog sweeping across the sandhills. The light and shade formed everchanging shapes: ghosts lurking in the hedgerow; men stepping out from gateways with their staves of ash; the silhouette of Old Boney creeping across the path. The silence was deafening.

Pull yourself together, Winnie. It can't be far now.

Her feet were ravaged by chilblains and blisters. Her belly was dragging her down. She could hardly go on, but she had no choice. If she let the ponies find their own way home to Abel Brockman at the mill, she doubted he would hire them out to the sisters again. He was a true horseman – his horses' welfare came first, because without them, he had no business.

She walked to Deal, then on to Walmer before turning up the hill where the fog was clearing, the sun appearing like a giant yolk through a hazy sky. The mill's sails were still, and the curtains open in the house next door. Winnie intended to turn the ponies out into the meadow then slip away without interrogation, but she had to pass through the newly built stable yard to reach it. As she entered through the gate, she encountered a woman on horseback. A dark bay lady's hack, fine-limbed with pricked ears and kind eyes, stood stock-still on the cobbles, her rider sitting side-saddle and wearing a bonnet trimmed with feathers, and a beautifully cut habit made from dark twill that draped down the mare's side.

'Mornin', Winnie.'

She stopped abruptly and the ponies came to a halt behind her as she glanced around for the owner of the deep, masculine voice.

'It's me. I'm over here.'

'Abel?' She looked up at the rider who removed his bonnet with a flourish, revealing his blond hair and side-boards. Like Jason, he had started wearing his hair short and curled. 'I'm sorry. I didn't realise it was you ... How strange.'

'I hope you will excuse my appearance.'

She didn't know what to say, wondering who was most embarrassed by their encounter: Abel garbed like a woman, or her, with a bellyful of illegitimate child?

He unhooked his right leg from the top pommel of the saddle, took his left foot out of the stirrup and dismounted, sliding to the ground where he landed lightly on his feet. He gathered up his skirt and stood gazing at her, his face flushed.

'I don't like anybody seein' me like this – that's why I start early in the mornin'. My cousins – Jason especially – would never let me hear the end of it if they found out. You won't tell a soul, will you?'

'I'm not sure—' It was just the kind of titbit of gossip that would slip out by accident one day when she was with her sisters.

'It's part of my job. Mares like Emma here – I named her after Lady Hamilton – are worth more than fifty guineas each if they're broken to ride side-saddle and are used to the flapping of a habit, and next to nothin' otherwise. If you promise to keep your silence, I'll forget that you've brought Gubbins home lame and quite exhausted.'

She looked behind her – Gubbins's muzzle was almost touching the ground and he was resting a leg.

'Let me put the mare away, then I'll have a look at the pony.' He smiled briefly, reminding her why many of the young women of their acquaintance had set their caps at him. In his mid to late twenties, conventionally handsome and a bachelor, he was a good catch. He made a comfortable living from dealing in horses, and he was set to inherit a small fortune on his father's death. Old Mr Brockman was one of Jason's uncles who had made enough money from smuggling to buy the mill and the surrounding land, proof to Winnie that it wasn't impossible to escape the free trade.

She waited for Abel to leave the mare in one of the stables. When he emerged without the bonnet, he took the harnesses off the ponies and checked Gubbins's feet.

'There's some heat in his near fore,' he said. 'I'll apply a poultice to draw out any poison.'

Winnie apologised, feeling guilty, even though she didn't know what she could have done to prevent it.

'Where are your sisters?' Abel moved closer. 'And what have you done to your face?'

'Louisa and Grace are at home. And my face …' she touched her temple, feeling for the bruise. 'It was dark – I walked into a branch, or something.' She couldn't remember.

'Let me deal with Gubbins, then I'll change my dress and give you a ride into town. 'I'm goin' that way anyway,' he added, when she hesitated.

'It's very kind of you, thank you.'

'It'll be my pleasure,' he said with a bow, at which she broke into a smile, somehow having expected him to curtsey.

'What are you grinnin' at?' he asked, looking hurt.

'Nothing,' she said quickly. 'It's the relief of knowing I'll soon be home safe and sound. I hate the free trade. I wish we didn't have to do it.' She bit her lip, then continued in a small voice, 'I shouldn't have said anything. Louisa wouldn't like it.'

'Then I won't tell if you don't.' He smiled back. 'There are ways and means of distancin' oneself from the business of runnin' goods. I'm sure that one day you'll find a way out of it. Let me call for my groom after I've changed my clothes.'

Within the half-hour, Winnie was sitting beside him in his trap, a blanket around her shoulders, another across her knees and a hot water bottle at her feet. Snuggled up with the smell of camphor and horse in her nostrils, she watched Abel flick the whip gently across the horse's rump. The trap rolled forward, picking up speed as the high-stepping hackney went into a flying trot.

'Have you heard anythin' from Billy?' Abel asked.

'No, but I live in hope.' Tears sprang to her eyes.

'I'll always regret not being able to give enough warnin' of the gangers' approach. I rode the horse as hard as I dared, but it was too late for the men to launch the boats.'

'You did your best,' she said, although she felt that he had looked rather a coward, galloping away and leaving the boatmen to their fate.

Winnie recollected the women's anger and distress as they watched the men being rowed out to the tender in the Downs.

Louisa said that they had launched the *Curlew* into a calm sea, but Winnie's mind harked back to a restless swell that slowed the progress of several other boats that had launched at the same time, carrying the wives, children, mothers, sisters, cousins and aunts of the men who had been captured by the gangers. Louisa said it had been bright sunshine, but Winnie knew better. A storm cloud like a giant anvil had towered above them, spewing rain, but it didn't really matter. Whether the weather had been fair or foul, it had been raining in Winnie's heart.

Winnie had taken the tiller while Grace and Louisa set every stitch of the *Curlew*'s canvas to take advantage of the squalling winds. On reaching the tender with her naval colours nailed to the mast, Winnie had joined the other women in begging for their menfolk's freedom. Having grown weary of the intrusion, the tender's crew had gestured at them to go away, and then when they hadn't, one of the guards had fired a pistol, sending the ball whistling past the *Curlew*. Deciding that discretion was the better part of valour, Louisa and Grace had dipped the lug and turned about.

'An inch closer and I would have lost my ear.' Pale-faced and shaking, Louisa had insisted – against Winnie's wishes – that they should go home and think again.

On the way into town, the horse slowed to a walk. Abel yelled at the carter ahead of them to move out of their way, and they trotted past a cartload of squawking hens in baskets on their way to market.

'I can get down here,' Winnie said, when they reached the castle.

'I would take much pleasure in conveyin' you all the way to your house,' Abel said. 'If that isn't too much of an imposition ...'

'It's hardly an imposition on your part,' she smiled. 'It is I who is imposing on you, if I am taking you out of your way.'

'It isn't by much. What impression would I be givin' if I dropped you here in your cond—' He broke off abruptly and remained silent apart from giving the horse curt instructions to whoa, bringing it to a halt outside Compass Cottage, where Winnie felt like a lady of the ton, taking

Abel's hand as she disembarked from the trap in front of the neighbours who'd come to see what was going on.

'I hope that we might continue our acquaintance, Miss Lennicker,' he said stiffly. 'Perhaps we will see each other at church, or at one of the dances at the Waterman's Arms.'

'As we have always done,' she said lightly, before remembering that she wouldn't be doing much dancing after the infant was born, and even if she did, it wouldn't be with Abel, if that was what he was asking. She thanked him again for his time and trouble and expressed her hope for the pony's rapid recovery. 'I wish you good day.'

'Good day to you.' He sprang back into the trap and picked up the ribbons, at which the horse moved off, heading down the narrow alleyway in the direction of Lower Street.

'Thank goodness you're back, Winnie.' Grace hauled her in from the doorstep. 'Louisa and I have been worried sick. I've been out with Cromwell looking for you. Yes, Mrs Witherall, we'll look after her. No, Mrs Edwards, we have plenty of brandy, thank you.' She pushed the door closed, shutting their neighbours out.

'Pinch me,' Winnie said, removing her glove.

'Why?'

'Because I want to know this is real.'

Frowning, Grace plucked at the flesh on the back of Winnie's hand.

'Ouch. Not that hard.'

'You asked me to do it.'

'Yes, but ... oh, never mind. I've never been so glad to be home.'

'What's wrong with your face? You're bleeding.'

'It's all right. It's stopped,' she said.

'Look at your feet – why are you wearing an old man's footwear?'

'It's a long story – I'll tell you everything when I've washed and changed my clothes, and I'm sitting comfortably by the fire.'

'Let me help you unlace those dreadful boots.' Before Winnie could protest that she was perfectly capable, Grace squatted at her feet and took them off, scattering pieces of straw. For once, Winnie didn't say a word. 'You'll find Louisa in the parlour. I'll order some refreshment from the maid.' She was teasing, making light of the situation, Winnie thought, when it could have turned out so much worse. 'You can wash later when the water's hot.'

Winnie went into the parlour and Louisa greeted her with a cry of delight, struggling to her feet.

'My dear sister.' Her smile turned to confusion. 'Your face?'

'I'm well,' Winnie said quickly. 'What about your ankle?'

'It's giving me much pain, but it will mend.' Louisa sat back down on the chaise and Winnie joined her. 'I feel such a fool.'

Grace appeared and filled the glasses she'd brought from the kitchen from the half-anker they kept under the table in the parlour for what they described as medicinal purposes. She handed the glasses round.

'Tell us about your meeting with Mr Cork,' Louisa said. 'You did manage to deliver the goods and the papers?'

'I did, but I had a narrow squeak on my way to the rondy. I was attacked—' Winnie took a swig of cognac as Grace gasped. 'This terrible man – I thought he was going to murder me.'

'Did you not scream for dear life?' Grace's eyes were like saucers.

'I didn't dare – he had a pistol and a knife, and I had no doubt that he'd use them.'

'We should go straight to Constable Pocket with this,' Grace said.

'There's no point. I was breaking the law, running goods inland. I'm not going to risk being dragged in front of the magistrates for a second time.'

'Did he try to have his way with you?'

'Grace, please,' Louisa said.

'He didn't. In fact, even as he rummaged me, he didn't show any interest in me in "that way", which is a blessing because I don't know what I would have done if he had.' She refrained from mentioning that he had been lying in wait for the Lace Maiden, not wanting to put Louisa through unnecessary worry, because it didn't matter now. If Louisa carried despatches for Mr Cork again, she would make sure that she and Grace would be there to protect her. 'I did my utmost not to antagonise him – I merely did as I was told. I felt that if I argued and fought back, he would finish me off, and then –' she burst into tears '– you would have found me lying cold and alone in the sandhills.' She hated the free trade more than ever. 'There is one thing more,' she sobbed. 'He stole Jason's watch – I'm so sorry.'

'It's all right.' Louisa put her arm around her. 'Try not to dwell on what happened. You are to be congratulated for your bravery – you have served King and Country well.'

'That's what Mr Cork said.'

'The same King and Country who have taken Billy,' Grace contributed.

'We should be grateful for small mercies,' Louisa said. 'It was kind of Abel to bring you back into town.'

'It was a most chivalrous gesture,' Grace added. 'Perhaps he has taken a fancy to our Winnie.'

'I shouldn't read too much into it,' Louisa warned her. 'Abel is a confirmed bachelor.'

'And I am already spoken for,' Winnie said emphatically, 'although I did wonder if he was flirting with me.'

'He's pleasant enough,' Louisa said.

'He smells like a horse – I expect he washes in saddle-soap,' Grace chuckled.

Winnie almost let on about how she had found him dressed in a habit, but she bit her tongue just in time. There was something a little odd about Jason's cousin that she couldn't quite put her finger on, and anyway, she was Billy's girl, and always would be. She glanced towards the panel in the limewashed wall beside the fireplace, recalling how they had found Billy slumped inside the hiding hole one night. Louisa had checked he was all right, holding a candle to illuminate his face and fine head of curly hair, before he gave out a giant snore that blew the flame out.

Winnie found that she could smile at the memory: Billy had been ape-drunk.

Chapter Seven

The Other Side of the Blanket

'You should be in bed,' Grace commented one January morning when she was putting the crockery away from supper the night before, and Winnie was on her knees trying to coax the fire alight. 'You are not well.'

She couldn't deny that she had cast up her accounts in the pisspot soon after she had woken up.

'I blame it on the bloaters,' she confessed.

'Nobody else is sick,' Grace pointed out. 'You can't keep secrets in this house, it being one of the county's smaller establishments.' Peering down her nose, she held up a set of teaspoons fanned out in her hand. 'I expect you could spend your whole life living somewhere like Mundel Manor without ever seeing a soul. I feel sorry for Miss Marianne Flinders,' she declared, flicking her wrist so the spoons flashed across Winnie's vision. 'With her sister married and gone off to Portugal to follow her husband in the army, she must be quite lost.'

'You are exaggerating,' Winnie smiled.

'At least you have the company of your sisters who care about you very much,' Grace said softly. 'If you are ailing, you must say so.'

'Thank you, but I'm sure I'll feel much better when I've filled my bellows with fresh air.' The sound of squeaking bedsprings broke into her consciousness.

'It's those pesky meakers again.' Grace rolled her eyes. 'Jason hasn't gone out yet?'

'He returned from a hovelling trip in the early hours. Didn't you hear him slamming doors and laughing? I could hear him telling Louisa about how the *Whimbrel* had beaten Black Dog and the Rattlers in a race to rescue a merchant ship that had slipped her moorings and drifted broadside towards the Sands.'

'I must have slept through it.' The fire burst into life, freeing Winnie to go and fetch the broom and a bucket of water from the lean-to at the rear of the house, one of the improvements Jason had made to the cottage to give them a little more space. When she and her sisters had lived there with their parents and Billy, it hadn't seemed especially crowded, but it was different living with a pair of newlyweds.

She went outside and began to sweep the pavement in front of the house for all she was worth.

'Mornin', Winnie.' Mrs Witherall paused from scrubbing her doorstep, her arms dripping with suds. 'Oh, my poor ol' knees. Give me your 'and and 'aul me up, will you?'

Winnie helped her up.

'Thank you.' Mrs Witherall gazed at her, her eyes mere slits behind her puffy eyelids. 'I expect you're fed up with everybody askin', but I'll ask anyway – out of politeness, not because I'm one of those who sticks 'er nose into everybody's business. 'Ow are you, my dear?'

'I'm well.' She forced a smile and turned away to carry on sweeping up the mud and mess, but a wave of pain pulled her up short. It rose to an agonising peak, then tumbled through her belly and loins and spread down her thighs.

'Are you sure about that?'

'Quite,' she said abruptly, as the pain faded, leaving just a dull ache.

'She's been sick, Mrs Witherall,' Grace said from the doorstep. 'Winnie, I've warmed some of that broth – I thought you might like some.'

'That's very thoughtful of you – I'll have some after I've done the chores.' She carried on sweeping while Grace and Mrs Witherall chatted on the doorstep, until another wave of pain took her in its grip.

With a popping sound and a rush of hot liquid running down her legs, the pain began to subside.

'I think you've burst a bladder at last,' Grace exclaimed, 'but why are you carrying …?'

'I'm not,' she said, feeling exposed and deeply embarrassed.

'That isn't brandy and it's nothin' to be ashamed of. It's perfectly natural.' Mrs Witherall seemed to be taking far too much delight in her misfortune. She was beaming at the prospect of a new baby to join the other littluns who lived and played in Cockle Swamp Alley, and not in the slightest part worried that the poor little mite was going to be born on the wrong side of the blanket.

'Your waters 'ave broken. Stop your sweepin' and box the compass as they say at sea. Turn about and get yourself indoors. You're just about to drop.'

Too scared to argue, Winnie allowed their neighbour to bundle her to bed as she shouted instructions to Grace and called to Louisa who appeared at the bedroom door, half dressed and yawning.

'Louisa, tell my boy to go out. This is women's business. Go and find clean cloths and sheets, and a jug of brandy.

'For Winnie?'

'For us. It's goin' to be a long day.'

Befogged by pain, Winnie laboured for hours, daylight turning to dusk. Her sisters and Mrs Witherall were at her side, mopping her brow and trying to persuade her to sup a little broth to keep her strength up, but she couldn't take it.

'Is she going to die?' she heard Grace whisper.

'Whatever makes you think that? This is nothin' – your mother laboured for two days and a night to bring you into the world.'

Winnie prayed as her body weakened. All she wanted was for it to stop.

'I can't do it.' She was shaking all over, her voice tremoring. 'I can't go on. It's too much.' She longed for the ice-cold sea to engulf her and wash away her pain, and for the waves to gather her up and carry her to Billy where she could rest in the safe harbour of his arms, close her eyes … and …

'Come on, ducky.' She was startled by a sharp jab in her ribs. 'You can't sleep now. The babe is almost 'ere – I can see the 'ead. One more push. That's all it will take. One 'uge, long push.' Mrs Witherall was at the end of the bed. Louisa and Grace were supporting Winnie by the shoulders. At Mrs Witherall's bidding, Winnie made one more effort, and the pain suddenly fell away.

There was a gasp, then silence, and just as Winnie was beginning to think there was something terribly wrong, she heard the baby cry.

'Well done, my dear. It's all been worth it – you 'ave a beautiful little girl.' Mrs Witherall wrapped the baby in a woollen shawl and placed her on Winnie's chest. Winnie stared at her newborn daughter, drinking in her features and laying them down in her memory. From the ginger tone of her wet curls, and the shape of her nose, there was no mistaking that she was Billy's child.

'She takes after her father,' Louisa observed, still critical perhaps of the fact that the child was illegitimate and had brought a level of unwanted interest and scandal to their door.

'What will you call her?' Grace asked.

'That's easy. Pamela Jane – Pamela after Ma, and Jane after Billy's mother.' She pressed her lips to the baby's silken forehead, inhaling her scent.

'That's a pretty name,' Grace smiled. 'Welcome to Compass Cottage, Pamela Jane. May you be blessed with a long and happy life.'

'She's a marvel, a sight to be'old.' Mrs Witherall clucked and cooed, as proud as if she had given birth herself. 'I always wanted a girl, but God gave me four brave boys instead.'

Winnie glanced up as Louisa left the room, closing the door behind her.

'Don't worry,' Mrs Witherall said. 'She's feeling a little sore.'

'She's ashamed of me.'

'It isn't that. I keep tellin' 'er, 'er turn will come soon enough.'

'I didn't realise …'

'Louisa isn't one for baring 'er 'eart.'

'She wants a child?'

'It's the way of the world – you get wed and soon after, you expect to 'ear the patter of tiny feet.' Mrs Witherall smiled ruefully. 'It isn't a bad thing to 'ave to wait awhile – a woman's feelin's for 'er 'usband are subject to change when an infant arrives, puce and squalling, and diverts 'er attention from 'im. When an 'usband continues to make 'is usual demands, 'e can easily snuff out the affection she felt for 'im in the first place. And of course, when the wife finds out that there's another infant on the way, she is then reluctant – even stubbornly opposed – to risk fallin' for a third and a fourth. There are exceptions – poor Mrs Roper's 'ad

98

one a year, regular as clockwork, throughout 'er marriage, but there won't be any more … God rest Terrier's soul.'

'Then either Mr Roper was very inconsiderate, or they were very much in love,' Grace said thoughtfully.

'What do you know of such things, young lady?' Mrs Witherall said lightly. 'No, don't answer that.'

'I hope that I would have enough love in my heart for my children *and* my husband,' Winnie said. 'I wish I had a husband …'

'Any husband, or Billy in particular?' Grace asked.

'That's a strange thing to say,' Mrs Witherall said. 'Of course she wants it to be Billy.'

'I'm only asking because Mrs Lavender whose husband went away to fight last year, is getting married to Mr Turner, the pawnbroker on Golden Street. Mr Lavender is missing, presumed dead.'

'How could she do such a thing?' Winnie murmured.

'She is calling 'erself a widow,' Mrs Witherall said. 'She 'as three children, three 'ungry mouths to feed. She's makin' a practical match.'

'And if Mr Lavender should come back? What then?'

'Winnie, there's no need to upset yourself – it'll stop your milk comin' in,' Mrs Witherall warned. 'There's a lot more to marriage than mutual respect and affection. How are you feelin'?'

'I don't know how to hold her, or what to do.' She had little recollection of Ma looking after Grace when she was born.

'It's simple. All you 'ave to do is feed 'er, wind 'er and wipe 'er bum.'

'And love her, surely,' Grace added.

'That goes without sayin'. Without it, a child won't thrive.' Mrs Witherall turned back to Winnie. 'You aren't goin' to give her away?'

'I couldn't,' she whispered. The littlun was Billy's. How could she possibly let her go? She would rather live on the street than be parted from her.

'Then we should 'ave a little somethin' to wet the baby's 'ead.'

Louisa appeared with a tray of cups and a jug of steaming milk, fragrant with the aroma of cognac.

'You must have 'eard me,' Mrs Witherall said. 'This is most welcome.'

Louisa put the tray on the dressing table and began to serve the drinks, saying, 'We will rally round and bring her up together. We're family, after all's said and done.'

'What about Jason?' Winnie asked apprehensively. 'You've discussed it with him?'

'Yes, and we are of the same mind.'

'Thank you,' Winnie said, a lump in her throat.

'Then we can count on you to continue in the free trade with us to earn your keep?'

She nodded. What choice did she have?

Her sisters and Mrs Witherall left her to feed the baby and rest, but she couldn't sleep, alert for every snuffle and cry. She picked her up from the crib Grace had made for the new arrival from a drawer placed across two chairs, and rocked her gently, telling her about her father, and the last time she had seen him.

When Winnie went back to the beach with her sisters after dark on the same day as they had gone to confront the guards on the tender without success, they were questioned by an officer of the militia. Lieutenant Tempest, whom Winnie understood to be the future husband of Miss Flinders of Mundel Manor, interrogated them, curious to know why they were going fishing at night. Not only did Louisa lie to him, saying that it was the best time to catch cod and flatfish, but she also persuaded him to help them launch the *Curlew* down the rollers and into the sea.

Louisa claimed that while Winnie had been trembling with nerves, she'd been smiling, confident in her plan, but Winnie remembered Louisa's pallid and fearful face as she instructed Grace to brush black paint across the *Curlew*'s name.

'What exactly is your plan?' Winnie asked, aware that amongst their blankets and provisions, there was a box containing Pa's musket – a Brown Bess – stowed in the bow. 'You've kept your cards close to your chest all day. It's only fair that you reveal them, so we know what we're doing.'

'We're going to cast a long line, rather than shooting a net, then we'll pass the tender and wait for our chance to distract the guards, under the pretence that we're fishing.'

It took a moment for Louisa's words to sink in.

It was as if she'd dropped a codling down the back of Winnie's neck.

'We can't do that – Billy can't swim.'

'What else do you suggest? It's the best I can come up with.'

Unfortunately, when pressed, Winnie failed to come up with an alternative.

Having watched Louisa set up the musket while she and Grace trimmed the canvas and fed out the line, Winnie caught sight of Billy along with the other men, coming up through the hatch, accompanied by two guards.

'Pull the line in,' Louisa hissed. 'Set the canvas.' And then Winnie heard the report of the musket, followed by shouting and yelling breaking out on the tender. The guards fired back, but the *Curlew* was already under sail and on her way towards the shore. And the men? Where were the men? She heard splashing …

'Louisa, what are you doing? We have to turn about,' Winnie argued.

'We can't do that – we'll all be killed!' Grace cried, but all Winnie could think of was Billy struggling in the water, fighting for breath as his bellows filled with brine.

'How will you sleep at night with their blood on your hands?' Winnie exclaimed, wondering how she could relieve Louisa of the musket and use it to threaten her, before Louisa yelled at the guards and told them – yes, she actually had the nerve to order them to stop firing.

'I beg you not to fire on us, but to go after the lugger, the *Good Intent*. She almost ran us down,' Louisa called out.

Winnie could hear the sound of oars in the rowlocks and the horror in the guards' voices as they realised that their prisoners had taken to one of their jollyboats, and then the wind picked up and carried the *Curlew* away.

'Louisa, what if they didn't make it on to the boat?' Winnie said. 'I've told you we have to go back and find them.'

'And I've told you why we can't. They must sink or swim.'

'You are callous and cruel.' She felt sick as the *Curlew* rose and fell through the waves. Her throat was raw. 'I'm ashamed to call you my sister! You have no heart!'

'Don't you think I'm afraid too? I know Jason and I have fallen out and I wish that we hadn't, but I don't want him to die. We must trust that he and Billy will help each other. If we go back, we'll be caught up in it – we could be shot at, arrested, anything. I'm responsible for you and Grace – Pa would have expected me to put my sisters first.' Louisa sounded hurt. 'If I'd listened to my conscience as far as you and Grace are concerned, I'd never have gone out this evening. I'd have stayed at home like every other woman of our acquaintance.'

'I'm sorry. I'm sorry,' Winnie sobbed, realising her mistake. When she looked back into the darkness, she couldn't see anything but the lanterns on the ships in the Downs and the lightship marking the Goodwin Sands. There were so many lights, she could no longer pick out those of the tender.

'We'll hover a little way from shore and wait until dawn – maybe we'll see Jason and Billy arriving on the jollyboat, or swimming towards us side by side.'

Winnie prayed, but God didn't answer her. As the sun rose, the boys on the beach dragged the *Curlew* up the shingle. The press gang moved south to Dover, while Winnie waited on tenterhooks to hear Billy's cheerful whistling as he swaggered along the alley, and his 'Anything for dinner? I'm starvin'.'

It was the little things that she noticed: his oilskins missing from the hook in the hall; the empty place at the table; the way a loaf of bread lasted so much longer ...

The next day the tender had gone, and so had Jason and Billy.

Returning to the present, Winnie stroked her daughter's cheek.

'So you see, I don't know where Billy is, or what he's doing,' she murmured, 'but you mustn't worry about a thing – I will be your ma and pa until he comes back, and I'll love you for both of us.'

After the birth, Winnie welcomed a stream of visitors to the house: Mrs Edwards; Mrs Roper who, although still grieving and struggling for money, brought along a well-used cap and barracoat as a gift; the vicar who said that she was welcome to attend church, despite her being an unmarried mother.

'Everyone's been very kind,' Winnie said when Grace came upstairs to sit with her for a while a few days later.

'Kind, or curious?' Grace said.

'Have I been the subject of much gossip then?'

'Truthfully?'

Winnie nodded.

'There's been a lot of talk, but it won't be long before something else takes over. Louisa has instructed me to ask you to dress and come downstairs for a while. There's work to be done and it's only fair that you help.'

'I know,' Winnie sighed. 'I've been enjoying spending time with Pamela. She's such a distraction that I've almost forgotten about the world outside this room.'

'Jason looks like he needs a decent meal,' Grace grinned. 'As you've no doubt noticed, our sister has taken over the cooking – she's trying to prove herself.'

'I did wonder. I was very grateful that Nancy brought those pies for us the other day.'

'So was Jason. Please, Winnie. Don't hide yourself away.'

'I'm not sure I can face going out. Everyone will be pointing the finger and laughing at me.' Just like they did with Billy, she thought.

'Let he – or she – who is without sin, cast the first stone. Our neighbours have committed all manner of misdemeanours – they steal, fight, drink to excess. You must remember what they are guilty of when we walk along the street, side by side with our heads held high.' Grace changed the subject. 'Now, may I cuddle my dear little niece?'

Chapter Eight

Ne'er Cast a Clout Till May Be Out

The boatmen were forced to remain ashore for a while by a quantity of snow. The high winds sent it drifting to a height of several feet, rendering the roads impassable. It took weeks to melt before January faded with barely a whimper. February was bitterly cold, and March blew in with storms and heavy seas and news from abroad: the Russians had entered Berlin and Prussia had declared war on France.

Winnie grew accustomed to the rhythm of the days, caring for Pamela, laundering, cooking and cleaning with Grace alongside her, chattering endlessly. When Jason was at home, they dined together in the parlour. They talked of their neighbours, of their escapades in the Downs – Jason about his hovelling trips with the *Whimbrel*, and the sisters about the provisioning they had done, limited by the lack of fresh food available during the winter and spring.

One evening towards the end of April, Winnie was at home and Pamela was crying in her crib.

'Oh dear, you have the gripes again. Come with your mama and she'll find you a dose of medicine.' Winnie went down to the kitchen with the baby squirming and sobbing in her arms. As she pushed the door open, she came face to face with Jason, who was naked down to the waist. His hair was wet, and the tin bath was steaming by the fire.

'I beg your pardon?' she said, hastily reversing.

'Don't worry,' he called. 'I'm quite used to company while I'm bathin', unannounced or otherwise. Besides, it sounds as if the littlun needs her daily allowance of geneva.'

'I'd never dream of giving her gin. It would ruin her.'

'Calm down. I'm shammin'. Of course you wouldn't, although I don't know what's in that gripe water you bought the other day. Does it not contain strong spirit?'

'A little brandy, according to the apothecary, Mr Spottiswoode, but it's so diluted as not to be detectable. Where's Louisa?'

'I'm right here.' Her sister was sitting in the inglenook, reading one of their mother's tomes by the light of the fire. The only books they possessed were a gilt-edged Bible, a volume on botany, a treatise on painting in watercolour, and Hannah Glasse's recipes.

Jason put on his shirt and began fastening the buttons. 'Where is my waistcoat? My favourite one?'

'Why do you ask me?' Louisa said. 'Don't you think I have enough to do without having to look after your clothes? It'll be where you left it.'

She was a good person, a loyal sister and a scratchy wife. Winnie smiled to herself. Louisa and Jason bickered and made up frequently.

Winnie found the bottle of gripe water and tried to measure out a teaspoonful. Each time she started to pour out a dose, the baby grabbed at the shiny spoon.

'You have to take your medicine, my darling.'

'You have the patience of a saint,' Jason said. 'Louisa, why don't you take her for a moment?'

'I'm in the middle of my book.'

'You've read them all before,' Jason said somewhat scornfully. 'Never mind. Let me take the child. Don't look at me like that, Winnie. I won't drop her.'

She handed Pamela over, and to her surprise, the baby fell silent, transfixed by Jason's face.

'You've worked magic,' Louisa commented. 'Peace and quiet at last.'

Jason sat down at the table with the baby in his arms, holding her hands as Winnie put the spoon to her mouth and tipped it up. The baby spluttered and coughed.

'She can't have had more than half of that,' Jason laughed. 'Is it enough?'

'I think so.' Winnie sat down opposite him. 'It seems that your presence has effected a cure for the gripes. She is already better.'

'She reminds me so much of Billy. I wonder where he is now,' Jason said.

'Oh, don't start her off, my love,' Louisa said.

'It's all right. I like to talk about him,' Winnie replied quickly.

'I keep askin', lookin' out for him, but I haven't seen him since the mornin' after you went out with Louisa and Grace, and distracted the crew on the tender.'

She'd heard the story – she'd asked him to repeat it many times in the past – of how several of the prisoners had managed to escape on the jollyboat, then row towards the white cliffs. Before they reached land, a naval frigate intercepted them, but rather than accept the captain's offer of a return trip to the tender, Billy and Jason had jumped into the sea. It turned out that Billy could swim well enough when his life was hanging in the balance, because they both managed to reach the rocks and scramble to the top of the cliffs, where by mischance they came face to face with two elderly ladies who were out for a walk.

Having been taken by surprise, they had got into a funk, their screams attracting the attention of a passing detachment of soldiers. Billy went one way and Jason went the other. He never saw him after that, his assumption being that he was picked up and transferred back to the gangers.

'It's possible that he's chosen to stay away,' Louisa said. 'Look how his father walked out when Billy was born. Perhaps there is some truth in the saying, like father, like son.'

'He wouldn't do that,' Jason said. 'I know him too well – he likes his home comforts. He had a share in the *Whimbrel*. And he was courtin' you, Winnie. Why would he run away?'

'Because he knew about the child,' Louisa ventured.

'He didn't. He has no idea that we have a child together. Why do you hold him in such low regard?' Winnie said hotly. 'Pa wouldn't have taken him as his apprentice if he'd thought badly of him. He had a lot of respect for Billy – he treated him like a son.'

'That's true,' Louisa conceded, 'but circumstances forced him to move in with us – it wasn't entirely a choice of our father's making. Ma liked having him here – she made sure that Pa paid him then docked the money for his keep plus a little extra for the inconvenience of him having the room that should have been mine.'

Ma was good at handling Mr Lennicker's finances, but Winnie had never thought of her as skinflinty.

'Billy was always very obliging, Louisa. He went out of his way to help our father and look after the boat.'

'I'm not criticising Billy – all I'll say is that he's a little too happy-go-lucky and too fond of his drink. Don't you remember the time we found him asleep in the hiding hole in the parlour?'

'Yes.' Winnie bit back tears as she gazed down at her hand where Pamela was now hanging on to her finger, just where a wedding ring should have been. How she cursed Old Boney and the American wars which had taken Billy away from her.

'You should put her down, not keep handing her around, or she'll never learn to sleep on her own,' Louisa said.

'What do you know about rearing a child?' As soon as she said the words, Winnie wished she could unsay them.

'A little.' Louisa's cheeks turned pink. 'Every time she cries, you pick her up to give her a cuddle or you ask someone else to hold her.'

'What's wrong with that? It's cruel to leave her.'

'Ma used to let you and Grace cry – it's done you no harm.' Louisa's voice softened. 'Never mind. Let's not argue.'

'Did I hear someone taking my name in vain?' Grace entered the kitchen in a state of undress, wearing her nightgown and slippers, with a shawl over her shoulders. She blew out the candle she was carrying. 'I couldn't sleep with everyone talking.'

'I'm sorry,' Louisa said. 'There's tea in the pot if you'd like some. Come and join us.'

As Grace looked around for a clean cup, Jason diverted their discussion on to his plans for the next run.

'This is not to go any further,' he said.

'We know that.' Louisa glanced towards Grace.

'Why do you look at me?' she asked, indignant.

'I know we can rely on you bein' discreet, Grace,' Jason went on, 'but it's especially important now. Over the past three months, Winnie's been attacked and there have been one or more gentlemen asking questions about Louisa. Let's not bring further trouble to our door.'

'Everybody in Deal knows we'll be doing another run,' Grace said somewhat scathingly as she sat down. 'You can't keep a secret round here.'

'We have to keep the details to ourselves and our associates. That's all we're sayin'.'

'Perhaps we shouldn't smuggle any more contraband,' Winnie suggested. 'That way, there's no chance of anything going wrong, or anyone getting hurt ... or arrested.'

'We've talked about this before,' Louisa said. 'Whatever you say won't make any difference – it's the money.'

'And the chance that one day, we'll make our fortune,' Jason grinned. 'Have you had any contact with Mr Cork, Louisa?'

She frowned and shook her head. 'I've been expecting to find a note left in one of the usual places, or for him to call, but nothing. Haven't you spoken to him?'

'All I've heard is that he's arranged for the merchants to have the goods ready at Gravelines for a date in May.'

'It's odd that he hasn't been in touch to discuss the other business,' Louisa said thoughtfully. 'The carrying of further despatches that will help the British army and navy or Napoleon. The intelligence may be of value to either side.'

'What do you mean by that?' Winnie said. 'Whose side are you on? Are we on?'

'Whichever will make us the most profit.'

'You would commit treason?'

'What do you think will happen when the fighting stops?' Louisa riposted.

'We will have peace and we'll be able to get on with our lives without worrying about our men being taken and Old Boney sailing up the Thames and into London.'

Louisa looked exasperated. 'If we can confound the men in power by carrying notes on armaments, morale and the number of troops, true and false, thus extending the conflict, it is to our advantage. I can't imagine returning to the life we had before.'

'You would make it impossible for my Billy to come home soon?' Winnie said, her voice cracking.

'I'm sorry, but that's the way it is. I'm sure that Mr Cork will want to continue with our contract, but ... oh Jason, why are you looking at me like that?'

'I worry that you may be disappointed. I've heard a rumour that the aforementioned gentleman, although content to carry on with our usual arrangement for carrying lace and other goods, has been engaging some of the Rattlers to act as couriers.'

'Who? And why?' Louisa exclaimed. 'And does this mean that Mr Cork has changed his mind about entrusting us with the gold?'

'Slow down, my dear. Let me answer your questions one at a time,' Jason said. 'I suspect that the situation with Winnie and the stranger has made him twitch. If a French agent, for example—'

'The man who attacked me wasn't French,' Winnie interrupted.

'If someone is out to sabotage the movement of intelligence between British spies, then it makes sense for Mr Cork to choose fresh couriers unknown to him.'

'Or her,' Louisa said acidly.

'Or her,' Jason said, humouring her. 'As to whom he's picked – well, if it's true, he's made a big mistake.'

Winnie leaned closer. 'Tell us – I'm on tenterhooks.'

'Those two clodpoles who came on side with us when their leader passed away. Since then, they've been nothin' but a liability. I told them to sling their hook when I found out that they'd spilled the beans about that idea we had for stashin' contraband under the sand in the sandhills. Isaiah couldn't help crowin' about it. Anyway, they're back with the Rattlers, and good riddance to 'em.'

'You mean Lawless and Awful Doins?' Louisa uttered a hollow laugh. 'I knew they were incapable of turning over a new leaf. They are wicked and inept in equal measure, a dangerous combination. It will never work.'

Winnie knew the men – they had kidnapped Louisa on One Eye's instructions in the past, taking her to the Rattling Cat whence she had escaped with Nancy's help. Awful Doins had looked up to their leader, going as far as wearing one of his teeth in his memory.

'Be that as it may, the plans for the guinea boat are on hold for the present. I will organise a meetin' with Mr Cork after the next run to see if I can twist his arm to entrust us with the gold.'

'This news is most unwelcome,' Louisa said. 'How could he do this to us?'

'It's his choice – he has the money, power and influence.' Jason tried to calm her, but she seemed to be taking Mr Cork's rejection badly. 'These are difficult times – we're all at sea, subject to the whims of the tide of gentlemen's opinions, and generals' failures and successes. We still have the means to make our fortune in the free trade. You still have lace to sell before the next run?'

'You're right.' Louisa pulled herself together. 'Tomorrow, we're going to take some to Mr Gigg – he's expressed a renewed interest in our wares, having been reluctant to purchase from us recently. He claims that our visits to his shop have piqued the interest of the Comptroller of Customs and his officers.'

'I'm not going with you,' Winnie said mutinously.

'We'll go together – you'll bring little Pamela. That way, we can say – if anybody asks – that we're looking to buy some linen to make sheets for her cot.'

'You will carry the lace?' Winnie realised when she was asking the question that she was wasting her breath.

Yawning, Louisa changed the subject. 'Are you ready to give the baby back and retire, my dear husband?'

With a grin, he placed Pamela into Winnie's open arms, saying, 'Early to bed, early to rise, makes a man healthy, wealthy and wise.'

And helps him test the bedsprings, Winnie thought a while later when she was trying to sleep.

In the morning, Winnie dressed Pamela in a layer of light clothing, then wound a length of lace trim around her middle, before wrapping her in a lace shawl and placing her in the handcart with a blanket tucked up to her chin.

'I don't like it, Louisa. She is too hot. Look at her.' Red-faced and whimpering, the baby fidgeted, trying and failing to escape the swaddling as Winnie pushed the handcart along the street, following her sister. Two gentlemen in black uniform rounded the corner and walked towards them. Louisa crossed the road, leaving Winnie to acknowledge their greeting.

'Good day, missus,' the taller one said, while the other removed his hat and took a long look at the baby.

'What a dear little boy. What rosy cheeks he has,' he said. Aware of the insignia on his hat, Winnie couldn't bring herself to meet his gaze. They were Customs men out to get them, and even though Ma had always said that they'd never rummage an infant for illegal goods or those on which duty hadn't been paid, she couldn't help worrying that one day, they might. 'You are out doing a little shopping?'

'I am taking the air, that's all.' Why had she said that? *That's all.* It would make him think there was more to her morning walk than that. 'And doing a little shopping for drapery in Walmer.' Now they would wonder why she didn't go to the shop in Deal ... She felt a little nauseous. 'It's all perfectly innocent.'

'Anyone would think you had something to hide, missus,' he smiled. 'We won't hold you up any longer. Goodbye.'

She caught up with Louisa further along the street.

'They were Customs officers,' she hissed.

'Why do you think I crossed the road?'

'I reckon I put them off the scent,' Winnie said, hoping against hope.

'They've been spending a lot more time out of their offices recently,' Louisa said. 'I'd like to sell as much of the goods that we have stored at home as possible. The hiding holes in the house are full to overflowing and there are barrels in the parlour. If they turned up today, they would spirit it all away from us, so to speak.'

'It isn't funny.'

'I know. I'll talk to Jason about using some of the alternative hiding holes where Pa stored contraband in the past.' Louisa walked on, apparently deep in thought, until they reached the draper's shop.

'You'll have to leave the handcart outside,' Louisa said. 'Unwrap the baby and bring her in. I'll bring the goods. Watch and learn, Winnie.'

The bell rang as they entered the shop, bringing an elderly man with small dark eyes set in a pudgy face to the counter.

'Come through.' Mr Gigg invited them into the private room at the back of the shop. 'Hurry, hurry. I hope this won't take long – the ladies of the ton must have their muslin, or the world will fall apart.'

'Allow me to introduce my sister, Mrs Fleet.'

He gave Winnie a cursory glance.

'I have a particularly fine lace shawl that I was planning to keep back for one of my other buyers,' Louisa said.

'There is also a length of black Chantilly and some scalloped trimming.'

Out of habit, she glanced quickly around the room to check that nobody was watching, before laying the lace out on the table. Mr Gigg put on a pair of gloves and picked the shawl up, holding it up to the light before putting it back down again, and poring over it with his quizzing glass.

'Mrs Fleet, I'm sure the flaws are as clear to you as they are invisible to Mrs Witherall here.'

Winnie hesitated, the baby in her arms.

'I'm not an expert in lace,' she said, but aware of the pressure of Louisa's boot on her toe, she changed her tune. 'Show me, Mr Gigg.'

He pointed out an area where the lace had snagged, and the loose thread that Winnie had seen Louisa sew back into the pattern on a previous evening.

'I've never seen such perfection.' She listened for Louisa's sigh of relief. 'I don't know what you mean, sir. Have you considered purchasing a more powerful quizzing glass?' She raised one eyebrow at her sister, who frowned. 'It's so beautiful I'd ask my husband to pay the earth for it.'

'I wouldn't go as far as to ask the earth,' Louisa said, amused. 'Why don't you make me an offer, Mr Gigg? One that I can't refuse?'

He stared at her, his head to one side.

'Three pounds and that is my limit. I have to make a profit as well, you know. I have overheads: I employ my son and two apprentices, then there's the rent on the shop and wholesale costs …'

'Four pounds – in coins, not banknotes, as usual.' Winnie knew why: a banknote, even one drawn on the account of Hulke and Sons on Lower Street, was merely a promise on paper, easily broken or forged.

He rubbed his chin, considering.

'Three pounds, ten shillings.'

Louisa turned to Winnie. 'I think we are wasting our time. Thank you for your offer, Mr Gigg, but it really isn't enough.'

'Perhaps I'm trying to drive too hard a bargain,' he said quickly, giving in. He paid Louisa the full four pounds from his safe and she transferred the coins into her purse. As the sisters walked home, Louisa thanked Winnie for her assistance.

'I know I come across as domineering and cross some-times, but I do my best, and I want to say that I'm sorry if I don't tell you how appreciative I am of your help around the house and everything else that you turn your hand to.'

'Well, thank you,' Winnie said, touched by her sister's praise. 'I'm sorry that you lost the contract with Mr Cork for carrying the papers.'

'So am I,' Louisa said. 'He will live to regret it, though.'

Chapter Nine

The Wages of Sin

'The wages of sin is death!' Reverend North's words jolted Winnie out of her reverie. Was Billy being taken from her, their punishment for what they'd done out of wedlock? Or was it the Lord's judgement on their part in the free trade, having completed a successful run in May, and being in the middle of preparations for another in a few days' time?

As for the rest of them – she looked around at the boatmen and their wives, sitting in the pews – what were they plotting as they half listened to Reverend North? How to make the tea go further, cutting it with rose leaves and dust? How to eke a little extra reward from their salvaging activities with a few white lies? If the vicar was right, most of his congregation should be dead and gone.

'We pray for the souls of those who transgress!' the vicar went on.

Winnie glanced along the pew. Across the nave, she caught sight of Abel who gave her a small smile. Had he been watching her? Or had his eyes been wandering out of boredom?

She bowed her head and began to pray silently for God's protection. On the last day of July, tide and weather permitting, the *Whimbrel* would be returning from France, laden with lace and cognac, baccy and tea, silks and watches, and jewellery.

At last, the Sunday service came to an end, and the vicar came to stand at the door to see his parishioners out.

'Miss Lennicker – Winnie,' he said. 'I wanted to say that I've heard of your recent generosity of spirit towards an invalid sailor who is facing penury. It gives me great pride and pleasure, knowing that a member of my congregation has been listening to my sermons on the subject of charity towards those less fortunate than ourselves.'

She blushed at the unexpected recognition of her actions towards Mr Jones.

'One must not let adversity stifle one's inclination towards kindness,' he went on. 'By that, I mean that you should carry on, according to your nature, not allow your-self to bend to fit the expectations of others.'

She wondered what he meant. Did he suspect that she was under pressure from Louisa to avoid becoming involved with other people's troubles?

She walked home with Grace, having left their sister minding Pamela as an excuse not to attend. When they arrived at the cottage, they joined her in the kitchen where she was making notes in a ledger. Pamela was lying on a blanket on the floor, chewing on the handle of a wooden spoon. When she saw her mother, she beamed.

Winnie scooped her up and kissed her hair as she extracted the spoon from her grasp. 'Thank you, Louisa.'

'You did me a favour, giving me an excuse to avoid the fire and brimstone,' Louisa smiled.

'Do you consider Abel handsome, Winnie?' Grace asked, changing the subject. 'I think he's taken a fancy to you. He was paying a lot of attention to you in church – and after the service.'

'I did catch him looking at me once or twice,' Winnie admitted.

'You must allow that he has an almost perfect visage: his eyes are cornflower blue; his nose well shaped – not too large, not too small; his teeth clean and his jaw square. Don't look at me like that.' Grace turned to her eldest sister. 'I had to have something to keep me from falling asleep during the sermon – I made a study of Abel's features, seeing as he had deliberately taken up space in the pew on the other side of the nave from ours, to be closer to Winnie. He kept glancing across at her.'

'I'm sure you're reading too much into it. He's been kind to me, knowing of my situation, that's all.' Winnie hardened her tone. 'If you must know, I have a favourable opinion of his character, but no comment to make on his appearance.' She almost let slip again about having seen him dressed in a habit but remembered just in time.

If she was pressed to give an opinion, she would say that he was too perfect. Tall, broad-shouldered and well formed, he was rather dull and stolid compared with Billy who was gawky, wiry and incredibly strong. Billy had a lightness about him: Fleet by name, fleet by nature.

'What do you think, Louisa? What is your view?' Grace persisted.

'I'm married – I only have eyes for Jason,' Louisa said adamantly.

'When I marry, I want my husband to be dark and dangerous.'

'Grace! You are young and foolish.' Louisa smiled fondly. 'A husband should be handsome and brave, but above all kind. Love without kindness isn't love.'

Winnie had found a pair of white satin wedding slippers under a bed while she'd been cleaning one day. Louisa had written an inscription on the soles, a report

119

of her wedding in Gretna Green. Reverend North had expressed his reluctance to perform a marriage ceremony without Louisa being able to provide evidence of a guardian's permission since she didn't have one, Pa having died without nominating someone in his place. He had suggested that they might call the banns, but once they'd set their hearts on it, Louisa and Jason had refused to wait another moment to become man and wife, so they had travelled to be married over the anvil.

Their cousin Beth had wed the old and countrified Mr Norris, and Winnie was beginning to feel left behind.

'Grace, you can help Winnie mind Pamela while you're cooking dinner. I have much to occupy me—'

'With the plans for the run,' Grace and Winnie finished for her. Louisa looked at them sternly before breaking into a giggle.

'Am I that predictable?' she laughed.

'Yes, you are,' Winnie said, laughing too.

Grace joined in, and soon the baby was gurgling happily along with them, until they'd forgotten what they were laughing about.

A few days passed before Louisa sent Winnie to speak to Nancy about the run. As Winnie walked along the street towards the pot house, she noticed two ruffians dawdling a few steps ahead. Since the attack, she'd made sure to keep her wits about her, wherever she went.

One of the men stopped and turned about to face her.

'Ah, Miss Lennicker. Where are you off to on this fine sunny mornin'?'

'I'm not sure it's any of your business,' she said stiffly, recognising Awful Doins and Lawless, the two smugglers who had worked with the Rattlers when One Eye had been leader. They had dissociated themselves from the gang after his death, but had reverted to working for Isaiah since then, much to Jason's relief. He'd always maintained that they were about as much use as a pair of sleeping night-watchmen.

'You are goin' to Molly's?' Lawless said.

She nodded.

'Allow us to give you some assistance.' He waited while she put her basket over her arm and took Pamela out of the handcart. Awful Doins pushed the handcart inside the porch while Lawless held the door open for her.

'I'm very grateful,' she said, stepping inside before they swaggered past her and took the table at the window that overlooked the street. Winnie sensed that Mrs Stickles was going up in the world, having recently acquired new furniture, and red and white gingham tablecloths.

Awful Doins clicked his fingers.

'Mrs Stickles. Mrs Stickles! What does a well-'eeled gen'leman 'ave to do around 'ere to attract the attention of the comely proprietor?'

Mrs Stickles came to the counter, a cloth over her arm and a dripping spoon in her hand. 'Don't you click your fingers at me,' she said lightly. 'I'm not the kind who comes runnin' to customers who don't take their turn.'

'I reckon you 'ave all the menfolk runnin' to you.' Lawless tittered.

Mrs Stickles stared at him, her eyes narrowed. 'May I remind you that I run this 'ouse and it's up to me to decide who's welcome. There are others 'ere who arrived before you, waitin' to be served. And I'll 'ave you know I'm bein' courted by a very special gen'leman, a man of honour who would never push 'is way to the front of a queue of 'ungry customers.'

'I apologise for my friend,' Awful Doins said loudly. 'Lawless, sit nicely and shut yer gob.' When he smiled, he revealed a line of misshapen upper gnashers, his lower gum being smooth and shiny, and devoid of teeth. Winnie couldn't be sure which of his teeth he had adopted from One Eye after his death – or whether it was an original or already second- or third-hand.

'Apology accepted. Ah, 'ow is the littlun?' Mrs Stickles said, beaming.

'She's well, as you can see,' Winnie said proudly. 'Am I to understand that you and your gentleman are to be married soon? What's his name? You did tell me, but I've forgotten.'

'My dear Mr Gambril.'

'Then you must have discovered his occupation by now,' Winnie smiled as she began to recall their previous gossip about the mysterious stranger. She felt guilty that she hadn't enquired about him before, but so much had happened since that it had slipped her mind.

'No, I 'aven't just yet. 'E asks me a lot of questions, but don't answer many of mine.'

Mrs Stickles's comment jogged Winnie's memory. She hadn't made the connection before and it seemed an unlikely coincidence, but could Mr Gambril be the same man who'd attacked her on the way to Nomansland Farm?

'Didn't you say he was asking after the Lace Maiden when he called in the first time?' Winnie clutched the ribbons on her bonnet as Pamela tried to pull them undone.

'I believe that 'e used that as an excuse to engage me in conversation. 'E's rather backward in comin' forward.'

'I expect he'll come out of his shell when you're better acquainted. Does he call on you often?' She wouldn't normally pry, but she was asking for good reason.

''E's dined 'ere every time 'e's been in Deal on business – that's at least thrice. He's a very handsome man, I'll have you know.'

'What exactly does he look like?'

'He has some imperfections – a beak like an eagle's and a broken tooth –' Mrs Stickles smiled fondly '– but they marry together perfectly with the rest of his features.'

Winnie hugged Pamela closer, almost certain now that her attacker and Mr Gambril were one and the same. She didn't know what to say, if anything.

'I can guess what you're thinkin' – the same as Nancy – that I'm a silly old fool for fallin' for him at my time of life, but I can tell a man's character and Mr Gambril isn't like the rest of them. What can I do for you, my dear?' Mrs Stickles went on as Winnie pulled herself together.

'It's more about what I can do for you – I have found these in one of the drawers in the dresser at home. Here.' She removed two dishes from her basket and handed them over.

'I've been lookin' for these – no pots, no pies.'

'Is Nancy at home?'

'She's out the back. Go on through. She'll be delighted to see you and the babe.'

Winnie stepped past the counter and into the kitchen at the rear of the pot house, a dark lean-to with a cracked and dusty window looking out on to the brick wall of the cottage behind it. Nancy was at the sink, scrubbing dishes, wearing a dirty white dress, apron and cap.

'How lovely!' she exclaimed as she turned to face Winnie. 'Let me dry my 'ands. May I 'old the babe?' She lifted her veil, revealing her pocked face. Nancy considered herself ugly, but her serene expression lent her an ethereal beauty – at least, that's what Winnie thought.

'Of course you can. Pamela, go to your aunt.' She placed the infant in Nancy's open arms, taking great pleasure in their mutual smiles and coos of delight.

'It is a shame that you do not call on us,' Winnie said. 'You are always welcome.'

'I'd love to, but my mother keeps my nose to the grind-stone.'

Winnie felt sorry because it seemed that Nancy had swapped one prison for another.

'I wonder if she would release you from the chains of the kitchen sink for a while?'

Nancy looked up from the baby's face. 'You mean, the run?'

Winnie nodded.

'I keep an ear to the ground. Our customers talk in riddles, thinkin' that it's enow to put me off the scent, but I know very well what they're discussin'. I 'ave a fancy for a bit o' hauntin' if that's what you're askin'.'

'That's wonderful … I'll let you know the details.'

'The Fey Lady's been quiet for a while, as if 'er spirit 'as found eternal rest – I think it's time to wake 'er up.' Nancy's mouth curved into a crooked smile, revealing her teeth, the line spoiled by a crescent of missing incisor, a reminder of One Eye's brutality.

'We decided to call upon you to help us, not only because we suspect that the Rattlers have their eye on our goods, but because of the rumour that the Customs men are being unusually diligent.'

'I've 'eard people say so. Oh, I wish I didn't 'ave to give the littlun back.' Reluctantly, she handed Pamela over and Winnie left her to her dishes, returning to the dining room just in time to find Awful Doins and Lawless arguing over their bill.

'I will settle it,' Lawless said, crowing like a rooster.

'Oh no. I shall. I insist,' Awful Doins said.

'It's an unusual turn of events when the pair o' you want to pay for your wittles,' Mrs Stickles said. 'You seem remarkably flush.'

'It will be your turn next time.' Lawless counted out a few coins from his pocket.

'We've recently received a retainer for our services,' Awful Doins explained. 'It won't be long before we come into possession of riches beyond your wildest imagination.'

'Do tell us more.' Mrs Stickles took the money and slipped it into the purse at her waist.

Lawless gave Awful Doins a nudge. 'We're not supposed to say nothin'.'

'Your secret will be safe with me,' Mrs Stickles said.

'Lawless is right – I shouldn't 'ave mentioned our stroke of good fortune. I can't say any more.' Awful Doins tapped the side of his nose with his forefinger. 'We've made a solemn promise to a person who will remain nameless, not to reveal the secret mission that 'e's asked us to carry out.'

'It can't be an honest way of making a livin', if it pays that well,' Mrs Stickles mused.

'It is for a noble cause: you are lookin' at the faces of the men who could be responsible for the end of old Boney.'

Winnie couldn't believe her ears. Mr Cork really had chosen this pair of clodpoles to carry the despatches in Louisa's place. As she watched them leave Molly's, she felt surprised at his lack of judgement and offended at the same time.

Walking home with Pamela, she reviewed her theory about Mr Gambril, but the more she thought, the more she doubted herself. On one hand, it seemed to be too much of a coincidence. On the other, if it was correct, she hadn't any proof. It would be her word against his.

The run went ahead as planned, and on a balmy evening in July when Marlin was due back with the *Whimbrel* and *Spindrift*, and Black Dog with the *Good Intent II*, Winnie and her sisters were waiting on the cliffs with the ponies at Kingsdown, looking out to sea. Mrs Witherall was minding Pamela, while her husband was lurking near the shore with Cromwell and the *Curlew*, waiting for the signal that would bring the landside smugglers to the beach.

An hour passed, the full moon rising higher above the sea, its rays picking out their faces, the approaching luggers, the ships in the Downs.

'We didn't pick the best night for this,' Louisa observed.

'How does it go? The best laid plans of mice and men,' Winnie said.

'And women,' Grace added. 'The menfolk like to believe that they've thought of everything, but it was Louisa who remembered to call on Nancy to do a bit of haunting. You know, Winnie, Abel was very friendly to you when we collected Gubbins and his friends here.'

'Oh, stop it,' Winnie sighed. 'I'm trying to concentrate. There, I've seen it – the blue flash from the *Whimbrel*.' She had the spout lantern at her feet, lit in readiness to return the signal.

'Are we ready for them?' Grace asked.

'What do you think? It's all quiet. No, listen ...'

'What is it?' Louisa said impatiently.

'I hear voices ...' The ponies shifted. Gubbins pricked up his ears and whinnied.

'Over there!' At the sound of masculine voices and approaching hoofbeats, Winnie's heart sank.

'They're on to us,' she whispered. 'It's the gobblers. Why? Oh, why won't they leave us alone? And Gubbins, what did you go and do that for?'

'He's dropped us right in the mire,' Louisa said quietly.

'There's nothing they can do – we aren't carrying any goods. The luggers will stand up a safe distance away until we give the signal.'

'I wonder how they knew of our whereabouts,' Grace said.

Winnie wondered too. Had they come across them by sheer coincidence, or had they been given prior knowledge of the landing place?

A pair of figures on horseback appeared.

'Ladies, we meet again.' It was Officer Chase who addressed them. 'It's a fine night for an outing.'

'It is indeed,' Louisa said.

'I see you are taking Mr Brockman's ponies for a walk.' When none of the sisters responded, he went on, 'Why would you employ a lantern of the type that is customarily carried by smugglers, if you are not involved in the free trade?'

'It is merely for guiding us in the dark,' Winnie said. 'The clifftop is a hazardous place. One trip on a tussock and that would be the end of it.'

'That lantern would also be useful for signalling to the luggers that are hovering – against the law – over there.'

'Luggers?' the three sisters exclaimed at the same time.

'What luggers? I can't see any,' Winnie went on.

Officer Chase laughed. 'They are over there – as clear as day. Here, I'll let you borrow my spyglass.'

'Is that wise?' his associate said, but Officer Chase continued to go along with Winnie's shamming. She wasn't sure what he was trying to prove, but she took the spyglass when he handed it down to her.

'Oh, you are right,' she said in mock surprise, as she held it to her eye. 'I can see ships standing in the roadstead, hundreds of them.'

'My friend, we are wasting our time,' the other officer protested. 'We can arrest her, but we'll have to prove to the old vicar in the morning that she was intending to use the lantern to signal to the luggers. I told you, we should have waited until they were unloading the goods before we pounced, but you insisted on riding up here to have another go at catching one of the Lennickers. Let's go. The boats won't come in tonight.'

The gobblers spurred their horses into action – Winnie suspected they were trying to impress with a spectacular gallop, but they only managed a lazy trot back the way they had come.

'What will we do now?' Grace asked.

'We'll have to go home and come back tomorrow,' Winnie said. 'I'll give the signal to stay out, but we must make haste.'

'Why the hurry?' Louisa said. 'We have time to kill thanks to the gobblers.'

'Ah, I don't want to be here when Officer Chase comes back looking for his spyglass,' Winnie smiled. 'I have it in my pocket and I have no intention of letting him have it back.'

'Winnie, well done,' Louisa laughed.

'It's a pity you didn't get the case for it as well,' Grace added.

Winnie signalled towards the north: three quick flashes of the lantern to tell the landside smugglers that they had abandoned the landing.

'That was in nobody's interest,' Winnie said. 'The gobblers know we'll wait for a day or two, and they'll have to turn out again.'

With heavy hearts, they returned the ponies to the mill and made their way home.

Two nights later, having left Pamela with Mrs Witherall as before, they set out again, travelling into the sandhills and choosing a spot deep into the deserted coast, beyond the looker's cottage and the Chequers Inn.

'Will Officer Chase be out tonight?' Winnie wondered aloud.

'It makes no difference whether he is or not. There's no need for subterfuge,' Louisa said. 'We're going to land the goods come hell or high water. We've employed extra batsmen, our friends from Dover and Sandwich, to make sure we outnumber the Revenue and any militia they might persuade along with them. Light the fire. Let them know we're waiting.'

The day before, they had collected materials for a beacon and covered them with an oilskin pegged down with stones. Grace removed the oilskin and folded it up. Winnie took the tinder box from one of the ponies' saddlebags and struck the flint, cajoling the kindling alight. She set it among the dry sticks and straw, and within seconds, flames leapt up into the darkness, bringing the luggers sailing towards the shore.

'Look, there's the *Guinevere*,' Winnie said, panicking when she spotted the Revenue cutter, painted black, and carrying her white gigs and galleys hoisted on her deck, astern and each side of her, lurking behind them. 'Louisa, what are we going to do?'

'There are five luggers now and the *Spindrift*, and they are all armed. Let's hope that the commander decides that discretion is the better part of valour.'

'She's retreating,' Grace confirmed. 'I expect they'll oversee our operations from a safe distance.'

Reassured, Winnie threw more wood on to the fire.

They had abandoned the idea of using the small boats on this occasion, deciding to employ as many men as possible landside. The sight of the fire brought a column of smugglers from the cover of the dunes, the batsmen protecting them on both flanks. As they reached the beach, the batsmen, brandishing their six-foot staves of ash, formed a seemingly impenetrable semi-circle between the sea and the sandhills.

'Mind your backs!' someone yelled as the Riding officers arrived at a gallop, accompanied by a small band of dragoons. They pulled up on the rise behind the batsmen. Officer Chase dropped his ribbons and cupped his hands around his mouth, shouting, 'Good evening, ladies and gentlemen. You are all under arrest!'

'Oh, what nonsense,' Winnie heard Louisa say from beside her. She felt nervous despite standing within the semi-circle among a crowd of at least two hundred and fifty people.

'On what charge?' one of the tub carriers from Limepit Acres called back.

'You know very well. It's patently obvious what trade you follow. The captain and his men will round you all up and march you down to Deal. No, I'll send you to Dover, where the magistrates will give weight to my evidence, not sit with closed minds and cloth ears, and the smugglers' money in their pockets.' Officer Chase's voice faltered as the captain of the militia rode up to him, the brass buttons glinting from his red coat.

The captain started to gesticulate. Winnie couldn't hear what he was saying, but Officer Chase didn't appear to be entirely happy about it.

'They can't possibly arrest us – we are too numerous.' Louisa was smiling, unperturbed by the Riding officer's threat. 'All they can do is look on while we get on with our work. We'll form a convoy as we carry the goods inland – they won't touch us.'

'There's nothing to stop them following us and picking us off one by one, as we disperse,' Winnie pointed out, but it seemed that the captain had better things to do than wait for hours on the beach with his men, because he ordered them to ride straight back to Deal, leaving Officers Chase and Lawrence, and their superior who had joined them, looking on, despondent.

The men brought the luggers in close to the beach and unloaded the goods. Before they had finished, the Revenue moved away, letting the landside smugglers disperse, melding with the shadows as they made their way inland.

Winnie and her sisters headed towards Deal, taking the tracks to the north of the town to avoid further detection. Having met with Nancy, Mr Witherall and Cromwell on the way, they continued to the Tar Path which led to St Leonard's, the parish church proper. Nancy was dressed in white, the exposed skin on her arms daubed with ash or limewash. Cromwell was struggling to carry a half-anker, while Mr Witherall limped along at the rear with a bale of silks on his back.

Entering through the lychgate, they moved silently around the perimeter of the churchyard where the grave-stones, old and new, loomed up in front of them from grass that was bootshoe high. They stopped beside a mossy tomb with the inscription: *Here lieth Michael Kent, a mariner of Deal, gone aloft on this day 17th March 1702.* Winnie knew it well – the last time they'd come up here was with Billy. He and Louisa had gone down into the maze of chambers and tunnels underground to look for Pa's stash – their inheritance – only to discover that it had gone, taken by One Eye and the Rattlers. They hadn't used it as a hiding hole since their father's passing.

'You open it, Cromwell,' Louisa said. 'All you have to do is move the end slab aside.'

'What if I don't want to, missus?'

'Let me do it.' Mr Witherall pushed past and squatted down to move the slab, revealing a dark hole through which a man of small stature or a boy like Cromwell might pass. Grace aimed the lantern spout into the hole.

'There's plenty of room,' Winnie said, surprised to see that the chamber below them, lined with stone and brick, was large enough for a goodly number of tubs, bales and boxes. In the past, she had avoided looking inside, preferring to remain above ground.

'I'll go down first,' Nancy said. 'I don't feel queasy about goin' down there.'

'Are you sure about this?'

'Ma says I can make a bit o' extra money out of it. I 'ave everythin' I need to be comfortable for a few days. It won't be no longer, will it?'

'We'll be moving the goods as soon as we can,' Louisa assured her. 'This is a temporary measure.'

'I've done this before – anybody who dares show their face down 'ere will be more scared of me than I'll be of them. I'll give 'em the frights, all right.' Nancy slid down through the hole, taking the lantern she'd brought with her. Louisa followed.

'Mr Witherall, you stand guard as we agreed. Grace and Cromwell, you lower the goods down to us. Winnie, you're with me.'

Winnie crawled into the hole, trying to ignore the stench of damp and stale air, and the sight of a skull that lay in front of the splintered remnants of a coffin. A rat the size of a dog scuttled away.

'Ouch. I always forget.' A shower of stones scuttered across the earthen floor as Louisa bumped her head on the ceiling. Winnie took care not to do the same.

'I've found the entrance to the next chamber,' Nancy called. 'This is where I normally do my 'auntin' from.'

'Aren't you frightened?' Winnie asked.

'I'm used to livin' 'idden underground – the thought of it doesn't give me no petrification.' She chortled with laughter, rather too loudly for Winnie's liking. 'There I go tryin' to talk proper like my sisters. Let me 'elp you stash the goods, then I'll settle down for the night.'

'Won't you be cold?' Although it was warm outside, a distinct chill permeated the hiding hole.

'I 'ave food, ale and blankets. And the chance to 'ave a rest from washin' pots and clearin' tables.'

'You won't fall asleep?' Winnie worried.

'I'll 'ear 'em all right. I 'ave the sharpest ears of anybody I know – and I always set up a thread across each passageway leading into my sleepin' chamber to alert me if someone should come stumblin' in. Old One Eye showed me 'ow to attach them to my person, but I'm givin' all my secrets away and we 'ave too much to do to waste time gossipin'.'

Reassured, Winnie joined Louisa, Grace and Cromwell in handing the bales along to Nancy who stacked them in the deepest chamber while Mr Witherall acted as lookout.

'Tu-whit!' Winnie jumped at the sound of an owl, then another, calling back. 'Tu-whoo!' This was followed by an attack of coughing, then scrabbling and the grating of one stone being moved across another.

'Our spotsman 'as spotted someone,' Nancy hissed.

'And let them know where we are,' Louisa said ruefully.

Mr Witherall was wheezing and wiping his forehead with his crumpled hat as he joined them underground.

'Someone's on our tail,' he said. 'I noticed two figures creepin' around near the porch of the church. They're up to no good, for sure. I reckon we should lie low for a while.'

'What about the ponies?'

'I gave 'em their orders. A whoa there, and the three of 'em went off at a gallop. We'll look out for 'em on our way 'ome.'

'We've unloaded all the goods.' Cromwell leaned against the wall. 'I s'pose all we 'ave to do now is wait.' His face looked pale in the lanternlight. 'I don't like it. Mr Appleton used to lock me in 'is 'ut on the beach of a night if I talked back to 'im. When I grew too big for 'im to man'andle, he gave it up.'

'Whist!' Mr Witherall said. 'Did you 'ear that?'

Winnie's heart almost stopped. She reached out for Grace's hand.

'No talkin', belchin' or the other,' Mr Witherall whispered. 'The Fey Lady will take her turn.'

The stones grated from the distance. They were two chambers away and quite safe, Winnie thought as she clutched Grace's hand. Someone's teeth were chattering – the boy's, she assumed – as an object went clattering to the ground. A lantern, perhaps?

'I don't think this is the best idea you've ever 'ad, Lawless,' came a voice.

'Well, if you can think of a better one, you'd better say so because we're in a bit o' a bind, thanks to you.'

'I was only doin' what that gen'leman who we met at the tavern for a game o' cards suggested if we got into a tight spot with the delivery.'

Winnie's ears pricked up further as she realised they had not been discovered by a gang of rival smugglers with their broad-shouldered batsmen, or a bunch of opportunistic armed thieves who had knowledge of the local area. Even so, they were still in danger – Awful Doins and his companion were likely to be carrying small arms and knives for their own protection.

134

'For your reference – that's what 'e said – you'd be wise to l'arn a few tricks o' the trade of subterfuge.'

'You aren't makin' no sense as usual – and neither was 'e, because I'm feelin' rather queer.'

'It's all that runnin' you did, gettin' away from the greasy genl'man. Right slippery, wasn't he?'

'The way 'e looked at you, it made yer feel all cold and huvvery,' Lawless said.

'We made the wrong call – we should never 'ave ate the papers.'

'If you'd done as your ma 'ad told you and chewed each piece twenty times afore you swallered, you'd be all right.' Winnie felt Grace stiffen beside her, heard her stifle a giggle as Lawless went on, 'We can't give the papers to this Mr Cork fellow until we pass 'em out the other end, and even then I'm not convinced that they'll be of any use to 'im.'

Grace's hand was pressed to her mouth, and her shoulders were shaking. Winnie swallowed back a sob of mirth.

'What was that?' Awful Doins said.

There was a long silence.

'Nothin'. Come on. Let's 'ave a look around. Someone might have left somethin' of interest.' The hapless pair of couriers began to move around the adjacent chamber. 'The gen'leman we played cards with, said that the words will come out the other end of the body as they went in: whole. If you were listenin' to 'im instead of givin' the eye to that new barmaid, you'd 'ave 'eard 'im go on to say that, if the words emerge in the wrong order, an eddicated man can straighten them out again. Mr Cork's 'ad a lot of schoolin'.'

Winnie felt the touch of a hand on her shoulder, but she managed to bite back a scream as Nancy pushed past her, emitting a howl that echoed about the walls.

'It's the Fey Lady! God 'elp us. What are we goin' to do now?' Awful Doins cried.

There was the sound of a sharp slap, perhaps an attempt to bring him back to his senses if he'd had any in the first place.

'It can't be 'er. She 'asn't done any 'auntin' for ages, not since young Nancy left the Rattlin' Cat,' Lawless reasoned. 'There never was no ghost. She was an apparition dreamt up by One Eye for 'is own purposes. Although, 'ow can this be Nancy when she'll be sleepin' at the pot 'ouse at this time of night?'

'I don't think we should stop to find out,' Awful Doins said.

'Woo woo ...' Nancy began again, and the intruders fled without closing the slab behind them.

'I'm very cross with you, Grace,' Louisa said.

'I couldn't help it,' she giggled. 'Oh dear, I've never felt such pain, trying to hold it in.'

'I don't think they'll be back,' Winnie said.

Apart from the fact that Mr Cork wouldn't be receiving his papers, all seemed well. They had hidden the goods, giving them time to deal with them later. Nancy was in place until they'd moved them on, and the run had been a success. If only Billy had been here to share it.

Chapter Ten

A Golden Opportunity

Louisa employed Winnie and Pamela to carry lace to the draper, and Miss Flinders called on them at home twice, accompanied by her maid, to purchase the same. They sold the cognac alongside their provisioning trips and donated a barrel of wine to the church. The watches went to one of the jewellers in Golden Street and the silks to Canterbury.

By the anniversary of Billy's disappearance towards the end of the first week in August, there were few goods left to worry about.

When she had finished her chores, Winnie dressed Pamela in a white knitted bonnet with ribbons and a plain barracoat and pushed her along Beach Street in the hand-cart. The baby chewed on her rattle, smiled and drooled, and soon fell asleep.

'I don't know where that time has gone,' Winnie murmured as she propped a parasol up to provide shade from the hot summer sunshine, unable to believe that her daughter was already seven months old.

She stopped at the capstan grounds and stared out to sea, at the mosaic of cobalt-blue and emerald-green water, and the golden sands exposed by the tide. There were ships moored in the Downs, over three hundred of them, along with a naval boat returning to the provisioning yard, and several fishing boats – the smaller luggers that they called cats – returning with their catches from the fishing grounds that lay to the east of Dover. Using the spyglass that she had filched from Officer Chase, who hadn't yet chased her up to retrieve it, she spotted an East Indiaman and a brig, a tall ship, square-rigged with two masts.

'Good day, Winnie,' Mr Witherall said, walking over to her. 'Or is it?'

'That depends.' She glanced up at the cloudless sky. 'The weather's set fair.'

'You're thinkin' of Billy,' Mr Witherall guessed. 'It's a year now, isn't it? I remember it well. The gangers were goin' to take me – an old man riddled with gout – until I fell to the ground. That's when they let me go, thinkin' I'd be an 'indrance.'

'To the day,' she acknowledged, a lump in her throat. 'I haven't heard a word from him. I can't help thinking that I must begin to assume the worst.'

'I'm terr'ble sorry for you, and the littlun, but you're right to start plannin' for the future.'

'I ask everyone I meet if they know where he is, if they've seen him, and the answer is always the same. I've even written to the navy at Greenwich, but they had no answer.'

'There should be a record of 'im, if he went abroad,' Mr Witherall said thoughtfully.

'That's what I'm afraid of, that he never got as far as embarking on a journey on a man-o'-war. That he fell from the cliff that morning when Jason lost sight of him and the sea has kept his body from me.'

'What do you think 'e would say if 'e could speak to you now, my dear?'

Something ordinary, she thought. Knowing Billy, it wouldn't be anything romantic or poetical, just a 'How's my girl?' or 'What's for supper?' Either would be enough.

''Tis a pity for a child to grow up without a father.'

'You mean, not knowing her father?'

'You're still ready against Billy comin' back,' Mr Witherall said, 'but you do 'ave to start thinkin' about what you'll do if 'e doesn't.'

Winnie felt her eyes glaze over as he went on about how Billy would want her to be happy, no matter what, and that it would serve her well to consider seriously any offers she might receive.

She knew what he was up to. Louisa had hinted at it too several days ago when they were walking back from Mr Gigg's. They wanted her to forget Billy and consider marrying someone else, but with the war, there were very few eligible men her age and certainly none that she would entertain as a husband, even if they should ask her, which they wouldn't, seeing as she was an unmarried mother.

'You 'ave much to offer in return,' Mr Witherall went on. 'Mrs Witherall says you always 'ave the pavement outside the 'ouse spick and span. My boy avows that you are an excellent cook and 'ousekeeper. You must see the advantages that marriage can bring.'

She nodded. She could see them, but she couldn't and wouldn't marry anyone but Billy. Her heart belonged to him, and him alone.

The same evening at suppertime, Winnie cleared the table ready to bring out an apple tart.

'Jason would like the blanket on the custard,' Louisa said.

'Unless anyone else wants it,' he said quickly.

'No, you have it,' Winnie and Grace said at the same time.

He cleared his plate – twice – which was gratifying, Winnie thought. The house shook, the result of a barrel being rumbled along the hidden pathway on the roof.

'The Rattlers are busy tonight,' Jason remarked.

'Do you think they know something we don't?' Louisa asked.

'I can hear voices and footsteps from the alley,' Grace murmured.

The smile disappeared from Jason's face. 'I wonder if the Comptroller of Customs and his men are nearby.'

Louisa took charge. 'Grace, go and hide that half-anker of cognac in the hang – cover it with the fresh woodchips. Jason, there's wine in the lean-to – it should go in one of the hiding holes.'

'I'll snuff out the candles to make it look as if there's nobody here,' Winnie said, but it was too late. There was a sharp rap at the door.

Winnie froze, a pulse throbbing at her temple.

'It's them. What are we going to do?'

'Bluff our way out of it as we've always done,' Jason said lightly.

'Winnie, you should fetch the littlun,' Louisa said. 'Who can fail to be distracted by the sight of her innocent smile?'

'Leave her to sleep,' Jason sighed.

'If we wake her now, she won't disturb us later,' Grace said.

There was another series of raps at the door.

'You'd better answer it, Jason.' Louisa followed him out to the hall. Grace and Winnie went too, standing at the bottom of the stairs as Jason slowly opened the door.

'Mr Cork here,' came a voice. 'I've come to see Miss Winnie Lennicker.'

'You mean Louisa? Mrs Witherall?' Jason said.

'I have business with her sister, Marlin.'

Jason turned. 'Winnie, are you expectin' a caller? Shall I show him in?'

Winnie felt that she would welcome almost anyone, knowing it wasn't the Customs officers who had arrived on the doorstep.

'I have something that may be to this young lady's advantage.'

'Then you may enter.' Jason showed him into the parlour. 'Winnie,' he called.

'This conversation is to be held in private,' Mr Cork said.

'I'm not sure—' Louisa began, but Jason cut her off.

'Let Mr Cork speak to Winnie if that is acceptable to her. Winnie, what do you say?'

'I will entertain a brief meeting,' she said, wondering what on earth he wanted to see her about.

'We thought you were the Customs men,' Grace said gaily, at which Winnie frowned at her. Would she ever learn to hold her tongue?

Winnie took a seat on the chaise in the parlour while Mr Cork sat at the table.

'Miss Lennicker, I brought my association with your sister to an end because of the danger she was in from third parties looking to interfere with the flow of intelligence between Britain and France.'

It was a pity he hadn't made that clear before, she thought. It would have saved Louisa much grief, having assumed that Mr Cork's silence had been down to her being forced to entrust Winnie with the despatches when she'd twisted her ankle.

'The Lace Maiden has become increasingly notorious for her role in the free trade. Her name and reputation go before her, which is why I can no longer employ her as a courier. I have since deployed others who are familiar with the area ... this was not a resounding success.' Winnie refrained from smiling, recalling the conversation she'd overheard between Lawless and Awful Doins. 'Reflecting on an alternative, I recalled how you had stepped into your sister's shoes that night, how you had overcome adversity in your determination to serve King and Country. I had some reservations – you are related to the Lace Maiden by blood and you are easily recognisable from the colour of your hair. But you have proved that you can be relied on to complete the task in hand, in a timely manner and with discretion.'

'Mr Cork, I'm honoured, but I'm not sure—'

'You are in an ideal position to provide us with further information: although snippets of gossip about passing vessels and rumours from the capstan grounds might seem insignificant, they are parts from which we can build up the bigger picture.'

'You would like me to take notes?'

'With care, yes. One must strive to avoid arousing suspicion about one's activities, but a woman such as you with a quiet, unassuming manner, and a young child, is unlikely to attract attention.'

'I haven't actually agreed to work for you,' Winnie objected. 'I don't want to cause offence, but I'm ... I wasn't born to be a spy.'

'And that's the beauty of it. You've lived in Deal all your life. When you are working for me, it will appear that you are carrying on your usual business. Let me go on. You will have a small but essential role in our efforts to win the war against the man who would be Emperor of France, of England and the rest of the world.

'As well as receiving intelligence, our network of British agents – also known as correspondents – spread false information and undermine the loyalty of French officers. Like many of us, I'm sure that your one wish for your child is that she grows up in a time of peace and prosperity.

You can help to make that happen. It is to your pecuniary advantage, but that is nothing compared with our desire to overthrow Napoleon and make an end to this terrible war that tears families apart and maims and kills our men.'

It was a heartfelt speech, she thought, but he was a clever and successful gentleman who knew how to get what he wanted.

'You are very persuasive, Mr Cork, but I'm not convinced. As you've so eloquently observed, I am a mother and I can't have it on my conscience to make my child an orphan.'

'I understand your concern, but your actions could save thousands of lives, and make you a fortune. Everything in life is a gamble. Are you prepared to choose this card?'

'I wish that you would have asked someone else,' she said in a small voice.

'I have explained my reasoning. When I was picturing the ideal candidate to travel with the gold on the guinea boat, you came to mind. Your brother-in-law Marlin has a vested interest in protecting you, keeping you out of danger and thereby aiding the secure transfer and delivery of the despatches. You and he are family, after all.'

'You expect me to travel to France?'

Mr Cork nodded. 'It's important for reasons that I cannot discuss at present that the papers are placed straight into the hands of the courier in Gravelines, a lady whom we refer to simply as "Madame". They will be delivered to you by one of our trusted men. On your return, you will simply meet with him in a place of our choosing and hand over the despatches and any other intelligence you have gleaned. What do you think?'

'I don't ... I can't ...' but then she thought of Louisa and how she had accepted the challenge. She had envied her courage and now Mr Cork was giving her a chance to prove that she wasn't merely the meek and mild-mannered mother of a bastard child. It was her opportunity to play her part, just as she hoped Billy was doing, fighting for their country on the high seas. What would her sister say to Mr Cork? 'How much are you offering in return for this work?' she asked.

They agreed terms and Mr Cork took a pre-written agreement from his bag, along with a pen and bottle of ink, and blotting paper.

He filled in the amount of remuneration she could expect – paid up to a few months in arrears – then signed it with a flourish of his pen before handing it to her. She signed as well. He blotted the ink and completed a second copy for himself.

All it said was, *For services to be rendered ...*

'Please keep this somewhere out of sight,' he said. 'I have deliberately withheld the details of the services you will supply. This matter must be carried out with utmost secrecy, but I will give you the bare bones of how intelligence flows between England and France. We have English agents embedded in Paris and Switzerland to obtain secret intelligence that may or may not be useful to the Prime Minister, the Secretary of State for the Home Office and for War and the Colonies, for the First Lord of the Admiralty and ultimately to the King.

'A few of our men have infiltrated Napoleon's army to gain insight into the morale of his troops, the state of their weaponry and the mood of his generals. My contacts recruit trusted men and embed them in enemy territory to establish a secure line of communication back to London – that is where you come in.'

'How will I know when there are despatches to be carried?'

'We employ signals – much like the free traders do – to pass messages along the line to indicate when an agent is ready to submit intelligence. We use all manner of locations for our exchanges, or you may be required to make a plant.

'Do not be alarmed, Miss Lennicker. All that means is that you transfer items to a secret destination: a hollow in a particular tree; a gap in a wall behind numbered bricks. You will always receive a plan; it may be written in a sympathetic stain – if so, you need to warm the paper gently over a flame to reveal the hidden lettering. Oh dear, perhaps I am revealing too much, but this only goes to show in no small measure the depth of my appreciation and the level of confidence I have in you.'

She almost smiled. If only he knew what she was thinking: that he was a smooth-talking, shiny bloater of a gentleman, and as slippery as they come.

'I have a network – no, a veritable spider's web of contacts, trusted men … and a few women on whom I depend. I correct myself – on whom King and Country can rely!'

'That is a very grand speech, sir.'

'There's more,' he said. 'You may wonder why the papers are not sent via the General Post Office – that is because they have a secret office of their own, employing translators and decipherers to intercept and monitor the mail and despatches sent on the Packet Service between Britain and foreign governments. I prefer to circumvent this system to maintain full control of the intelligence. Is there anything else you'd like to ask me?'

'No, sir. Thank you. You've been most … enlightening.'

The only question, the one burning on the tip of her tongue – even as Mr Cork left Compass Cottage – was, whose side are you on? If she'd been shocked at Louisa's lackadaisical response to the question, she was even more perturbed by her meeting with the smuggler's agent. She concluded that whether he was assisting the French or the English, he seemed more intent on helping himself.

'What did he want?' Grace asked as soon as Winnie had closed the door behind him.

'You must have some idea – in fact, I expect you heard the gist, if not our entire conversation.'

'What makes you think that?'

'Because you had your ear to the parlour door the whole time – I heard it creak from time to time.'

'My ear?' Grace said lightly, trying to divert her.

'No, the door. When you lean on the handle, it makes a noise.' Winnie grinned. 'Oh Grace, I love you.'

'Are you going to tell Louisa?'

'Are you going to tell Louisa what?' Their elder sister appeared at the kitchen doorway, along with her husband.

'What did Mr Cork want with you?' Jason asked.

'Ask Grace – she knows all about it,' Winnie smiled.

They celebrated Winnie's good fortune with milk and brandy, having decided that it was indeed a stroke of luck and potentially a highly lucrative extra string to their bow, making up for their loss of income now that Mr Cork had decided that Louisa was no longer his choice of courier. Jason would give Winnie safe passage on the *Whimbrel* or the guinea boat, and charge Mr Cork for it. From then on, though, she was on tenterhooks, waiting for the signal.

The remainder of August passed quietly with Pamela learning to crawl and babble, then September came bringing autumn mists and cold mornings to Deal. The hop pickers moved into the countryside, harvesting from the bines until twilight, while Winnie and her sisters continued selling their French lace to Mr Gigg and the ladies of Deal, provisioning the ships in the Downs and catching and selling fish. Occasionally, Winnie and Grace went mushrooming in the fields, being careful what to pick. Ma had taught them that all mushrooms were edible, some of them only the once.

One morning, Winnie was playing happily with Pamela in the kitchen.

'Pat-a-cake, pat-a-cake, baker's man ...' Pamela was on Winnie's lap, smiling and showing off her new tooth. 'Make me a cake as fast as you—' Winnie paused when she heard the knock at the door. 'Whist, littlun. They'll go away if we ignore them.'

Pamela gurgled and cooed.

'Pat it and prick it and mark it with P—' There was another knock. 'And put it in the oven for baby and me,' she chanted softly.

Rat-a-tat-tat.

'Oh, who is it? Mr Cork? No, I think he'll send some mysterious sign – perhaps, in his arrogance, he has made it so mysterious that I have missed it. Could it be your auntie? Louisa said she'd be out all day.' With a sigh, she stood up. 'We'll have to make it look as if we've been as busy as bees while she's been out.' With the baby on her hip, she grabbed a handful of vegetables followed by the crock of salted pork and placed them on the table, before rushing to open the front door.

'Abel?' She looked a fright, she thought, not having run a brush through her hair that morning.

'I was told you'd be expectin' me.' He frowned, his head slightly to one side, and his hands behind his back.

'I had no idea.'

'My cousin must have forgotten to mention it.' His foot was against the doorjamb. 'May I come in?'

Pamela grabbed at the front of Winnie's dress and clung on, turning her face away from their unwanted caller who was dressed like a dandy in a blue cutaway coat and white breeches.

'I suppose you better had,' Winnie said, aware that the neighbours were bound to misconstrue the situation. 'Come through to the ... I was going to suggest the kitchen, but seeing as you're dressed up like that, you'd better take a seat in the parlour. You can wait for Jason there while I get on with my chores. Louisa will have words with me if they aren't done by the time she gets back.'

'I'm here to see you, not Jason. I suppose you could say that it's about a new venture on my part.'

Bemused, she showed him into the parlour and opened the curtains. The bright light of day made the baby squint as Abel strode up and down the room, taking four strides each way. He was too large for Compass Cottage, Winnie decided, and the kind of man who belonged outdoors with his scent of fresh cologne and horse.

'Would you like a drink, some tea perhaps?' she asked, thinking that it would give her an excuse to leave the room and run a comb through her hair, but he declined.

'Do sit down,' she said, taking a seat. He followed suit, resting his hat on his knees with a posy of flowers that he'd been hiding behind his back on top. He picked at the petals, discarding them one by one, until they made a small carpet on the floor.

'What is it you wish to say to me?'

'I'll be blunt. There's no point in beatin' about the bush. I've come to make you an offer.'

'I beg your pardon?' Winnie held Pamela a little tighter – the baby wriggled, trying to get out of her embrace, as Abel blundered on.

'You are a cheerful and capable woman – my cousin speaks highly of your culinary skills. You have a foal at foot, so to speak – a sweet, innocent child – who will entertain and delight her mother, fulfillin' her maternal desires, and my own mother's expectation of becomin' a grandmother. I am more than willin' to take her on as my own.'

'Please, stop,' Winnie begged.

'You must allow me to continue, or I will forget somethin' of importance,' he said, cutting her off. 'You have expressed a wish to give up the free trade. Marry me, and I promise that you'll never have to watch your back again. I will look after you, support you, if you'll do me the honour of acceptin' my hand in matrimony. There, I have done it. We will ask the vicar to have the banns read – we can be married in one month.' He forced a smile. 'Why wait and have a long engagement when you've made up your mind?'

'Abel, forgive me, but I haven't given you any encouragement, no reason to expect that I would accept an offer.' She thought she had made her situation perfectly clear. Billy had been gone for over a year, but it made no difference to her feelings. It was as though Abel had been wearing blinkers.

'I would have thought, given your position livin' at Compass Cottage with Mr and Mrs Jason Witherall –' he sounded oddly formal '– you'd appreciate havin' your own home. I'll have a house built for us on the meadow behind the stables. We'll have three bedrooms at least, one for each of us, and one for the littlun.'

She began to panic, wondering how she was going to get away from him without hurting his feelings. 'This is too much.'

'Oh dear. I have forgotten to speak of my admiration for you … Winnie, I think you are the loveliest woman I've ever seen, and that's important because – accordin' to Mr Brockman, my father – a sickly wife is a great eyesore to a man. Although we both come from lowly stock, I would have guessed that you were a woman of quality.'

'That is a strange compliment.' She stared at him in wonder.

'My mother has advised me to select a wife as I would a horse: runnin' one's eye over her to check her conformation, spendin' time with her to judge her manners, and findin' out about her ability to perform the tasks one is expectin' her to do.'

'You are beyond the pale, sir,' she said, shocked. 'You are comparing me to a horse?'

'I'm tryin' to explain. Let me speak.'

'Are you sure you wish to go on? You are digging yourself a rather large hole with your proposal of marriage, and I can't see if you go on any deeper that you will ever be able to get out of it.'

'What is it that a young lady is lookin' for in a proposal? Mrs Brockman suggested the posy which I seem to have ruined.' He leapt up. 'I will fetch another, a larger one.'

'No, no, no,' she said, shaking her head.

'Then I will use more flowery expressions of affection to persuade you?' To her relief, he faltered. 'Who am I tryin' to fool? Winnie, I am offerin' a marriage of convenience that works both ways. People look on me differently when they know I'm not yet married – our union will help my business, my reputation.'

She frowned.

'The women are always after you, then … when they come to choose a hack or hunter?' The idea amused her. 'There is no point in trying to make me jealous.'

'I'm not one for playin' games. I need a wife and you fit the bill.'

'I can't possibly accept,' she said softly.

'Why not, when I have an income of six hundred pounds a year?'

'You cannot buy me.'

'I assure you that there will be no beddin'. It is not necessary for the success of our union.'

'There will be no union,' she exclaimed.

To her horror, he took a handkerchief from his pocket and blew his nose. Pamela twitched with alarm at the noise and started to cry.

'I'm very grateful for your consideration even though it has come as a great surprise, but I couldn't be a good wife to you,' she said. 'My heart belongs elsewhere.'

'Did I see Abel leaving the cottage?' Louisa asked later when Winnie was sewing, adding a new section to one of her skirts to replace the frayed hem.

'You did,' she answered curtly.

'Did he leave a message for Jason?'

'No … he came to call on me.'

Louisa sat down heavily on the other end of the chaise. 'Oh Winnie, what did he say?'

'He made me an offer.' She knotted the end of her thread and stuck the needle into the material to make a start on the seam, but she tugged too hard and the knot came straight through.

'That's … wonderful news.'

'I turned him down, Louisa.' She glanced up at her sister. 'Whatever makes you think I'd accept? You had some idea that this was going to happen, didn't you? Don't deny it. Mr Witherall hinted at it the other day.'

'You should have told him you'd think about it. He'd make an ideal husband.'

'Not for me,' Winnie replied firmly.

Chapter Eleven

A Golden Moment

November 1813

'The finest cod you've ever seen! Dabs fresh from ol' briny!' Winnie's throat was hoarse from shouting, trying to make her voice heard above the screaming and coarse language of the other fishwives in the bustling market. She looked down at the handcart – she still had a dozen freshly smoked bloaters left, along with their recent catch. Could she get away with reducing her prices without Louisa noticing, so she could get home to Pamela? Even though she trusted Grace implicitly, she was envious of the fact that her sister was indoors with her daughter, while she was freezing to death at the market on a grey November day.

'Winnie! Winnie!' Cromwell came hurtling along the street towards her, dodging the crowds of shoppers and the stray dogs hoping to snatch a few scraps. He stopped, skidding into the handcart. 'Sorry!' He hardly paused for breath. 'Will you give me a penny for my news, miss?'

'That depends on what it is,' she said.

'It's good news, the best.'

'Go on then.'

'The penny first,' he said wisely.

She fumbled in her purse and pulled out a coin, dropping it into his grubby palm.

'Well?'

'It's Billy Fleet – 'e's back in Deal. I thought you'd want to know.'

'Oh!' Her hand flew to her mouth. 'Where is he? Why hasn't he come to find me?'

''E's at the 'ospital. The new one.'

'Then I must go to him. Take this back to Compass Cottage for me.' She gestured towards the handcart. 'Tell Grace I've gone to see Billy.' Without waiting for his answer, she turned on her heels and ran, her heart pounding, an ache in her chest. She didn't know whether to laugh or cry, so she did both. The moment she had been praying for had finally arrived.

Billy was home.

Except that as she approached the hospital, her joy began to turn to apprehension. He must be injured, but how badly? Would he still recognise her? Would the man she loved be the same?

She entered the naval hospital, rebuilt after the original burned down the previous year, and approached the desk in the reception hall where a young man stood in front of an open ledger.

'Please, I'm looking for a Mr William Fleet. I've heard that he's a patient here. Can you help me, Mr …?'

'Mr Arthur. Let me see,' he said kindly. 'Do you know when he was admitted?'

'Yesterday? This morning? I'm not sure, but it will be recently.' She grew impatient as he ran his finger down the list, turned back one page and then another. 'I can't find a record of him. Are you sure he's here?'

'Perhaps there's been a misunderstanding,' she muttered, disappointment welling inside her. She wasn't sure she could bear it if Cromwell had been mistaken.

'Ah, here we are – he was admitted on the sixth of this month.'

'That was a week ago! Why did nobody say so? Why didn't he send word to me straight away? I don't understand.' It was as if her blood had completely drained from her body, leaving her weak.

'Some of these men have terrible wounds and a few arrive insensible,' Mr Arthur said. 'Contacting next of kin is often of secondary importance when they have an urgent requirement for intensive treatment and rehabilitation. I assume you are his ... wife?'

'Mrs Fleet, that's right,' she said, because that was whom she wanted to be, Billy's wife who lived in a homely cottage on Beach Street, with a red tiled roof, pale stucco and a blue front door.

Did he not want to see her? Had he broken his head? She couldn't think of any reason why he wouldn't have got in touch with her.

'Take a seat over there, while I go and ask him if he's fit to receive a visitor.'

'Then he is conscious? He is in possession of his faculties? Oh, then there is no need for you to talk to him. He will see me. I know he will.'

'It's the rules, Mrs Fleet. Sit down and wait, and I'll return shortly.'

With great reluctance, she sat down and waited. The scent of lye soap and boiled vegetables drifted into her nostrils and she could hear distant screaming and the clattering of pans from the kitchens. Soon after, a man in his thirties, dressed in a loosely fitting shirt and pantaloons, walked past her towards the exit. Noticing that he was barefoot, she stood up and hurried to block his way.

'Excuse me, sir. You seem to have forgotten your boots.'

He looked at her wildly as though he couldn't comprehend the meaning of her words, before two of the hospital staff, women who reminded Winnie of the fishwives in the market, ran to catch him and turn him back.

'Get yerself back to bed,' one said roughly, putting their errant patient in an armlock. 'Mrs Bone, call for the ward master for the cuffs.'

'Will do, will do, Mrs Cook.'

'The poor man has lost his mind,' Mr Arthur muttered, returning as the women bundled him away. 'Mr Fleet wishes to see you, but I'd remind you that no man returns from war unchanged.'

'Thank you,' she said, hardly listening. All she wanted was to see Billy again.

'You'll find him in the ward on the second floor, opposite the staircase, third bed on the left. I would show you there myself, missus, but I shouldn't really leave my post. The ward master's name is Lieutenant Cobb – he's expecting you.'

She thanked him and rushed to the ward, stopping in the entrance to look along the room. The pale sun slanting through the long windows cast a light across Billy's bed. He was sitting propped up with pillows and swathed in a grey blanket, staring straight at her, his carroty hair short and rumpled, his eyes bright, his complexion pale beneath the freckles. He smiled, and her heart turned over.

'Billy,' she cried as she dashed to his side. 'I'm so glad to see you.'

He's unwell so calls Winnie his sister here, but it's odd that this is not referred to later. Why didn't you send for me? I'd have come straight here if I'd known.' She reached for his hand, tangled her fingers with his and gave them a squeeze.

'I 'aven't been able to speak – I couldn't make the words come out. The doctors say it was the shock that turned me mute. Who'd rabbit it, eh? Me not talkin' for a month.'

'That is extraordinary, but at least you have found your tongue again. All will be well now you are home.'

'I'm sorry, but –' his shoulders slumped '– you don't want me like this. I'm a liability – I can't go out with Marlin and the crew. I'll never skipper the *Curlew*. I'll never realise my dream of becomin' a boatman like Mr Lennicker.' He choked back a sob before going on, 'It breaks my 'eart to think of it.'

'Whatever has happened, it will mend. Time heals.'

'I wish they 'adn't brought me back to Deal – I won't be a burden to you.'

'Billy, stop!' She wiped her eyes. 'I love you just the same as I did when you got taken. We'll get by. I know we will.' She looked up and down the ward. 'Let's get you home where I can look after you.'

'It's me who's supposed to look after you.'

'I mean until you've made a full recovery,' she said.

'My leg won't grow back,' he said abruptly.

'I beg your pardon?'

'I've lost my leg, the left one below the knee – a musket ball shattered the bones and the ship's surgeon 'ad to amputate. He 'ad it off in less than two minutes. You see, it upsets you … I knew it would.'

'It's a bit of a shock, that's all. There are plenty who have suffered the loss of their limbs. Look at Admiral Lord Nelson – he lost one arm and an eye, yet he was given HMS *Victory* as his flagship. He was at sea, even at the end when the French musketeer shot him.' Pa had recounted the stories of Nelson's heroism many times, and of his death eight years before. She was trying to make Billy feel better, but she sensed that her words weren't

156

having the desired effect. He seemed wild-eyed and upset, like the patient who had attempted to leave the hospital. 'Have the doctors told you when you can go home?'

'They've said I must leave soon – there are more injured sailors arrivin' every day, and there's nothin' more that they can do for me. The danger of gangrene is past.'

She recalled how Pa had died when his wound had mortified.

'Can you move about at all?'

'I can walk a little way with the crutches they've given me. I 'ate them, Winnie. People will stare.'

'We can arrange for you to have a wooden leg, perhaps.' She sensed that although Billy was back in Deal, there were going to be a few obstacles to overcome before they regained the level of happiness that they had grown accustomed to before he left.

The ward master came striding into his domain, his shiny shoes squeaking across the floor.

'You've had long enough, young lady,' he barked. 'I gave my permission for you to see that your husband is alive and kicking, not to wear him out with an inquisition. There'll be time for that later. He needs his rest.'

'I beg you to allow me to stay just a little while longer – I haven't seen him in over a year, and we have much to say to each other.'

'We make no exceptions. Come back at four o'clock when you may stay for a full hour.'

'You'd better leave, Winnie,' Billy said, releasing her hand.

'I'll be back,' she said. 'Don't go anywhere.'

''Ow can I?' he said miserably.

She smiled, knowing that he would feel better when he came home.

She hurried back to the cottage to tell her sisters the news.

*

157

'He's here in Deal!' Grace started dancing around the kitchen. 'It's a miracle.'

'I always knew he'd turn up like a bad penny,' Louisa said.

'You knew nothing of the sort.' Winnie pushed Pamela's highchair close to the table and fed her some goat's milk and pap. Pamela grabbed at the spoon, flicking the mixture everywhere: in her hair, in Winnie's eye and across the floor. 'Oh, you are a yucky child.' She started to mop up the mess. 'Louisa, you were the one who said he'd run away on purpose.'

'Where is he? How is he?'

She explained.

'I've said he can come home as soon as the doctors say so. I hope that's all right.'

'This is Jason's house now,' Louisa said. 'It isn't really up to me.'

'Where else can he go? There are reports of patients who've been discharged, making their homes in the attics of the hospital. I don't want that for him. Imagine how he'd feel – rejected, unloved ...'

'I'm concerned that the cottage is overcrowded – we're always tripping over each other. And where would Billy sleep?'

'He can have my room – his old room – and I'll share with Winnie and Pamela,' Grace said.

'That's very generous of you, but it doesn't feel right asking you to give up your bed,' Louisa said.

'Needs must,' Grace replied.

'What about the propriety of it?' Louisa tapped at her temple as though thinking. 'Winnie, you are not married. There will be further gossip if Billy moves in with us.'

'We'll be married soon enough,' Winnie said. 'In the meantime, he needs nursing and who better to do that than me? Please, Louisa, I'm begging you to let him stay with us in the heart of our family where he belongs.'

'I'll have to speak to Jason,' Louisa insisted. 'We'll see what he says about it.'

'Thank you.' Winnie threw her arms around her and gave her a hug.

'I'm not making any promises.'

'I know.'

'Billy will be able to meet his daughter for the first time,' Grace said. 'Imagine that.'

'I won't tell him he's a father until I can bring the two of them together.'

'Perhaps it would be prudent to give him warning,' Louisa suggested. 'Springing it on him might be too much of a shock.'

'I want to see the look on his face when I place her in his arms and say, "Meet Pamela, our daughter." It will make up for all the trials and tribulations we've been through.'

Nothing could spoil her happiness, not even the thought that Jason might say no to the idea of Billy living at the cottage. Grace helped her put her hair up and fasten the bodice of her flowing chemise gown – a pale pink confection with a ribbon beneath the breast and an embroidered hem, which she had put aside in anticipation of Billy's return.

When she arrived at the hospital at four, she found Billy sitting in the reception hall with his luggage beside him: he didn't have much, just his duffel and another cloth bag.

'I'm free,' he smiled wanly. "Avin' met you, the ward master assumed that I had a home to go to. 'E called one of the medical officers to discharge me.'

'Do you think you can manage to make your way as far as Cockle Swamp Alley?' she asked tentatively, not wanting to let on that Jason hadn't yet given permission for Billy to live with them. 'I wish I'd had a chance to ask Abel to carry us in his trap.'

'You are as thoughtful as ever,' he sighed. 'I don't deserve you.'

He pulled himself up and one of the crutches fell to the ground with a clatter. Winnie made to pick it up, but Billy stayed her, his hand on her arm.

'I'll do it. I don't need your pity – I can see it in your eyes, and I can't bear it.'

'Come with me,' she said gently, tearing her gaze from the stump of his left leg, the empty trouser leg fluttering in the breeze.

He looked pale and thin as he leaned on his crutches, his elbows hanging out of holes in the jacket. His swagger had gone, and he seemed so fragile that the wind might blow him over. Winnie slung his duffel over her shoulder and carried the second bag across her stomach.

'This is heavier than I was expecting,' she said. 'What's inside it?'

'A few souvenirs,' he said, grunting as he struggled to swing himself along.

'Billy, I have cried every night since the gangers came because I had no word from you. Why didn't you write?'

'You know I'm not one for letters.'

'You could have asked someone else to scribe on your behalf. I'm sorry,' she added when she noticed the shadow crossing his eyes. 'Let's put it behind us.' She changed the subject. 'Don't you think it would be easier to use a stick? I think there's one in the hang.'

'Don't start mitherin'.'

'I'm only trying to help.'

'I don't want your 'elp – I want to do things for meself.' He stopped and looked out to sea. 'I apologise – I shouldn't 'ave said that.'

'I'm sorry too.' She blinked, staring at the harsh November sunshine that was cutting through a sea fret, making the vessels in the roadstead appear like ghost ships, floating above the water. Billy was ill and not himself, she thought, yet it was hard to stifle the ache of even this tiny rejection. It wasn't quite the homecoming she had dreamed of, but he would mend. She would give him his favourite beef pie and gravy, and buy him a tonic from the apothecary, and – Pamela's lungs permitting – give him time to rest.

'Let's go 'ome,' he said eventually, and they walked slowly on.

Cromwell and the other boys stopped scrapping with each other and came charging up the shingle slope, pointing and shouting.

'It's true. Billy's come back! 'Ow are you, sir?' Cromwell was the first to greet him, all smiles. 'Oh?' His eyes settled on the crutches. 'You've been injured.'

''E's an 'ero,' one of the others said, his mouth dropped open. 'Mr Fleet, what was it like? I'm thinkin' of volunteerin' for the King's shillin'.'

'That's an honourable sentiment but takin' up arms at sea isn't for everybody. Come and see me about it sometime.'

'Leave him alone now,' Winnie said, trying to push them away. 'He wants some peace and quiet.'

'I don't want anyone else seein' me like this,' Billy said in a low voice.

'I fear that it's too late.' Winnie watched as the boys went ahead, knocking at doors and calling their neighbours into the alley. As they made their way to the cottage, they were swallowed up by a growing crowd, eager to welcome Billy home.

Mrs Witherall appeared, hands pressed to her cheeks as she exclaimed, 'Well, I never, well I never did,' over and over again. Mr Witherall came to greet Billy with his hand outstretched, but when he noticed the crutches, he gave him a pat on the back instead.

'This calls for a celebration,' he smiled. 'There'll be milk and brandy, and dancin' at the Waterman's Arms tonight. We'll get Mrs Stickles to bring some of 'er pies.'

'Thank you,' Winnie said, 'but I don't think Billy's up to dancing.'

'I can speak for myself,' Billy reminded her gently. 'I'm sure I'm up for a bit o' drinkin' and chinwaggin' with my old friends.'

Winnie had hoped they would find some time to be alone together, kissing and cuddling, and talking as they used to, but she understood his wish to renew old acquaintances. She could be patient. It was going to take time for him to readjust to ordinary, everyday life, she thought as Louisa appeared at the cottage door.

Smiling, her sister held her arms out in welcome.

'Billy, I didn't think I'd ever be this pleased to see you. But Winnie, you have put me in a difficult situation ...'

'The hospital has discharged him. I didn't have a choice.'

'Is there a problem?' Billy asked. 'Am I no longer welcome?'

'It isn't that. Our circumstances have changed while you've been away,' Louisa said. 'It's only right that I should speak to my husband first. Come in, though – I'm sure he'll let you stay for a few days at least.'

'I'm very grateful,' Billy said. 'You and Marlin? You are ...?'

'We are married – I'm Mrs Jason Witherall,' she said, her eyes shining. 'Grace,' she called. 'Where are you?'

'There's someone I'd like you to meet,' Winnie said, leading Billy into the house.

'Go into the parlour,' Louisa suggested. 'I'll find Grace.'

162

Stifling her impulse to help him, Winnie watched as Billy struggled to remove his boot and make his way into the parlour where he sat down heavily on the chaise. Winnie waited for Grace to arrive, with Pamela in her arms. She seemed flustered and the baby had her buttons done up wrong on her knitted coat.

'I didn't realise you were bringing Billy back today. If I'd had notice, I'd have put her in clean clothes. Billy, it's wonderful to see you – I thought ...' Grace bit back tears and turned to Winnie, uncertain what to do with the baby who was smiling and flapping her arms and legs at the sight of her mother.

'Allow me to introduce you to Pamela Jane,' Winnie said.

'Louisa and Marlin didn't 'ang about,' Billy marvelled.

'Go to your mama.' Grace handed her over to Winnie who held her close and kissed her forehead.

'Oh?' Billy said in a shocked tone. 'You didn't wait for me – you are married?'

'She's yours, silly,' Winnie said, smiling. 'She's your daughter.'

'How can that be? How old is she?' She heard the tremor in his voice and the flicker of doubt.

'She was born in January. She's ten months old.'

'Billy, you don't really think Winnie would go with anyone else?' Grace interrupted. 'She's never stopped talking about you. She asks every Jack Tar she meets if they've heard or seen anything of you, and she reads the newspapers whenever she can get hold of them. I've seen her drying her eyes when she thinks nobody's looking. I've heard her crying at night.'

Winnie gazed at Billy who was staring up at her, his expression a mixture of affection and astonishment.

'Would you like to hold her?'

He nodded. Winnie knelt and placed his child into his arms, watching his eyes light up as Pamela's frown turned into a smile.

'For once, I am speechless,' Billy murmured. The baby reached for his hair and tugged at it. He pulled a face. She tugged harder. 'Ouch!' he yelped, and she let go. Her face began to crumple and for a moment, Winnie thought she was going to cry. Instead, she stared at Billy, then with a chuckle, grabbed at his hair again.

'She will have you twisted round her little finger before you can say Jack Robinson,' Grace laughed. 'She has the rest of us running around at her beck and call.'

'I need that milk and brandy after this,' Billy marvelled. 'What a surprise. Well done, Winnie. You've made my day … my year. I'm a father – it's goin' to take me a while to get used to it.'

Winnie's cheeks ached from smiling – it was golden moments like these that made up for their involvement in the free trade. She knew she should mention the guinea run to Gravelines, but decided not to spoil his homecoming.

Chapter Twelve

All that Glisters is not Gold

Winnie sent Grace out for a hot beef pie as she took a chair for Billy to sit on just outside the front door while he supped his drink. She placed a blanket around his shoulders and a fleece across his knees to protect him from the winter cold, and then she stood next to him with Pamela in her arms, watching the world go by.

The maze of narrow streets and alleyways was abuzz with gossip and exclamation.

''Ave you 'eard? 'E's back. Billy.'

'Billy Fleet?'

'You could 'ave knocked me down with a feather when so an' so told me.'

'Billy!' Jason and the crew of the *Whimbrel* came running towards him, cheering and laughing.

Jason was first to greet him.

'Don't get up. I'm sorry we weren't here – we've been out for a few days.' He grinned as his mother and father walked by, arguing with each other. 'My mother was waitin' on the corner to give me the news, but my father caught us as soon as we beached the *Whimbrel*, deprivin' my mother of her moment of glory.'

'Nothin' much 'as changed then,' Billy said, looking up, a smile on his face. Marlin was his hero, the man he looked up to. 'Was it a good 'ovel?'

'There was a small brig foundered up the coast – I don't know what her captain was thinkin' taking her that way. When we untied him from where he'd fixed himself to the mast, I told him that he should have taken on a pilot. Still, he's learned his lesson. We'll have made a few bob from the salvage.'

'It sounds like you had a great adventure, Marlin,' Billy sighed.

'You'll be back out with us soon.'

'I dunno about that. I can't help meself, let alone anybody else, bein' a poor ol' pegleg.'

'Oh? I didn't know ...' Jason's expression fell, then brightened again as he clapped a hand on Billy's shoulder. 'There's nothin' to stop you havin' a wooden one. You should see what they can do nowadays. I've seen a gentleman with one made from papier mâché. It's light and shapely, and you wouldn't know the difference.' He changed the subject. 'Let's go inside. Are you comin' in, lads?'

The crew descended on the cottage, filling the hall, kitchen and parlour.

Louisa took Jason aside and a little while later, they approached Winnie and Billy and told them that Billy could live with them for as long as he wanted to.

'Thank you,' Billy said, shaking Jason's hand. 'Your 'ospitality is very much appreciated. I'll pay me way as soon as I can.'

'I know you will,' Jason said.

What with her husband having agreed to an extra person living at the cottage and the rowdiness of the *Whimbrel*'s crew, Louisa looked a little cross at times, Winnie noticed, but she was too happy to let anything spoil the day in the slightest. Billy was home and their family was complete.

Eventually, the party moved on to the Waterman's Arms, leaving Billy behind to spend some time alone with Winnie. Grace offered to mind Pamela and Louisa made the sleeping arrangements plain to Billy, much to Winnie's annoyance. Sometimes her sister treated grown men and women as if they were children.

While Jason and the crew were out drinking and her sisters were with Pamela in the kitchen, Winnie and Billy sat up in the parlour, side by side on the chaise, holding hands. It seemed so strange. Having waited for this moment for over a year, she didn't know how to begin.

'At last,' she said after a long silence. 'I thought they'd never leave.'

'I just want to look at you.' Billy's voice grated with emotion. 'I've been waitin' for this for … well, I can't believe it. It's like a dream … When I was low, not knowin' 'ow to reach you because of the breadth and depth of the ocean that lay between us, I thought o' you. I dreamed o' you, Winnie. I looked for you too, and I saw your face in the stars at night. In the daytime, I saw the sparkle of your eyes in the way the sun catches the tops of the waves. I 'eard your whisper carried on the wind and felt your caress in the breeze. I blew kisses, prayin' the wind would carry 'em to you.'

'I felt your presence all around me too, Billy,' she said softly.

He leaned across and kissed her, and the memories of how they used to be, his scent and his warmth flooded back. She wasn't sure how long they remained in each other's arms before he drew back.

'Ouch,' he said, grimacing in the candlelight. 'It's my leg … The pain is unbearable at times.'

'I'll go to the apothecary tomorrow and buy you something to dull it,' she said. All would be well – she would make sure of it.

167

As the candle flame trembled in the draught from the fireplace where the embers were beginning to die out – there were no more logs in the basket, Louisa's ruse perhaps to make sure they didn't sit up all night – Winnie's mind turned to their situation.

'We're going to have the best life from now on, Billy.'

'I'm glad,' he said, biting his lip.

'I've so much to tell you. Jason and Louisa went away to Gretna Green to marry, because they didn't want to wait until the banns were read, and Louisa had no legal guardian to give them permission. Then we had to sell Compass Cottage to cover Pa's debts.'

'It doesn't belong to the Lennickers?'

'Jason bought it at auction. He said we could stay for as long as we liked. It's still our home.'

'It isn't, though, is it? You're under an obligation to Marlin. 'E and Louisa could send you – us – packin' whenever they like.'

'You know they wouldn't do that. Jason is an honourable man, the perfect brother-in-law.'

'Even so, there's nothin' to stop 'em. Do you pay rent?'

She shook her head. 'I contribute to the household instead. I do the cooking and cleaning, and I go out provisioning—'

'With the baby?'

'Mrs Witherall minds her now and again.'

'What about the other thing? The free trade?'

She smiled ruefully. 'I play my part in it against my will, because I have sailed very close to the wind in recent times. I've been arrested and put in the stocks, and I've been assaulted. The gobblers accused me of carrying a half-anker of cognac in the handcart.'

He looked horrified. 'Is that all it was?'

'You can be hanged just as well for a lamb as a sheep. I'm not sure that's the saying exactly, but it's close enough. Anyway, I was dragged up in front of the magistrates. Officer Chase had it in for me, wanting me to be tried at the next Assizes, but Reverend North did some clever talking and I ended up with an hour in the stocks.'

'I wish I'd been 'ere to save you,' he said, close to tears. 'I can't stand the thought of you bein' laughed at and pelted with eggs.'

'Our friends and neighbours turned it into a day out. Everyone was very kind – well, almost everyone. They were on our side, Billy. I'll never forget that.' He seemed distressed, making her hesitate over telling him anything else – about the assault, for example. 'Now that you're home, we'll find our way out of it. How about you?'

'Me? It was the 'ardest, most challengin' year of my life. The boatswain's mate 'ad it in for me because I was popular with the men. Everybody looked down on 'im with disdain. 'E would call me a bilge rat, the lowest of the low, and quote the Articles of War and threaten to 'ave me keel'auled, somethin' that 'asn't been allowed by the Royal Navy 'igh-ups for seventy, eighty years. 'E'd tell me 'e'd 'ave me flogged around the fleet with the ship's doctor in attendance, but in the end, 'e gave me sixty lashes on the bare breech.' He half smiled. 'I could show you my scars ...'

'When we're married,' she said. 'You know how things stand with Louisa – I don't want to have bad blood between us.'

'I know,' he sighed.

'Did the boatswain's mate keep on at you the whole time?'

Billy shook his head. 'I managed to turn the tables on 'im, caught 'im stealing rum and slops from the purser to sell to the crew. When I suspected what 'e was up to, I alerted the purser to be on the lookout, and sure enough, 'e obtained proof of it and took it to the captain who ordered the villain to be thrown in chains and fed 'alf rations. It's strange 'ow another man's misfortune gained me much respect. The captain appointed me Able Seaman and after that, my time on board was tolerable ... except towards the end.'

He clammed up and Winnie didn't push him for any more details.

He forced a smile. 'You 'aven't asked me 'ow many young ladies caught my eye while I was away ...'

She stiffened. 'Of course I haven't. Billy ...?'

'I'm teasin' you. I never even looked at another woman, not that there were many to attract the eye. Most of the time I was at sea.'

'I was the same – I have only ever had eyes for you, you silly goose.'

'Then I'll retire to bed a contented man,' he said. 'I miss the way the 'ammock rocks you to sleep, but I don't think I'll 'ave any trouble noddin' off tonight. I can barely keep me eyes open. Goodnight, my darlin'.'

He didn't argue when she helped him stand up and make his way up the stairs.

It was Winnie who couldn't sleep. Having been disturbed by Jason returning from the Waterman's Arms, she went to work in the kitchen, polishing the brass candlesticks and the copper pans until they shone. At dawn, she collected Pamela from her crib where Grace had put her to sleep the evening before, fed her and took her into the yard to watch the birds fighting over a few crumbs and a rind of bacon. She wished she'd got around to telling Billy about Abel and the proposal – she supposed she would have to do it soon, before anybody else did.

Winnie found a renewed zest for life, caring for Billy and Pamela and continuing with her work around the house and outside. Even so, on the fourth night after he moved back in, she found herself struggling to keep the baby from crying so as not to wake the rest of the house, then Billy had an attack of the night terrors, and Jason went in to calm him down, when she felt it should have been her.

'Why do you wait on Billy hand and foot?' Louisa asked, coming downstairs in the morning to find Winnie already dressed and cooking porridge. 'He can't laze around for ever.'

'I wish you had more compassion. Don't you remember how you limped about when you twisted your ankle? He has lost a limb. Your injury mended. His won't.'

'That's what I'm worried about.'

'He's only been back for a few days.' With her face burning from the heat of the fire and her sister's criticism, Winnie stirred the pot. 'I'm going to the apothecary later. I'm borrowing some money from the housekeeping – I'll put it back, I promise.' She had some modest savings put by, but she didn't want to break into them, preferring to pay Louisa back from the next instalment of the allowance she received in return for her labour. 'Billy will have some money of his own soon – he has a ticket to claim his wages from the navy. There's supposed to be a pension he can apply for too, so we won't be on our beam ends.'

'I'm not trying to press you, Winnie,' Louisa said, indignant. 'I'm sure we'll work something out, depending on when Billy goes back to work. You know what it's like. Life's hard – we can't afford to carry passengers who don't pay their way for too long, that's all.' Her tone became less hectoring. 'I can help you find out how to go about applying for that pension, if you like.'

'Thank you.' The porridge was ready, the oats smooth and creamy. Winnie took it off the fire and put it on the table, then she dished up a portion for Billy and took it up to him.

Later, when she had done the household chores and returned from Mr Spottiswoode's with extract of willow bark and a tonic, because the laudanum she had given Billy for the pain in his leg had upset his constitution, she sat with him for a while in the parlour while Pamela crawled around the floor with a doll that Grace had found in the attic. Winnie wasn't sure she liked the way that Pamela kept chewing the poor thing's wooden head and sucking at its painted hair.

'There's a run planned for the next sennight – it's different, Billy,' Winnie began. 'Jason's taking a guinea boat to the smugglers' city … I'm going with him – to France.'

'You?' His face changed. 'I'm not lettin' you go. I forbid it.'

'I can't back out now. There are reasons – promise me you won't repeat this.'

'You don't 'ave to tell me anythin' – because you aren't goin'. What about Pamela? You would leave 'er motherless?' His voice became querulous. 'What about me? Where is your respect for my opinion?'

'Grace will look after the baby – it's all been arranged. We won't be gone long, four days at the very most. You can't tell me what to do.'

'You don't love me any more,' he said morosely. 'I'm no use to you now that I'm a pegleg.'

'I've never said that.' Tears stung her eyes. 'Let me explain. Mr Cork is paying me handsomely to carry despatches to France. I can't afford to turn the work down.

And I don't want to either because this is information that could help us against Old Boney. And you must remember how I feel about him.' She felt sick, torn, going against Billy, but this was for the nation, the Prince Regent and the King. For the future of their daughter. 'Jason will look after me.

'You went off to fight – you were volunteered, but you took your turn,' she continued. 'It's my turn now.'

'You are a woman, a member of the weaker sex.'

'Weaker? Oh, I he's back now found more strength than I ever imagined possible when you disappeared. As I've told you, I've faced the Bench, been thrown in the stocks, and suffered censure and criticism as an unmarried mother. You can't stop me. I've found my voice and I will no longer be pushed and pulled one way or another. I have made my decision.'

'What 'appens next time?'

'There won't be a next time. I've given my word that I'll do this last run, and then together, we'll find another way to make ends meet. All I ask is that you allow me to go without sulking or holding it against me. Let's kiss and make up. Please, Billy.'

He nodded reluctantly. She wrapped her arms around his neck, and just as she planted a soft kiss on his lips, a howl erupted from the floor. She heard Billy's sigh of frustration as he pulled way.

'You'd better pay the littlun some attention,' he groaned. 'Spend as much time with 'er as possible in case you don't come back.'

'Billy, you said—'

'*You* said, remember? I can't 'elp feelin' sore about it when you're goin' against me.'

What had happened to them? When she had first fallen for him, he had been funny, cheerful and passionate. She understood that the pain was niggling at him, but she hadn't realised that he was such a one for arguing and holding a grudge. And she was terribly afraid that something bad was going to happen and he was going to let her down in the end over the wedding that she'd been relying on to make her a respectable woman.

'Where are you goin'?' he said as she stood up and smoothed her skirts.

'I'm going to take Pamela out for some air. It doesn't do her any good to be stuck indoors all day. The smoke from the fires makes her cough, and she always sleeps better after a walk. I'll leave you to rest,' she said firmly, wanting to discourage him from coming with her. She needed time away from him to think.

'I'll come with you,' Grace said, when Winnie was in the kitchen, dressing Pamela in layers of clothes and a knitted bonnet against the cold.

'Thank you. I'd appreciate the company.'

'Were you and Billy fighting?'

'Maybe a little,' Winnie responded. 'Make haste – I think the weather is on the turn.'

'We won't need Ma's old parasol to keep the sun out of your eyes today, littlun,' Grace smiled as she pinched Pamela's rosy cheeks.

They left the house in a milky haze, but by the time they reached Beach Street, any brightness had been extinguished by a feisty wind, gusting charcoal clouds across the sky.

'We should go straight home,' Grace said, as a shower of hailstones clattered down around them.

'No,' Winnie said abruptly.

'Is this because of Billy?' The wheel on the handcart squeaked as Grace pushed it along.

'It has nothing to do with him. I had it in my head that we would walk to the castle—'

'You go that way almost every day!'

'I know – and I shan't let a little rain divert me, although it is coming down hasty.'

'Very well. Let's go to Molly's first,' Grace suggested. 'We can take shelter there and walk back when it stops.'

Winnie agreed. It wasn't much further to walk, but by the time they reached the pot house, her cloak was soaked through.

'Come in and dry yourselves by the fire,' Mrs Stickles said, greeting them.

'Do you have any gossip?' Winnie said as they divested themselves of their cloaks and draped them across the fireguard where they started to steam.

'I don't know what you're talkin' about,' she said with a sly smile.

'You know very well.'

'I 'ave 'igh 'opes, Winnie. 'E's quite charming, but business 'as kept 'im away from Deal, more's the pity. What about you? 'Ow is dear Billy?'

'He's very well, thank you.' It wasn't true, but she wanted to give a good impression of her united little family.

'Did you 'ear that Abel Brockman asked one of the Kesby sisters to marry 'im?' Mrs Stickles asked.

'Apparently she turned 'im down, more fool 'er, I say,' Nancy interrupted, bringing a tray with teacups and a teapot.

'Perhaps she didn't have any romantic attachment to him,' Grace said.

Winnie glared at her sister, unsure how many people knew that he had proposed to her.

"E's a cold fish, that one,' Mrs Stickles opined. "E delivers our flour.'

"E's charmin',' Nancy said.

'Abel 'as no interest in women in that way. At the tavern, the barmaids used to set their caps at 'im, showin' off their wares and brushin' past 'im in a way that would inflame any other man, yet 'e never took no notice. They say 'e has other preferences – 'e takes care of 'is 'orses with a ridiculous parade,' Mrs Stickles said. "E wouldn't make a suitable match for a young lady, not if she desired the comfort of a physical connection.'

"Ow is the littlun?' Nancy asked, quickly changing the subject as they sat down to tea and slices of cobnut cake, fresh from the oven.

The hail eventually slackened off a little, enough for Winnie to persuade Grace that a stroll to the castle was not entirely unreasonable.

'My feet are wet, and my stockings are chafing my legs,' Grace complained.

'You can go home, if you wish.' Winnie gave the hand-cart an extra push, and Grace hurried to keep up. They passed the Shutter Station with its six octagonal shutters, standing on the seafront where the glassmen watched day and night, waiting to send signals to the Admiralty in London. Having left the barracks behind, they reached the castle with its massive walls and castellated keep, the captain of Deal's residence within. The Union flag was flying and there were guns mounted on the bastions facing out to sea.

'Wait there with Pamela,' Winnie said, as she found the spot she was looking for: a tiny dark mark in the wall which – as you moved closer – became a small crack that allowed you to slip your hand inside. Beyond that was an empty void, except this time, Winnie's fingers touched an object that was smooth, apart from the strings keeping its contents together. Her heart missed a beat. This was it. This was what she had been waiting for since Mr Cork had sent her a letter as promised, explaining where to find the hiding hole for the plant. She was in possession of the despatches. It wouldn't be long before she was on her way to France.

Chapter Thirteen

Sending a Cow to Catch a Hare

It was a late November night, and there was the merest splinter of a moon visible in the dark sky when Billy accompanied Winnie to see the guinea boat off. He had mastered getting along relatively quickly with the crutches, but he soon tired, and it took them over two hours to reach the beach on the seaward side of the sandhills where they spotted the monstrous vessel with a single mast and twelve oars each side, moored in the shallow water.

'Good luck, my darlin'. You travel with my blessin',' he said before turning to Jason, who had come to join them. 'I swear, Marlin, if you don't bring 'er back—'

'Trust me. We'll be home before dawn the day after tomorrow.'

'The box?' she asked.

'It's stowed away. Everythin' is on board.'

'But not above board, I hope,' one of the crew called over.

'Goodbye, Billy,' Winnie said, hardly able to see for the salt spray mingling with her tears as a ripple of laughter ran through the crew. 'Look after Pamela.'

'Don't talk like you aren't comin' back,' he said gruffly, before leaning in and snatching a kiss. 'God speed.'

Jason gave Winnie a piggyback to the guinea boat and when everyone was on board, the men took up their oars.

'Prepare to row!' Jason yelled. 'Three, two, one …'

178

The twenty-four oarsmen leaned forward, dropped their blades into the choppy waves, then pulled them through the water, but the sweep of the oars to starboard and larboard didn't match, and the boat lurched like a drunken pond skater.

'Stop!' Jason yelled, as her bow turned back towards the shore. 'What are you doin'? You will have her wrecked before we've gone more than a cable's distance. You two at the stern, swap places to even things up.'

Winnie huddled in the bow, wrapped in blankets and oilskins, and remembered Pa telling her and her sisters about maritime measurements – a cable was approximately one hundred fathoms or a tenth of a nautical mile, but that didn't matter now. The crew weren't exactly inspiring her with confidence.

'Pull together, lads. The Rattlers did the crossin' in seven hours – we'll cock a snook at them and show them it can be done in less.'

'We'll show 'em, Marlin,' the crew called in unison, and this time, as they took a stroke, they turned the boat about and headed towards the Downs.

Moving under the cover of darkness, the oars muffled in the rowlocks and with Jason keeping his voice down so as not to attract attention, the guinea boat wove between the vessels at anchor, their lanterns glittering in the cold night air. As they emerged from the relative shelter of the roadstead, the wind got up and the waves began to break across the bow. Splashes of ice-cold water blurred Winnie's vision and stung her cheeks.

'Pull, lads. Pull,' Jason yelled.

'Whist, Marlin! You'll have the Revenue after us.'

'Put your backs into it then,' he snapped back. Normally unflappable, he was feeling the strain as well he might, Winnie mused, when he was responsible for carrying an unimaginable number of guineas on behalf of the financiers in London. Rumour had it that it was in the region of five thousand pounds' worth, but it could well be more. She wondered where it was – she couldn't see any sign of the guinea boat's precious cargo.

'Where's your sense of rhythm, lads?' Jason's voice was swept away in a cacophony of sound when they were well into open water: the wind; the waves; the splashing oars; the grunting oarsmen.

One missed a stroke, his blade smashing against the one behind.

'I'm sorry, mate. I caught a crab,' he gasped.

'Watch what you're doin'!'

The swell grew larger, the boat beginning to pitch fore and aft. Water was seeping between the boards as well as splashing over the bows. Winnie got bailing – as did Jason and the helmsman – but all she had was a pie dish with the inscription: *If this dish dare to roam, box its ears and send it home to Molly's Pot House, Middle Street, Deal.*

'Ship to larboard!' someone shouted, and Jason paused and took out his spyglass. Winnie watched what she thought was starlight reflected in the crests of the waves, but as they travelled on, she realised the lights were moving towards them: the Revenue were hoisting their colours on a vessel with high bulwarks and ports for seven guns on each side.

Jason swore. 'Row for your lives! It's the gobblers.'

Winnie dropped the dish and curled up on the boards, her pulse racing, her limbs weak at the thought that lightning was about to strike twice. Any vessel that was caught within one hundred miles of the coast with illegal goods was liable for impounding and forfeiture. Any convicted smugglers would be sent to serve aboard a king's ship for five years. As for her, she was certain they'd find a suitable punishment: a lengthy spell in gaol.

'Head back to the Sands,' Jason ordered. 'We can lose them there.'

'We are turnin' back on ourselves.' Gunner was one of the oarsmen who had swapped places, and not one of Jason's usual crew.

'It can't be helped.' Winnie could hear the panic in Jason's voice. There was much at stake: a fortune in gold, their lives and liberty, if they were caught.

'We can outrun them, Marlin. It's like sendin' a cow to catch a hare.' Another of the men who had been co-opted into the crew as an extra – a burly man with a port-wine blemish on his cheek whom Winnie wouldn't have wished to meet alone on a dark night – joined the mutiny.

'It's a dangerous strategy,' Jason maintained. 'On the open water in the Channel, there's a risk that another ship – a privateer, perhaps – will intercept us while we're tryin' to escape the Revenue. We'll do this my way and if there's anybody here who wants to go against my orders, they can give up their place on our return to Deal, and they'll never work with the Witheralls and Lennickers again. Got that?'

'Yes, Marlin. To the Sands …'

They turned south. Concerned by his talk of a privateer, especially remembering what had happened to Terrier, Winnie sat up and peered over the gunwales as she started bailing again. They were beginning to put clear water between the guinea boat and the Revenue cutter as the roar of the breakers on the sandbanks grew louder, but as far as Winnie was concerned, they were between the Devil and the deep blue sea. On one hand, they had the cutter's guns trained on their boat. On the other, was the Goodwins, the everchanging profile of sandbanks and channels where

181

hundreds of vessels, great and small, had been wrecked. There were foxholes too, where the unwary on foot might sink and disappear for good.

The oarsmen flew into a fierce rhythm, leaving the frustrated Revenue officers and their captain behind as they entered Trinity Bay within the Sands.

'Easy oars,' Jason called softly, and the men stopped rowing and rested their blades on the calmer water. They sat in silence, ears strained, listening to the booming of the waves on the sand, the ringing of a bell marking the end of a watch on one of the men-o'-war anchored in the roadstead, men shouting and laughing in the distance, and then the sharp, imperious bark from what could only be an officer on the cutter.

'Identify yourselves! Or I'll give the order to fire!'

Winnie was almost sick with nerves.

'It'll be all right, miss,' one of the men said, but she didn't see how, when they were stuck in a dead end inside the giant ship gobbler with the Revenue heading towards them.

Shivering, she wrapped the blankets and oilskins tightly around her.

'They've launched a jollyboat,' Gunner shouted at the sound of splashing. 'Marlin, when are we goin' to make our move?'

'Now!' Jason said. 'Row to the bank, jump out, pick her up and carry her. It's but a short distance across this part to the next channel.'

'She is too heavy!'

'I've heard that it's been done before. The gobblers can't possibly follow us.'

They moved swiftly, helping Winnie out. Having shaken the stiffness from her limbs, she ran to keep up with the men who had lifted the boat from the water and were dragging her across the sandbank, before helping Winnie back in and pushing the hefty guinea boat and her hidden cargo into the next channel, thus flummoxing the Revenue officers.

'I don't believe it, sir – they're on foot.'

'You've had too much to drink.'

'I swear on the life of my children that I haven't touched a drop.'

'Follow them, then.'

'How? The jollyboat is too heavy for the three of us to lug across the sand, and we can't get through with the cutter. We'll be stranded if we take her any further.'

'Turn her about! Take a sounding – we are heading for the shallows. I said, turn her about!'

'Row, lads, row,' Jason ordered, and within the hour, they were back on their way across the Channel, moving faster than Winnie had ever travelled in her life.

'I'm startin' to feel a great deal of affection and admiration for this boat,' Jason chuckled. 'Keep your eyes peeled,' he went on when the lights of the north coast of France came into view, guiding them to Gravelines. Napoleon's *ville des Smoglers* was originally a fortress built on the River Aa where the watercourse cut through the sand dunes fifteen miles south-west of Dunkirk. Until a couple of years before, the *genti terribili*, as Old Boney described the smugglers, worked from Dunkirk, but because of their riotous behaviour and the fact that Napoleon wanted his military security escorts to keep an eye on them, he transferred the centre of the free trade in France to Gravelines.

'We'll soon be ashore,' Jason said more cheerfully, as he urged his exhausted oarsmen on.

Winnie was frozen to the core by the time they reached the wharf, having had to wait for another guinea boat to leave, sparing them her space.

'It's a busy place,' Jason said. 'There can be hundreds of boats docked here at any one time.'

Winnie remained sitting on the boards, with the box containing the despatches beneath her cloak and the hood pulled up over her head to hide her distinctive golden hair. Jason gave their papers for admittance to an official who gave them permission to secure the boat and unload her hidden cargo on to a waiting carriage.

'Come with me – I've booked a room for you,' Jason said, when the carriage moved off. 'I'll take you to meet Madame in the mornin'.'

'I rather wish it was all over and done with.' She bit back tears, not wanting him to think her weak.

'It's different for you because you have a littlun. I enjoy the challenge of makin' sport with the gobblers and priva-teers, and keepin' possession of the items we've brought with us.' He grinned. 'You're right to be wary, though. Make sure you keep your door locked tonight.'

'Why? Do you know something I don't?'

'It's a common-sense precaution, that's all,' he said, but his momentary hesitation was enough to raise her suspicions that there was more to it than he was letting on.

'Will you be nearby?' she asked.

'I shall be takin' my turn to guard the boat while we're loadin' the goods for the journey back. May I assist you by carryin' the box?'

'No, thank you.' Mr Cork had entrusted her with the despatches, and she would look after them. 'It is not particularly heavy.'

'As you please. Your lodgin's are within the compound at the rear of one of the warehouses.'

The room was pleasant enough: clean, with plenty of candles and a welcome fire ablaze in the grate. After Jason left, Winnie ate the bread, cheese, veal and boiled cabbage that had been brought up to her and drank a little wine, before praying for Billy and Pamela, for Jason and the crew, and for herself.

She checked the despatches in the box on the pretence that she was taking them out to dry them – they had suffered from the wet conditions on the boat. The newspapers that were held together with brown paper were of little interest, but the packet with them that had been sealed with wax was beckoning to her. What exactly were the messages she was carrying from the British to their agents in France and Switzerland?

Riddled with guilt but unable to restrain her curiosity, she held the packet over the flame of the candle, letting the wax melt. The paper almost caught, but she managed to pull it away in time. The seal softened and came away. She unfolded the sheaf of papers and examined them. There were letters, written in a neat copperplate hand, from a gentleman in London, talking of his club, the cost of port and the social events he had attended, addressed to 'my brother'.

Frowning, she looked closer. As she held the first letter to the candle to study it, she noticed how words began to appear between the lines, the lettering darkening from the colour of orange peel to burnt sienna. It wasn't scriven in the King's English, nor was it in French.

'Ah, it is in code,' she muttered. Having spent a while trying to work out what it meant, she admitted defeat. Feeling frustrated and uneasy, she folded the letters again and dripped candlewax on to the remains of the original seal to secure them, before retiring to bed.

She couldn't sleep for thinking of home, and of the coded messages and what they might mean.

*

The following morning, Winnie heard Jason knocking at the door: two taps then a gap before two more, their pre-agreed signal.

'Are you ready?' he called.

She walked across the room to let him in.

'Did you sleep, Winnie?' he asked, placing a tray of rolls and coffee on the small table near the fireplace.

'Not a wink,' she sighed, 'but at least I had a bed. How about you?'

'I snatched an hour or so on the guinea boat – it wasn't terribly comfortable, but I can sleep almost anywhere.' He poured the coffee and handed her a cup.

'What can you tell me about Madame?' she asked, sitting down.

'She's one of the merchants, an unusual position for a woman among the seventy or so who work from Gravelines,' he explained. 'That's how Mr Cork came by her acquaintance – through his interest in dealin' in lace.'

'Why does she wish to meet me? Why can't you hand over the despatches as you have in the past? Louisa never came to Gravelines. Why the change of tack?'

'Monsieur Alexandre, Madame's right-hand man, usually brings the lace to the wharf, collectin' the des-patches and takin' them to Madame by return. She picked him for his pugnacious nature and his threatenin' appearance – he's just shy of seven foot tall and has a deep scar across his chin. Unfortunately, he's disappeared without trace and it's feared he has come to harm. Madame is no longer sure whom she can trust so she's requested a meetin'.'

'Have you met her before?'

'On a couple of occasions. I suppose you would say that I know her more by sight than to speak to. Don't worry, Winnie. You're only the courier, not a spy. But don't say too much. Just answer yes or no, *oui* or *non*. You have the box?'

Winnie collected it from where she had hidden it under the bed.

'Old habits die hard,' she said, forcing a smile. 'Where are we going?'

'To Madame's shop on the other side of the compound. It isn't far.'

They made their way from the warehouse through the narrow streets, passing an encampment of huts and tents where men in winter clothes stood outside, smoking and watching the world go by.

'They're free traders like us – there's room for three or four hundred men,' Jason said. 'Napoleon had the compound built to encourage smuggling – for his own ends, of course. He didn't do it out of the goodness of his heart – he has no heart.'

Having turned the corner from the encampment, Winnie found herself in a street lined with shops and stalls, reminding her of the market in Deal. The vendors were selling fresh fish and strings of dried onions, flour and potatoes, tea and coffee and hot chestnuts. The shop windows advertised colognes, jewellery and clocks for sale.

'This is where we will find Madame.' Jason stopped in front of a window draped with colourful luxury fabrics: patterned silks and lace. As he pushed the door open, a bell rang, bringing a young girl running out from the back of the shop.

'*Madame vous attend. Par ici*,' she said, and they followed her up a spiral staircase to an upstairs room with a leaded glass window that looked out over the street. A woman sat in the window-seat beneath it. Slowly, she turned towards them.

'*Bonjour, Mr Witherall* ...' She stood up, the bracelets on her arm clinking as she moved gracefully towards them. Far from being the old crone that Winnie had expected, Madame was a striking young woman, a little older than Louisa, with piercing blue eyes and perfect teeth. Below a simple headpiece adorned with ostrich feathers, her brown hair fell in soft curls around her face. Her neckline was dangerously low, the waistline of her yellow silk dress high, and her sleeves short.

'*Bonjour, Madame,*' Jason said. 'You remembered ...'

'I make it my business never to forget a face.'

'Allow me to introduce—'

'I'm sure the Golden Maid can speak for herself. I am delighted to meet you.' She gave a small curtsey and Winnie curtsied back. 'You have something for me?'

'*Oui*, of course.' Winnie handed over the box, praying that she wouldn't examine the seals on the letters. Madame had a quick look inside then closed the box again.

'*Merci beaucoup*. I have this to give to you in exchange.' She gave Winnie a small packet of what she guessed to be letters. 'I very much look forward to meeting my English friend again.'

Winnie forced a small smile – she didn't share the sentiment.

'Next time, I expect you to come alone – we will be freer to talk, as one woman to another.'

'It's done – we can go home now,' Jason said as they hurried back past the encampment with the steady march of footsteps behind them. Winnie glanced over her shoulder to see four men in green uniforms following them.

'Keep walkin' and don't look back,' Jason warned. He lowered his voice. 'They are the Douane, part of Napoleon's customs unit. The goods are loaded and the crew are ready to go – we don't want any unnecessary delays.'

With a shudder, Winnie did as she was told, her hands curled into tight fists until the officers turned down a side street and their footsteps faded.

'Well done, Golden Maid. That's what we'll call you from now on,' Jason said. 'The wharf is in sight.'

She was running by the time they reached the boat. Jason helped her on board, and a couple of their fellow free traders from Folkestone pushed them off. As the crew picked up their oars, Winnie spotted a man hastening along the wharf towards them.

He was shouting, gesticulating at them. He stopped at the edge of the water and shook his fist. She recognised her attacker from the slope of his shoulders and his battered hat.

Had he been following her? What did he want? And why couldn't she seem to shake him off?

If he wanted the despatches, he was too late. Madame had the ones destined for the English agents in France, while she had the ones for their King and Prince Regent. As for the goods, the crew had attached sinkers to the barrels of cognac in the bottom of the boat and fastened them on a warp one behind the other, tying it fast through a hole at the end of the guinea boat's keel. The bales of textiles and pouches of baccy were wrapped in oilskins, secured with knotted string.

Darkness enveloped them as they rowed away, the sun setting behind them. Two hours from Gravelines, the sombre mood among the oarsmen began to lighten.

'We're in the clear,' Gunner shouted.

'Don't speak too soon,' said another.

'We're flyin'! Marlin, if I were lookin' for a boat for a mistress, I'd choose this one – she's shapely, obligin'—'

'Mind your language – we have a lady on board,' Jason called back, amused.

'I'm sorry, missus. It slipped my mind that we 'ad a woman among our number.'

'Put your backs into it, lads,' Jason said. Winnie spotted the glint of his pocket watch – a new one Louisa had bought to replace the one that had been stolen – as he checked the time. 'It's lookin' like a five-hour crossin'.'

Winnie scooped out some water, hoping to lighten the load. She couldn't wait to drop the despatches off as arranged and get home to Pamela and Billy to celebrate with the rest of the boatmen and their families with milk and brandy, and music on the beach.

As they approached the Kent coast, the white cliffs barely visible in the darkness, Jason diverted the guinea boat towards the cliffs at Kingsdown where the landside smugglers were waiting for them.

'Hold up!' he called, and the oarsmen rested their oars. 'We'll stand here until we're given the all-clear. Smoker, do the honours.'

After fumbling around in one of the boxes, Mr Edwards loaded the flintlock pistol and sent up a blue flash. They waited, but there was no answering signal from the cliffs.

'They 'aven't lit the fires,' Smoker observed.

'They're keepin' us out, that's why,' Jason said, making Winnie's heart sink because she knew what that meant. 'The gobblers must have heard somethin'. We'll go south and find shelter until tomorrow night.'

'I wonder who blabbed.' The crew began to speculate.

'It could have been anyone – maybe one of the Rattlers who heard we were going to break their record for the crossin'.'

Could it possibly have been Billy? Winnie wondered if he might have let slip their plan one day when he was in his cups, but she didn't believe he would have drunk enough to loosen his tongue that much.

'Let's move,' Jason said. 'We don't want to be caught hoverin' out here.'

They set off again, turning down the coast towards Romney. They would have to hide up in marshes and sleep on the boat with sheep bleating in the background, Winnie thought sadly, but it would be worth it to keep them out of trouble with the Riding officers. She pictured Officers Chase and Lawrence sitting proud on their horses, happy that they had thwarted the smugglers for once, as they made steady progress past the white cliffs and Dover. By the time they passed the Martello towers at Folkestone, the oarsmen were tiring fast.

'This is killin' me,' Gunner grumbled. 'Can't we stop?'

'Not yet,' Jason said.

'It's a long way to the marshes,' Smoker observed, swearing.

'Don't waste your breath arguin',' Jason hissed. 'They're on to us – the crew of the *Guinevere*! The cutter!'

'We aren't goin' to outrun 'em this time – we're over-laden,' Gunner muttered.

'No, we aren't.' Smoker dropped his oar, as did the other men, and they hauled the casks from the bottom of the boat and dropped them over the side. 'What about the rest o' it, Marlin?'

Winnie noticed how he looked across the water, assessing how soon the cutter would arrive. With her sails set and her colours raised, she was moving ever closer.

'Everythin' will have to go overboard. We can't risk bein' caught with it. It's a terrible shame to lose the goods, but we've done all right so far – we've made a fair bit out of the outward journey. Let's not push our luck.'

There were several loud splashes before the crew picked up their oars again and battled to row against the drag created by the line of casks that they were towing along behind them just beneath the waterline. The cutter was right on their tail – Winnie thought she could hear the casks knocking against her keel as she closed in.

Jason cupped his hands to his mouth and shouted, 'Ahoy! What boat are you?' even though he knew very well who they were. It was part of the act, Winnie realised, carrying on as though the captain and crew of the guinea boat were innocent of any crime.

'We are a King's boat. Heave to. Stop rowing, sirs. Desist immediately, or we will fire!'

The crew rowed for a few more desultory strokes, then stopped, knowing they were well and truly caught in the Revenue's net.

The cutter launched one of her jollyboats, sending four officers over to interrogate Jason.

'What language do you understand?' one asked, holding up a lantern.

'We are Englishmen of the finest sort,' Jason replied. 'Boatmen, Cinque Ports men from Deal, members of the Sea Fencibles who can be relied upon to go out in the fiercest of storms, riskin' their lives for others whose vessels founder on the Sands.'

'For what purpose is this vessel registered? Show me your papers.'

'We will do that willingly,' Jason said as Winnie crouched in the bow, the despatches tucked inside her bodice. He made a play of opening the box that contained the information. 'This is our licence for catchin' mackerel.'

'The papers are ... in order,' the officer said, having perused them thoroughly. 'But we will board and rummage the boat anyway.'

'I can't see the sense of you wastin' your time when you could be chasin' after those who are breakin' the law of the land. We have a woman aboard, a young lady who wishes to return home forthwith.'

'You are some way from home,' the officer frowned.

'They are shamming us – where is your catch?'

'Ah, we have suffered the misfortune of losin' our nets,' Jason said.

'That's most convenient.'

'I'd say that it's been quite the opposite,' Jason countered.

'We will make a search according to our orders.'

'You're welcome,' Jason said, and two of the officers came aboard.

'I can find nothing, nothing at all,' one of the officers concluded as Winnie sat hardly daring to breathe on the one bale of lace that they had omitted to throw into the water – Pa had done likewise in the past: hidden goods in plain sight.

'There must be something, Officer Porter,' his fellow officer said.

'I tell you, there is nothing incriminating here.'

'I find it hard to believe that you and your crew, Captain Witherall, have come back from France empty-handed.'

'I told you, we've been fishin',' he maintained.

'We're wasting our time,' Officer Porter decided, and the men returned to the jollyboat which headed back through the gloom to the cutter.

'They aren't wise to our tricks yet. It's lucky that they didn't find the false boards,' Jason chuckled when they were out of earshot and out of range of the commander's spyglass. 'Next time, we'll have to change tack, so to speak.'

There wouldn't be a next time, Winnie thought as Jason continued, 'Haul them in, gentlemen.'

They dragged the casks back into the boat, but there was no hope for the textiles – they were lost: waterlogged and fallen to the bottom of the sea.

'We'll come back with the creepin' iron tomorrer,' Smoker suggested.

'No, don't risk attractin' further attention from the Revenue for somethin' that isn't likely to be salvageable. The ladies and gentlemen will have to live without their lace and silks. We have worse things to deal with than they do, the first bein', where are we goin' to bring her in, lads?'

Winnie followed Jason's gaze. The shoreline remained in darkness.

Thwarted, the men rowed south and took shelter in the marshes beyond Hythe where they waited for dawn before taking Winnie as close to Deal as was prudent, considering the height of the waves crashing against the foot of the white cliffs at South Foreland. In the end, they dropped her off on the beach at Kingsdown where a pair of fishermen, pipes in their mouths, were preparing their boat for a day's fishing.

'Good mornin',' one said, expelling smoke from his nostrils.

'Was that Marlin's gang, missus?' the other asked.

She hurried away without replying, one hand holding her hood in place against the blusterous wind, the other feeling for the despatches tucked inside her bodice. Jason had proposed she take a chaperone with her, but she had refused. The fewer people who knew her business, the better. She trudged along the coastal road until she reached

Walmer Castle, the home of the Warden of the Cinque Ports, keeping her eyes and ears open for trouble, thinking of Billy and Pamela, of the money she would receive to help them set up a home of their own, and dreaming of a plateful of huffkins and jam to quell her pangs of hunger.

Carrying on along the shore, she noticed a few scrubby trees struggling to flourish in the windswept landscape, before she crossed the grass to the Strand, turned right and carried on past the North Barracks, a three-storey building with a clock tower, to the back of Deal Castle.

On reaching the castle, she planted the despatches in the same place that she had picked up the last ones, relieved yet regretting the fact that she hadn't had a chance to read them. Glancing around to check that nobody had seen her, she set off for home.

She had promised herself that she would never travel to Gravelines again, but on reflection, having opened the despatches and found the secret messages encoded in the letters, she wanted to find out more about their provenance and whom they were destined for. If they contained intelligence for the French, she had to find out who was involved in the double cross and stop them. She couldn't have it on her conscience to do nothing.

Chapter Fourteen

A Turn for the Worse

Winnie let herself in to the cottage, took off her boots and cloak and quietly made her way along the hall. The kitchen door was open.

'I promise you, my little darlin', that I'll never walk out on you, no matter 'ow bad things get,' she heard Billy solemnly declare. 'I won't do what my father did to my ma.'

Winnie's throat tightened as she heard him go on, 'I'm not like 'im anyway. When I went away not knowin' you were even a twinkle in your mama's eye – or in her belly, strickly speakin' – I didn't go of my own accord.'

Winnie crept forward, catching sight of Billy sitting in the inglenook with Pamela on his knee. 'You should 'ave seen what I wore around the ship: a pea jacket and petti-coat trousers; a shiny black hat; a blue neckerchief to stop the tar getting to my pigtail when my 'air grew long.' He saluted, touching the imaginary brim of a hat between his index finger and thumb. Pamela beamed and cooed, then stuck her fist in her mouth. 'I wore stockin's and shoes with the most marvellous pinchbeck buckles. Ah, you want your mama. She'll be 'ome soon.'

'I'm here,' she whispered.

'Thank goodness,' he sighed, looking up. 'Oh Winnie, are you all right?'

'Of course. Jason and the crew looked after me as they promised, and I've completed the mission I was given by Mr Cork.'

'All we 'ave to do now is wait for 'is money. 'Ere, take the baby,' he said, lifting Pamela towards her.

Winnie swept her up and cuddled her close, holding out her free hand to take Billy's and give it a squeeze. He struggled up from the seat and threw his arms around her and their daughter, showering them both with kisses.

'I don't know 'ow you do it, lookin' after the littlun,' he said, when they were settled at the table with bread, ham and eggs. 'You must 'ave the patience of a saint.'

How long had he minded her for? she wondered, amused. An hour, maybe?

'Where are my sisters? I thought Grace was supposed to be looking after her.'

'They went to find out if there was any news about the landin'.'

'That side of the run went asprawl. It's a pity, but everyone's returned safely. That's what matters.'

'Winnie's back – her boots are here,' she heard Grace exclaiming, and her younger sister came flying into the kitchen – without removing her own boots, Winnie noticed, but it was no time to be pernickety. Winnie felt Grace's arms around her neck as she leaned down to kiss her cheek. 'We're so glad to see you. How was France? What was the journey like?'

'Give her a chance to answer.' Winnie turned to find Louisa, her eyes alight with happiness. 'Welcome home.'

'Did you see any sign of Old Boney?' Grace went on, playing with her hair.

'I'll tell you what France was like,' Winnie said. 'It was cold and wet, and just as I expected.'

197

'Go on ...' Grace said, giving one of her curls an impatient tweak.

'It was full of Frenchies.'

'And? There must be more.'

'Everyone eats garlic,' Winnie elaborated. 'And frogs' legs and snails.'

Grace's mouth fell open. 'Did you partake of any of this?'

'I tried everything,' Winnie said, straight-faced, but on seeing Grace's expression of utter horror, she broke out laughing. 'I did not – I wouldn't touch anything but English fare. I did have hot chocolate and bread rolls that were not as sweet or as light as the huffkins we buy from the bakery in Deal.' Winnie kept the rest to herself. If Billy came to know about the dangers that she'd faced in Gravelines, he wouldn't let her go again. She would have to trust Jason and the crew to keep the details of their adventures to themselves.

It seemed that Billy had had plenty of adventures of his own that he had kept from Winnie. One day, she was in the hang taking down the bloaters when she smelled the aroma of pipe-smoke and overheard the men talking in the kitchen.

'We were fightin' the Yankees – they called it Mr Madison's War, and said it might not 'ave 'appened if the British 'adn't gone and pressed men from America's naval ships. This isn't somethin' I can talk about with Winnie. I don't want 'er upset,' Billy said.

'I'll keep it to myself,' Jason responded. 'What was it like out there, crossin' the ocean?'

'It was rough at times, and we 'ad no idea what we were goin' to come across next: 'ostile ships, privateers ... There was a merchant vessel flyin' Dutch colours. She struck her topsail in salute, then put all hands on deck. I saw 'em 'oldin' the riggin', but it turned out that they were trickin' us into thinkin' they were showin' peaceful intent.' There was a long pause. 'They'd already taken 'er as their prize.'

'What did they do next?'

'They sent a shot across our bows. We fired back, holin' their ship, and in return, they shot away one of our ensigns. It was quite a battle, practice before we engaged with the enemy.

'After that, we took the crew prisoner and salvaged what we could, then sailed on. But I lost one of my best friends that day. A toast to Johnny Boy, one of the best who ever walked on this earth.' Winnie heard the thump of a glass being slammed down on the table. ''Ow's your glass, Marlin? It looks like there's a south wind in it to me.'

'I won't have any more.'

'We sewed 'im into an 'ammock with cannonballs at 'is feet, and I put the last stitch of the sailmaker's needle through 'is nose to make sure 'e was dead and gorn before we cast 'im overboard. We 'ad the remainin' ensign 'alf-masted – we 'adn't got a spare to replace the one that got shot away. The next day, the purser auctioned 'is gear for 'is estate. I've only been in the navy for a dog watch, yet it felt like all my life. It's 'ard to come 'ome and settle down, knowin' you'll never go back to sea.'

'You'll go out with us on the *Whimbrel*, though,' Jason said.

'It's a gen'rous offer, but you know very well I can't do that in my condition. I'd be an 'indrance, not an 'elp.'

'If you won't come out on the lugger, there are other things you can do. You can caulk a seam and turn your hand to a bit of carpentry, like you used to. I remember how you and Louisa repaired the *Curlew* after your misadventure.'

Winnie recalled the day that she and her sisters launched the *Curlew* for the very first time. Louisa had bought her from Mr Jackson who was anchoring ashore to enjoy his retirement on the profits he'd made from fishing and the free trade. She had been in a sorry state with some of her boards rotted through and encrusted with barnacles, but Terrier's son had made her seaworthy again. Against the advice of one or two of the older boatmen who could see all the signs of a storm brewing on the horizon, they'd set off on a fishing trip with Billy.

Believing that they knew better, and not having Pa to guide them, they had gone to one of the fishing grounds and cast their net. The weather deteriorated, and the *Curlew* kept turning in the strengthening wind. As they pulled the net in, a gust turned her broadside to the wind and the net snagged, fouling the tiller so they couldn't steer her. Billy sliced the net away then rigged the lugsail for the trip back. The *Curlew*'s canvas billowed, driving her away from the coast, while the gulls dived at them, their screams caught and carried away on the rising gale.

Winnie swapped places with Grace who was suffering from seasickness, taking a turn at the tiller, but although she pushed and pulled at it, it wouldn't budge.

'Billy,' Louisa shouted as they drifted. 'We're too close to the Sands.'

'We're nowhere near 'em,' he called back, but Winnie knew him too well.

'I don't want to die,' she cried out.

'We aren't goin' to die,' Billy yelled back, and Winnie began to believe him until the mast broke with a snap, and the weight of the wet canvas dragged it into the water.

Billy sawed it away while Louisa picked up the oar and began to paddle furiously against the wind and tide, but her efforts were fruitless. The howling winds moved them ever closer to the sandbank, until the *Curlew* scraped across the sand with a horrible scrunch, and grounded herself.

They were stuck, they couldn't swim, and they were frozen to the bone. All they could do was scream and holler as loudly as they could with the waves crashing down over their heads, bringing a fresh rush of water each time, filling the boat to the gunwales.

Louisa held Grace in her arms, while Billy and Winnie huddled together, waist-deep in water.

'I'm sorry, Winnie,' Billy whispered into her ear. 'I should never 'ave agreed on this expedition—'

He broke off when Louisa exclaimed, 'Look!'

Winnie had stared through the rain and spray as the silhouette of a giant lugger appeared. She was manned by oarsmen, her sail close-hauled, and captained by Jason who shouted, 'We've found the *Curlew*.'

He'd called them dunderheads, as his crew managed to get them off the *Curlew* and on to the *Whimbrel*. Having floated the *Curlew* and towed her back to Deal, they took the remains of her mast and canvas for their trouble.

'Say you'll have a go, Billy,' Jason said from the kitchen.

'Oh, I dunno.'

Winnie's spirits sank. She wished he would find something to occupy his time – she thought it would make him feel better if he had a purpose.

'You have two arms,' Jason said. 'What's stoppin' you? It isn't something to be proud of, lettin' Winnie support you and your child. Winnie is a good worker – reliable, sweet-natured … Sometimes, she's too soft.'

'Are you suggestin' that I'm taking advantage of 'er?'

'You have to step up, Billy.'

'Has she been sayin' things about me?'

'She would never cast aspersions on your character. She's mightily fond of you – you should have seen her sorrowin' after you the whole time you were missin'. Don't lose her respect – you'll regret it. Come down to the beach in the mornin', spend some time at the capstan grounds renewin' old acquaintances, and I'll find you some odd jobs to do. You've nothin' to lose.'

'Thank you for 'aving faith in me, Marlin. I'll do my best.'

'Don't worry about me – think of Winnie and Pamela.' Following a brief pause, Jason went on, 'I envy you.'

Winnie pricked up her ears – this was an unexpected turn of events. Who would have thought that Jason would be jealous of Billy's situation?

'You're a Deal boatman – all I ever wanted to be, but never will be now,' Billy said. 'You're a captain with shares in more than one boat. You 'ave a loyal crew, a beautiful wife, an 'ome …' He tailed off.

'I acknowledge that I have everythin' I could wish for – except for that one blessin' that brings great happiness and makes a family complete.'

'That will 'appen soon enow,' Billy said.

'It hasn't so far – I'm beginnin' to suspect that somethin' is amiss.'

'It's rare for an 'usband and wife to remain childless,' Billy went on. 'Isn't it? I'm guessin'. I'm sorry for being maudlin – I've been so bound up with my own troubles that I 'aven't noticed anyone else's sufferin'. Winnie is the kindest person I know, and you're right – I should be lookin' after 'er.'

'Then we'll meet at dawn and make our way to the beach. Why don't I buy you a drink at the Waterman's Arms later, leaving the women to their gossip? There are times when their constant chatter drives me to distraction, and I have to get away.' Jason was chuckling as their voices faded.

'Are you sure you should be going out drinking?' Winnie asked when Billy came to tell her after supper.

'I 'ope you aren't turnin' into a nag,' he smiled.

'I'm thinking of you and your health – you can hardly stand up at the best of times, let alone when you come home from the tavern a trifle disguised.'

'That's unfair – I'm much steadier than I was, as long as I 'ave my crutches to lean on.'

'I'm sorry – it's cruel of me to keep reminding you …' Her voice faded.

'There's nothin' wrong with being truthful,' he said harshly. 'It makes no difference – I think about it all the time.'

'I wish I could help you …'

'Please, don't say anythin' else. I'm goin' out with Marlin and that's all there is to it.'

She couldn't help herself, blundering on, 'You will be careful?'

'Stop fussin', Winnie.'

She glanced towards the bottom of the stairs where Jason was collecting his boots and coat.

'Leave him alone.' He grinned. 'Billy's a grown man.'

Although confident that Jason would look after him, Winnie felt apprehensive, recalling the many past occasions on which Billy had staggered home from the Waterman's Arms or the Rattling Cat. She wondered if she was worrying unnecessarily. Although he had been keen on his drink before he was taken by the gangers, he hadn't, as far as she knew, taken more than a drop of milk and brandy and perhaps a little ale since he'd been home.

*

'He had a few too many – I should have been keepin' a closer eye on him,' Jason said the next morning when he appeared in the kitchen, shoving Billy – who seemed much the worse for wear – in front of him.

'Don't apologise – you aren't his nursemaid,' Louisa scolded.

Winnie cuddled Pamela, turning the baby's face away because she didn't want her seeing her father drunk.

'I don't want nothin' to eat or drink,' Billy grimaced. 'Marlin, I'll stay 'ere …'

'Oh no, you won't. You said you'd do some work for me today. Besides, the fresh air will do you good.' Jason collected the basket of provisions that Winnie had put aside for the men the previous evening. 'Good day, ladies.' He stepped close to Louisa and kissed her cheek. 'I'll be back as soon as I can, my dear wife.'

Winnie read her sister's lips.

'I love you,' Louisa mouthed. Winnie wasn't sure she could bring herself to say the same to Billy. She contented herself with expressing her wish that his head would soon clear.

'My head's clear enow,' he said bad-temperedly.

'What do you think possessed him?' she exclaimed when Billy and Jason had gone, the front door slamming behind them.

'The other men were egging him on, apparently,' Louisa said. 'Jason said they were all at the Waterman's Arms last night.'

'I don't like him drinking – it's disrespectful and childish of him to go against my wishes.'

'Men are renowned for staying young at heart,' Grace suggested. 'Mrs Witherall next door says they never grow up.'

'I hope you aren't making a habit of observing those of the opposite sex, Grace. It's unfeminine and leaves you open to criticism,' Louisa said.

'She's looking for a husband,' Winnie chuckled.

'It's all right for you, Louisa. You have Jason, and Winnie has Billy,' Grace said.

'Billy and I will marry when the time is right.' Winnie was confident that that was her destiny, but when he came home a few hours later with a cut on his hand and his face as black as thunder, she wasn't so sure. She didn't think it was a good time to point out that the tar on his clothes would never come out.

'You're home sooner than I thought.'

'There's nobody keepin' an eye on me on the beach, an' I've 'ad enough of sawin' timbers for one day.'

'Would you like some ham and bread? You must be starving.'

'I've 'ad a pie and the 'air of the dog at the pot 'ouse. Tell the truth, I didn't want to come back. Winnie, 'ow could you? You've always been a stickler for honesty, but it turns out that deep down you're a liar!' He took a step back and minced across the hall, his hand outstretched. 'I've never so much as looked at another man since you've been away, Billy,' he said in a high-pitched voice. 'I've kept myself pure in thought and mind for you, my love.'

'I've done nothing wrong,' she shouted to make herself heard.

He stopped, turned and snapped at her, his face contorted with grief and anger. 'Abel Brockman offered 'is 'and! Yes, I know. Jason mentioned it – in gen'ral conversation.'

'I'm not denying it.'

'Then you must 'ave looked at 'im – more than that. You must 'ave encouraged 'im in some way. Did 'e kiss you?'

'No! We talked about mundane, everyday goings-on when I returned the ponies to the mill and after church, that's all. I didn't do anything to lead him on.'

'What 'appened then? Did 'e stroll up to you out of the blue and ask you to marry 'im?'

'That's exactly how it went, although I suspect that Mr Witherall and Mrs Brockman had a hand in it.'

Billy snorted in disbelief.

'I didn't tell you because I knew you'd be upset – the more time that went by, the easier it seemed not to stir up the past. Billy, I love you. That's why I turned him down straight away.'

'Are you sure about that? You weren't tempted by 'is chiselled features and pretty golden locks? Or 'is money?'

She hesitated.

'Oh, you were …?'

'There was a fleeting moment when I considered it – not with my heart, with my head. He promised me that I'd never be part of the free trade again, something that you know I've always wanted, and he said he would look after Pamela as if she was his own. Tell me what you would have done in my position,' she said fiercely. 'I didn't know if you were coming home. Listen to me, I beg you. The proposal took me completely by surprise. I didn't ask him to call on me … and I'd never have gone through with it, because –' she burst into tears '– I love you with all my heart.'

'Your cryin' don't wash with me,' he said. 'I don't know if I can forgive you for makin' a fool of me.'

'I've apologised. There's nothing more I can do,' she said icily. 'It seems pointless wasting time arguing and bearing grudges, when we should be making the most of each other's company, but if you don't love me … if your feelings have altered, then you must tell me.' With that, she walked away, heading up the stairs to find Pamela and cry in private.

It was hard to avoid him, although she tried. Three days passed before she realised that the situation couldn't go on. One of them would have to bend.

In the morning, she got up to find fern-like patterns of ice on the inside of the bedroom window, and Pamela babbling to herself in her cot.

'Hello, littlun,' she said, reaching out to touch the tip of the baby's nose. 'Oh, you are cold.'

'Ma-ma-ma.' Pamela held out her arms. Winnie scooped her up and carried her downstairs to the kitchen to warm up.

'Has Billy gone out yet?' she asked Grace, who was stirring porridge in the pot over the fire.

'Not as far as I know.' She stretched and yawned. 'You'll have to speak to him one day. You can't carry on like this.'

'I know,' Winnie said, contrite. 'I should have told him about Abel straight away, not kept it to myself.'

'There's no point in crying over spilt milk, as Ma would have said. You never did anything to lead Abel on.' Grace stopped abruptly, looking past her. 'Billy!'

'Mornin',' he said softly as Winnie turned to face him. His hair was rumpled, his eyes shadowed and his fingers white as they gripped his crutch. 'Winnie, I'd like to talk to you, if you'll listen. I've been a fool.'

'You certainly have,' Grace said. 'Making mountains out of molehills. Go and listen to what he has to say for himself. I'll mind the baby.'

Murmuring her assent, Winnie let Billy hold the doors open as she made her way to the parlour.

'I want to say from the depths of my 'eart, 'ow sorry I am. I make no excuses. I 'urt your feelin's.'

'Oh Billy ...'

'I can't bear the thought that I've ruined things between us.'

'I should have told you about Abel at the beginning.'

'You 'ad your reasons and I appreciate that you were thinkin' of me, but I'm not some delicate ornament to be 'andled with excessive care. I can take it. And Marlin's right – I need to do somethin' about gettin' my pay from the navy, and find a way of earnin' a livin' wage so we can be married. I 'ave that ticket to cash at the Admiralty – payin' in arrears is their guarantee against desertion, you see.'

'We could hire Abel to drive us to London.'

'I don't want anythin' to do with 'im,' Billy said harshly.

She shouldn't have suggested it, she thought. 'Someone else, then?'

'I'll see Mr Turner, the pawnbroker – 'e'll pay me for the ticket and take 'is cut.'

'What about the pension?' She thought of Mr Jones and how he'd said that it wasn't enough to keep body and soul together.

'Winnie, I want to go back to 'ow we were before I lost my leg, before the press gang came.'

'We can't go back, but we can start anew. How about that?'

'I don't know where to begin,' he confessed.

'Kiss me, just as you did the very first time.'

'What about your sisters?'

'Forget about them. They can mind their own business. Kiss me, Billy,' she whispered, and he did.

The sound of Louisa's voice cut into her consciousness, bringing her back to earth.

'Winnie, where are you? It's gone nine o'clock and you know what that means.'

'Yes,' she called cheerfully, clutching Billy's hand as she took a small step back. 'I'm breaking the law.'

'You're making rather a habit of it,' Louisa went on.

A local bye-law, the Pavement Act, obliged the residents of Deal to clear the pavements outside their homes by the allotted time. Several of their neighbours had been taken in front of the magistrates to be fined or put in the stocks for neglecting their duties.

'I'd better go,' Winnie said.

'I'll 'elp you,' Billy offered.

'Really?'

'I'm used to scrubbin' the decks. It strikes me that you're always workin' – why don't you go and put your feet up for a while?' Winnie hesitated. 'I'll do a proper job. This is just the beginnin', my love. I'm goin' to make it up to you. I'll never touch a drop o' drink again.'

Winnie returned to the kitchen while Billy collected the broom.

'Does he know how to use that?' Grace asked when he had gone, broom in one hand and a crutch in the other.

'I'm sure Mrs Witherall will demonstrate,' Winnie said, smiling.

'You've kissed and made up,' Grace grinned. 'I can tell – you're blushing.'

'Did I hear that right?' Louisa bustled into the room, accompanied by the smell of fresh bread. She placed her basket on the table.

'All is well between Billy and me,' Winnie confirmed.

'Thank goodness for that,' Louisa said. 'I never thought I'd say this, but I prefer to see you two mooning around, making sheep's eyes at each other, rather than put up with the slamming doors and angry silences. I've been to the baker's, by the way. I thought we could do with a treat.'

'You've bought huffkins,' Winnie exclaimed. 'Thank you.'

'But I've made porridge,' Grace said.

'Then we won't starve,' Louisa smiled.

When Billy came back into the house, they sat around the table and ate the traditional flat bread rolls with honey and tea, while Louisa told the story of how the huffkins had come to have the imprint of the baker's thumb in the centre. The rest of them had heard it many times before, but Louisa said that Pamela should hear it too.

Pamela listened to her aunt intently, occasionally banging the wooden spoon Grace had given her, against her highchair.

'It's like Winnie telling her tales,' Grace said. 'She's too young to understand.'

'How do you know?' Louisa said before returning to her story, starting again at the beginning.

'Once upon a time, there was a baker who had a beautiful but bad-tempered wife. One day, she was in a huff because he refused to buy her a piece of lace.'

'Are you sure it was lace?' Grace interrupted.

'It doesn't matter what it was – I'm using it as an example. Anyway, she stuck her thumb into every loaf, ruining them all. When he said he would sell them, she laughed in his face, but he sold every single one, making her even crosser. Eventually, he forgave her though, and bought her the lace because she had made his fortune from huffkins.'

Winnie didn't think she would make her fortune from carrying despatches, but with Billy's decision that he needed to make an income, she felt more optimistic that they would be able to marry sooner rather than later. She knew of couples who had been affianced for years, unable to wed until they were past twenty-five years old, because the husband-to-be couldn't afford to keep a wife. With a favourable tide and the wind behind them, she hoped they wouldn't have to wait that long.

Chapter Fifteen

The Goose that Lays the Golden Egg

By Christmas, the worst winter in living memory had caught Deal in its iron fist and refused to let go. Ice formed inside every pane in the cottage, except for those in the kitchen window, and the idea of having to go outside to the privy filled Winnie with a sense of trepidation each time. The whole family spent their days huddled in the kitchen with the fire roaring and smoke clinging to their clothes. Winnie cooked broths and stews to keep them warm.

On Christmas Eve, Winnie and Grace had been excused from attending church to mind Pamela. Billy had gone with Louisa and Jason, having been encouraged by the latter to risk his neck in the snow.

Winnie sat at the table, bouncing Pamela on her knees.

'Giddy-up!' she said, and Pamela laughed.

'There will be tears before bedtime,' Grace said from her place beside the fire, where she was making a new section of net to splice into the old one that had been ripped by the claws of a large spiny crab.

'Are you all right, Grace? You're beginning to sound like Louisa.'

'I hate being stuck indoors, that's all. It drives me to distraction.'

'You went to the market yesterday.'

'I know, but there was hardly anyone there to talk to. The stallholders can't get their barrows into town. The road up to Limepit Acres and the one to the mill are blocked by snowdrifts. There's no way of bringing provisions in by horse and cart.'

'I thought you had plenty of people to talk to here.'

'You're all so … well, Louisa's married and you're as good as married. It isn't the same as it used to be when it was the three of us.'

'Time moves on.'

'There, you sound like Mrs Witherall. Old, Winnie.'

'I will take that as a compliment – with age, comes wisdom.' Winnie smiled. 'It won't be long before spring comes and you'll be back to your merry self. Do you remember how Louisa used to tell us stories when Ma and Pa were out and about?'

'I remember the one about the star-crossed lovers and the origin of lace.'

'I'll tell the one about the goose. Now, Pamela, listen carefully to your mama. Once upon a time, there was a farmer.'

'Like Uncle Laxton?' Grace interrupted.

'If you wish. Once upon a time, there was a farmer called Uncle Laxton who lived with his wife. He was already wealthy – not as rich as Sir Flinders, but comfortably off and well able to employ men to labour on his behalf. One day, when his wife was collecting the eggs from their flock of geese, she found a golden one in a nest of straw.'

'I can't see Aunt Mary collecting eggs, Winnie.'

'Grace, don't keep interrupting – you're spoiling the story.' Winnie continued, 'She showed her husband. Would there be another golden egg the next day? he wondered.

Lo and behold, there was. His wife found a golden egg every day for a full sennight. The farmer rubbed his hands with glee.' Winnie took Pamela's hands and rubbed them together. Pamela giggled. 'He watched his flock of geese night and day until he'd worked out which one laid the golden eggs, and then he separated her from her friends and placed her in a gilded cage, giving her the best food. "How can I make her lay more than one egg a day?" he asked his wife. She said to feed her up until she was as fat as a pig.' Winnie snorted, making Pamela jump. 'Snort, snort, snort. So they did, but she laid only one egg a day.

'The farmer grew impatient. He wanted more eggs and he wanted them straight away, so do you know what he did? He went outside and wrung the goose's neck and then he plucked her feathers and looked inside her, but he didn't find a single egg. Out of greed, he had killed the goose that laid the golden eggs.'

'She's too young to understand,' Grace said, amused.

'It's never too early to start learning about the world,' Winnie said.

'Now you sound like Ma.'

'I hope I can be even half as good a mother as she was, God rest her soul.' Winnie gazed at Pamela who yawned. 'Oh dear, am I boring you?' She held her close.

'Talking of golden eggs, have you received your payment from Mr Cork?' Grace asked.

'I'm still awaiting my windfall,' Winnie responded. 'Everything is paid several months in arrears. I wish it wasn't so, but that's the way it is.'

'I suppose you'll be leaving us.'

'Billy and I would like to get married and set up home together … Grace, don't be upset. We'll find lodgings in Deal. We won't be far away.'

'I'll miss you,' she said, 'and Pamela.'

'Unless Billy can pick up some more work, I doubt very much that we'll be able to afford to move out. Hark, what was that?'

'They're back,' Grace said, getting up. 'They'll be expecting a meal, and we aren't ready.'

'It was a beautiful service.' Louisa blew on her hands as she walked into the kitchen. 'The church was decked out with holly and ivy, and candles, and Reverend North kept his sermon short and sweet.'

Billy and Jason followed her and pulled their chairs up to the table.

Winnie placed a sleeping Pamela into her cradle, then served up bread and bloaters, and mutton stew. Grace poured mulled wine and they sat talking.

'I apologise for speakin' of this over supper, but there was a body found this afternoon,' Jason said.

It wasn't unusual for a body to be washed up on the shore, Winnie thought, only half listening.

'Smoker and his cronies were out with the creepin' iron, still thinkin' they might find the goods we threw over-board all that time ago. They never give up when there's a sniff of money to be made. I don't know how many times I've told them that it's hopeless – the textiles will be ruined.'

'Can't they be washed?' Billy asked. 'Louisa, you'd know about that.'

'Lace can be lightly steamed and an iron run over it with a piece of clean linen in between, but scrubbing won't do it any good,' she said. 'Do they know who this poor man – or woman – is?'

'He had no papers, but from the length of his bones, Smoker reckoned he would have been unusually tall, close to seven feet,' Jason said. 'He had a scar across his chin and bruisin'. Smoker's convinced – this is to go no further

215

– that it's the mortal remains of a Monsieur Alexandre from whom we used to collect lace at Gravelines.'

Winnie recalled Jason telling her of Madame's missing right-hand man. It appeared that he had met with a violent end as Jason had surmised.

'The hooners are in town.' Jason changed the subject. 'I've invited them to call in and entertain us.'

'Oh, you haven't?' Louisa said. 'They'll drain our cellar.'

'We haven't got a cellar,' Grace said.

'I'm speaking metaphorically. I suppose it will be all right if we don't allow them to help themselves to ale. And we'll keep the brandy under lock and key.'

'All they're expectin' is cake, some ale and a few pennies,' Jason said.

'As long as they don't wake the baby,' Winnie replied.

'Where is your sense of enjoyment and honour for our ancient customs?'

'Them jackanapes always make me laugh,' Billy said. 'When will they be 'ere?'

He was answered by a rap at the door and the sound of deep voices carolling in tune with a fiddle and pipes.

The family stood up as Jason let the hooners in, welcoming them and shaking their hands. First came a trio of red-faced jovial musicians, followed by a man leading the strangest of beasts by the bridle. Winnie recognised the waggoner, as he was called, as one of the labourers from Limepit Acres. He had a crooked finger – it was universally known that he had deliberately broken it to preclude him from military and naval service. The beast was a horse – strictly speaking, a carved horse's head carried on a four-foot pole by a personage who was hidden underneath a sackcloth. The horse's head was elaborately painted: smuggler's black with brown eyes made to look wild and alive with splashes of white, scarlet nostrils and mouth, and two rows of white wooden teeth. It had a horsehair forelock and mane and its lower jaw was attached by a complex arrangement of string, by which the mouth could be opened and snapped shut.

The horse pranced around the kitchen, growling and snapping its teeth while the last of the entourage entered the kitchen. A lady? No. Winnie caught Grace's eye and wished she hadn't because they had both recognised Mollie – not Molly Stickles, but the character associated with the hoodening.

It was Abel, carrying a broom and wearing women's clothing: a bonnet trimmed with silk flowers that Winnie assumed he'd borrowed from Mrs Brockman whom she'd seen wearing it about town; a flowing Grecian gown; a redingcote that was too small for him; ladies' gloves and his riding boots.

As he moved around the crowded room, the pipers began to play and the fiddler plucked his strings, promptly dropping his bow. He picked it up before 'Mollie' could sweep it up, and continued playing 'Greensleeves' for the audience while 'Mollie' chased Grace, then Louisa and then Winnie with the broom, as was the custom. Jason cheered and Billy roared with laughter as the horse said a few words. Louisa joined in, clapping while Winnie and Grace pushed the table aside and danced.

As the strings faded and the pipes stopped with an abrupt toot-toot, Louisa served cake and ale, and they were very merry until past midnight, long after the hoodeners had gone on their way.

Winter maintained its icy grip, but there was news to brighten the short, dark days entering the New Year: Sir Flinders, his wife and other dignitaries were to make a formal visit to Deal.

On a cold dry day when much of the snow had been cleared from the streets, swept into the gutters where it began to melt, a large crowd assembled outside the Royal Naval Hospital. Winnie waited, leaning on the handcart as she chatted with her sisters and Mrs Witherall while Pamela slept, her nose and cherubic mouth visible between her woollen hat and blanket.

'Mr Witherall wanted to come along with me, but 'e 'as a terrible attack of gout and gravel.'

Winnie had guessed he was unwell – they had been subjected to his moaning and groaning through the adjoining walls of their houses the previous night.

'I hope he's better soon,' she said.

'For all our sakes,' Grace added.

'I beg your pardon? I didn't quite catch that,' Mrs Witherall frowned.

'I said for your sake,' Grace corrected herself, her cheeks pink as Winnie gave her a poke in the ribs. 'We are honoured that Sir Flinders is gracing the town with his presence.'

'It's all for show,' Mrs Witherall said. 'One of my cousins 'as a daughter who's a scullery maid at the manor. 'Is Lordship 'as an 'ouse guest, a Monsieur Boule.'

Winnie's ears pricked up as she continued, ''Is staff say that the aforesaid gen'leman is keen for Sir Flinders to introduce 'im to the great and good: the Captain of Deal and Port Admiral Folet. 'E's also taken a great interest in 'is Lordship's connections to the 'ospital and barracks and 'is charitable doin's. Sir Flinders seems more than willin' to oblige 'is friend while 'e makes a tour of the county. Apparently, 'e's 'ired a chef to create French dishes for 'is guest – they've 'ad pheasant 'angin' in the larder for so long that they've gone green. Can you imagine?'

Winnie didn't like to.

'What's in it for Sir Flinders?' she wondered aloud.

'Power and money,' Mrs Witherall said wisely. 'Sir Flinders is a wealthy man, but it's rumoured that Monsieur Boule is worth five, maybe ten times as much. If Sir Flinders can find a way of persuadin' 'im to contribute to the government's coffers in return for … well, I don't know what, but it'll be a case of you scratch my back, I'll scratch yours … Anyway, I reckon 'e'll become Prime Minister one day.'

'Make way. Make way.' Constable Pocket was in the middle of the street, blowing his whistle as not one but four carriages came towards them, sparks flying from the horses' hooves. The constable jumped out of the way as they pulled up one by one in front of the hospital. There was a stately coach drawn by six horses and sporting the Flinders' coat of arms on the doors, two carriages each pulled by four horses and an open chaise drawn by a pair of cream ponies, tossing their heads as the ostrich plumes attached to their black harnesses fluttered in the light breeze.

The sight of such magnificence sent a thrill down Winnie's spine and the crowd pressed in to watch the passengers alight.

Firstly, from the coach, came Sir Flinders and his wife, followed by two gentlemen wearing formal attire. Lady Flinders held on to her bonnet, a spectacular creation in peacock blue to match her redingcote.

An entourage of ladies and gentlemen, including the Port Admiral who was responsible for overseeing the naval shipping stationed in the Downs, emerged from the hospital gates to greet the arrivals as a young woman Winnie recognised as Miss Marianne Flinders, the younger of the Flinders sisters, stepped down from the chaise. Louisa intercepted her and her companion, her lady's maid, perhaps.

'Good day, Miss Flinders,' she said.

'Ah, it's you. The Lace Maiden,' Miss Flinders said with a small smile. Winnie noticed that her long gloves were adorned with a row of exquisite silk buttons. 'My sister often asks after you in her letters.'

'I don't wish to delay you any more than necessary, but I would like to enquire after Mrs Tempest's health.'

'She is very well, thank you. I look forward to the day when she and Harry return triumphant from the Continent, because we must always hope for an end to this dreadful war, mustn't we?'

'Indeed,' Louisa said smoothly. 'If you require my services at any time, do get in touch, won't you?'

'Of course. I had better move on – my father expects me to entertain Monsieur Boule.'

'How do you find him?' Winnie couldn't resist asking.

'I shouldn't speak ill of a house guest, but he is a fawning toad who makes impertinent enquiries about our friends and acquaintances. He and my father's apparent respect for each other is only skin-deep. He has a habit of being late for dinner, something my father can't abide, and he's used up all my writing supplies. I cannot wait for him to return to London.' Miss Flinders walked away towards the hospital gates.

'She looks very odd with her high forehead and thin eyebrows,' Grace whispered.

'Her looks are fading,' Winnie agreed. 'I'm afraid that she will be left on the shelf.'

'Surely her appearance is à la mode amongst the ladies of the ton,' Mrs Witherall said, 'although I don't understand why.'

'She could be described as pale and interesting,' Louisa said. 'I don't know where I heard of it, but some ladies have mice trapped for them so they can make false eyebrows from the fur.'

'No, Louisa. You are gammoning us,' Winnie chuckled.

'I'm not. The likes of Miss Flinders have nothing to do except worry about finding a suitable husband – they are slaves to fashion.'

The dignitaries disappeared into the hospital building, leaving the coachmen standing around with the horses.

'Shall we go to Molly's?' Louisa said. 'There's nothing more to see here.'

They walked to the pot house.

'Welcome! Ma, it's my sisters,' Nancy exclaimed, opening the door to them. 'Are you stoppin' for refreshment?'

'We'll take tea if we may,' Louisa said, removing her gloves as Winnie carried Pamela inside, and Grace followed.

'To what do we owe this unexpected pleasure?'

'We came to see the dignitaries arrive on their tour of Deal. You should have seen the ladies' bonnets and the carriages,' Grace said.

'I am not so easily impressed by ostentatious displays of wealth,' Winnie said. 'The money that Sir Flinders spent on his turnout would have allowed the staff at the hospital to treat many more injured sailors.'

'I believe that his income is more than adequate to do both,' Louisa observed. 'I apologise for Winnie – she's become rather dull and motherly.'

'I have much to occupy my mind,' Winnie allowed.

'Tell us what is so absorbing that you no longer laugh with us,' Grace said.

'I can't.'

Grace looked disappointed.

'I'm sorry,' Winnie said. Much as she yearned to share her secret, she didn't dare let slip the details to anyone, even her sisters. She'd hoped that light would suddenly

221

dawn, revealing what she should do next about her suspicions over the despatches, but the more she thought about them, the more clouded her options seemed to become.

As they took their seats at the table in the window, Mr Jones came over to speak to Winnie.

'Hello, missus,' he said.

Louisa frowned.

'Good morning, Mr Jones,' Winnie said. 'Allow me to introduce you to my sisters.' Having made the introductions, she enquired how he was.

'I wanted to give you this token of my appreciation for what you've done for me.' He took a small parcel wrapped in rags from the pocket of his coat and handed it to her. She opened it, finding a bracelet made from plaited thread and shells.

'It isn't much, I'm afraid.'

'It's beautiful,' she said, glancing towards Louisa. 'I can't accept it though.'

'I can't give it to anybody else – I made it with you in mind.'

'Then thank you. I'm very grateful.'

'It's the small gestures that wreak the greatest changes, missus. With food in my belly, I 'ad the strength to get walkin'. I was idlin' on the beach when, with my 'alf-good eye, I spotted a coin shinin' from the pebbles. I picked it up – it was a gold coin, a guinea. "What a bit 'o luck, Mr Jones," I said to myself. "I can use that."

'I bought food for my children and a greatcoat from Mr Turner's on Golden Street. It was a fortuitous meetin' because 'e let slip that 'e 'ad a room in the attic for rent, so I took it.'

Winnie knew of Mr Turner, the pawnbroker who made his fortune out of other people's misery. And there was a lot of misery if one judged it from the number of people who queued up outside his shop every day.

'Since then, I've been collectin' shells, coloured stones and driftwood, and makin' them up into trinkets that I sell in the taverns and at the market.'

Winnie wished Billy was equally assiduous about earning a wage. Mr Jones excused himself and she placed the bracelet of shells around her wrist.

'You aren't going to wear that, are you?' Louisa said.

Winnie took it off and slipped it into her purse. To avoid any misunderstandings, she would ask Billy first, she decided, as Mrs Stickles appeared with a tray.

'Winnie, can I 'ave a word with you?' she said, once she'd put the tray down and poured the tea.

They spoke in the kitchen where the fire was raging, and an aroma of beef and scallions filled the air.

'Is this about your fancy man?' Winnie enquired.

'I 'ave his book – the one I told you about. I wondered if you could make sense of it for me – I'm itchin' to know what 'e's written about me.'

There was a time when Winnie wouldn't have touched a gentleman's personal diary, but breaking into the despatches had changed all that.

'What are you expecting?' she asked as Mrs Stickles stood on a chair and reached up to the top of the dresser. She removed the book and handed it to Winnie, before struggling down again.

Winnie examined the cover – it was bound with navy calf's leather with no embellishment, no title or author's name. She opened it and turned the pages.

'What does it say? Look, there are 'is notes, 'andwritten in the margin.' Mrs Stickles peered over her shoulder.

'It's just a list – several lists of letters and words. No, they are groups of letters. It isn't written in English – it's gobbledygook.' A pulse pounded at her temple. She knew what it was: instructions as to how to break a code, or

223

codes. She was even more sure now that the seductive Mr Gambril was the very same gentleman who had been looking for Louisa, and who had attacked her in the sandhills. The hairs on the back of her neck stood on end as she recalled seeing him on the wharf at Gravelines, watching the guinea boat shrink into the distance.

Was he responsible for creating the coded messages? His notes were in English, which suggested it was more likely that he was trying to break the code. More importantly, now that she was in possession of the book, would she be able to read the information contained in the papers and written in invisible ink?

'Are you sure there's nothin' of a ... romantic nature? Or a mention of my name?'

'I'm sorry to disappoint you, but the scribbles in the margins is notes, questions relating to the lists. The only other addition is an address here for an establishment in Kensington.'

'Perhaps 'e couldn't find the right words,' Mrs Stickles said sadly. 'I'd better 'ave it back – I'll return it when I see 'im.'

'I'll hold on to it for now,' Winnie said. 'Give me time to read it from cover to cover – maybe I'll find some reference to his affection for you.' She felt mean giving Mrs Stickles false hope, but she needed the book. 'When are you expecting him to return to Deal?'

'I have no idea. 'E's the type who keeps 'imself to 'imself.'

'Will you let me know when you see him again? I'd like to meet him.' On her terms, she thought, not lurking about in the sandhills or among the warehouses at Gravelines. She wanted to know what kind of man he was and what he was looking for.

Chapter Sixteen

Over a Barrel

'Billy, wake up.' A sennight after their happy reunion following their disagreement over Abel and a few days after a small celebration that they held in honour of Pamela's first birthday, Winnie pushed the door open to find him lying on his back, snoring like one of Uncle Laxton's fat pigs. 'You must be worn out, my poor love.' Her heart went out to him, knowing how much walking he was having to do in his quest for work. Jason's offer of a place on the *Whimbrel* still held, but Billy refused to put the rest of the crew at a disadvantage. He'd done a few odd jobs for Jason and now he was trying the boat-yards.

She walked across and opened the curtains, then returned to his bedside and leaned down to kiss him.

'Ugh,' she said, backing away from the stench of spirits that oozed from his skin. She gave him a sharp dig in the ribs.

'Can't you see I'm sleepin'? All that traipsin' about yesterday's fair done me in.'

'You didn't traipse any further than the Waterman's Arms or the Rattling Cat. Don't lie to me. You've been drinking.' She slumped on to the edge of the bed. 'How could you do this to me? You promised.'

Groaning, he tried to sit up but sank back again, his hands over his eyes.

'I didn't mean to. I went in for a little somethin', a small beer to slake my thirst, and then Isaiah offered me another on the 'ouse, and another.'

'He isn't renowned for his generosity – you're lying to me,' she said scathingly.

He tried to get up again, sweat dripping from his brow, his face greener than sea lettuce.

'Stay there. I'll make up some excuse as to why you aren't up and about today.' She wasn't sure it would wash with Louisa, but she'd been practising lying for some time.

She went downstairs to the kitchen.

'Where's Billy?' Louisa said straight away. She didn't miss much. 'I thought he was intending on making an early start.'

'His leg's playing him up – he's taking his time …'

Louisa stood with one hand on her hip, the other holding a basket.

'He could at least try to lend a hand, Winnie. It isn't fair that Jason goes out hovelling and we lug these provisions around, while Billy lazes about. As for Pamela – she kept us all awake with her crying.'

'How am I supposed to keep her quiet?'

'I don't know – you're her mother.'

Winnie had fed her and put her back in the crib, at which she had screamed the place down. Afraid she was going to do herself harm, Winnie had picked her up and rocked her gently, and Pamela had begun to settle. When her tiny sobs had subsided, Winnie put her down. She had just got back into bed and pulled up the covers when Pamela opened her bellows again. Winnie had repeated the process three times and when Pamela had finally fallen asleep, Billy came home. He stomped up the stairs, having forgotten to take his boots off, and woke her up.

With Billy in the house, and the presence of her family around her, Winnie had been in despair. She had never felt so alone.

'I'm going to ask Mrs Witherall if she'll mind Pamela for a few hours.'

'Can't Billy look after her?' Louisa eyed her with suspicion, but the lies slipped straight off Winnie's tongue, like syrup.

'When he's taken something for the pain and he's feeling better, he's going out looking for work. Mr Christchurch at the boatyard said he'd see if he could do anything for him, and if not, there are other boat builders he can try.'

'That's promising at least,' Louisa said.

Reassured that she had pacified her, for the present at least, Winnie left the baby with their next-door neighbour and went out with her sisters, waddling along in extra layers of petticoats and stockings with two bladders of cognac knocking against her legs, and wearing a pair of mittens that Grace had knitted from scraps of wool.

'It's a proper blustery day today,' Cromwell said when they reached the beach, and Winnie wondered if he was trying to get out of the provisioning trip on the *Curlew* that they had planned. He helped her load several baskets of potatoes and cabbages from Mr Laxton at Limepit Acres, and some apples, along with a barrel of salted pork.

'What's wrong?' she asked, noticing that he was close to tears.

'My sister's lost 'er baby. In 'is infinite wisdom, God 'as taken the poor little bastard up to 'eaven. That's what the vicar said when 'e came to baptise 'im and pray for 'is soul.'

227

'I'm sorry.'

''E can't be all that wise,' Cromwell said miserably. 'My sister's takin' it terr'ble bad. It wasn't 'er fault, you know. She got taken advantage of by a soldier who loved 'er and left 'er. Even though I begged 'er not to, Mrs Appleton's thrown 'er out of the 'ouse.' As was the custom for many, Cromwell called his mother by her married name.

Winnie's chest tightened, and she swallowed back a sob at the thought of an innocent child a few days old being snatched from his mother's arms. She thought of Pamela and how she hated leaving her, even with Mrs Witherall who was delighted to have a few hours with her in return for half a dozen apples, or a pound of potatoes.

'Please convey my condolences to your sister.' They were empty words for a poor woman with no husband, no home and no baby.

'I dunno where she'll live – it looks like she'll be 'eadin' to the poor'ouse. I wish I could afford to buy 'er a place, even rent a small room.'

How she wished she could help them. She cast a glance towards Louisa who gave a slight shake of the head. Like the Witheralls and Lennickers, the Ropers and Edwards, the Kirbys and Startups, the Appletons would have to help themselves.

Against a clear blue January sky, they launched the *Curlew.* She flew down the beach and plunged into the water, drenching them with spray. Winnie got bailing, and Louisa and Cromwell set the sail, while Grace took the tiller, wiping water from her eyes.

As the wind filled the lugsail and set the *Curlew* gently on course, Winnie paused to look out towards the Downs, her nostrils filling with the sharp scent of salt and pine tar. Ahead of them, one of the many merchant ships that crowded the roadstead lowered a jollyboat into the water.

The purser, whom they had met before, sat in the stern while two officers rowed him towards them.

'Ladies, what delights apart from your pretty selves do you bring for us today? I have a hankering for fresh meat.'

The purser was rude and uncouth, not bothering to stand as a gentleman would. He made Winnie feel uncomfortable, especially the way his gaze settled on Grace, whose long ebony hair was trailing from beneath her sou'wester.

She hoped Louisa was prepared to lower her prices so they could sell quickly and go home, but there was no chance of that – she would squeeze out as much money as she could.

'And something to buoy the spirits,' he went on with a wink.

'It comes at a price,' Louisa said.

'A very fair one, I'm sure, because you are all remarkably fair young ladies.'

Louisa gave him the cost of the bladders, at which he visibly blenched.

'If your pockets are not deep enough to purchase both quantities, I will allow you to buy just one.'

'No, missus. We will have both,' the purser suddenly decided. 'I shall make myself a nice little profit out of it.'

The deal was done and after further negotiation, the purser relieved them of the potatoes, cabbages and salted pork, leaving them with little left to sell.

Louisa was delighted, and because they were cold, she suggested they return ashore early. Having beached the *Curlew* and made her fast, Cromwell looked out for the other shore boys. It hadn't been such a good day for him, not with his family troubles and being out for such a short time, Winnie thought. She waited until her sister's back was turned and slipped a couple of coins into his palm. His mouth formed an O of uncertainty.

'It's yours,' she whispered. 'A gift from me. Use it wisely – and don't tell Louisa.'

'That's worth keepin' yer mouth shut for,' he said softly. 'Thank you. I'm ever so grateful.'

'What have you got to be grateful for, a little tyke like you?' Louisa said fondly, walking towards them.

'Nothin', missus.' He frowned and corrected himself. 'Everythin'. Oh, I dunno. I'm all betwattled.'

'We'll see you again soon,' Louisa said.

'Tomorrer?' he asked.

'It depends on the weather and how long it takes us to get hold of fresh stock.'

'We could always go fishin'.'

Winnie sensed his desperation and determination to help his sister.

'I'm sorry we can't give you regular work, Cromwell,' Louisa said.

'It won't be many years before you're old enough to go out on the luggers,' Grace added.

'Yeah, I s'pose,' he sighed. 'Thank you anyway, ladies.'

'He's a good boy,' Grace said, as they walked through the capstan grounds towards the street. 'I don't think he ever washes though, not even once a month.'

Winnie smiled, putting thoughts of Cromwell aside in favour of looking forward to collecting Pamela from Mrs Witherall. Louisa was reluctant to let her bring her home early because she had plans for them to let down more cognac for their next provisioning trip, but Winnie and Grace overruled her.

When they arrived back at the cottage with the baby in Grace's arms, Billy's boots were missing from the hall.

'Perhaps a miracle has happened, and he has turned over a new leaf,' Louisa said.

'We will be very proud of him in overcoming adversity,' Grace joined in. 'We were right to be patient. Come with me, littlun. Winnie, may I feed her?'

'Yes, thank you,' she said, realising too late that Louisa – who hated seeing idle hands – would immediately enlist her help to move the barrels of cognac from the hiding hole into the parlour. They drew the curtains and lit the fire and three smoking tallow candles to work by. Winnie opened the first barrel which contained about four gallons of strong cognac.

'Those fumes will knock us senseless.' Chuckling, Grace came in, carrying a pan of caramel syrup, her hands wrapped in cloth. She placed it on a mat on the table.

'Where is Pamela?' Winnie asked.

'I've put her down in her cot.'

'Then she will not sleep tonight,' Louisa warned.

'I don't like her to be around when we're letting down the cognac,' Winnie said. 'It's dangerous for an infant – I couldn't forgive myself.'

'You're worried that exposing her to the mere presence of strong drink will send her the way of her father?' Grace said.

'What do you mean by that?'

'You know very well – Billy likes his drink.'

'No more than any other man of my acquaintance.'

'My husband drinks in moderation,' Louisa said. 'Billy gollops it down like a fish.'

'I wish you'd leave him alone – he's still adjusting to life at home.'

'I feel sorry for him, but he doesn't lift a finger around the house. Perhaps you can have a word with him, Winnie.

I don't like to nag, but I worry that Jason will lose patience with him. You know how hard he works.'

'When he returns from the boatyard with good news, I'll speak to him, but you can't expect too much. He gets these terrible phantom pains, and although I've given him laudanum and tincture of willow, neither makes a difference.' Winnie opened the first barrel while Louisa mixed the caramel with a measure of water. Winnie tipped out half the cognac into a spare barrel, then poured Louisa's mixture into both barrels and mixed the contents. She stepped back to allow Louisa to drop their set of glass beads inside, then waited to see which one bobbed up to the surface, indicating the strength of the spirit.

'That'll suit the English taste.' Winnie waited for Louisa to retrieve the beads before she resealed the barrel. 'Next.'

Grace rolled another barrel out of its hiding hole, and having opened it, Winnie sniffed at the contents.

'Ugh. It smells ... odd. Like seawater. Is this one of the barrels that came off the guinea boat? It was towed under-water while Jason was seeing the gobblers off.'

'No, it's from the same batch as the first one.' Louisa was frowning. 'Put some in the cup over there.'

The liquid was watery with a brown tinge, and tasted of bad eggs, not brine.

'That's very much like the elderflower wine that Aunt Mary used to bring as a gift for Ma,' Winnie said.

'Like cat's piss then,' Grace contributed.

'Mind your language,' Louisa said, and Grace pursed her lips mutinously. 'This is very strange. I've never seen it before. Either the merchant has done us out of our goods, or someone else has ...' She turned and stared straight at Winnie. 'Billy's done this.'

'It could be anybody,' Winnie said, her heart racing. 'How can you accuse him when he isn't here to defend himself?'

'Ask yourself why that is. Because he's out drinking. It's funny how he can walk as far as Ringwould and beyond to reach a tavern, but he can't make it to the capstan grounds.'

'You're wrong. Billy can't get to Ringwould – he's told me so.'

'Then he must have an identical twin. Mr Witherall saw him up there – he was in no doubt that it was Billy.'

'We should give him the benefit of the doubt, Louisa,' Grace said. 'He fought for us – it wasn't his fault he lost his leg.'

'He can't live on that excuse for the rest of his life, much as I respect and appreciate what he's done.'

'Louisa, if you're right, fair enough, but you can't accuse him without any proof,' Winnie said, her voice querulous.

'The proof is there – two per cent, if that, the lowest concentration I've ever recorded.'

'He's a hero. He saved some of the men on his ship, but he also saw his best friend die. He blames himself for surviving when his friend didn't. Look, it's only half an anker – I'll pay for it myself,' Winnie said meekly. She'd been putting a little aside in a wooden box under the mattress, whenever she could, and she was upset to think that she was going to have to throw it away on Billy's indiscretion. 'I'll make him promise not to do anything like this again.' The trouble was that it was a terrible breach of trust. She remembered how angry One Eye had been when their father had appropriated some of his run goods. It ran against the unwritten smugglers' code of honour. You didn't take from your own kind because one day you might have to rely on them to watch your back.

When Billy returned home in the middle of the after-noon, Winnie intercepted him before he could slip upstairs to his room without being noticed.

'Louisa has something to ask you. I'm sure it's nothing and the matter will be quickly cleared up.' She took his hand and led him into the parlour.

Louisa showed him the contents of the cup.

'What is the meaning of this?' she asked.

'I 'ave no idea.' His brow furrowed, but the flicker of his expression before it changed into one of stubborn denial was enough to convince Winnie that he was lying, and she was deeply disappointed.

'It came from one of the barrels,' Louisa went on.

'It looks like seawater,' Billy said. 'I've seen it before – when you sow the crop and leave it underwater for a while, sometimes you get seawater leakin' in and spoilin' the brandy. It's what's known around 'ere as a veritable stinkibus.' He belched. 'My apologies, ladies.' He excused himself, seemingly unable to get away quick enough.

Upstairs, Billy's door slammed, rattling the window-panes.

'Pa never did train him not to do that,' Grace observed. 'How many times do we have to remind him not to wake the baby?'

Winnie held her breath, listening for the cry ... but it didn't happen.

'This isn't fair. I'm going to have words with him.' She scurried up the stairs, then knocked on his door and walked in without waiting for an answer.

'I know you're lying. Explain yourself,' she said tersely, then when he hesitated, sitting dumbly on the edge of the bed in darkness, his face barely illuminated by the light

234

coming through a chink in the curtains, she went on, 'I'm staying here until you tell me what's going on.'

After a long pause, he began to speak. 'I couldn't 'elp it. I 'ad a terr'ble achin' tooth for a tot of brandy while you were out one time, knowin' it would numb the pain. There's plenty more. I didn't see no 'arm in it.'

'Louisa knows you're lying – I could see it in her eyes.'

'Louisa's always 'ad it in for me. She flew to the conclusion that it was my fault, because she's always thought the worst of me.'

'Stop play-acting, pretending you're surprised.' Winnie thought back to the past and Billy's liking for drink, how he'd become more than a trifle disguised and turned up late for fishing trips with their father, or fell asleep in the hang among the buckets of briny fish, or failed to show his face when he'd agreed to crew for Jason on the *Whimbrel*. 'Oh, it doesn't matter. I'm tired. All I will say is that a dog shouldn't steal from its master.'

'Are you sayin' you think I'm a dog?'

'No, it's a saying. That's all. What I mean is that Jason and Louisa were kind to me and Pamela while you were away. They've been generous to you too, giving you a roof over your head, when they didn't have to. I can't reason with you when you're like this. You've changed – you don't feel like my Billy any more. You've been so bound up in your own problems, you've hardly asked about me.'

'I'm sorry,' he said. 'Truly, I am. I should 'ave thought …'

'You're back, yet we've barely talked about tying the knot.'

'Marryin' you would make me the 'appiest man in the world, but 'ow can I make an honest woman of you without a regular wage?'

'You could work, if you took up Jason's offer.'

'We've been through this afore – the crew doesn't carry passengers.'

'I hate these arguments. All we do is go around in circles. There are times – and this is one of them – when I wonder what it would have been like if I'd married Abel.' Her hand flew to her mouth as Billy's face fell. 'I'm sorry. I didn't mean that I wish I had married him.'

'But you do,' he countered. 'You wouldn't 'ave said it otherwise.'

'When we were younger, I always stood up for you. Do you remember how when you were fifteen, you ate all that apple sauce that Ma had made to go with a joint of pork?'

'I 'ad a rumblin' belly for it, I recall,' he said morosely. 'I was starvin'. You told Mrs Lennicker you'd seen one of the Rattlers' cats creep in and lick it from the jug.'

A thought occurred to Winnie. 'You know, I don't think she believed me – she just went along with it.'

'She was very kind. She took me aside a few days later an' told me if I were ever 'ungry to the point where I couldn't wait for the next meal, I should ask 'er for bread and a mite of jam. After that I often found an extra egg on me plate.'

'I wish she was still here with us.' Ma would have known what to do, how to advise her. 'I never meant that about Abel – I mean it from the bottom of my heart – but I was so cross. Can we stop fighting and look to the future?'

'What about Louisa?'

'I'll square it with her.'

'Oh Winnie, it won't 'appen again, I promise.'

'I know you'll do your best,' she said, aware that promises were frequently made, then broken. She had forgiven him but couldn't quite bring herself to lean closer and give him a kiss.

She returned downstairs to the parlour to find Grace and Louisa sitting on the chaise.

'We've given up,' Grace said in explanation.

'We aren't in the mood for work any more,' Louisa added.

'I'm sorry.'

'He's admitted it, hasn't he? He's such a goose.'

'I'll pay for what he's wasted – I have some savings. And I'll make sure he doesn't do it again.' Winnie felt like a mother who had lost control of her errant child.

Louisa clearly had the same idea. 'You're the mother of his child, not his mother,' she complained. 'He'll do it again, as sure as eggs is eggs.'

'He's promised me ...'

'Winnie, sometimes you have to be cruel to be kind. You're letting him walk all over you. You run after him, clear up after him and this is how he rewards you. Don't let him drag you down with him.'

'Leave her alone,' Grace interjected. 'She loves him.'

'Love is kind and respectful. This is making Winnie feel bad. I tell you, if Jason lied to me over drink, I'd kick him up the—' Grace giggled. Louisa stopped and glared. 'I was going to say the alley, not what you're thinking.'

'Jason ...' Winnie's voice faded. There was no point in arguing with Louisa – she was always right. 'I'm going to my room,' she snapped, and she turned and slammed the door behind her, just like Billy had, before storming up the stairs. Although it gave her a fleeting sense of satisfaction, it was short-lived, for just when she wanted some peace and quiet to think, Pamela woke up.

Chapter Seventeen

A Leopard Doesn't Change its Spots

'I let you down, Winnie,' Billy said the following morning. 'I'm goin' to change, I promise.' He was almost in tears, she realised when he continued, 'It's no excuse, but the drink 'elps block out the pain ... and bad memories.'

'I'm trying to understand.' She recalled the conversation she had overheard between Billy and Jason. 'I suppose we deal with adversity in different ways. If I have any troubles, I share them with my sisters, or go for a long walk,' she said, hoping to inspire him with alternative modes of distraction. 'Shall I go to the apothecary to see if there's anything else he can prescribe? I saw an advertisement for a sleeping potion in his shop window.'

'It's kind of you to offer, but I don't expect it's any different from takin' a nip o' gin, and probably a lot more expensive. No, Winnie, I'm goin' to 'ave to grin and bear it.'

'Oh Billy.' She put her arms around him and gave him a hug.

'Ah, that makes me feel a lot better,' he sighed.

'I'm available for a cuddle at any time,' she said, flirting with him.

'I'm goin' to ask Jason if 'e knows of any work ...'

'What happened at the boatyard? I thought Mr Christchurch might have something for you.'

'Ah, I meant to tell you.' Her heart sank as he went on, ''E wasn't too 'appy with the things I done, so 'e let me go. 'E only found me some work as a favour to Marlin.'

'I see.'

'But it will be all right. I'll find somethin' – I'll try one of the other boatyards, Elson's on Middle Street. I'm goin' to make my girl proud of me and earn enow for us to get married and move out.'

'I'm delighted to hear it,' she smiled. 'We'll succeed, if we both take a share in it.'

'I know. This 'as been a misstep on my part. I've seen the error of my ways.'

'I knew you would, Billy. I just wish ... I wish you hadn't had to go through so much, the loss of your friend ...'

He gazed at her. ''Ave you been eavesdroppin'?'

She nodded. No more lies.

'Let's say no more about it,' he said. 'We've agreed to start anew.'

Winnie's peace of mind lasted for over a sennight. Despite the cold weather making Billy's leg ache, he went out to do a little work for Jason now and again, although he'd limp home after an hour or two, with congbells dripping from his nose, and his fingers swollen and covered in tar. The luggers and fishing boats went out as usual, and whenever Louisa obtained enough goods and produce to make it worthwhile, they took the *Curlew* out provisioning and fished on their way back.

One morning towards the beginning of February when Billy was still abed, Louisa had Grace and Winnie packing the baskets in the hall. Pamela, red-faced and smiling, had pulled herself to her feet, and was moving along from one basket to the next, disturbing their handiwork.

'The brandy won't freeze, but we will.' Being tall and slight, Grace felt the cold worse than Winnie did. 'Perhaps I should stay at home and mind the baby.'

'I've arranged for Mrs Witherall to have her,' Louisa said.

Billy didn't bring in much of a wage, so Winnie felt doubly obliged to keep Louisa happy. She didn't mind making the largest contribution to the household, as long as Billy kept away from the drink.

There was a thud as an apple fell and rolled across the floorboards.

Pamela squealed with delight as a second fruit followed.

'No, darling,' Winnie said, amused. 'Will you look at her!'

'She is the sweetest, funniest baby,' Grace exclaimed, but Louisa wasn't quite so impressed with Pamela's new trick, even though the apples were already shrivelled and bruised from having been in storage over the winter.

'She's unpacking the baskets as soon as we've filled them,' she said. 'Winnie, take her next door, then we can get on. Cromwell will be waiting for us.'

Reluctantly, Winnie gathered Pamela up and went to knock at Mrs Witherall's door, stepping over the piles of dirt and ice, the remains of the recent snow.

'Morning,' she said, as the door opened very slowly to reveal their neighbour dressed in her nightgown and cap. She was holding a handkerchief to the side of her face.

'You look poorly,' Winnie said. 'I thought something was wrong. You should have said – I'd have cleared the pavement for you this morning.'

'I'm afraid I'm goin' to 'ave to let you down. It's one of my teeth. It blew up sudden during the small hours.'

'Can I do anything to help?'

'You're very kind, but Mrs Edwards 'as brought me some oil of cloves that she 'ad in the back of her cupboard. If it don't settle, I'm goin' to 'ave Mr Witherall pull it out.'

'Well, I hope it doesn't come to that. If you need anything, you know where we are.' She wished their neighbour a peaceful day and returned to the cottage to explain the situation to Louisa.

'It means that Grace will have to stay here after all,' Winnie said.

'No, no, no,' Louisa said. 'That won't do. Grace is our lucky charm – her flirtatiousness is far more effective than a horseshoe or rabbit's foot. We always sell more when she's out with us. Billy's at home, isn't he? He can mind her.'

'I don't know. He finds it tiresome and he won't like being teased about it if any of the other menfolk find out,' Winnie said.

'He is her father.' Louisa looked askance. 'Pa used to mind us – he used to take us out on the boat with him if Ma had business elsewhere. But it's too cold to take the littlun out with us today – she'll freeze to death.'

'I'll ask him then,' Winnie said.

'Tell him,' Louisa corrected her. 'Make haste. Grace, go and fetch Cromwell – he can help us carry the baskets.'

Billy was keen to mind Pamela, confessing that he appreciated an excuse not to venture out in the cold. Winnie worried that he would find it tedious, but he assured her that he would enjoy having their daughter to himself.

'It isn't often I get a look-in with all you women about,' he said, when she sat Pamela on the floor in his room, telling him that, until she returned home, he would have to have eyes in the back of his head. He laughed.

'Oh, get on with you. It isn't that 'ard to look after a littlun, especially such a sweet and innocent babe like our

241

Pamela. Look at 'er.' She was gazing adoringly at her father. 'Butter wouldn't melt in 'er mouth.'

Smiling, Winnie didn't enlighten him about her antics with the baskets.

The provisioning trip was not a great success. The cold seemed to have frozen everyone's purses firmly shut. The sisters returned with most of what they'd taken out with them, apart from a loaf of bread and some cheese that they'd eaten while they were fishing. The fish wouldn't bite either. Seeking deeper water, they had disappeared from the usual fishing grounds.

'I c-c-can't w-w-wait to be h-h-home,' Grace stuttered from her place at the tiller.

'Almost there,' Louisa said brightly, as Winnie and Cromwell took in the lugsail. 'Billy will have the fire blazing. Grace, have a care!'

Grace had overdone her touch on the tiller, bringing the *Curlew* in broadside to the beach. With great presence of mind, Cromwell grabbed an oar and pushed the boat away from the shingle.

'Straighten 'er up!' he called. 'Gently does it.'

The *Curlew*'s bow nudged the shore and a wave pushed her up the beach. Cromwell jumped out and attached a rope while the other shore boys came running down to help haul her up the slope. They had been lucky, Winnie thought. In a heavier sea, the boat would have been thrown sideways against the beach, causing damage that they could ill afford.

They unloaded the baskets and the bucket that contained the fruits of their labour – seven codling and two small crabs – before hurrying home. Winnie glanced up as a pair of seagulls began screaming at each other from the roofs on either side of the alley. Every chimney had a column of yellow-grey smoke rising from its pot, except for Compass Cottage.

'He must have let the fire go out,' she said aloud.

'He'd better not have,' Louisa said, opening the front door.

'Billy?' Winnie called, as she helped Grace drag the baskets inside.

'He isn't here,' Louisa said. 'His boots are missing.'

'It's freezing,' Grace shivered.

'I expect he's taken Pamela out for some fresh air,' Winnie said hopefully. 'She has driven him to distraction with her games.'

'He's been gone some time – the ashes are still warm, but not hot ...' Grace called from the kitchen. 'I've never felt so cold.'

'I'll light the fire, then go and look for him,' Winnie said, joining her. 'Sit down. I'm worried you're going to catch a chill now.'

'Billy won't stay out long with the weather like this,' Louisa contributed.

'Unless he's gone to the pot house, or ...' Winnie took the tinderbox from the mantel and knelt beside the fireplace, trying to coax a flame from the ashes, but it was too late. She built a new fire, using dried grass and small twigs from the basket, then used the flint from the box to create a spark to ignite the kindling. It began to smoke as delicate golden threads of fire spread through the dried grass. She added larger sticks, followed by a small log and then a larger one.

It took her a while to establish the fire, but the flicker of fear and anger that had ignited in her breast at the thought of where Billy might be, had burst into flame much more quickly.

By the time Grace was settled with some cognac and hot tea, her teeth no longer chattering, and her lips no longer blue, Winnie was desperate to find her errant lover. Surely he hadn't let her down again, not after all his promises, and not with the baby.

She waited, but when he wasn't back after another hour, she went to look for him.

'I don't know why you're going out again. He's old enough and ugly enough to look after himself,' Louisa said as Winnie put on her hat and coat. 'And he wouldn't do anything silly because he's minding Pamela.'

She wasn't sure what it was – a mother's intuition, or that Grace's mistake with the *Curlew* had unnerved her – but she felt that something was wrong and the sooner she put it right, the better.

She stepped outside the door and looked left and right along the alleyway, wondering where to start.

She began at Molly's where the invalid sailor, Mr Jones, was sitting hunched over the fire, his boots almost in the grate.

'Fancy seein' you 'ere, Winnie – we 'aven't seen you for ages. 'Ave you brought the babe? She'll be all grown up by the time we meet 'er again.'

Mrs Stickles's face was glowing like a furze beacon as she emerged from the kitchen.

'I've been very busy, spoiling Billy now that he's home. And that's the reason I'm here – I'm looking for him.'

'I 'aven't seen 'im, I'm afraid. Ask Mr Jones – 'e's been out and about. I invited 'im in for yesterday's leftovers and 'e's been sittin' there ever since. It's mortal cold out there.' Mrs Stickles looked past her. 'Mr Jones, 'ave you seen Billy Fleet anywhere?'

'What does 'e look like?'

''E 'as a pegleg, red hair and big ears,' Mrs Stickles contributed.

'He has the baby with him,' Winnie said.

'I can't say that I've seen 'im, but from your description, 'e should be pretty easy to spot. 'Ere, let me 'elp you find 'im, missus. It's the least I can do after your kindness to me.' He stood up and stretched, before picking up his tattered black greatcoat from the back of his chair.

'There's nobody else 'ere but me and Nancy,' Mrs Stickles said. 'I 'aven't seen 'ide nor 'air of Billy for a while. You'll probably find 'im natterin' to the old men at the capstan grounds.'

'Not in this weather,' Winnie pointed out as Mr Jones made a contribution to Mrs Stickles's purse in return for his meal, put on his coat and hat and collected his stick from the stand in the corner.

'There's always someone there, lookin' out to sea,' Mrs Stickles said.

'I'll go into town and work my way around the market and Golden Street,' Mr Jones offered. 'You carry on along as far as the Three Kings. If I find 'im, I'll tell 'im to come and find you.'

'No, tell him to go straight home – the baby will catch her death if she's outside any longer.' Would he really have taken Pamela to one of the local watering-holes? In a way, she hoped that he had, because at least the baby would be safe and warm.

When she arrived at the Waterman's Arms, Mrs Causton was serving behind the counter.

'What can I get you, miss?' she asked, raising one eyebrow.

'Nothing, thank you. I'm looking for Billy.'

'He's over there.' She nodded towards the table in the corner where the men looked up from their cards, and a shamefaced Billy tried to stand up. His false leg gave way and he sat down heavily again.

'Where's Pamela?' She rushed across to him. 'Where is the baby?'

'My love!' Billy wiped his mouth on his sleeve. 'Don't fret – I asked Mrs Causton to put 'er be'ind the bar for me.'

'You did what?' she exclaimed, turning towards Mrs Causton who spat on a glass and rubbed it with a cloth.

'He's mistaken. There's no babe here, my dear. He didn't bring her on this occasion.'

'You mean, he's brought her here before? Oh, no matter.' She grabbed Billy by one ear, pinching it tight. She could have cheerfully strangled him. 'Where is she? Tell me!'

Wincing, he grasped at her wrist, but she held on.

'Give a man a chance. You are confuddlin' me with your yellin' and shoutin'.'

'I'll yell as loud as I like.' She didn't care that she was making a scene. All she cared about was being reunited with Pamela. The poor little mite would be petrified – and hungry.

'I'll tell you … if you'll just loosen your grip …'

'Go on then.' She let go of his ear, watching the blood rush back into the rim.

'I gave her some pap like you said, dressed 'er and took 'er out – she wouldn't stop screamin' because she was missin' 'er ma. You've never seen anythin' like it – 'er face went dark, like a blueberry, and she wouldn't look at me, or listen to a word I said. You don't know what it's like, Winnie. I was afraid it would send me mad, and then I don't know …' He lowered his voice. 'I was afraid of what I might do to 'er in a temper, so I got out of there and then this terrible thirst took an 'old of me, and I thought I'll nip in and 'ave a drink, just a small one to soothe my nerves because they were right jangled.'

'I don't care about your nerves. Where is she? Where have you left her? If anything's happened to her, I'll never forgive you.'

246

'I went into the Rattlin' Cat …' Billy swayed as he grabbed and missed his crutch which was leaning against the wall.

Winnie didn't wait for him. She hitched up her skirts, ran outside and raced to the other tavern where she shoved the door open and burst in, sending the cats on the counter scattering, the bones on their collars rattling.

'Where is she?' The door banged back. 'Where is my daughter?'

'It's all right, Mama,' Isaiah said sarcastically. 'She's 'ere.' He walked through from the back room, with Pamela in his arms.

'If she's come to any harm, I'll—'

'What do you think I am? An ogre?' He touched Pamela's cheek. She whimpered.

'Give her to me,' Winnie said.

'Let Uncle Isaiah say farewell first.'

'You are not her uncle. She has nothing to do with you.'

'That isn't true – I've been lookin' after 'er as if she was my own flesh and blood while Billy who's supposed to be 'er lovin' pa, came in here, drank too much, then forgot 'er, despite claimin' she was *the apple of his eye*.'

'How can he drink when he has no money?'

''E asked for credit – I saw no reason not to give it to 'im.'

'What kind of landlord encourages a penniless father to drink himself senseless?'

He grinned. 'Billy didn't have no sense in the first place. I'm 'ere to make a profit – for myself and my staff, and for the benefit of my patrons. I can't afford to keep the fires burning for 'em out of charity.'

Winnie noticed the dog slinking towards Isaiah then sitting down at his feet, strings of drool dangling from its jowls. She snatched the baby and pulled her close, pressing

247

her lips to her hair. She smelled different, violated by the stench of beer and baccy, smoke and musk.

'Billy won't be setting foot in here again,' she said, as on cue, Billy came falling through the door to surprise followed by laughter.

'You've found 'er,' he said, looking up from the floor, his crutch still in his hand.

'Either you come home with me now or you don't come back!'

'Oh, I do like a domestic,' someone said. 'She's got you right under the thumb, Pegleg. You'll be volunteerin' for the navy next.'

''Elp me up, Winnie,' he muttered. 'Give us an 'and.'

Disappointed and devastated, she stared at him, torn between helping him – because she still loved him, no matter what – and leaving him there as punishment for what he'd done to her and Pamela. It was time to accept that her lover, the man she was going to marry, was a drunk.

'I can't help you any more,' she said, defeated. 'You'll have to help yourself.'

She turned and walked away with the baby like a lead weight in her arms, but she held her head high.

'How could he do that to you?' she murmured. 'Calls himself a father, does he? I'm never going to let you out of my sight again, I promise.'

As she made her way along Cockle Swamp Alley, she noticed Mr Jones shuffling towards her, his hand raised.

'Ah, missus. You 'ave found the child!'

'Yes, thank you,' she said.

'And Billy?'

She nodded, her eyes pricking with tears.

'That's grand,' he said. 'All's well that ends well.'

Knowing that it wasn't the end of the matter, Winnie let herself into the house. Her instinct was to run upstairs and hide, but she knew she would have to face her sisters sooner rather than later.

'Ah, you've found her,' Grace said when Winnie entered the kitchen where a draught of hot, muggy air enveloped her. 'I've made a start on supper for you.' Winnie barely noticed the pot of stew bubbling over the fire. She placed a cloth on the table and laid Pamela on top of it, then proceeded to strip off her clothes, checking every inch of her skin for any spots or bruising.

'What are you doing?' Grace asked.

'I want to be sure that she's come to no harm.' Winnie explained how Billy had left her with Isaiah at the tavern. 'He was so addled with drink, he forgot her. Louisa was right. I can't make any more excuses for him.'

'Are you taking my name in vain?' Louisa said, walking into the room with a pile of laundry in her arms. She placed it on the other end of the table. The clothes were stiff, frozen into shape by the wintry weather. 'What's Billy done now? Where is he, for that matter?'

Winnie had to explain all over again as her elder sister stared at Pamela.

'The baby,' Louisa said. 'Something isn't right.'

Winnie's skin pricked with antagonism. She was Pamela's mother – she'd know if there was something wrong. But she looked again.

'Her breathing – it's always quick and shallow, but it's more obvious today,' Louisa said.

Winnie gazed at the baby's chest. As her belly hollowed out below her ribcage, she could hear a faint whistle.

'She has caught a chill,' she cried in horror. 'Grace, fetch her crib and blankets. I'm not letting her sleep upstairs. She'll stay here by the fire so I can watch her.' This was Billy's fault, she thought as she picked Pamela up and held her close. The whistle was louder, coming with each breath, and her cheeks were an unnatural, dusky pink. Pamela closed her eyes and rested her head against her mother's shoulder, her mouth open and drooling.

'I don't think I can bear it.' Winnie began to cry.

'It's only a chill.' Louisa tried to reassure her. 'We'll send for Doctor Audley if it gets any worse.'

'But he's no good with children – everybody says so. Oh, what has Isaiah done to her?'

'It's Billy's fault. Isaiah's done you a favour, looking after her for you, Winnie,' Grace said, still in the room. 'He would never harm her. He loves all God's creatures. He adores his dog. I've seen him plant kisses on its head when he thinks no one is watching. As for the cats, he is generally kind to them, except when they get under his feet.'

'What about the kittens?' Louisa said. 'He is cruel to them.'

'He is not. He sends them out to farms all over Kent to keep the rats down.'

'That's what he's told you. I know for a fact that he puts them in a weighted sack and drowns them at sea.'

'I don't believe you,' Grace said sharply. 'Louisa, you'll have to help me with the crib – it's too heavy for me to lift down the stairs.'

Her sisters set up the crib in the corner of the kitchen, making sure it was away from any draughts. Winnie dressed Pamela in her nightgown and put her down.

'Louisa, would you mind asking Mrs Witherall to come around?' she asked. 'I need her advice.'

'I'm not sure she'll be up to it, but I'll go and see,' Louisa said.

Mrs Witherall accompanied Louisa to the cottage, her curiosity apparently getting the better of her.

'I hope you can help me,' Winnie said. 'How are you?'

'Much better, thank you. Mr Witherall took a set of pliers to my bad tooth, effectin' an instant cure. What's wrong with the littlun?'

'She has a fever and I don't know how to help her.'

'Keep 'er well wrapped up. There's no need to remind you to close the windows in this weather. Make sure she as plenty to drink: barley water or chicken broth. Although the provision of adequate sustenance is important in this situation, the most essential tonic is a mother's love. Watch over the poor little scrap, Winnie. And pray for her.'

Filled with guilt for not having been at home to protect her, and furious with Billy for letting her down, Winnie sat at the table and wept.

'Oh dear, oh dear,' Mrs Witherall said. 'Why don't you go and get some rest? Your sisters and I will watch over 'er.'

'I won't sleep a wink – I won't leave her side until she's well again.'

Mrs Witherall took her leave after an hour, and not long afterwards, Billy arrived.

'By rights, we shouldn't let you in after what you've done.' Winnie heard Louisa scolding him in the hall.

'I'm 'ere because of Pamela. 'Ow is she?' He pushed his way into the kitchen where Winnie and Grace looked up from watching over her as she slept fitfully between bouts of coughing. He stopped at the side of the crib. 'It's bad, isn't it? Oh Lord, what 'ave I done?' The realisation that he had caused his daughter terrible harm seemed to have sobered him up.

'She has taken a chill,' Winnie said bitterly. 'When you left her behind at the tavern, Isaiah must have put her in a draughty spot while he waited for one of us to go back for her.'

'I am the worst father anybody could 'ave. What can I do to make 'er better?'

Louisa stepped in. 'Billy, you are like a brother to me and Grace, and our parents would have wanted us to do our best for you, but this can't go on. You have outstayed your welcome.'

Billy stood there, open-mouthed.

'You are turfin' me out?'

'No, Louisa. Can we talk about it?' Winnie interrupted.

'We've given him every opportunity to give up the drink, but he can't help himself. It's all very well trying to protect him, but what about us? One slip of the tongue when he's in his cups and he'll have the Customs men here, searching the house. If he mentions our other lines of work in the taverns or on the beach, he'll put you and the rest of us in mortal danger.'

Winnie understood. With the guinea run planned for March, there was more at stake than ever. Jason had talked of a family of brothers – bankers who, having invested in gold from the East India Company, were keen to loan it. to both the French and English armies on the guarantee that the victor would honour the debts of the vanquished. Either way, the bankers couldn't lose, but the smugglers were under considerable threat when carrying what was rumoured to be up to thirty thousand guineas on each trip across the Channel. A guinea was worth twenty-one shillings in England, and thirty shillings in France.

'You and Pamela can stay, but Billy must find lodgings elsewhere.' Louisa looked down her nose at him, her expression a mix of annoyance and compassion. 'We're all fond of you, but your presence has become a liability. My husband has supported you and helped you get work. He's even put himself out to obtain a false limb for you – it was no mean feat, finding someone to make one to fit. It isn't fair to expect him to keep carrying you. We have our own burdens ...' She smiled suddenly and touched her belly. 'I have hopes that soon we will have our own child.'

'I-I-I don't know what to say,' Billy said.

'It doesn't matter now,' Louisa said briskly. 'You haven't helped your cause by your tardiness in making an honest woman of my sister. A gentleman with any decency would have put her reputation and feelings ahead of anything and married her.'

'Perhaps I 'ave been wallowin'.' He hung his head. 'I'm truly sorry, and I'm sayin' that even though I know it's too late to change your mind.'

'Please, Louisa. Give him one more chance,' Winnie begged. 'Let him stay until after the next run and then we'll go – I'll have the money by then to set up home.'

'You're going to support this lazy good-for-nothing?' Louisa exclaimed. 'It's not right.'

'If he goes, then we go too,' Winnie said. 'I mean it.'

Louisa thought for a while. 'I can't have it on my conscience to allow you and Pamela to leave with Billy. It isn't right – she has a fever. You can't drag her out into the night air and off to some poky room somewhere – it'll finish her off.'

Louisa had a point, Winnie thought, but she was torn.

'I won't stay without him,' she said stubbornly.

Louisa had to give in. 'Then he can stay for now, but I'll be watching him like a hawk. Have you got that, Billy?'

'Yes, thank you,' he muttered. 'I'll be eternally grateful.'

Winnie thanked Louisa for letting him stay.

'It's only until after the run,' she confirmed. 'He won't stop drinking. A leopard doesn't change its spots.'

After her sisters had retired to bed, Winnie stayed up in the kitchen with Billy and the baby. Pamela grunted and snuffled in her crib, perspiration running down her forehead.

'Would she be better sitting up?' Billy asked.

'What do you know about it?' Winnie replied snappily.

'While I was away, the ship's doctor treated one of the sailors for a right graveyarder of a cough. 'E made 'im sit up – 'e said it would 'elp clear 'is chest. He gave 'im a concoction of 'oney, rum and lime to drink.'

'You can't give our daughter rum.'

'I'll go and get some milk and 'oney – there's no 'arm in tryin' it.' Without waiting for her response, Billy fetched the mixture, warmed in a bowl, by which time, Winnie had sat the baby up on her lap. Pamela cried and coughed, but after a spoonful of her father's medicine, she settled.

'You see,' Billy said. 'I'm goin' to do everythin' in my power to make 'er well again.'

Two days and two nights passed. Pamela's condition was about the same. Sometimes Winnie thought she was rallying, and sometimes she thought she was worse, unable to take milk and honey, or sweetened tea for coughing. Early in the morning of the third day, she took her from her crib in the kitchen and carried her upstairs to the landing where the door to Billy's room was open.

'Winnie? Is that you?' she heard him say. ''Ow is she?'

Winnie pressed her lips to Pamela's fevered forehead. 'She's worse. Didn't you hear her coughing all night?'

'I'm sorry.'

She stepped into his room. 'I'm going to speak to the vicar.'

Slowly, he got to his feet, the coverlet around his waist, then he moved towards her, his eyes on the baby.

'The poor little mite,' he sighed. 'Is she really bad?'

'Billy, I think she's going to die ...' Winnie's voice cracked.

'Let me come with you.'

'No.' She regretted having convinced Louisa to let him stay. She blamed herself for not challenging him over the drinking sooner, because she had felt sorry for him. 'I don't want to have anything to do with you. You disgust me.'

'I'll go to the vicar for you then,' he said. 'You stay 'ere.'

'I don't trust you. If I want something done, I have to do it myself.'

'Then let me mind our daughter ...'

'I can't leave her with you, not after last time. Grace will look after her. You can't look after yourself, let alone a child.' She could hardly bear to leave her, not for a minute, but this was a crisis of her own making, and it was up to her to see if she could persuade Reverend North to help them before it was too late.

Winnie went to St George's but the vicar wasn't there, so she walked all the way to St Leonard's. She pushed the church door open and stepped inside. Her footsteps echoed on the stone floor as she made her way to one of the pews, where she knelt to pray that Reverend North would make an appearance.

'Good day, Miss Lennicker.' She turned and saw him emerging from the sacristy. 'I'm sorry for disturbing you. Would you like me to pray with you?'

'I'm not sure, vicar,' she said, getting up.

'Is there anything I can help you with? How is your child?'

'That's just it,' she said, dashing away a sudden tear. 'She's taken a chill. She's very sick and I was wondering if there was any chance of having her baptised so she can be received into the church before—'

'You are afraid for her life?'

Winnie nodded. 'I realise there are difficulties ...'

'You are not yet married, that's true, but it is possible. The parent may be recorded as a spinster of this parish and the child as base born. This will allow her to be christened and – should God admit her to the glory of Heaven – she can be buried in consecrated ground. It is hard to speak of, but you have done right by your daughter in coming here.'

'How soon can it be done?' she asked.

'I can call at your home and carry out a private ceremony as early as this afternoon. Is that convenient?'

'Yes, thank you.'

'Your family have always been very generous to the church. I have no doubt that they will continue in the same vein. One more suggestion on my part, though – I would advise you to apply your mind to marriage now that Mr Fleet is back. Failing that, it would be wise to deprive yourself of the power of further propagation. I shall see you at two o'clock sharp.'

'I'm very grateful. Now I must hurry back to her.'

'Of course. A child needs its mother at a time such as this.'

Distraught and ashamed, Winnie didn't stop to listen to his farewell. She ran home where she washed Pamela's face and hands and wrapped her in a clean gown. Listening to the rattle coming from the baby's chest, she spooned honey and cooled water into her mouth.

'Reverend North is coming to baptise her,' she said as Grace looked down at the baby.

'I'll fetch Billy,' Grace said. 'You probably don't want him here, but it's important. Perhaps the vicar's prayers will put him back on the straight and narrow. Then I'll help you with your hair.'

Winnie thanked her sister, who went to inform Billy and Louisa of the vicar's imminent arrival before she brushed Winnie's hair, plaited it and put it up. Winnie waited in the parlour with Pamela in her arms, rocking her gently, stroking her blotchy cheeks, and begging her to fight for her life with the strength she had left.

'I'd do anything to make you better,' she whispered.

'Welcome, Reverend North.' She heard Louisa greet the vicar and then he came into the room, accompanied by her sisters and Billy, who had put on his Sunday best for the occasion. As Pamela started to cough again, her small frame shaking, Billy could hardly meet Winnie's eye.

She was fading, Winnie thought, her heart breaking. The christening would be only just in time ...

Reverend North took a vial from his robes and sprinkled the contents on to Pamela's forehead.

'I baptise you, Pamela Jane Lennicker, in the name of the Father, the Son and the Holy Spirit.' He paused before going on, 'Let us pray.'

Unable to speak and with tears running down her cheeks, Winnie bowed her head, listening to the others saying the Lord's Prayer. Billy's voice was low and filled with contrition. As they said the final 'Amen', Winnie reached out and touched his arm to comfort him, realising that he was in as much pain as she was.

Chapter Eighteen

A False Dawn

Winnie watched over Pamela day and night. On the morning of the fifth day, the child's skin lost its mottled heat and her cough diminished, and Winnie dared to hope that she might be past the worst.

'She is much improved.' Grace smiled when she found Winnie feeding her milk and a dry biscuit at the table in the kitchen. 'Have you told Billy? He's been worried sick.'

'I haven't seen him yet. What's the layabout doing?' She was half shamming when she said this, aware that he had at least been out and about since he'd left the baby at the Rattling Cat.

'I can't say. I promised ...'

'You are in league with him now,' Winnie said. 'It isn't right that you protect him.'

'You misjudge him,' Grace responded. 'You'll find out what he's been up to soon enough. He'll be home at dusk.'

When dusk fell, there was no sign of Billy and Winnie's faint sense of optimism that he was bringing good news faded.

'Be patient,' Grace said, and within an hour, he arrived home. Winnie heard him taking off his boots and oilskins in the hall before he burst into the kitchen, beaming from ear to ear.

'How is the baby?' he asked. 'I suppose it'll soon be time to stop callin' 'er a baby.'

'She'll be known as the baby of the family until another littlun comes along,' Winnie smiled. 'Anyway, you can see for yourself.' She stepped aside to show him Pamela sitting on a blanket on the floor, playing with a wooden rattle. When she saw her father, she raised her arms.

'Ah, she wants you to pick her up,' Winnie said.

'First things first. I have somethin' for you.'

Pamela coughed.

'Oh no,' Winnie exclaimed as Pamela puffed her cheeks, grimaced and coughed again, three times over. 'You poor little thing. Come to Mama.'

'No.' Grace stayed her with a hand on her arm. 'She isn't having a relapse – she is gammoning you.'

'Our sweet, innocent daughter?' Billy said. ''Ow can that be?'

'She's worked out that every time she coughs, someone pays her attention.' Grace chuckled. 'Let me have her.' Whisking her up, she took Pamela across to the pantry and collected an apple from the crate they were keeping for Christmas. 'I will cut this up for you.'

'It is rather shocking that she manages to be so devilish at this tender age,' Winnie said, confident that Grace's theory was correct.

'Like father, like daughter,' Billy grinned.

'Why are you so cheerful?' Winnie asked.

'Close your eyes and 'old out your 'and. No cheatin'.'

She did as he bade her, hearing the chink of coins as a purse landed in her palm.

'My wages from Mr Elson's boatyard,' he said triumphantly, as she opened her eyes. 'Every penny.'

'Oh Billy, I'm so proud of you,' she cried.

'It will be the same every week from now on. I'm truly sorry for what I've put you through, and to prove my love to you and Pamela, I've made a vow never to drink again.'

'Not even a drop of milk and brandy?'

'It's become clear to me that if I take one drink, I 'ave to 'ave another, and another until I'm ape-drunk and no use to anyone. I will never touch the stuff again. I promise you, on our daughter's life. What's more, you give Louisa my keep out of this and put the rest by, because I don't want to wait any longer. I've been to see Reverend North at St George's – that's why I was delayed. 'E's agreed to post the banns for our marriage ... I 'ope I 'aven't overstepped the mark.'

'Where will we live?' Winnie asked.

'We'll find lodgin's – it won't be much, a room or a couple o' rooms, but it will be our 'ome. What do you say?'

'It's what I've dreamed of for a very long time,' she said, a lump in her throat.

'I've worked it out. We can be married as soon as the next run is over and done with.'

Winnie threw her arms around his neck and showered him with kisses.

'Hey, not until you're husband and wife,' Grace commented. Blushing, Winnie took a step back. 'Congratulations. You deserve it. You've both waited long enough.'

'Thank you, Grace. We'll still see you all the time,' Winnie said.

'Excuse me. Not *all* the time,' Billy grinned. 'We'll live nearby so you can mind Pamela now and again.'

'Which gown will you wear?' Grace asked.

'The pink one,' Winnie said.

'I'll sew on some ribbons for you. Perhaps Louisa can be persuaded to buy you some slippers like the ones she had for her wedding.' Grace pressed her finger to her lips, thinking for a moment. 'Who will come to the wedding breakfast?'

'I haven't had a chance to think about it, but it will be a very small affair,' Winnie said.

'There's lots to arrange,' Grace said, and Winnie smiled to herself because her sister couldn't have been more excited than if it had been her own marriage.

'I'll let you ladies continue with your talk of gowns and slippers.' Billy smiled wryly. 'I'm goin' to sit down and rest my leg for a while before supper.' He sat down and removed his false limb, unbuckling the leather straps and leaning it against his chair. 'That's better.'

Billy kept to his word for another week, going diligently to work every day, but towards the end of the third sennight in February, he returned home early.

'Why are you back so soon?' Winnie was dragging a basket of logs into the kitchen when Billy came charging in, his boots leaving sandy footprints across the floor. 'How many times do I have to—'

'Don't worry about that. Mr Elson's given us the rest of the day off. Nobody can do nothin'.' He picked Pamela out of her highchair and rested her on his hip where she giggled and tugged at his hair.

'The yard has closed down?'

'No!' Billy was laughing, red-faced with sheer happiness and excitement. 'Louisa, Grace, come 'ere! I 'ave news!'

'What is it?' Louisa appeared from the hang, her apron spangling with fish scales, and Grace came in from outside where she'd been hanging out the laundry, her hands blotchy with cold.

'You'll never guess – Old Boney's dead and gorn!' Billy punched the air.

'Would you mind repeating that?' Grace asked.

'It's true. Napoleon is dead. Port Admiral Folet – the gentleman who commands the Royal Naval ships stationed in the Downs – 'as received a letter from a lieutenant colonel and aide-de-camp to Lord Cathcart. It says that a ship from Calais called *L'Aigle* 'as landed 'im near Dover. 'E's on 'is way to London to bring the news that the allies have obtained their final victory in Paris.'

'Go on,' Winnie said, almost overwhelmed with excitement.

'Old Boney was overtaken by a group of Sachen's Cossacks – they 'eld 'im up and killed 'im, then divided 'is body between 'em. The white cockade is on display all over France to celebrate the peace. Oh, I wish Mr and Mrs Lennicker 'ad lived to see this day.'

'Thank the Lord,' Winnie sighed. 'The war with France is over.'

'We are going to have the greatest celebrations anyone has ever seen,' Grace said.

'Louisa, are you all right? The news seems to have left you speechless,' Winnie observed.

'It has rather taken the wind out of my sails. It's something we've yearned for, yet ...' she frowned '... this alters all our plans.'

'For the better,' Winnie said, taking Grace's hands and dancing in circles until they were out of breath. She wouldn't have to go to Gravelines and meet with Madame again. There would be no more guinea runs.

'We'll be dependent on hovelling and smuggling goods – there'll be no way of making our fortune from gold,' Louisa went on.

'Hark,' said Grace. They stood stock-still and listened to the crescendo of sound rising from the streets: shouting, laughter, the boom of a cannon and banging of drums.

The people of the town were on the march, called together by a hue and cry to revel in their good fortune.

The celebrations in Deal went on all day and long into the night. When it was deemed too cold to dance on the beach, the townsfolk retreated to the taverns and their neighbours' houses to talk of their hopes and dreams for the future now that the threat from the erstwhile Emperor of France was over and the French monarchy was about to be restored.

Winnie was a little sorry that she wouldn't have her moment of glory or earn a fortune from delivering despatches, but it was more than made up for by the fact the little upstart had received his just deserts. Her nightmares of the bogeyman sailing across the water to invade England were over. What was more, her dreams of leaving the free trade seemed closer to coming true, because without Old Boney, the blockade on French goods would be overturned, making the smugglers' role far less lucrative than before.

As for Billy, although she half expected him to return home the worse for wear, he came back to the cottage in the early hours as sober as a judge.

However, their joy was short-lived.

The following day, Billy came home from Elson's with tears in his eyes.

'There's been a terr'ble mistake,' he began. 'Old Boney isn't dead. Far from it – 'e's alive and kickin'.'

Winnie's heart plummeted.

'It was an 'oax. A sham,' he went on bitterly, his arm around her shoulders. 'The gentleman who wrote the letter is one Charles Random de Berenger. 'E was sitting in the Ship at Dover, dressed in a military cap and scarlet uniform, supping ale as 'e scribed the false missive, but 'e's no officer. 'E 'as nothin' to do with the military.'

'Why would anyone do that?' Winnie was in tears. Even the baby was silent, apparently overwhelmed by the enormity of the deception. 'What is the point?'

''E was doin' it for money. 'E thought to create a rumour that would inflate the value of government securities. I 'ad to ask Mr Elson what that meant, and 'e explained that if the gentlemen who invest in stocks and shares believed that there was going to be peace, they would buy more, thus raisin' the prices. The criminal syndicate of which Mr de Berenger was a part, bought up government bonds in advance of sendin' out the letter.'

'At the lower price?' Winnie said.

'That's right. When the London Stock Exchange opened the other day, the price of government bonds went up and the fraudsmen sold their bonds for 'uge profits. After the rumour was proved to be untrue, the prices slumped again. De Berenger and his associates have made a vast fortune from gammonin' the Stock Exchange.'

'One has to admire their nerve,' Louisa said, joining in.

'It is too much,' Winnie argued. 'It is all very well making money from the rich to help the poor, but to have deceived us ordinary people to line their own pockets … I hope they are caught and brought to justice.'

'The authorities already 'ave the name of the writer of the letter. I don't think it will take 'em long to identify the rest of the culprits,' Billy said.

'I hope they find them – I thought this was my way out of the free trade.'

They sat up in the parlour, Billy resting his head in Winnie's lap, and Louisa didn't say anything about them stopping up late when she found them asleep there the next morning. The atmosphere was subdued.

'Life must go on,' Louisa kept saying and although it grieved her, Winnie couldn't help thinking that her elder sister was pleased that the war wasn't yet over.

Winnie couldn't be sore for ever, because the bright spring days were on their way and she had her wedding to look forward to. March blustered in, following a bitterly cold February. The snowdrops had faded and the windflowers were beginning to make an appearance in the chestnut wood near the mill where Winnie sometimes took Pamela, picking up sticks for the fire and hiding them under her blankets in the handcart. The Brockmans owned the land and, although they didn't mind her walking there, they were precious about their firewood, even though all she ever collected was a few twigs. She felt that Abel owed her for disturbing her peace of mind with his proposal anyway.

There was still talk of the scandalous fabrication of Napoleon's death, and seven of the men responsible had been caught. According to rumour, however, the authorities were still searching for one more.

On a clear afternoon, Winnie was hurrying back from the market with ingredients for a mutton stew when she decided to divert to the beach for a little peace and quiet, taking advantage of the fact that Grace was minding Pamela for a while. Billy – she hoped – was working on the guinea boat which was berthed in one of the channels among the sandhills. With her basket over her arm, she strolled along past the hut that Pa had built from discarded boat timbers to provide shelter and space for storage. She paused for a moment, the better to recall his presence and the days she and her sisters had spent out fishing with him when they were very young.

'Psst.'

Winnie almost jumped out of her skin.

'Who is it?' she said urgently, glancing along the shingle to check that she wasn't alone. 'Show yourself,' she added, noticing that some of the shore boys were kicking a pig's bladder around. 'I said show yourself!'

'Miss ... Mademoiselle ...' said a disembodied voice with an accent that made Winnie's skin prick with suspicion.

'Who are you? What is your name?' she asked, her imagination running wild. Had her biggest fear come true? Had Napoleon and his army invaded England's shores?

'Pierre,' came the voice. '*Aidez-nous*. Please, my friend needs help.'

Summoning her wits, she turned to face the hut. She and Billy had often hidden in there among the detritus of Pa's fishing trips: tools; leaky buckets; fragments of old nets and floats. She heard the wooden door creak and saw a dark crack appear.

'*Ici. Nous sommes* ... over here, miss. We won't harm you. Nor do we expect you to put yourself out to give us some assistance, but my friend here – he is very sick.' The voice wavered. 'I don't know what I can do.'

'How do I know that you aren't shamming me?' Winnie hoped that the shore boys wouldn't spot her talking to herself.

'It's a fair question. Look, I have something for you.' A hand appeared, dangling a pocket watch from a chain. 'Take it.'

'I can't possibly accept,' she said firmly. 'You are a stranger to me. And a Frenchman, and we are at war. I can't have anything to do with you.'

'I beg you to take it as proof that we are speaking in good faith, and as a reminder that for my companion, time is running out.'

'How do you know I won't walk away with it?' She frowned.

'We have nothing to lose. If you should decide to help us, it is only a small part of the reward you will receive for our safe deliverance. If not, my friend will die on this godforsaken English beach.'

Was he trying to blackmail her? It sounded like it, but if he was telling the truth, she couldn't have it on her conscience to walk away.

She stepped forward and pulled the door ajar to find two men looking up at her, their complexions pale and their brows deeply lined. She guessed that the speaker, Pierre, was the gentleman who was kneeling beside his sickly friend, holding his hand. His friend was lying on his side, looking gaunt.

'You see,' Pierre said, 'we are *prisonniers de guerre* ...'

'You are on the run?'

He nodded. 'We made it this far, but now we are *dans la merde*. We can't travel any further without assistance.'

Winnie didn't know what to do. They were the enemy, Old Boney's men. It went against her principles to offer them help. What was to stop them returning to France and rejoining their fight against the English? Having expected to see wickedness pooling in Pierre's dark eyes and hear evil pouring from his mouth, she was surprised to find that he seemed very much like an ordinary gentleman.

The sick man coughed. From his appearance, there seemed little chance that he would ever take up arms again.

'What's wrong with him?' Winnie asked.

'He is suffering from consumption. Have you heard of it?'

She nodded.

'The disease causes an inevitable decline. My friend's wish is to see his dear wife and son before he dies, but I fear it may already be too late. I'm an intelligent man and I've extricated myself from many a scrape before, but I can't see what I can do. I don't want to keep moving him, yet we can't stay in one place for long. My friend holds high office, being an admiral of the French fleet, so they will be looking for us; our parole agent; the commissioners; the – how you say – Bow Street Runners.'

Winnie hated the French, thanks to Napoleon, yet she had warmed to Pierre for his compassion towards his friend and his gentle manner. She thought of the Admiral's wife and son, and the dying husband and father. Wasn't it wrong to prevent their very last meeting, no matter who they were and what they had done? As well as the fire and brimstone, Reverend North preached of the virtues of charity and forgiveness. Didn't he say to her that she should follow her heart? But she was torn because she knew that aiding and abetting escaped prisoners of war was an offence against the law, and if she was caught, she would end up in gaol.

'I will help you,' she said eventually, 'if you give me the watch as security.'

'You are an angel, miss.' Pierre handed her the watch, grasping her hand at the same time. 'You will be rewarded.'

'I don't know how much it will cost for your passage across the Channel,' she said, thinking that Jason would see it as an opportunity to make a profit.

'I am a wealthy man, and I will honour any debts that my friend and I accrue.'

'I'm sorry, missus.' Cromwell came running up to her. She closed the door quickly and turned to find the pig's bladder that the shore boys were playing with, at her feet.

He pushed it aside with his toe. 'Who are you talkin' to?' He eyed her curiously.

'To myself – you must think I'm slightly touched.'

'No,' he said, but she could tell he was lying.

'Good day, Cromwell.'

'If you're lookin' for the extra floats for the nets, they're on the shelf in the back of the 'ut.' He made to step past her. 'I'll show yer.'

'Don't! Leave it to me. I'll find them when we need them.' Now he really did think she'd gone mad, she thought with a wry smile, but then he was suddenly distracted by a shout from the water.

'It's the *Whimbrel*. Ahoy there!' He picked up the bladder, tucked it under his arm and ran down the slope, following the other boys.

Winnie pulled the door ajar. 'Wait here. I'll be back as soon as I can. Are you hungry?'

Pierre nodded. 'My friend hasn't eaten for three days.'

'I'll see what I can do about that.'

Jason and his crew were beaching the *Whimbrel* and the shore boys prepared to pull her up the beach. Was she doing the right thing? Would she be putting Pamela and her sisters, and Billy and Jason, in danger with what she was asking of them? She had been trying to get away from the lies and deception of the free trade, yet now she found herself considering breaking the law again.

Out of compassion, she would stand up for the escaped prisoners and beg her family to help them. Then she wondered if she was more like her sister than she'd realised, because she saw that there was a chance of making some money out of it. If Pierre was telling the truth, she might earn enough to get her own little family away from smuggling. It would be ironic if she could find her way out of the free trade by entering fully into the spirit of it.

Seeing that it would be a while before Jason returned to the cottage, Winnie fetched two portions of pie and ale from the pot house, borrowing a basket to carry them in.

'I didn't expect to see you,' Mrs Stickles said.

'I thought that Billy and I would treat ourselves.' She smiled, but the familiar sense of fear – of being found out – began to creep up on her.

On arriving back at the beach, she ran into Mr Witherall making his way home from the capstan grounds.

'Where are you off to? It's gettin' late,' he said.

'I'm going to meet Billy.'

'You're a brave one to go wanderin' through the sand'ills on your own.' He eyed her quizzically. 'Billy's a grown lad – he can find 'is own way 'ome. Winnie, I don't want to alarm you, but there's a rumour about some froggies bein' in the area. You know what I mean, garlic eaters.' Grimacing, he went on, 'As you must 'ave 'eard, there are several agents willin' to take escaped prisoners of war from 'ere to Gravelines for a fee. Those who leave their parole towns or manage to get off the 'ulks, make their way 'ere to Deal and Dover, 'opin' to get back to France.'

'I don't see what that has to do with me.'

'They are men whom desperation 'as made dangerous. They'll rob anybody for their money, clothes ... I thought you would 'ave l'arned your lesson after what 'appened to you. There's safety in numbers. If you insist on goin' to meet Billy, let me come with you.'

This was the last thing she needed.

'I promise I won't walk into the sandhills alone,' she said. 'I'll wait for Billy at the Three Kings – I have a friend there, one of the chambermaids. Go home, Mr Witherall. Mrs Witherall will be waiting for you.'

Having convinced him she would be safe, she watched him go, before returning to the hut on the beach. She knocked softly on the door and pushed it open.

'Take this,' she whispered. 'I'll be back later.'

'Come to Mama,' she said, as Pamela grinned and held out her arms from her chair in the kitchen when Winnie returned home. 'Has she been good, Grace?'

'She's been angelic,' Grace smiled. 'Where have you been, though? You've been ages.'

'I'm 'ome,' she heard Billy call before he joined them in the kitchen, closely followed by Jason and then Louisa.

'Winnie, you haven't told me what delayed you. You left me here holding the baby.'

'I saw Mrs Stickles on the way back,' Billy said. 'She told me you'd bought pie for supper.'

'I didn't ... I mean, I didn't buy them for supper.'

'You haven't been spending the housekeeping on waifs and strays again? Oh, Winnie, really! This has to stop,' Louisa exclaimed. 'My husband goes out almost every day for his hard-earned living. It isn't fair that you squander it.'

'Your sister is kind-hearted to a fault,' Jason said. 'I think we should give her a little latitude when it comes to decidin' who deserves our charity.' Winnie thought that he looked a little embarrassed. 'I like to believe that we can contribute in a small way to the welfare of man- and womankind.'

'Perhaps you should have enlightened me about your aspirations of becoming a philanthropist before,' Louisa grumbled.

'I have something to say—' Winnie began.

'"I'm sorry" would be a good place to start.'

'I'm not going to apologise for the investment I made in pies and ale. They were for an excellent cause, as I'm

271

sure you will all agree after you've heard my story. When I was walking along the beach, I heard a voice coming from the hut and I found a pair of Frenchmen, one who claims to be wealthy, the other an admiral whose dying wish is to return home to see his family one last time.'

'This is quite a tale,' Louisa said lightly.

'They're afraid that there are people looking for them – they need a safe place to shelter until they can find someone willing to take them across the Channel. It won't be long before Jason takes the guinea boat back to Gravelines with the next cargo of gold – I thought that these men could travel with him.'

'Why are you helping them? You hate the French,' Grace said.

'They are people like us, caught up in the war and far away from home.'

'It's too dangerous,' Louisa said. 'If we are found out for taking them in, not only will they be arrested, but we will too. I thought you'd had enough of taking risks.'

'They'll pay for the journey – there is a profit to be had.'

'We don't know these men. There's no guarantee that they'll ever cough up. The only way I'd consider it is if we could get the money up front,' Jason said.

'That isn't possible. They can't pay us until they reach France.'

'Oh, I wasn't born yesterday,' Louisa sighed. 'They have sucked you in with a sob story.'

'They are wealthy men.' Winnie took the watch from the basket and handed it to Jason. 'They gave me this to prove their intent.'

'Let me see.' Jason's eyes lit up as he examined the timepiece, opening the back and studying the movement. 'This is very fine, very fine indeed. Look at the quality of the filigree. It is the work of a Parisian or Swiss craftsman. Keep it in your care for now.' He handed it back to her.

'He could have stolen it,' Louisa said. 'Remember our motto: trust no one.'

'We should meet these men,' Jason decided. 'We can make a judgement then.'

'What if they are spies?' Louisa persisted. 'Or would-be thieves, planning a way of stealing the gold we've been entrusted with? What if they attract the attention of a privateer? Or the two of them try to overwhelm you and the crew when you're out on the water? It's a bad idea. I don't like it at all.'

'There are others who make a tidy sum from aidin' the escape of French prisoners, especially officers,' Jason said. 'I'm surprised at you encouragin' this, Winnie, knowin' of your moral stance and dislike of deception and law-breakin'.'

'I know I said I wanted to get out of the free trade, but circumstances have changed,' Winnie said. 'I'd already decided to continue working for Mr Cork. I have my reasons, and it isn't just about the money.'

'What do you think, Billy?' Jason asked.

'The further you are away from yer loved ones –' Billy looked at Winnie and smiled softly '– the sweeter the idea of 'ome becomes. When you're sick or injured, you would do anythin' to see your family again.'

'It's another string to our bow, if you and Louisa agree to it,' Winnie said, addressing Jason.

'What would we do with them until we're ready to go?' Louisa said.

'They can stay here,' Winnie said.

'We don't have the space,' Louisa retorted. 'We can't have them sleeping in the hang or the privy.'

'They wouldn't be here for long. Don't you recall what Pa used to say about hiding goods in plain sight? Our

273

neighbours know that the cottage is full to overflowing – Mrs Witherall tells everybody that Grace and I are forced to sleep top to tail even though we have our own beds. They'd never guess there were two more people living here. If anyone should come nosing around, the men could disappear into the hiding holes.'

'I don't like it,' Louisa repeated. 'They'll find the goods we've stashed away. What's to stop them doing a runner with them?'

'Most of the goods are gone – either sold or hidden up at St Leonard's,' Winnie said. 'Besides, the Admiral couldn't run to save his life – he's on his last legs. He can hardly breathe for coughing.'

'What if he should take his last breath here? How would we deal with that?' Louisa asked. 'No, it's a terrible idea. I'm dead set against it.'

Winnie glanced towards Jason who was rubbing his chin, deep in thought.

She continued, 'They stay here in hiding, and then when the weather's right and the coast is clear, you can row them to Gravelines with the guineas. I will look after them while they're here and during the crossing and carry the despatches for Mr Cork.' Enthused by her plan, Winnie turned to Billy. 'The crew of the guinea boat will look after me in turn, as they did last time.' Her heart thudded as she looked back towards Jason.

'There'd be no harm in meetin' them, I suppose,' he said eventually.

'Then we should go straight away.' Winnie wanted to strike while the iron was hot, but Louisa was more circumspect.

'Wait until it's dark,' she advised.

*

Under cover of darkness, Winnie, Billy and Jason went down to the beach, Billy leaning on his crutch, Jason carrying a lantern, and Winnie with a basket over her arm and a light woollen blanket for the invalid cast around her shoulders.

The sea was calm and the streets quiet apart from the occasional rattle of carriage wheels, laughter from the Jack Tars who had stumbled out of Deal's watering holes, and the ringing of a bell from a vessel in the Downs.

'Is anyone following us?' Winnie murmured.

Jason turned and swung the lantern, its arc of light picking out the nearby heap of lobster pots and the silhouettes of the boats hauled up on the beach.

'I can't see nothin',' Billy whispered, finding Winnie's hand, as Jason crept up to the hut, his feet barely making a sound on the shingle. He pushed the door ajar and shone the lantern inside.

'Ah, I've met these men before,' he said. 'When I was pacin' the beach the other night, I found them tryin' to make off with one of the boats. I thought I'd made myself clear – that you were to take yourselves off elsewhere.'

'My friend here is very sick – I didn't know what else to do. The lady here said she might be able to help us.'

'We are going to help you,' Winnie asserted, afraid that Jason was having second thoughts. 'We've already agreed and settled on a plan.'

'We'd be better off taking the reward for your capture,' Jason said. 'There's bound to be one, if you are truly gentlemen of rank.'

'I'll allow that we look like vagrants, but we are men of influence and owners of extensive properties in France. Have mercy on us. Take us in your boat and we'll reward you more handsomely than the authorities will. I'll pay you one hundred and fifty guineas for each of us, if you land us on our home shore.'

'How will you pay, if we agree terms?' Jason asked.

'We'll send the money through one of the banks. Sir, I would not risk my life and liberty, if it wasn't for my friend.'

'Then we will shake hands on it.'

'Thank you,' Pierre replied softly.

'You will have to stick to our rules,' Jason said. 'That is the deal.'

The gentleman whom Winnie knew as the Admiral raised his hand. It hovered, pale and ghost-like from the darkness inside the hut, then fell back as he uttered a few words in French.

'It's my honour to escort you home,' Pierre said. 'You would do the same for me.'

'You'll stay with us until the boat's ready and there's favourable weather,' Jason said. 'You'll be obliged for your own protection – and ours, because we don't want to risk arrest for shelterin' you – to stay indoors during daylight hours, and if you go out at night, you will wear a disguise.'

'We will follow your orders, sir. My friend's strength is failing, though. Have you any idea how long it will be before we can travel?'

'I can't commit to a date, not yet. Are you in?'

Pierre muttered something to the Admiral, then turned back to Jason.

'We accept your offer of assistance on the terms we've agreed. Shall we remain here for the night?'

'You need to come with us,' Jason said gruffly. 'Can your friend walk?'

'I'll get him up and give him my shoulder to lean on,' Pierre said.

Winnie walked ahead, carrying Pierre's duffel bag as the men made their way slowly along Beach Street to Cockle Swamp Alley. A small detachment of soldiers marched along the road towards them, and she wondered what they might make of their unusual procession. Billy hobbled along with his crutch, his stump on the false leg apparently causing him pain, while the Admiral moaned and groaned as Jason and Pierre supported him, half carrying, half dragging him with the blanket over his head and shoulders.

'Good evening, officers,' Jason said, but the soldiers were apparently on a mission and not interested in them.

As they turned the corner, Winnie noticed a light in the bedroom of the house opposite. The curtains twitched.

'Hurry, we're being watched,' she whispered over her shoulder, before scurrying to the front door of Compass Cottage. Having let the men in, she closed the door behind them and locked it securely, fetching a chair from the parlour to lean against it for good measure. So far, so good.

'These are Winnie's foundlings?' Louisa appeared in the darkened hallway, holding a candlestick. 'Welcome to our home.'

'Madame, I haven't the words to express the depth of my gratitude to you and your family for giving us shelter.' The Frenchman spoke quietly and with consideration, and Winnie observed Louisa's manner softening. 'My friend needs to rest.'

'Does he require the services of a physician?' Winnie asked.

'I'm afraid that a doctor's visit will attract the attention of your neighbours. The fewer people who know we are here, the better.'

'I wouldn't send for Doctor Audley anyway,' Jason said. 'He's in the pay of Black Dog and the Rattlers. I don't know if he can be trusted to keep his silence and I'm reluctant to put him to the test. We should keep this to ourselves, within the family. Do you agree?'

'Most definitely,' Winnie said and Billy nodded in agreement.

'Winnie will provide food suitable for an invalid and, if medicine is required, we can always call on Mr Spottiswoode,' Louisa said.

'The quack?' Jason raised one eyebrow. 'Oh no, I don't trust him either. The fewer changes we make to our daily routines, the better.'

Billy and Jason helped the Admiral into the parlour and put him to bed on an old mattress that Louisa had borrowed from next door. Pierre was to sleep on the chaise. Winnie prepared warm milk and brandy, and supplied hunks of bread and cheese, then retired with Grace to their room upstairs.

'It's a very romantic turn of events,' Grace said, as they talked late into the night. 'Who would have thought that we'd end up harbouring a pair of Frenchies? I wonder how long they'll stay?'

'It depends on when Mr Cork finishes harvesting the beans.'

'Since when has Mr Cork acquired an interest in farming?'

Winnie giggled. 'I'm referring to the gold ... the guineas.'

'Oh, I see. You don't have to talk in riddles with me.' Winnie could see Grace's teeth gleaming in the dark. 'I wonder if Louisa mentioned the Frenchies to Mrs Witherall when she borrowed the mattress.'

'If she did, everyone in Deal will know the identity of our house guests by now.'

'Are you scared, Winnie?'

'A little,' she confessed. 'There are plenty of vultures circling out there, ready to fall on the reward for information leading to the recapture of escaped prisoners. We would be sorely punished for aiding and abetting them, but we must concentrate on the greater reward: the joy to be found in reuniting the Admiral with his wife and son.'

She heard Grace chuckling. 'You would say that. You're kind and generous to a fault, and I love you for it.'

Chapter Nineteen

Of Tonics and Blisters

Winnie's fugitives settled in, taking baths and changing into fresh clothes. Winnie arranged for their dirty ones to be laundered and returned, then, having gained Louisa and Jason's consent, went out with Grace to the apothecary to buy a tonic for the Admiral. With the patient's condition deteriorating, they were more worried about what they would do with his mortal remains, than they were of being caught harbouring him.

As they left the house with Pamela sitting up in the handcart, Winnie heard the town crier raising a hue and cry on the corner of Cockle Swamp Alley and Beach Street before moving on to his next stop.

'Oyez, oyez.' The crier rang a handbell, bringing several children to his feet, staring up at him in awe. 'There are prisoners on the loose. Oyez.'

'They are looking for the Frenchies,' Grace whispered.

'Whist,' Winnie said. 'Keep your mouth shut and keep walking.'

They hurried along towards the town, stopping briefly to read a poster that had been pinned to the board outside the Customs House.

'I don't recognise those men,' Winnie said loudly, having read the descriptions and glanced at the artist's impression of the fugitives.

'Would you be able to identify them if you ran into them on the street?' Grace said. 'They are both quite non-descript, although the one on the left has a rather large nose, and the other is ... moderately handsome.'

'Oh Grace.' Winnie chuckled, but the sound of her laughter rang hollow, because she knew how much trouble they'd be in if anyone found out that they had anything to do with the wanted men.

They reached the apothecary where coloured glass bottles with labels that Louisa said were written in Greek were lined up in the window, catching the sunlight as it slanted down between the rooftops and higgledy-piggledy chimney pots.

'Welcome, young ladies.' Mr Spottiswoode, an elderly gentleman who looked remarkably well for his years, greeted them from the counter where he was weighing out various powders on his scales, ready to mix according to his secret formulas. 'How may I assist you? You are looking a little peaky, if I may say so, Miss Lennicker,' he said, addressing Winnie, 'I believe it's the fashion among young ladies to remain indoors, hidden away from the elements to nurture such a complexion, but it isn't condu-cive to health, in my learned opinion. I have a tonic that will help – it's been most popular, and I have only a small vial left.'

'No, thank you. Another time,' Winnie said quickly. 'Our lodger is suffering from weakness, loss of appetite and a fever. In addition, he has a cough. I'd be grateful if you could supply a medicine to alleviate his symptoms.'

'You are referring to Mr Fleet? I remember that you called here several times for pain-relieving preparations. Is he still taking them?'

'He has no need of them any more.'

'Tell me, is he confined to bed? Is he taking fluids?'

'No, he isn't abed,' Winnie said, growing flustered at the apothecary's intrusive questioning.

'He is abed, Winnie,' Grace corrected her. 'He is prostrate.'

'You are right,' Winnie said. 'Perhaps you should do the talking.'

Grace went on to elaborate, remarking on the high colour in Billy's cheeks, the way his eyes had sunk into their sockets, and how he was so delirious sometimes that he sounded as if he were talking in tongues.

'Then it is very serious,' Mr Spottiswoode said. 'I recommend keeping up a steady perspiration to sweat out the poison from the patient's skin. In addition, a gentle dose of an antimonial taken with wine will do wonders. If that fails, then apply this paste to the side of the neck.'

'I don't know how to do that,' Winnie said.

'Use this spatula.' He placed one on the counter. 'Don't leave it too long or it may excite the fever. Remove it when the patient detects a decided sensation of smarting, but should the skin become fully raised into a blister, take scithers and snip it, then dress it with this healing ointment applied on a linen rag.'

She thanked him as she placed the medicines in her basket.

'I'll invoice you as usual. Don't hesitate to return and confer again, if these measures turn out to be insufficient. As you know, there are times when the patient is beyond help.'

'Oh,' Grace exclaimed, touching the corner of her eye with her handkerchief. 'Poor Billy. I can't bear the thought of it.'

Grateful for her sister's presence of mind, Winnie slipped her arm through Grace's, and with great wailing, they stepped outside the shop and collected Pamela from where they'd left her waiting in the handcart, gazing happily at the bottles in the window.

'I hope we didn't over-egg the pudding,' Winnie said as they walked back.

'We'll have to be more careful not to give the Frenchies away.' Grace smiled and tickled Pamela's cheek. 'Have you thought about what colour ribbons you'd like for your wedding gown? I was thinking that – as it's almost impossible to find a good match for the pink – you should choose a shade of cream. The haberdasher has some in stock.'

'We should go and have a look,' Winnie said, delighted by Grace's enthusiasm for her and Billy's nuptials.

Within the half-hour, Winnie had paid the haberdasher for a length of cream ribbon along with a length of primrose yellow for the gown Grace was intending to wear at the church.

With the ribbons safely tucked away at the end of the handcart, they returned to the cottage, where Grace took over minding the baby while Winnie went to administer the apothecary's medicines to the Admiral. Pierre was sitting quietly on the chaise, reading a newspaper. He looked up.

'How is the patient?' Winnie asked.

'He's sleeping. Shall I wake him for you?'

Nodding, she placed her tray on the table and poured seven drops of the antimonial into a glass of wine.

'He needs to drink this,' she said.

'I'll help him.' Pierre knelt at his friend's bedside and shook him gently by the shoulder.

'Ah, I was having such a wonderful dream …' the Admiral moaned.

'The young lady has brought you something to reduce the fever,' Pierre said. 'Let me sit you up.'

Between them, they managed to haul him into a sitting position just long enough for him to drink the potion before he slumped back, exhausted.

'Thank you,' Pierre said. 'Please, come and sit with me. We can watch over him together.'

Winnie wasn't sure – the chores didn't do themselves.

'Just for a little while,' she decided. She stoked the fire then took a chair at the table. Pierre began to talk.

'I was an officer on a privateer. I was sent to Alresford in June 1808. It's a parole town in one of the shires, where I met up with the Admiral and a number of other French army officers. In fact, it felt like a *petit* France. It was unfortunate that when Napoleon started refusing to send English prisoners of war home, the English decided to stop sending ours back on the cartel ships in return.'

'How were you treated?' she asked.

'We were lucky. It's ordinary French sailors who end up on the prison hulks in Chatham, dying from dirt and starvation. I've heard that their conditions are disgusting. The English doctors are afraid to attend to the prisoners – they are said to feel the pulses of the sick with the ends of their canes. I'm sorry. I shouldn't have mentioned it, I've upset you.'

'I have never heard of this. It makes me feel ashamed.' What if Billy had been captured by the French or the Americans? She had little doubt that he would have been treated just as badly.

'Parole wasn't the end of the world. The British authorities paid half a guinea a week for expenses.' Pierre smiled. 'Not enough for my friend here – he has extravagant tastes. Anyway, I have no concerns about my financial situation – mine was a successful ship and we won many valuable prizes, of which I managed to convey the bulk of my share to France, before I was captured. While in Alresford, the

284

Admiral and I supplemented our income by giving language lessons.'

The Admiral must have been listening, because he mumbled, 'Pierre, you gave lessons in love.'

'To whom, may I ask?' Winnie said.

'To the most beautiful of English roses, Miss Sarah Meadows. I lodged with her family, having sworn to behave with honour and decency. I was forced to teach her and her four sisters for my pains, but it was worth it to spend time in her presence.'

'He has given up his pursuit of love to help me return to France,' the Admiral observed weakly. 'It is more of a sacrifice than his manner lets on.'

'When I know you are safely reunited with your family, I will return to her. I've given her my word,' Pierre said.

'You won't be able to come back until the war is over. We have broken our parole.'

'That is true, but I'll find a way.'

'If you're caught, you'll be thrown on to one of those prison ships. I told you that you should have left me to make my own way home.' The Admiral coughed and fell silent.

'What were the conditions of your parole?' Winnie enquired. 'Were you locked away at night?'

'The commissioners of His Majesty's transport service enforced a curfew. We weren't allowed to go further than a mile out of town on the great turnpike road, and we had to be back in our lodgings by five in the winter and eight in the summer. If anyone was found wandering the fields, they could be taken to prison and the person who apprehended them paid ten shillings.

'We weren't supposed to have any correspondence with family or contacts in France unless the letters were shown to the commissioners' agent and approved by his superiors. We managed to get around that though – I paid a certain amount of necessary attention to the lady who runs the post office.'

He went on to explain how he and the Admiral had given their parole agent the slip, then changed into smocks and brown stockings, and hid their faces beneath broad-brimmed hats, enabling them to walk out of town unchallenged. A carter had given them a lift, assuming they were merchants buying and selling potatoes and swedes.

The more Pierre spoke, the more Winnie liked him. He was kind, thoughtful and intelligent. He had no particular fondness for garlic – apparently Miss Meadows hadn't appreciated the way that it lingered on the breath – and he wouldn't be drawn on his opinion of Old Boney and the war.

'Have you any idea when we will be away from here? Being cooped up makes me nervous and sends me a little mad.'

'Be patient,' she said. 'It won't be for long.'

If time dragged for Pierre, it flew by for Winnie.

She was sitting with Pamela, taking advantage of the Admiral being asleep, and of Louisa and Grace's absence while they ran an errand to sell lace, when she noticed a tiny black spider scuttling across the kitchen table.

'Look, a money-spinner,' she said, delighted.

Pamela peered at it cross-eyed.

'We must be kind to it,' Winnie explained. 'It will bring us good fortune.' She let it run on to her fingertip and turned it three times around her head, before carrying it to the safe haven of the dresser-top. After returning Pamela to her crib where she sat chattering nonsense, she heard Billy's footsteps.

'Where is my lovely lady?' he said, joining her. 'Before you start frettin', Mr Elson 'as given me an hour off, as long as I make it up later. I thought we'd go and look at a couple of lodgin' 'ouses. Is there any way you can find someone to mind Pamela at short notice?'

'Not Pierre,' she said quickly, in case Billy was thinking of him. 'I'll ask Mrs Witherall.'

Having left Pamela with their neighbour, they made their way through town.

'The first place is in Middle Street,' Billy said. 'It's next to the boatyard so I wouldn't 'ave far to walk for work, and it's within shoutin' distance of your sisters.'

The landlady turned out to be a whiskery maiden aunt of the sisters from the bakery. She showed them a grand but shabby room on the second floor, from which Winnie could hear hammering and shouting.

'I think it will be too noisy for the baby,' she said.

The landlady frowned.

'No children. Did I not make that clear, Mr Fleet?'

'This isn't suitable for our family,' Winnie replied sharply. 'I'm sorry if we've wasted your time. Good day.'

'She was quite the 'arridan,' Billy said as they walked away. ''Owever, our choices are limited by our finances. We'll go and look at Golden Street. If that isn't right, we'll 'ave to think again.'

'We could pawn the watch,' Winnie suggested, willing to do anything to find somewhere they could call home.

Billy shook his head. 'We don't want to attract attention, remember. The last thing we need is "uncle" askin' awkward questions, like where did we acquire such a fine article.'

'You are speaking of Mr Turner?'

'That's right. In fact, that's where we're goin' now. 'E 'as a room to let above the shop.'

Winnie hesitated. 'I don't like the idea of living above a pawnbroker's – it doesn't feel … respectable.'

287

'Beggars can't be choosers,' Billy said. 'I don't care where I live to begin with, as long as it's with you.' He smiled and her optimism returned as she recalled the money-spinner.

There was no queue outside the pawnbroker's on this occasion, and they walked straight into Mr Turner's shop. He kept them waiting – deliberately, in Winnie's opinion – as he perused a gold ring through a quizzing glass, turning it over several times before returning it to a glass case that he locked and slid under the counter.

'How may I be of assistance?' he asked, getting up and slipping on a pair of spectacles. He was decidedly broad in the beam, Winnie thought, and he wore a gold chain around his fat neck and a jewel on every finger. His dress was flamboyant, his shirt, waistcoat and trousers decked out in many colours and patterns.

'I have three matters of business, sir,' Billy said politely. 'The first bein' concerned with the pay that I'm owed by the Admiralty.' He showed him the ticket. 'Will you offer me anythin' for it?'

'I will give you half of its face value,' Mr Turner said. 'I have to make a living, and if you don't like it, you can always go to Greenwich on your own account.'

Winnie wondered about the wisdom of cashing it in for so little return.

'Shall we leave it?' she asked quietly.

'I should like to 'ave the money in my pocket. We 'ave need of funds to purchase a ring, which brings me on to the other reasons for comin' to see you. I'd be most grateful if you would show us a selection of weddin' bands, and the lodgin's you 'ave advertised in the window.'

Mr Turner smiled, a gold tooth glinting from the corner of his mouth.

'Allow me to show you to the room first, then we will examine the rings.' He showed them out the back and up the stairs where the walls were hung with curiosities of many kinds: tapestries; glass-eyed stags' heads; taxidermy fish; oil paintings. It was three flights to the attic where Mr Turner opened the door from the landing. Billy promptly banged his head on the ceiling as they entered a room that stank of rats and wet boots.

'I had to ask the previous tenant to leave because he wasn't keeping up with the rent. He was a pleasant enough sort, but sadly low on funds, being recently invalided out from the navy. Have a look around.'

There wasn't much to see. Winnie felt the draught coming in through the window – the frame was rotten, and the glass cracked. The fireplace was filled with soot, and on closer inspection, a dead seagull.

'Thank you,' she said. 'We'll let you know our decision.'

'Don't leave it too long – I have a list of people who are interested.'

Back in the shop, he showed them four rings – they were too big, too small, too scratched or too expensive, and Winnie couldn't deny that she was disappointed, but she could see that Billy was downcast too, so she tried to cheer him up on the way home.

'That wasn't a success,' he said. 'I'm sorry.'

'I'm glad you decided not to sell him your ticket.'

'I don't know what to do about the ring – we can't be married without one.'

'I'm sure we can improvise,' Winnie smiled. 'We can borrow a curtain ring.'

'Won't that be far too large for your finger?' Billy asked.

'It can be adjusted to fit and it's only a temporary measure until we find a proper one.'

'You're right,' Billy sighed. 'It's a shame about the room too.'

'I have faith that something will turn up – that attic would be no good for the baby's chest. I feel sorry for the gentleman who's lost the roof over his head. The last I heard, Mr Jones who gave me the bracelet of shells was living there. He has had a terrible run of bad luck. Thank you for the outing though – it was lovely of you to think of it, even if it didn't work out as you planned.'

'I'd do anythin' for you, Winnie. I wish I could afford to buy you an 'andsome 'ouse in the country where we could live 'appily ever after. Oh, I'd better go. I don't want to upset Ol' Elson.'

She watched him head towards the boatyard, walking steadily with one crutch. The vicar was going to read the banns for the third time on Sunday morning. It wouldn't be long until they were husband and wife, and when their money came in from the guinea run, they would be able to rent something better than Mr Turner's mould-ridden attic.

Chapter Twenty

A Blessing in Disguise

Three weeks passed, during which time Winnie made enquiries as to Mr Jones's whereabouts, but it seemed that nobody had seen him. Whilst out and about, she also went to the bank, Hulke and Sons on Lower Street, taking Louisa with her because none of her family had ever used the facilities of such an institution and she didn't know how she would be received, being a woman. She made an appointment with the manager who, to her surprise, treated her and Louisa with extreme deference, opening an account for Winnie and offering his advice on savings and investments.

Winnie and Grace continued with their preparations for the wedding. Grace attached the ribbons to Winnie's gown and let out the seams at the waist so that it fitted perfectly.

The prisoners remained confined to the cottage and Winnie learned how to make many dishes suitable for invalids. She cooked shank jelly, a long process involving leaving the lamb in salt for half a day, then brushing it with herbs and simmering it for hours until the kitchen steamed up. She also prepared toast and water to be drunk cold, and stewed rabbit in milk with mace.

The Admiral suffered from undulating fever: often dripping with sweat and hardly sensible; in between times he would appear gaunt and weak, but able to hold a conversation for a short while until he grew weary or started to cough, or the fever came back. Winnie went twice more to the apothecary who was surprised that his treatments hadn't yet cured – or killed – the patient.

One morning, Winnie made milk porridge and saloop with water, wine and lemon peel. She also added honey, thinking that it might soothe his hacking cough.

'You must eat … one spoonful to begin with.' Feeding the Admiral reminded her of giving Pamela her meals. Sometimes she would eat everything with enthusiasm, but often she would fuss and refuse, then deign to nibble on a buttered crust or the end of a carrot.

As she helped him, she noticed the oozing blister on his neck, the one she'd created according to Mr Spottiswoode's instructions. She wasn't impressed. It had made no difference to the Admiral's feverishness. In fact, it appeared to have made his condition worse.

'Where is Pierre? I've made porridge for him as well – it's here, getting cold.'

'He's …' The Admiral waved his hand in a gesture that encompassed every possible direction, so Winnie didn't know whether he meant that Pierre had gone to the privy or taken himself into the hang for some time alone.

'Oh?' Winnie said, nonplussed.

'He has gone out.'

'He can't do that!' she exclaimed.

'He has gone in disguise.'

'How? He isn't allowed out during the hours of daylight, and for good reason.'

'He isn't the kind of man who can be confined. Being forced to stay indoors in this cramped accommodation isn't good for his mind or constitution. In Alresford, he would walk for miles every day.'

'Weren't you under the thumb of the parole agent though?'

'We had ways and means of circumventing his control. For example, we went to dine some ten miles away from town. The following day, we were arrested for breaking our parole, but Pierre and I were *bons amis* with the local gentry who wrote letters to the commissioners in support. It went against the agent.' A smile played on the Admiral's lips. 'It wasn't all bad. We made the best of it, but then I fell ill. I know how the land lies, Mademoiselle. Time is running out.'

'We'll get you home – you have to have faith.' She reached out and touched the back of his hand, noticing how the veins ran dark and thread-like beneath his skin. 'You are cold? Let me find you another blanket.'

'I feel as if I'm being broiled alive,' he said. 'No more blankets.'

'I'm going to call on the apothecary to see what we can do to heal the sore on your neck. Is there anything else I can get you?'

'*Non, merci.*'

'I'm afraid that Jason and Louisa – Mr and Mrs Witherall – will be very angry with Pierre for breaking his word.'

'Perhaps they will not find out. He is wearing the disguise of a Deal boatman: a sou'wester, oilskins and boots, and a bandanna around his neck.'

'Then he will stand out like a sore thumb,' she smiled. 'You must go and attend to your child – your beautiful daughter – and your chores.'

'It's all right – I can stay a little longer.'

'I thank you for your companionship, but I can barely keep my eyes open.'

'I'm sorry – I should have thought …'

He smiled weakly. 'You're a good woman. You remind me of my wife – she is selfless, like you.'

She stood up from his bedside, glancing towards the handbell on the table beside him.

'I'm going out to look for Pierre,' she said.

'So the bell won't work.' He forced a small smile as he leaned back against his pillow and closed his eyes.

She took the tray with the barely touched porridge and saloop back to the kitchen.

'Was there something wrong with the oats?' Grace said, carrying Pamela around on her hip.

'He's lost his appetite completely. He's as weak as a kitten, but whether or not he gets back to France is the least of our worries. Pierre has left the house against Jason's orders. We have to go and fetch him back before Jason finds out.'

'And before anybody else notices him.' Grace's eyes were filled with alarm. 'How could he be so stupid? I'll go and look for him. You stay and mind Pamela – she's grizzly today.'

'She's teething,' Winnie said. 'It'll do her good to have some fresh air. We'll go together. We can look for Pierre, go and ask Mr Spottiswoode if there is anything else that he can prescribe for my patient, and take Billy some nuncheon – he's working on the *Spindrift*.'

'There's plenty of cold porridge,' Grace smiled.

'That won't go down too well. No, I'll take him some cold ham and egg pie to make up for the fact that he hardly sees me, because I'm always looking after Pamela and the Admiral.' Winnie scraped the porridge back into the pot for another day and poured the saloop into a jug, putting a plate over the top to stop the spiders falling in. 'When did Louisa leave the house?'

'Not long ago – she's gone to call on Mr Gigg and settle our account with Abel for the loan of the ponies.'

They put on their hats and cloaks, gloves and boots and wrapped Pamela up warmly before heading out towards the capstan grounds, thinking that that would be as good a place as any to start their search.

As they walked past the boats and lobster pots, Cromwell came running up to them.

''Ave you 'eard about the Frenchie?' he cried.

Winnie shook her head.

'We don't know anything about any French men, or persons of any other nationality for that matter,' Grace replied gaily.

Cromwell frowned. 'You must know 'im – 'e's lodgin' at your 'ouse.'

'How do you know that?' Winnie said at the same time as Grace said, 'The only person who lodges with us is Billy.'

'Oh dear,' Winnie sighed. 'Who else knows?'

'Everyone,' Cromwell said. 'It's no secret. 'E was at the butcher's this mornin'. Mr Flack was tellin' 'im 'e could buy a cut of beef, yellin' at 'im at the top of 'is voice as if 'e 'ad cloth ears.'

'"I don't want beef, *merci*," he kept saying, but Mr Flack was insistent, and eventually the Frenchie ran out of patience. "*Non bon, non bon!*" 'e cried, at which point, Mr Flack offered 'im a marrerbone. I laughed till I cried. We all did, because everyone except Mr Flack understood that 'e didn't want to buy any beef. 'E didn't want to buy nothin' at all.'

'Cromwell, you've been very helpful, but do you happen to know where the gentleman went after that?'

'You could try the Three Kings or the Rattlin' Cat. 'E asked me if I knew where 'e could get a drink.'

Winnie glanced towards Grace. Pierre could be anywhere – there were plenty of taverns in Deal and there was no reason why he wouldn't have gone further afield.

'Have you seen Jason?' she said, addressing Cromwell.

'The *Whimbrel*'s out.' He waved in the direction of the roadstead. 'They're takin' a pilot off one of the merchant ships and deliverin' a replacement anchor to another.'

Jason wouldn't be back for a while, Winnie thought. They had time to find Pierre.

'If you see the Frenchie again, tell him to go straight home.'

'Is 'e in trouble?'

'He will be.'

'And we will be too,' Grace said as they made their way back into town. They called at the Waterman's Arms, but it was closed, so they carried on to the market where they saw no sign of a Frenchman dressed in a boatman's garb. They diverted to the apothecary who expressed his great delight at seeing them again, as well he might, Winnie thought, holding on to her purse.

'What kind of alleviation or physic do you require this time? May I ask if the tonic you purchased last week effected the cure that you desired?'

'It was most satisfactory, thank you. Mr Fleet is quite well,' Winnie replied, deciding not to complain about the effect of the blister in case Mr Spottiswoode took offence and refused to serve them again. He seemed like a gentleman who would be easily offended. 'I wonder if you can recommend a tincture or salve for a festering sore.'

'Ah, this is a matter requiring some delicacy—'

'No, sir. It is my brother-in-law, not me who is suffering.'

'It is no surprise to me that your family experiences these painful and frequent afflictions. They are due to the vapours that arise from the spit on which the residents of Deal have built their houses.'

Winnie breathed a sigh of relief, but Mr Spottiswoode was a clever man, and she didn't think she could keep up the pretence for too much longer. She had thought of sourcing their own ingredients to prepare at home, but she was afraid of getting it wrong – she didn't want to be responsible for the Admiral's demise. Jason remained sceptical. He reckoned that if he put his mind to it, he could make more money from quackery than the free trade, which was saying something.

'Can you describe this sore? Where is it on the body?'

'Does it make a difference?'

'If you would permit me to visit the patient, I will be able to more accurately prescribe a treatment, if not an absolute cure.'

'That won't be possible,' she said quickly.

'If it is the expense that is putting you off, do not worry. I will set up an arrangement by which you can pay in manageable instalments.' He smiled slyly. 'What price is the restoration of one's health?'

'I'm sure you are going to tell me,' Winnie said, a little anxious about the suggestion that he should call at the cottage.

'I shall work it out, according to the strength of the formulation I prescribe. When it's ready, I'll deliver it to you personally to explain exactly how it should be used and how often. I insist.'

'What are we going to do now?' Grace hissed as they walked home. 'He knows, Winnie.'

'What makes you think that?'

'We've asked his advice four times recently …'

'You're reading too much into it. How can he possibly make the link between us and the Frenchies?'

Grace looked unconvinced. 'It's possible that he spotted Pierre out and about, or he's heard the story of the butcher and the bones. He'll have seen the posters, Winnie – it isn't difficult to work out that the best chance the prisoners have of escaping to France is to form an association with one or more of the free traders who make regular journeys across the Channel. When do you think Jason will take the guinea boat out next?'

'Soon, I hope,' Winnie said. Her nerves wouldn't stand much more.

'There's Louisa,' Grace warned, but it was too late to hide. She was almost upon them as they crossed the road heading towards the market. She smiled.

'Where have you been?'

'We've been searching for Pierre,' Winnie explained in a low voice. 'He slipped out of the house while we weren't looking.'

'Oh dear. I knew something like this would happen. It's imperative that we find him and drag him back; Abel told me that there are two officers from London nosing around Deal. Apparently, the chief magistrate at Bow Street has sent them to help in apprehending the escaped prisoners and anyone who has aided and abetted them. He's warned his officers not to apply to the magistrates of this town – Reverend North, Mr Causton and Mr Norris – because he suspects them of being in league with the smugglers and susceptible to bribery.'

'The guinea run must be brought forward if possible,' Grace said.

'There's no chance of that,' Louisa replied. 'We're expecting the gold on the twenty-sixth day of this month, that's in three days' time.'

'Should we move Pierre and the Admiral elsewhere? Up to St Leonard's, for example, or place them at Nomansland Farm?'

'We risk discovery whatever we do. Their descriptions have been circulated and it turns out that our Admiral is well respected for his contribution to Napoleon's war effort as well as being a successful privateer. The Bow Street Runners are keen to recapture him to prevent him commanding one of Boney's ships. *We* know that he's too frail to do that, but they don't.'

'What shall we do next?' Grace asked.

'Keep looking for Pierre,' Louisa replied. 'Make discreet enquiries with the neighbours. Have you tried the Rattling Cat?'

'Not yet,' Winnie said.

'We'll go there next. There's no telling what Isaiah will do if he finds out what we've been up to.'

Winnie remembered all too well how he had supplied Billy with drink on credit. She hurried to the tavern with Pamela and her sisters. Leaving the handcart outside, they entered the bar to find the floor strewn with damp sawdust and the tables still covered with tankards and platters from the night before. Two of the cats leapt down from the counter, the bones rattling on their collars, and the sound brought Isaiah's longdog trotting across from its blanket beside the fireplace.

'What brings you 'ere?' Isaiah emerged from the cellar beyond the counter, climbing up through the trapdoor, his hair adorned with cobwebs. 'Is it business or pleasure?'

Winnie didn't know what to say. She looked to Louisa who answered, 'Business, of course. An acquaintance of mine has requested a cask of geneva – I wondered if you might have some to sell?'

'At a price,' he said, amused. 'Well I never: a Witherall askin' a Rattler for goods. I've never 'eard of that afore. Why don't I see what I 'ave left and let you know 'ow much it's goin' to cost you? Come back after seven o'clock and I'll 'ave an answer for you.'

Winnie guessed why he'd invited Louisa to return when the tavern was thronging with the Rattlers and other villains – he wanted to lord it over them. Little did he know that they had no intention of coming back.

'Grace, I have somethin' else that might interest you,' Isaiah said. 'The mother cat 'as borne four kittens.'

Winnie noticed how her younger sister's face lit up.

'May I see them?'

'We should go,' Louisa said. 'We don't want to take up any more of Mr Feasey's time.'

'It won't be for long,' Grace said.

'They're over there in the box.' He gestured towards one of the tables. 'We put them up there to keep them away from the dog.'

'You see, I told you he cared for them,' Grace told Louisa. She turned to Isaiah. 'Have you found homes for this litter?'

'I will soon find 'em employment as mousers and ratters. Their mother is adept at killin'. They will take after 'er.'

Winnie took Isaiah's words with a pinch of salt, but it appeared that Grace was completely taken in as she gazed into the box of pure black kittens.

'We could take one – we have meakers in the hang,' she said hopefully.

'We don't want a cat,' Louisa said.

'Then you must 'ave one,' Isaiah said to Grace, ignoring Louisa as he picked out one of the kittens and placed it in Grace's palm where it mewed plaintively. 'Take 'er home, feed 'er on milk and bread, and some meat cut up into tiny pieces. Don't give 'er too much, or she won't l'arn to 'unt. Got that?'

Smiling, Grace nodded.

'Give it back,' Louisa said icily. 'The last thing we need is another mouth to feed.'

'That's the beauty of it though,' Isaiah said. 'A cat can look after itself.'

'I'm not giving her up.' Grace let the kitten nestle in the crook of her elbow and tickled it under the chin.

'It's too young to leave its mother. It's cruel.' Louisa's voice softened. 'Less cruel than the alternative, I suppose.'

'I don't know what you're implyin',' Isaiah said, 'but I don't like it.'

'Grace, you may have her,' Louisa relented, 'on condition that you are entirely responsible for her.'

'Oh, thank you. I'll look after her, I promise.'

'We'll call again later,' Louisa said before they made their excuses and left.

Winnie put a protesting Pamela back in the handcart and pushed her along while Grace carried the kitten tucked inside her bodice with its head poking out, and Louisa practised what she was going to say to Jason about them having taken on a mouser.

'Is that Pierre?' Winnie asked as they walked along Beach Street for a second time. 'The figure dressed in oilskins and sou'wester. I'm sure it's him – he stands out like a sore thumb.'

'What kind of disguise is that?' Grace exclaimed. 'Why would you wear rain-clothes when there is hardly a cloud in the sky?'

They watched him retreat into the alley, before following him home.

'What do you think you are doing?' Winnie asked when she saw him ringing the doorbell.

'Ah, Mesdemoiselles. I had business at the Post Office – I didn't want to trouble you with it.'

'You have broken the rules,' Louisa said, letting him in.

'You can't tell me that you recognised me in this garb.'

'We did,' Winnie confirmed, lifting Pamela out of the handcart.

'Oh dear,' he said gloomily, entering the kitchen behind the three sisters. 'It was all that I could find to wear.'

'What did you do at the Post Office?'

He raised one lively eyebrow as though surprised by Louisa's question. 'I sent a letter to Miss Meadows in Alresford.'

'How could you?'

'I had to send word – to put her mind at ease. I left in a hurry, without telling her where I was going. Anyone else would have done the same.'

'I don't think you realise what you've done. There are wanted posters up all round town and people ready to turn you in for the reward that's been offered. I wouldn't put it past the postmaster to put two and two together.' Louisa's cheeks were scarlet with annoyance. 'You've put us all in danger with your thoughtlessness – you can't stay here any longer.'

Winnie jumped at the sound of a voice from the hallway. 'Is there anyone at home? Miss Lennicker?'

She leaned against the kitchen door and nodded towards the exit into the back yard. Pierre made a rapid escape.

'Who is it?' Praying that it wasn't Constable Pocket or the Bow Street Runners, she entered the hall to find Mr Spottiswoode standing inside the front door.

'The door was open.' He removed his hat. 'I hope you don't mind, but I wanted to make sure I handed the tincture to you in person. Here it is.'

She almost snatched it from him.

'I wonder if I may visit the patient as I'm here.' He smoothed his hair which shone with Macassar oil. 'It would be of great benefit to his health ... and to your purse, miss.'

'Is all well, Winnie?' Louisa asked from behind her.

'Our caller is on his way,' she sang out. 'I'm very grateful for the tincture.'

'I hope it will be efficacious,' Mr Spottiswoode said, looking around the hall, his eyes settling on the pairs of boots lined up below the coat hooks as if he was counting them. 'Are you sure you wouldn't like me to instruct you on the method of application?'

'No, sir. That will not be necessary,' she said firmly. 'Good day.'

As she showed him out, she heard the handbell ringing. 'I have to go,' she added.

She locked the door behind him and went to attend to the Admiral, but as she mopped his brow, she felt uneasy.

'Excuse me for a moment,' she said, standing up from the chair at the bedside and walking across to the window. Her breath was coming hard and fast as she took hold of one of the curtains and slowly drew it across, letting in just a chink of light ... Something – or someone – on the other side of the glass suddenly ducked, then crawled as far as the neighbour's doorstep, then leapt up and ran away. Stifling a gasp, she closed the curtain again.

'Is everything all right?' the Admiral asked.

'Yes,' she responded, but after she had finished making sure he was comfortable, she called Pierre to sit with him, and warned him to keep the curtains closed.

When Jason returned, the family sat and talked of the day's events.

'Pierre can't be trusted,' Louisa said. 'It's common knowledge that the Frenchies are here at Compass Cottage. When the apothecary turned up, we all panicked.'

'It's worse than that,' Winnie cut in. She told them about the peeper whom she'd caught looking in through the window. 'We are being watched.'

'We should send word to Mr Cork to see if he can bring the delivery of beans forward,' Louisa said.

'If we can lie low for three more nights, we will be home and dry.' Jason tried to reassure his wife. 'The plan for movin' our house guests to the guinea boat remains in place, but it's more important than ever that we execute it perfectly, down to the very last detail.'

'I disagree. We should move them elsewhere as Winnie suggested earlier. If we are under surveillance, it is only a matter of time before we are found out. It will not be pleasant – they'll have to stay in the hiding hole at St Leonard's, but it won't be for long.'

'You're probably right, Louisa,' Jason sighed.

'I am right,' she said. 'We can't keep them here – we are sitting ducks.'

'How will we move the Admiral without being seen?' Winnie said.

'We'll have to beg a favour or two from Abel. He'll help us, if we pay him,' Jason said. 'It's too late to move them tonight. It'll have to be tomorrow, under the cover of darkness.'

'I 'ave an idea,' Billy said. 'I'll act as a decoy – I'll dress up in Pierre's smock and ask Smoker to 'elp me stuff an 'essian sack with straw and make it look like the Admiral. We'll push it along in the 'andcart, makin' our way towards St George's, leaving the rest of you to travel with Abel to St Leonard's as soon as the coast is clear.'

'That could work,' Louisa said slowly.

'Who will stay with the prisoners?' Grace asked, the kitten purring on her lap.

'Winnie, of course,' Louisa said. 'And Billy, until he's needed to play his part for a second time, when we move Pierre and the Admiral to the guinea boat.'

'I'll mind Pamela,' Grace said. 'Someone has to do it.'

Reluctantly, Winnie agreed. It was asking for trouble, expecting the baby to stay underground in the hiding hole with the dust and damp, and it would be no good for her chest.

'I'll speak to our house guests at first light, and then I'll go and call at the mill,' Jason said.

'What about the peeper?' Louisa asked. 'I don't like the thought that we're being watched.'

'During daylight hours, Pierre and the Admiral will have to retreat to the hidin' holes in the cottage,' Jason said. 'Billy, you'll be with me. Ladies, you will continue with your usual business. I think a quiet day carryin' out your usual chores will allay the watcher's suspicions, at least until we have achieved our aim. Avoid doing anythin' out of the ordinary.'

'As if we would,' Louisa said archly. 'We lead very dull lives.'

Chapter Twenty-One

Breaking the Code

At first light, the cottage was plunged into activity. Winnie helped Pierre settle the Admiral in the hiding hole in the parlour before sending him up to hide in the gap in the wall behind the linen press in Billy's room. Jason and Billy went out. Louisa answered the door – somewhat apprehensively – to Cromwell who had a message for Winnie.

'What is it?' Winnie asked, wiping her hands on her apron as she approached the boy.

'A gen'leman who says 'is name is Mr Cork is stayin' at the Three Kings. 'E is expectin' you at the signallin' tower at ten o'clock sharp. The driver of the post chaise will be wearin' a button'ole of pear blossom. I dunno why 'e told me that.'

Winnie gave him a penny, knowing that Mr Cork would have already rewarded him for his trouble.

'Are the Frenchies still 'ere?'

'I have no idea what you're talking about. Now, run along,' Winnie said.

'I'll see you again soon.' Smiling, he skipped away towards the beach.

Winnie turned to Louisa.

'I shall have to go out,' she said.

'At least you have Pamela – no one will think it odd if you take her out with you.' Louisa's voice sounded brittle, like breaking glass, and her complexion was unusually pale.

'Are you quite well?' Winnie asked.

'I'm fine – it's the worry of all this.' She waved her hand vaguely.

'Everything will work out for the best,' Winnie reassured her. 'Perhaps you should forget the chores and put your feet up.'

'I can't – there's too much to do, and I need to keep myself occupied.'

Winnie understood. The women had to prepare food for the oarsmen who would be crewing the guinea boat across the Channel. They were staying near Folkestone where they were paying a landowner to store the guinea boat away from prying eyes. A trusted acquaintance of Billy's was making alterations to her mast and timbers to create more hiding holes than ever before for the guineas that Mr Cork was having delivered shortly, under guard from London. Jason said that it was a vast fortune of up to thirty thousand pounds in value, more than Winnie could imagine.

'I'd better prepare myself,' she said. 'I'll be back as soon as I can.'

'Be careful,' Louisa warned.

'I'll watch my back, don't you worry.'

She stepped out of the cottage and put Pamela in the handcart. She screamed, unhappy at being taken from the comfort of the kitchen where she had been playing with Grace and the kitten. Much as her crying tore at Winnie's heart, she acknowledged that it was the perfect cover for her expedition.

When she reached the signalling tower, there was no ceremony or discussion. She didn't even see Mr Cork. His man walked across to speak with her, making out that he was asking for directions. As he did so, he dropped the package into the handcart. Pamela grabbed it and stuffed the corner into her mouth.

'Oh no, darling,' Winnie said, noticing the fleeting expression of alarm crossing the man's face before he returned to the post chaise. 'You can't have that – you don't know where it's been.' She removed it from Pamela's grasp, at which she began to cry. 'So much for not attracting attention,' she muttered as she let Pamela have her purse instead, before pushing the handcart past the tower.

'Good mornin', Winnie. 'Ow are you and the littlun today?'

She glanced up to find herself face to face with Mrs Stickles.

'Very well, thank you.'

'Who was that gen'leman?'

'Oh, just some driver wanting directions to … to Walmer.'

'It's a little odd that 'e drove off in the opposite direction then.'

'Maybe I didn't make myself clear,' Winnie sighed. 'What brings you this way?'

'I've been up to the mill to settle my account – Mr Brockman was threatenin' to close it and I can't do without flour. I saw Jason speakin' to Abel – they were castin' their eye over an 'orse. 'Ave you 'ad any luck with the book I gave you?'

'I'm afraid it isn't poetry or fiction. There's no mention of love.'

'What is it then?'

'I don't understand it.' Winnie decided to keep the truth to herself. 'Has Mr Gambril been back for it?'

'Not yet, but I continue to live accordin' to the proverb: while there's life, there's 'ope.'

Winnie wished her farewell and went on her way, turning right and right again, heading back to Cockle Swamp Alley. Caught up in her plans to deal with the despatches, she didn't notice what Pamela was up to until she heard the chink of her purse landing on the cobbles.

'Finders keepers, missus!' One of the Roper boys who was about six years old dived towards the purse and snatched it up. 'My oh my, what's in 'ere?'

'Give that to me,' she said, panicking. 'It belongs to the baby.'

He waved it in the air. 'It's mine now.'

'Don't talk nonsense. It's stealing. Haven't your ma and pa taught you anything?' Suddenly, he burst into tears, great racking sobs that shook his shoulders, and Winnie remembered that he had lost his father. 'I'm sorry. Give me the purse. I'll count you out a few pennies in return and we'll say no more about it. How about that?'

Smearing snot across his cheek, he nodded and handed it back.

Having given him some money, she hurried the last few steps to the house and let herself in.

It wasn't until after noon that she managed to retire to her room to look at the despatches. Pamela was lying in her crib, listening for her mama, her eyes flicking towards the washstand on which Winnie had placed a lighted candle. She opened the packet from Mr Cork and melted the seals on the four envelopes inside. She extracted the first letter and held it over the flame. Nothing. She tried with the second letter. The same again. Frowning, she tried the third. Gradually, the brown stain of the secret ink appeared between the lines on the page.

'Yes,' she whispered, her excitement and anticipation growing, along with the frisson of guilt that she was doing something she shouldn't yet again, breaking into intelligence for the British agents in Paris and Switzerland.

She took the code book from the money box and painstakingly deciphered the writing into ... it wasn't English. It was French. The skin on the back of her neck tingled with apprehension. Something wasn't right, but she didn't know what it was, and to her fury and frustration, she still couldn't find out. What she needed was someone who could translate the French into English ...

Immediately, she thought of Pierre. Could she trust him?

What was she thinking of? Imagine the damage she could do by showing a Frenchman intelligence obtained by the British for the British. If it was for the British ... Why would the information and instructions be written in French? Because Madame was French ... that must be it, she thought, but Madame was merely a courier, like Mr Buckley and herself, or so it seemed.

Had Mr Cork had a hand in the creation of these coded letters? She wanted to believe that he was an honest man, but how could she be sure? Appearances counted for little.

The question tormented her. Should she fold the letters, place them back in the envelopes, seal them up and forget about the secret writing? Or should she ask Pierre to translate the message she'd decoded into English on a separate piece of paper at the risk of him going on to alert the French authorities that she – Winnie Lennicker – was a spy for the British government?

For the sake of her peace of mind, she wished she'd never got involved.

Leaving Pamela to nap, she went back downstairs to the kitchen to prepare food and broth. She checked through the crate of onions in the pantry and threw out the bad ones. As she began chopping the rest, Louisa returned from the privy, looking pale and wan.

'Can I get you anything?' Winnie asked.

Louisa shook her head. 'There's nothing to be done. I've … lost the baby.' Her face contorted with distress and pain as she clutched her belly. 'I'm bleeding.'

'Are you sure it's gone?' Winnie asked, hoping against hope that it wasn't true.

'This isn't the first time …'

'Sit down,' Winnie urged her.

'I must keep going as if there's nothing wrong.'

'Louisa, do as I tell you for once.' Winnie pulled a chair away from the table. 'Sit down. I'll fetch you a drink.' She returned from the parlour with a small glass of cognac. 'Drink it,' she said as Louisa tried to push it away. 'How far gone do you think you … were?'

Louisa shrugged as she took a sip. 'I'm not sure … three or four months. Oh, I thought it was going to work out this time.' She broke down in tears. 'I thought I'd been made to suffer enough.'

'I'm so sorry,' Winnie said, leaning down and slipping her arm around Louisa's shoulders. 'I know how much it means to you.'

'I've always been able to do everything I wanted … within reason, yet when it comes to this one simple, straightforward and natural act, I can't do it. I don't believe I'll ever bear a child.'

Winnie couldn't think of any way of consoling her. It was no use telling her that she would be a mother one day, that she just had to be patient, because she didn't have a crystal ball. All she knew was that her strong, capable sister was distraught.

Suddenly, Louisa straightened, swallowed the rest of the cognac and rubbed her eyes.

'That's enough crying.' Her tone hardened. 'I don't want Jason to find out.'

'You have to tell him.'

'How can I? He'll be devastated. I've never seen anyone so excited about the prospect of becoming a father. Boy or girl, he's already been planning how he's going to take his child out on the *Whimbrel*.'

'All the more reason—'

'Not before the run,' Louisa interrupted. 'There's too much at stake. I don't want him worrying about me while he has all the responsibility of captaining an unfamiliar crew, carrying a fortune in guineas and making sure that the authorities don't catch up with Pierre and the Admiral. He must look after you as well. I'll tell him on his return.' She held up her hand. 'Don't try to sway me. I'm doing the right thing.'

'I'm sorry,' Winnie said.

'What for?' Grace said, entering the kitchen with a basket of provisions that she'd bought in town.

'Nothing,' Winnie and Louisa said at the same time.

'It doesn't look like nothing,' Grace observed, putting a jug of milk and loaf of bread on the table.

Louisa pinched her cheeks, washed her face and went upstairs to change her dress and brush her hair before returning to join them with glittering eyes and her head held high.

'There are some uniformed officers going along the street, knocking on doors,' she said. 'I've warned Pierre to keep quiet. Grace, go and tell the Admiral. Winnie, fetch Pamela.'

'She's sleeping, the poor little thing.'

'Just do it. Quickly. I'll stall them for as long as I can.'

'What are we going to do?' Grace began to panic. 'What will we say?'

'Let me do the talking,' Louisa said. 'I'll give you a nudge if I feel that it would be politic for you to swoon in front of them.'

'Can they search the house?' Winnie asked, feeling sick.

'We have the right to defend our home, but if they have a warrant for the arrest of the parole-breakers, they'll be crawling over the cottage like emmets. We must prepare for the worst.'

'How?' Winnie doubted that even Louisa would be able to explain away how they'd been completely unaware of the existence of their two extra lodgers.

'We're wasting time,' Louisa hissed. 'Do as I say.'

Winnie ran upstairs and picked Pamela up from her cot, at which the baby burst into tears at being rudely awoken. When Winnie returned to the hall, Louisa was at the door, holding it open to two officers in dark uniform, and behind them, Constable Pocket.

'You call us away from our chores, gentlemen,' Louisa said sternly, as Grace emerged from the parlour with the cup and saucer that she'd collected from the Admiral. 'And you have woken the baby with all your racket.'

Pamela obliged with loud sobs as Winnie held her tight.

'I regret the inconvenience, ladies. We have the authority to search these houses in order to apprehend two Frenchmen who are on the run. We have reason to suspect that they are residing at an address in Cockle Swamp Alley.'

'Then we are in danger?' Louisa asked. 'My husband is a Cinque Ports man, away hovelling, and there is no one to protect us. For a moment, I thought you had come to tell me that his ship had foundered and all was lost.'

'Please, don't be alarmed. Permit us to carry out a thorough search of the property and then we'll be on our way.' The officer who was speaking appeared to be the more senior of the two. 'Constable, you will remain on the doorstep to make sure that no one leaves the house while we are inside.'

313

'What about the backyard?' Louisa said. 'I don't want anyone making false allegations against us.'

'It's all right, missus. We have men posted at every exit on the alleyway, and others waiting at the rear of the terraces, because we don't want anyone to say we neglected our duty.'

'Of course,' Louisa said smoothly. 'Well, you'd better have a look round.'

Grace and Winnie waited in the hall as Louisa showed them the parlour, kitchen, hang and lean-to outside. They searched everywhere, even inside the privy, before returning indoors and heading upstairs. They'd missed the Admiral's hiding hole, Winnie thought, but what was to stop them finding Pierre? Hugging Pamela, she closed her eyes and prayed, as she heard them enter Billy's room and move the bed, before rummaging in the linen press. All they had to do was move it away from the wall, and they would find the loose panel that covered the entrance to the hiding hole.

'You are making quite a muddle,' she heard Louisa say. 'You have smudged the clean sheets. Do you know how long it takes to launder them?'

'It's always better to be safe than sorry,' the officer countered. 'Is there a means of climbing into the attic?'

'Oh, you have caught us out,' Louisa exclaimed. 'Sir, if you look up at the trapdoor, you will see that it hasn't been moved for a long time – look at the cobwebs. My sister was supposed to have made a start on the spring cleaning, but with the baby … She is a blessing, but time-consuming. She has only recently recovered from a fever – we thought we were going to lose her.'

'Thank you for your patience. Officer McMullen, there's nothing to see here.'

The two officers returned downstairs and bade them farewell as they left the cottage.

Winnie heard Louisa's sigh of relief as she closed the door.

'Well done, Louisa,' Grace said quietly. 'You saved our skins. I always knew there was virtue in not being overly house-proud. Thank the Lord for those cobwebs.'

'There's nothing in the attic anyway,' Winnie said.

'Jason tossed their luggage up there last night – there wasn't room for it anywhere else. He did his best to make the trapdoor appear undisturbed, a successful ploy, as it turns out.'

Winnie heard a faint thud from the parlour.

'Our guests have to stay where they are,' Louisa said. 'Give them some food and drink and tell them to be ready.'

Winnie handed Pamela over to Grace. She attended to the Admiral first, finding him sitting up in the hiding hole, his arms around his knees, his forehead glistening with sweat.

'We had a narrow escape,' he said, forcing a smile. 'I thought I was going to cough and give myself away.'

'I've brought you wine and warm broth, and a dressing for your neck.' She busied herself, changing the bandage. 'I'll be back later. Do you have a message for Pierre?'

'*Non, merci.*' Clutching a handkerchief to his mouth, he began to cough uncontrollably. When he eventually stopped, Winnie noticed splashes of blood on the white linen as he put the handkerchief aside.

She left him to take what nourishment he could, before carrying a tray of refreshments upstairs. The linen was scattered all over Billy's bed, so she was able to move the linen press without help and slide the panel away behind it.

'Pierre?' she whispered. 'The coast is clear, but you and the Admiral must remain where you are, Louisa's orders.'

'You spoil us, Mademoiselle, and you keep us going with your reassuring disposition. Without you, I don't know what we would have done.'

'I have a favour to ask you,' she said, deciding that she had to take the next step. She had to know what was written in the despatches before she travelled to Gravelines.

'Anything,' Pierre said.

'It is a delicate matter – I'd appreciate your complete discretion.'

'I have no desire to reveal your business to anyone else. All I wish for is a prompt return to France, nothing more, nothing less. What is it?'

'I have a document here.' She pulled the letter that she had decoded from her pocket and handed it to him. 'I believe that this is written in French. Can you tell me what it says?'

He began to read aloud.

'*Madame, your fears that we have been discovered are ground-less. Our mission continues apace ... Please find enclosed information acquired from the horse's mouth, the Port Admiral of Deal, no less.*' He paused. 'How did you come by this? Oh, I shouldn't ask ... It appears to be a sample of intelligence destined for my countrymen in the pursuit of an end to this war.'

'It was just some paperwork I found discarded near the market,' she said smoothly.

'How strange.' Pierre frowned because he didn't under-stand, but Winnie did, and the realisation that she had been working on behalf of Old Boney and his cronies made her feel sick to the stomach. She thought of Monsieur Alexandre's demise and the dangers she faced, having been caught up in the affair.

'Thank you anyway,' she said, taking the paper from him.

She moved the panel and cupboard back into place then returned to the kitchen, wondering what she should do. She was going to Gravelines to nurse the Admiral anyway. If she failed to deliver the despatches to Madame, there would be trouble, but if she handed them over, she would be giving away valuable intelligence. Furthermore, she needed to intercept the intelligence she was expected to bring back from France – she didn't know exactly what she might find contained within, but she hoped for evidence to incriminate those persons responsible for double-crossing Sir Flinders and Mr Cork ... unless the latter was also part of it.

Mr Cork's web of spies and couriers was turning out to be a very tangled one.

Winnie began to pack the items she would require for her spell in the hiding hole and the ensuing guinea run. She needed more paper, an expensive luxury. Deciding that she didn't want to go out for a second time that day, she went downstairs to take a couple of pages from the back of the ledger that Louisa used to record the household accounts, including their catches and whatever Jason made from hovelling.

Having checked that she was alone in the kitchen, she took the ledger from the drawer in the dresser. As she tore out the first page, she felt a tap on her shoulder. With a jolt of alarm, she turned.

'Oh my, I thought you were one of the runners come to get me.'

'If you want paper, you only have to ask,' Louisa said. 'I keep spare sheets in the parlour. There's no need to wreck my ledger.'

'I'm sorry ...'

'This is to do with Mr Cork?'

Winnie nodded.

'I hope you know what you're doing.' Louisa didn't press her any further.

'Going back to what we talked about before,' Winnie said tentatively. 'Do you think it's the upset of having the Frenchies here that's caused it?'

'It isn't the first time that I've thought I was with child, then suffered terrible bleeding. I didn't say anything. It makes me feel a failure. I can do anything, except give my husband a child. It's all very well Mrs Witherall telling me that it will happen in good time, but I can't bear her to keep going on about it. Sometimes I wonder if it's divine retribution for the way we live our lives.' Louisa held Winnie's gaze. 'Perhaps you have been right all along, and it's time we abandon the free trade.'

Winnie didn't know what to say.

'Don't worry about me,' Louisa went on eventually. 'Pack your bags – it won't be long before dark.'

'I have everything I need,' Winnie said, 'and the baskets of blankets and provisions are ready in the hall. I have one more thing to do before I kiss my darling daughter goodbye.' She stifled a sob. 'I'm not sure that I can leave her.'

'We'll look after her, I promise,' Louisa said.

Winnie hid in the room that she shared with Grace and copied the relevant letters from the despatches, missing out names and dates and replacing them with some of her own invention. She folded the copies and sealed them with candlewax mixed with the red wax she'd saved from

318

the originals. She was done, she thought, picking some hardened wax off the rug, hoping that Grace wouldn't notice because she was very proud of it, having made it herself from scraps of material during a long winter of dark evenings.

All that she had to do now was put the original letters away in her money box and spend time with Pamela, until the dreaded moment arrived when the men came home.

Jason and Billy turned up with Smoker and a hessian sack, stuffed and tied to resemble a manly figure.

'Look at the eyes,' Billy cried.

'They aren't in the least part realistic.' Still, Winnie had to laugh. There were circles painted on with white paint and fringed with black lashes.

'Has there been any trouble?' Jason asked.

'There has indeed,' Louisa answered. 'Constable Pocket and the runners turned up. They didn't find what they were looking for though.'

'Let's not delay, in case they should decide to come back. Are we ready?'

'Aye aye, cap'n,' Smoker said.

'Abel will be here within the half-hour,' Jason said. 'Louisa, I'll fetch our guests' luggage while you and Grace extract Pierre. Billy and Smoker, you help the Admiral out of his hidin' hole. We'll all meet in the hall, blacken our faces with soot from the bucket over there, and listen out for our driver. We'll know he's waitin' at the corner when we hear the signal: a seagull's cry. He's been practisin'. We thought that anythin' else would attract unwanted attention.'

Winnie wanted to point out that the gulls were usually quiet at night, but she kept her mouth shut.

'I'll open the door just a little,' she said, afraid that they wouldn't hear Abel's impression of a seagull.

It wasn't long before the cry came.

'He's here,' she hissed as those present took up their places in the hall.

'Let's go,' Jason whispered, and the procession hurried down the alley. Turning the corner, they found Abel who was barely visible, sitting in the driving seat of a cart that he'd painted black for the occasion. It was drawn by a black horse with its hooves wrapped in hessian. Any brasses that might have clinked or jangled had been removed from its harness.

Winnie loaded her basket over the side of the cart, while Jason and Pierre helped the Admiral in at the rear. Louisa and Grace placed more baskets, blankets, oil lamps and a half-anker of wine next to Winnie's, as Pierre helped Winnie into the cart, then jumped in beside her.

Winnie spread a blanket over the Admiral as he lay down on the floor of the cart, and they were off. The cart turned one way while Billy, limping alongside Smoker who was pushing the false Admiral in the handcart, turned the other. The wheels, which Billy still hadn't got around to oiling, squeaked away like a thousand meakers – Winnie fancied that she could still hear them long after the two men had disappeared.

Abel drove on. The cart jolted and lurched along, but they made good progress. As they cleared the busier part of town where a few Jack Tars were still wandering the streets, somewhat worse for wear, Abel pulled the covers from the carriage lanterns that he'd attached to the front and sides of their transport. The light they emitted was enough to give Winnie an idea of where they were.

When they reached St Leonard's, Abel set them down outside the lychgate. It was up to Winnie to take a lamp to show Pierre to the hiding hole in the shadow of the church and slide the slab aside. Somehow, the two of them managed to settle the Admiral in the second chamber and unpack the blankets and provisions.

She left one of the lamps glowing, turning the wick down to eke out their supply of oil for as long as possible.

'This is ... a most desirable residence, don't you think?' Pierre said dryly. 'We will be very comfortable here.'

Winnie stifled a gasp as something scuttled across her foot. She missed Pamela, was worried about Billy, and resented the fact that any respectable woman from a good family would be planning her imminent wedding day, not sitting in a cold, dark hiding hole with a pair of fugitives.

Two nights passed before they set eyes on anyone else.

'Oh, it's you, my darling,' Winnie cried when Billy's face appeared at the entrance to the chamber. 'We thought you might have been Reverend North or the gardener who looks after the churchyard, come to investigate the footprints around the tomb.' It was the only potential problem that Jason hadn't thought of – the wet and muddy ground that might give them away. 'I've been worried about you, not knowing if the decoy worked out.'

'Oh, it did,' he grinned. 'It scared the wits out of one of the Jacks we met on our way. Pamela is missin' 'er ma, even though Grace is spoilin' 'er. But my dear Winnie, 'ow are you?'

'Much better for seeing you. It's hardly a room at the Three Kings ...'

'The Admiral is well?'

'About the same,' Winnie replied. 'He's been very quiet. I don't think the vapours down here have improved his health.'

''Ow about you, Pierre?'

'*Très bien, merci*. Thank you for allowing us the services of your lovely lady who is kindness personified. Are we really on the move this time?'

'The transport will be 'ere at midnight.' Billy checked the watch in his pocket – a silver one, not the Admiral's, Winnie noted.

'Nobody's followed me up 'ere – I've been careful. As for the authorities, they came back yesterday and made another search, but they didn't find nothin'. It caused Louisa much amusement.'

'How is she?'

'Well, I think. Why do you ask?'

Winnie kept her voice low. 'Don't say anything to Jason, but Louisa was with child.'

'Oh, you don't say?'

'She begged me not to breathe a word of it to Jason before the guinea run. You will keep an eye on her while we're gone?'

'You don't 'ave to ask me. I'm goin' to be like a farmer, tendin' to 'is flock of 'ens.'

'You're going to make me a wonderful husband,' she smiled.

'By this time next week, we'll be married, my love. And you needn't worry about borrowin' a curtain ring – I've bought a proper one.'

'Oh Billy, that's wonderful.'

'It's nothin' special,' he said.

'It will be special to me because you took the trouble to choose it. I don't care if it's made from brass or wood. It doesn't matter.'

'Then I'm glad – and relieved. It's been preyin' on my mind, not bein' flush enow in the pocket to buy you the best.

'We'll be a proper family, the Fleets of Deal. That's all that matters to me, not the prospect of riches. I don't care about makin' our fortune – I'm 'appy working with my 'ands, cuttin' and sandin' timbers for Ol' Elson. When this is all settled, we'll lead a quiet, ordinary way of life.'

Billy's dream seemed a long way away as they hurried to the lychgate on hearing Abel's signal: the cry of the seven whistlers this time. Winnie didn't think it was a good choice: the call of the curlew was a bad omen. Billy and Pierre had to carry the Admiral this time – he had become too weak to stand, let alone walk to the cart.

'All's quiet,' Abel whispered as the horse chewed on its bit. 'The vicar is tucked up in bed in the rectory and I haven't met a soul on my way here.'

'Let's pray that it stays that way,' Winnie said as she settled herself down beside Pierre, checking for a third and fourth time that she had the despatches tucked inside her bodice, before they left Billy behind. With the Admiral groaning at every jolt of the cart, Abel drove them in a north-westerly direction to join the ancient tracks over down and farmland, avoiding Deal before turning east to enter the sandhills and meet with the guinea boat along the coast.

Apart from disturbing a pig that came snorting from the undergrowth, making the horse shy and the passengers start, they reached the meeting place without incident, but Winnie had no reason for complacency. She had at least six hours stuck on the guinea boat to look forward to, crossing the choppy waters of the Channel, exposed to the vagaries of the Revenue and sundry privateers, while she did her best to keep the Admiral alive. And she had no idea what challenges she would have to face when they reached Gravelines.

Chapter Twenty-Two

The Devil to Pay

Mr Witherall took the helm, Jason stood as lookout and the rest of the men took up their oars. With a signal from their captain, the men began to row, and the guinea boat, sitting low in the water, slipped away on a high tide from the sandhills.

'Where's your sense of rhythm?' Jason called. 'One, two, three. I reckon we'll be back in Deal by tomorrer nightfall for our usual on the beach.'

Winnie felt the Admiral's fingers tighten around hers. Concentrating on his welfare as a means of putting her worries about her meeting with Madame briefly to one side, she gave them a gentle squeeze.

'It isn't far now – you'll soon be home,' she said.

'There'll be a carriage on its way for us when we reach Gravelines,' Pierre said. 'With luck, it will be there already. I paid one of Jason's trusted acquaintances to deliver a message to one of the merchants there in advance.' Winnie assumed that Pierre had sent the note with another of the Deal smugglers. He had taken a risk in doing so, and she hoped that it would pay off.

The Admiral coughed, bringing up a spoonful of blood into his palm. Winnie gave him a handkerchief, but although he wiped the blood away, he continued to stare at the stain where it had been. Her hope that he might live to spend time with his family seemed increasingly faint.

The boat moved into an area of rough swell that made it rock and pitch.

'It's like – rowin' – through – treacle,' one of the men grunted.

'Keep goin', lads – do you want to be the crew who lost thirty thousand guineas to the Revenue or a Dutch privateer?'

'No, Marlin!'

'Then row as though your lives depend on it!'

'It's little wonder we're goin' slow,' called Dunk, one of the oarsmen. 'Who thought it was a good idea to overload the boat? That many beans, and passengers too? What's our share in this enterprise?' His voice hardened. From where she sat with the Admiral, Winnie noticed the sheen of sweat across his face and the corded veins in his arms. 'You're takin' advantage – treatin' us like dumb asses!'

'It's a very good share,' Jason shouted back. 'If you don't like it, don't sign up for the next run. I can find other willin' hands.'

'We should turn back, find a place to land and unload the spoils – this could be the biggest prize of our lives, lads,' Dunk went on.

Winnie froze. Was he suggesting a mutiny?

'I wouldn't go against me, if I were you,' Jason said coldly. 'If it wasn't for the venturers who've put their faith in me, I'd hole this vessel, and let her go down with you and the gold.'

'You wouldn't!' Dunk dropped his oar. It clunked into the blade of the man in front of him. He swore and the whole crew stopped rowing. 'Let's tie 'im up and throw 'im overboard.' Standing up, he gesticulated towards Jason who stared back at him, a weary expression on his features. 'We'll be in clover – we'll never 'ave to work again! Come on, lads. What are you waitin' for?'

'I'm not goin' against Marlin,' someone muttered. ''E's saved my neck many a time.'

'We're in this together. Break your word, and you'll never be able to show your face in Deal again,' said Cut-throat, the oarsman behind Dunk.

'Words don't mean nothin' when there's a fortune at stake. What a load of dunderheads! Can't you see these are the easiest pickin's you'll ever make?' Holding her breath, Winnie watched him unsheathe a knife from his belt. 'Who's with me?' he went on. 'Let's 'ave a show of 'ands.'

The boat rocked as a wave broke across her bow. Cut-throat took advantage of Dunk's temporary loss of balance by leaping on to his back and holding him around the neck, choking him until his skin turned dark and his eyes bulged.

'Let him take a breath,' Jason said as Cut-throat relieved him of the knife and threw it aft. 'Then tie him up – we'll decide what to do with him later. I'll be glad to see the backpart of him.'

Winnie watched as Cut-throat wrapped a rope around Dunk's wrists, knotted it and ran the other end twice around the mast as Dunk kicked and swore.

'I apologise to the lady on your behalf,' Jason said. 'You will never crew for me again, nor will you receive a share in the profits of this venture. I treat you like a dumb ass, because you are one. Pierre, take up his oar!'

Pierre moved to Dunk's place.

'Now, row …'

It took them seven hours instead of the five and a half that Jason had planned for and as such they had to queue for a mooring at Gravelines.

'I thought we were goin' to end up in Davy Jones's locker, no thanks to you, Dunk,' Jason complained. 'Never mind. What's done is done. Winnie, how is your patient?'

She mopped the runnels of sweat from the Admiral's brow with a damp cloth. He was deathly pale, but she didn't want to tempt fate by saying so.

'He is much the same. Don't fret, sir – by noon, you will be with your wife and son.'

'I thank you,' he muttered, before closing his eyes.

Three vessels left the wharf before they were invited by an official to row the guinea boat to a free mooring. Cut-throat and the crew hitched her lines to the mooring posts while Jason found their papers authorising their entry into the port. Dunk remained tied to the mast, shivering with fear and cold.

'What are you going to do with him?' Winnie asked.

'Leave him to stew in his own juices until we're done here.' Despite his apparent anger, Jason threw a blanket over the man's shoulders. 'Then I'm goin' to leave him behind.'

'You can't do that!' Dunk exclaimed, his teeth chattering. 'I want to go 'ome.'

'You should have thought about that before you crossed me,' Jason snapped. He turned back to Winnie. 'I suggest that you wait here with us until the gold has been unloaded and the Frenchies are on their way. Then I – or one of the crew – will escort you to Madame's. What do you think?'

'I think I should go alone – that's what she requested last time. I understand why. It's a covert operation ...'

'I admire your courage, but I really think one of us should keep an eye out for you. Gravelines is a dangerous place.'

'You're thinking of Madame's right-hand man, Monsieur Alexandre,' she said.

He nodded.

'I don't think it wise to go against her wishes.' Besides, what could Jason do if Madame realised that Winnie had interfered with the despatches and was bringing false intelligence? She would be putting them both at risk. 'I'll take them to her under the cover of darkness, giving you time to load the goods. If I'm not back within the half-hour, come and find me.'

'I'd never forgive myself if somethin' went wrong. How would I tell my wife that I'd failed to protect her sister?' Jason fretted, but he didn't insist on accompanying her – maybe he would have done, Winnie mused, if he'd known about her plan to double-cross Madame.

Transport arrived for Pierre and the Admiral. Again, the military security officer checked Jason's paperwork, and the credentials of the driver, before allowing the Admiral and Pierre into the carriage.

Pierre leaned out of the window.

'I thank you all, especially the maid with the golden hair, for everything you've done for us!'

'God speed,' Winnie shouted after them as the horses pulled away, the carriage moving swiftly behind them. She doubted she would ever see or hear of them again.

She waited, drinking coffee and eating bread rolls while another carriage arrived with outriders to take the gold to Paris. The sacks of guineas were quickly unloaded from the guinea boat, being extracted from the cavities between the double layer of timbers forming the hull, and from the hollowed-out section of the mast. Within a short time, the entourage was off, and another arrived to take the guineas from a second vessel that had arrived not long after Jason's crew.

'Come on, lads. There's no rest for the wicked,' Jason shouted. 'There are goods to load and my lady wife has requested that I make a few extra acquisitions before we return home. We'll be away by midnight. Don't drink too much and don't get into any kind of trouble. Anyone who isn't here at the allotted time will have to swim for it. Cut-throat and Drifter, you take the first watch, Mr Witherall and I will take the second.'

When darkness fell, Winnie told Jason she was on her way to Madame's. He sent Cut-throat with her, against her wishes. At first, as they made their way through the streets past the encampment, she was grateful for his presence, but gradually she became aware that he was none too steady on his feet.

'I apologise for my ungen'lemanly behaviour, miss.' He stumbled. 'I've 'ad a few too many.'

She began to wonder if it was wise, taking him along with her.

'Our destination isn't far away – you can wait outside while I attend to my business.' She walked ahead of him, passing the shops and stalls, many of which were open late into the night, selling food and drink to the hungry smugglers. 'Stand over there,' she said when they reached Madame's shop. The shutters were closed, and the door locked.

As she knocked, she couldn't help feeling that she was being watched, not by Cut-throat but by someone else. She blamed her nerves – the more anxious she was, the more convinced she was that she was under surveillance. Part of her wanted to run away, back to the relative safety of the guinea boat. *Forget about the spy ring, Winnie*, a little voice whispered in her ear. *It's none of your business. Go back to your child. Marry Billy and live happily ever after.*

Except she couldn't have it on her conscience to ignore the fact that she had been carrying despatches for Old Boney. The betrayal of her country's intelligence had to be stopped. She had the evidence. It was up to her to convince someone in authority to put a stop to it.

She knocked again.

It was Madame who let her in, showing her up the spiral staircase to the room above. There was an oil lamp burning in the corner and candles flickering from the wall sconces.

'*Je suis ravie de vous voir*, Golden Maid.' Her bracelets clinked as she held out her hand to take the papers.

Winnie took them from inside her cloak and gave them to her. She carried them over to the lamp and examined them, her long, slow perusal of the seals making Winnie's heart pound so fiercely she was afraid that Madame would hear it.

'I must hurry you,' Winnie said. 'I have a boat waiting for me.'

'All in good time.' Eventually, Madame unlocked a drawer in her bureau and took out a package. 'Now you may depart,' she said, as she handed it over.

When Winnie emerged on to the street, she looked for Cut-throat, but he wasn't there. It didn't matter, she thought, because she had the despatches, and with luck, she would return to England with the information that, like a pot of gunpowder, could blow the whole operation orchestrated against her countrymen by persons as yet unknown to smithereens.

She didn't hear him until it was too late. As she hurried away from Madame's, running along in the shadows of the towering warehouses, she was intent on getting back to the guinea boat, and as a result, he was upon her before she realised that he was there.

She felt the noose of an abrasive cord around her neck, compressing her voice box so she couldn't scream, or breathe. She struggled, squirmed and kicked. She craned her neck and sank her teeth into her attacker's hand. With a grunt, he loosened his grip, allowing her to gulp air into her bellows before he tightened the noose again.

Lord, save me, she prayed. Where was Cut-throat? Where was Jason?

'I 'ave a message from Madame.' The words spoken in a foreign accent gusted into her ear. 'She's seen through your ruse and she is bitterly disappointed. *Désolée*, in fact, because she thought she could trust you.'

Winnie managed to force one finger between the cord and her neck, giving herself the space to take a breath.

'You were disingenuous, thinking you could just reseal the envelopes and she wouldn't notice. Madame has the sharpest eyes in the business – the fine hairs that were planted across each seal have disappeared or been disturbed.'

Her attacker dragged her into an alleyway heading away from the wharf, away from the lights and the sound of voices, away from life ... An image of her baby flickered into her mind: a sobbing child left motherless. She couldn't – *wouldn't* – let it happen to Pamela.

She dropped her hands from the noose and thrust her elbows hard into her attacker's belly. With a howl of fury, he twisted the noose tighter until her vision filled with pulsing black circles.

As she began to lose hope and consciousness, she heard a crack, the sound like a butcher's knife cleaving bone. The noose slackened and her attacker fell away behind her, his body slumping to the ground. Gasping for breath, she glanced wildly around her, trying to retrieve her wits and her sense of direction, but it was too late to run, because there was someone else present, his hands tight around her wrists.

'Miss Lennicker, we meet again. I believe I have saved your life.'

'Don't ask me to express my gratitude,' she wheezed, recognising her attacker from their previous encounter on her way to Nomansland Farm. 'Unhand me and let me go on my way.'

'Not until we've discussed an urgent matter of business.'

'I'm sure that we can have no mutual interests whatsoever. Let me go,' she repeated. 'I have friends who will be looking for me.'

'This is how you reward me?' he said gruffly.

'I have nothing of any value on my person.'

'Ah yes, the watch. I apologise, but I thought to impersonate a vagabond thief. As it turns out, I've become rather partial to it – it keeps excellent time.'

'At least you are honest.' She stopped abruptly, feeling foolish. Why would she praise this rough, poorly dressed personage, who had clearly been stalking her, for his honesty? How did she know he was telling the truth?

'At first, I was looking for your sister, but then it turned out I'd been barking up the wrong tree. We haven't been properly introduced. My name is Mr Gambril.'

She had guessed correctly, she thought, recalling Mrs Stickles waxing lyrical about the gentleman with the code book.

'I have a child, a daughter.' With a shudder, she glanced along the alley into the darkness where the body of Madame's man lay on the ground, then in the opposite direction towards the narrow band of light from the lanterns on the wharf. 'I beg you to let me go.'

'Not yet. We need to talk. Let me assure you, though, that I intend you no harm.'

'What do you want from me?'

'I'm acting on behalf of the British government—'

'I don't believe you.'

'I can show you my papers of authority from the Home Service.' Releasing her, he took some papers from his greatcoat pocket and opened them with a flourish. 'You see …'

Straining her eyes, she read confirmation of his name and his role in the gathering and management of intelligence.

Without waiting for her answer, he folded the papers and put them away.

'There is a gentleman known as Monsieur Jean Boule. It is an alias, not his real name. He is a coxcomb who has ingratiated himself with certain influential men in Parliament, persuading them to send money to France to a royalist organisation to fund an uprising against Napoleon Bonaparte. However, having discovered some discrepancies in this gentleman's stories, I'm investigating the possibility that the money is funding Bonaparte's army and that Monsieur Boule is spying for the French. I have told you all this to show that I am genuine, that I seek the truth.'

'I don't believe you,' Winnie repeated. 'I've seen evidence of the codes you use to write your version of events in the despatches.' His brow furrowed as she went on, 'The book came into my possession.'

'Ah, Mrs Stickles … I pride myself on my attention to detail, but this is one occasion when I slipped up. I assumed she would keep it back for me when I left it behind.'

'She gave it to me, thinking I'd be able to read it for her – she wondered if you were writing a novel, or poetry.'

'I obtained it from Monsieur Boule's London residence – by foul rather than fair means, involving a maid in my pay. Miss Lennicker, I was trying to read the despatches for myself.'

'It's a good story,' she admitted, and Mr Gambril's view that Monsieur Boule was responsible fitted with the facts as she understood them.

'What will it take to convince you that I'm on the same side as you are?'

'You don't have any idea whose side I'm on,' she countered.

'I have Mrs Stickles' assurances of your honesty and good character. Besides why would I risk my skin to save you from Madame's aide's clutches if I thought you were on the side of the enemy? He was going to kill you and take the despatches back to Madame.'

He had a point, she thought.

'What do you know of Mr Cork, the agent?' she asked.

'I have yet to make a judgement. The evidence of his involvement in this plot against the British government is vague to say the least, but if it does turn out that he is a part of it, then he will be prosecuted. Miss Lennicker, I *need* that book.'

'I am ahead of you, Mr Gambril. I left the despatches in Deal with the code book – I read them, decoded the hidden lines then had them translated by a source whom I trust implicitly. They are, as you suspected, messages written in French for the purpose of aiding Old Boney. I created false papers and gave them to Madame who noticed that the seals were not right, which is why she sent her aide after me.'

Mr Gambril wasted no time in further deliberation. 'Take Madame's papers back to Deal and make the plant as arranged so as not to arouse suspicion that we are on to them. I will return to London to notify the higher-ups to let them know that they have misplaced their trust in Monsieur Boule. If we have enough proof of his nefarious activities, he will be arrested and tried. I believe he has caused much damage to our war effort and our government's reputation.' Winnie thought of Sir Flinders and how he had been shammed.

'What if Madame should send a note with someone else to warn Monsieur Boule?' she asked.

'I expect to make it back to London in good time,' Mr Gambril assured her. 'Let's pray that I reach my destination before she can get word to him.

'I'll be in contact with you forthwith to arrange collection of the ... items you've mentioned. Thank you, Miss Lennicker. I am eternally grateful to you. Before I leave you, let me reassure you that I don't make a habit of attacking people, especially members of the weaker sex.'

'Less of the weaker, sir. You mean *fairer*.' Her confidence had grown. She was in control, having gained possession of the evidence that could break a spy ring. She might not be clever like Louisa, but she had common sense.

She turned at the sound of shouting, catching sight of a figure running along the alleyway towards them, a lantern swinging from his hand.

'Jason?' she cried, as Mr Gambril slipped away into the darkness.

'Winnie, are you there?'

'Thank the Lord,' she breathed as she hurried towards him. 'I thought I was a goner. We must leave Gravelines right away.' She tried to explain. 'Madame's found out that I more natural speech looked at the papers ...'

'Oh dear,' Jason said, offering her his arm.

'Her man – he's dead, I think.'

335

'Save your breath for now,' he warned. 'We're ready to depart – that's why I came to look for you.'

'Where's Cut-throat? He disappeared.'

'I have no idea, but anyone who isn't on that boat by the time we get there, isn't comin' back to Deal with us. The goods have been loaded. Our papers have been stamped. If what you say is true, the Douane will be on our tail.'

She thought she heard yelling and footsteps, men in clod-hoppers charging after them, as she once more ran for her life. When they reached the wharf, Jason picked Winnie up and flung her into the boat. As Gunner pushed the boat away, Jason leapt across the black expanse of water, grabbed the gunwale and scrambled in. When the rocking had subsided, the oarsmen picked up their oars and started to row.

Shaking, Winnie covered herself with oilskins and sat in the bottom of the boat, her back against a bale of lace, her arms wrapped tightly around her knees, as she prayed for their salvation. This time, it seemed that her prayers were answered, because by first light the Kent coast hove in sight. Never had she felt so relieved to see the white cliffs of Dover.

'We've done well, lads,' Jason shouted. 'I reckon we'll soon be home and dry.'

As the crew rowed towards Deal, Mr Witherall, Billy and Cromwell came sailing to meet them. They brought the *Curlew* alongside the guinea boat, the waves gently lapping against her bow. The crew of the guinea boat unloaded the cargo of goods into the *Curlew* and the other boats that Smoker and some of the other free traders brought across from the shore.

'We made it. We've only gorn and done it!' There was no disguising the triumph in Billy's voice as Winnie hoisted herself over the gunwales of the guinea boat and into the

Curlew in a most unladylike manner. Laughing, he gripped her hand and helped to haul her in. 'It seems that we've 'ad a good catch today, the best one ever.' He offered her a chest to sit on and they perched side by side, watching Jason and his crew – minus Dunk and Cut-throat whom they'd left in Gravelines – as they removed the last traces of their association with the guinea boat.

Jason opened the box that contained the false papers and set them alight, then offered Gunner a hammer.

'I hate to do this, but there'll be another one where she came from.'

Gunner duly smashed a hole in her side before Jason and the remaining crew leapt on to the *Curlew* and the other boats.

They watched her go down, sinking beneath the water with a sigh and a soft rush of bubbles rising to the surface.

'Better to destroy the evidence than 'ang on to 'er for the sake of forty guineas,' Mr Witherall observed.

'Indeed. Let's go ashore,' Jason said.

'Aye,' Gunner agreed as Winnie turned her gaze towards the shore and the rooftops of Deal, longing to be home. Tomorrow was her wedding day.

Billy kissed her cheek. 'Cromwell came with a note addressed to you. Mr Cork requests the pleasure of your company at the Three Kings and you're to inform the manager when you arrive there.'

'Thank you,' she said, relieved that she wouldn't have to trek all the way to Nomansland Farm, or lurk around the outside of the castle, waiting for the coast to be clear before she dropped the despatches in their hiding hole.

'Let's go home,' Jason shouted. 'Full sail ahead!'

'Not for Deal. We should 'ead north for the sand'ills, my boy,' Mr Witherall said. 'The militia were out in force when we set out to do a little fishin'.'

'Ship ahoy!' Gunner called and all eyes turned to the *Guinevere*, who had suddenly appeared from between some of the ships in the roadstead and was sailing towards them, all canvas set.

Winnie felt strangely calm. She had narrowly survived her second visit to Gravelines and succeeded in helping Mr Gambril in his quest to break a French spy ring. The gold had been safely delivered, Pierre and the Admiral had arrived on home soil, and they were about to land a decent haul of run goods, if the *Guinevere* didn't catch up with them.

She shaded her eyes from the early morning sunshine as she looked back towards the Sands. The *Guinevere* seemed to be hovering in their wake, tacking slowly along behind them, like a dog harrying a flock of hens.

'Why don't she leave us alone?' Mr Witherall grumbled, shaking his fist at them. 'She must 'ave better things to do than 'arass a fleet o' innocent fishermen. Keep 'er steady, boy,' he barked at Cromwell who had his hand on the tiller. 'Stay on course!'

'I'm not sure,' Cromwell said. 'The cutter is movin' closer – I think she's tryin' to cut us off. What shall I do?'

'Follow my orders and don't back down.'

'But she's goin' to push us into the shallows ...'

Jason called across to the cutter's crew. 'You're runnin' us down,' he yelled, but the crew on deck didn't acknowledge him.

'Get rid of the goods,' Mr Witherall shouted. 'Throw 'em out, then turn towards the shore. Your new marks are the peak of the tallest sand'ill and the clump of alders. Got that, boy?'

'Aye, aye, captain,' Cromwell responded as Jason and Billy dropped bales of textiles and twenty half-ankers of cognac overboard. The crews of the other boats did likewise and Winnie began to breathe again. Her relief soon turned to alarm when a second vessel, a cruiser from Folkestone, appeared on their opposite flank, helping the *Guinevere* drive the flotilla inexorably towards the shore in a pincer movement, while the beach filled with uniformed officials.

Winnie began to quake with fear and Billy turned white beneath his freckles.

'Box the compass!' shouted Mr Witherall. 'Dip the lugsail, Marlin! I said, turn about, boy!'

'I'm tryin' to,' Cromwell cried.

'Who are those men?' Winnie asked.

'I dunno, but I don't like the look of 'em,' Billy said. 'Marlin, do you 'ave a plan?'

'Not yet,' Jason said, frowning.

'The priority is to get Winnie past 'em so she can deliver the despatches,' Billy said. 'I'll provide a distraction – you go with 'er.'

'Why don't I divert them while you and Winnie make your way to wherever you need to go?'

'You'll do as I say this time, Marlin. I can't run. You can.' Billy added fiercely as Winnie felt for the despatches that she'd tucked inside her bodice, 'You are an 'ero to me. You've saved my skin many a time, and it's the least I can do to return the favour.'

Jason scanned the beach. 'It looks like there's a detachment of dragoons waitin' with the Bow Street Runners and Constable Pocket, ready to arrest us for aidin' and abettin' the Frenchies, while the gobblers are about to grab us for importing illegal goods. We are between the Devil and the deep blue sea. If they catch anyone, it should be me. You have a little girl who's waitin' for you at home.'

'You 'ave to make it back, Marlin,' Billy said quietly. 'Louisa needs you.'

'Pamela needs her father more ...'

'You should be with Louisa at this time,' Winnie joined in. 'Jason, I'm sorry, but she's lost the baby.'

'No!' Winnie shrank at the pain etched on his face. 'You're lyin'. She would have told me.'

'She didn't want it to interfere with the run, knowing how important it was to get the guineas to France. She said it would keep ...'

'You should be at your wife's side,' Billy said. 'Let me do this.'

'Billy, no. You're bound to be caught.' Winnie sensed that Jason's resolve was wavering, torn between his duty to his men and his compassion for Louisa.

She touched her throat where the noose had left its mark – things were going from bad to worse.

'It's a chance I'm prepared to take.' Billy's fists clenched, emphasising his determination. 'When I give the order, you must all leave the boat and make your way 'ome as best you can. First, though ...' As Winnie stood up, he grabbed her, pulled her close and kissed her. 'I'll be back as soon as I can. Look after Pamela for me. Tell her 'ow much her pa loves 'er.'

'Oh Billy ... Take care, my darling.'

'Promise me you'll run as fast as you can,' he said. 'Take Marlin's 'and and don't look back.'

'Billy, 'ere's the pistol, primed and ready.' Mr Witherall handed it over to him before continuing, 'Cromwell, bring the *Curlew* on to the beach as far as you can before she grinds to an 'alt. The rest o' you be ready to jump over the side – keep down, usin' the boat to provide cover, then run for the sand'ills. After that, it's down to you and Lady Luck.'

'Father, come with us,' Jason said.

'No, I'll 'old you back. I'll take my chance with Cromwell 'ere.'

The officials on the beach were moving ever closer, and the *Guinevere* and the other ship were in as near as they dared without becoming grounded. Their routes of escape were cut off.

'It's now or never!' Billy raised the pistol and fired towards the sandhills over the top of their would-be captors' heads. The dragoons unsheathed their cutlasses, the Bow Street Runners pulled out their small arms, and the figure that Winnie had identified from a distance as Constable Pocket stumbled away in the direction from which he had come.

'Go!' Billy urged as the *Curlew* grounded with a lurch that sent Winnie bumping into Jason. Recovering her wits, she scrambled out, lowering herself into the shallow water and crouching beside the hull to shelter from the small-arms fire that began to rain down from the sandhills. A boom from the *Guinevere*'s guns sent Winnie running across the beach, her head down and her skirts hitched up, as she raced alongside Jason.

'Remember what Billy said. Don't look back. Don't think about anyone else,' Jason panted.

'Don't talk. Save your breath,' she gasped.

As they reached the tideline, the dry powdery sand slowed them down, but they kept running straight across the beach to the entrance to a narrow path into the dunes, the only gap that wasn't guarded by their potential captors. Except, as they reached it, Constable Pocket, looking sheepish, appeared in front of them.

'Stop!' he shouted, stepping aside. 'You must stop in the name of the law.'

Taking advantage of his apparent lack of appetite for arresting his friends and acquaintances, Jason and Winnie ran past him.

'There'll be somethin' in this for you,' Jason muttered. He grabbed Winnie's hand, pulling her up the shore, and guided her between the clumps of rough marram grass into a hollow where he began to dig, sending up showers of sand. Having revealed a few timbers from an old rowing boat, he gestured to Winnie to slide into the chamber underneath, where he joined her, pulling the boards over their heads.

Her bellows aching, she lay down on her stomach and waited, her palms damp with sweat and her tongue coated in grit. They were alive, at least, but what about Billy and the rest of the boatmen?

Chapter Twenty-Three

A Tale of Mixed Fortunes

Winnie remained as still as a rock until the shouting faded and stopped, then she turned her head to face Jason. He was looking at her, his brow furrowed.

'How will we know when it's safe to go out there?' she whispered.

'I'll have a look.' He rolled on to his back and raised one of the boards, letting in daylight. Winnie sat up, her neck cricked, as she peered through the gap. There wasn't much to see – just sand, spiky blades of grass and a snail shell, and the sky above the hollow.

'I'll hold the timber while you crawl out. Ladies first.' Jason smiled. 'No, on second thoughts, let me go out first, in case we come face to face with the enemy. We know that some of them are armed.'

'I'll go first,' Winnie countered. 'They're less likely to fire on a woman.' Without waiting for him to argue, she moved towards the gap and scrambled out. She crawled to the top of the slope to survey the sandhills and the beach. The little boats had dispersed – she could see two of them, like insects on the water. The Folkestone cruiser had gone, disappeared among the ships in the Downs, while the *Guinevere* had moored a little further offshore. As for the dragoons and everyone else, the only sign of them was the footprints left in the wet sand along the tideline.

A pair of grey and white gulls soared overhead, wheeling this way and that, and a rabbit popped its head out of a nearby burrow, then quickly retreated, showing its white tail.

'What do you reckon, Winnie?'

'We have a choice: move now and hope for the best, or wait until dark. I prefer the former.' She was keen to unburden herself of the despatches before Mr Cork heard about Madame's discovery and the attack on her aide by other means, and she wanted to go home, not just because of Pamela and wanting to find out about Billy's fate, but because she wanted Jason to be back at his wife's side where he belonged.

She waited for him to appear from the hollow before they made their way back along the beach towards the Three Kings.

'We should hold hands to make it look like we are lovers walkin' out together, in case our persecutors spot us,' Jason said. 'At least, if it doesn't feel too awkward.'

'You are my brother-in-law. I don't think there's any harm in it, if it helps us flam the authorities.' Winnie took his hand and walked beside him, trying to keep up with his long strides. 'Slow down. If we're to be convincing, we should dally a while.'

'I'm not doin' any dallyin' after what we've been through durin' the past few days. I want to get back to my wife – as you've said, she needs me.'

She felt very bad, having been the one who had told him that Louisa had lost the baby. He would be drowning his sorrows, not celebrating on the beach that night.

344

The sand turned to shingle underfoot, slowing their progress, but eventually they reached the Three Kings.

'I'll wait for you outside,' Jason said.

'I won't be long, if he's still here.' Having extracted the despatches from inside her bodice, Winnie made her way to the reception desk where the manager was dealing with an elderly couple who had lost their luggage on their way to Deal.

'I'm sorry to keep you,' he said to Winnie, then turned back to the couple and sent them on their way with a promise that he would send one of the porters to enquire with the owner of the post chaise they had hired. 'You have booked a room, or a suite, Mrs—?'

'I have an appointment with one of your guests, a Mr Cork.'

'Ah yes. You will find him in the dining room.'

'I don't like to interrupt—' She realised she hadn't any idea what the time was.

'He will see you. Let me show you the way.'

He was eating luncheon alone, his platter piled up with cold meats and piccalilli. As he looked up, his napkin slipped. He picked it up and tucked the corner back inside the collar of his shirt.

'You have something for me?'

She placed the packet on the table. He took it and dropped it into a bag at his feet.

'My clerk will be organising your payment and you will receive it in due course,' he informed her. 'I believe that we have come to the end of our arrangement. I shall not be requiring your services again.'

Her palms ran damp with perspiration. Had news reached him from Madame via one of the other guinea boats? Did he suspect that something was amiss?'

'If the rumours are true,' he continued, 'this damned war with France will soon be at an end.'

'Farewell then,' she said, but he didn't reply, stuffing his mouth with a slice of beef.

Wondering if Mr Gambril would find evidence that Mr Cork was involved in the plot, she went to find Jason.

'It's all done,' she said, and they walked back across the top of the beach. It was deserted – even the shore boys weren't there. The boats were hauled up on the shingle and the huts closed up.

'Where is everyone?' Jason asked. 'The music? The dancin'? The drinkin'? Mrs Stickles and her hot pies?'

'They must have gone home,' Winnie said. 'Something's gone asprawl. I can feel it in my bones.'

When they arrived at the cottage, the handful of neighbours who were gathered outside parted to let them through. Winnie went ahead of Jason into the kitchen where her eyes fell on Pamela, sitting on Grace's lap.

'Oh, let me have her,' she cried, picking her up and cuddling her, breathing in her scent. 'I do believe that you've grown in the past few days.' Gradually she became aware of the other people present and the expressions on their faces: Louisa, Mr and Mrs Witherall.

'What's the news, Father?' Jason asked.

'It isn't good. There's no beatin' around the bush ... Billy's been arrested, taken by Constable Pocket of all men.'

'No ...' Winnie's legs buckled. Louisa grabbed her before she could drop the baby and sat her on a chair.

'Smoker and Gunner 'ave been arrested as well.'

'Where are they?'

'In Dover gaol.'

'Why Dover, not Deal?'

'It's obvious, isn't it? They're 'opin' to put 'em in front of magistrates who will make a fair judgement.'

'Look after Pamela for me,' Winnie said, trying to hand the baby back to Grace.

'Where are you going?'

'To Dover. I will walk, if I have to.' It was more than eight miles away, if she took the road through Walmer and Ringwould.

'We should all go together. We can hire a carriage from Abel and travel in style,' Jason said. 'We are fairly flush in the pockets – perhaps we can find out who the magistrates are and offer them a little inducement to ...'

'I don't think we should,' Louisa said. 'It might make matters worse for the prisoners. There's no evidence that Billy and Smoker were involved in helping the Frenchies.'

'They'll find somethin' they can use to pin the blame on them,' Jason said. 'It wouldn't look good for the runners if they were let off; they have been brought in as experts in tracin' and apprehendin' those responsible for a crime that crosses border. The high-ups like Sir Flinders and his friends in London would be embarrassed if it became known that the Admiral had returned home and nobody had been convicted of aidin' and abettin' his escape. It'll be a show trial, makin' an example of them to stop others doing the same. I'm sorry, Winnie, but I think that's how it will go.'

'Let's see what happens first,' she said bravely. 'It might not turn out as badly as we imagine.'

'The 'earin' is bein' 'eld tomorrer,' Mr Witherall said. 'They're tracin' witnesses and takin' statements. Our men won't speak against them.'

'There will be others willing to have their say, though.' Winnie tugged at a loose thread on her shawl. It began to unravel.

'I'm going to do some askin' around,' Jason said. 'I'll find someone willin' to speak for them and I'll call on Abel to warn him to prepare for an early start.'

Winnie sat up with her sisters who entertained Pamela and tried to raise Winnie's spirits with milk and brandy, and some Folkestone pudding pie that Grace had bought from Molly's. It was sweet with currants and sugar, reminding her of Billy and making her wonder if he'd been fed.

As if reading her mind, Grace said, 'We'll take the rest with us tomorrow. Billy can eat it on the way home.'

'*If* he comes home.' Winnie started to cry. It was supposed to have been their wedding day.

'Jason will do his best to get him off the charges.' Louisa patted her gently on the back.

'I'm sorry for telling him before you had a chance to – I didn't have a choice,' Winnie said.

'Told him what?' Grace interjected.

'It's nothing of any importance,' Louisa said bravely. 'You should rest, Winnie. Grace and I will look after Pamela until she's ready for bed.'

'I won't sleep,' Winnie said, but after two nights at sea and the strain of her experiences in Gravelines, she didn't recall anything from the time her head hit the pillow until Grace woke her at dawn.

'Abel will be here soon. I'll help you dress, then I'll mind the baby.' Grace said.

The cold light of day brought back the misery she'd felt on hearing of Billy's arrest. He had sacrificed his liberty – and maybe his neck – for Winnie and Jason, but what price was he going to have to pay for his heroic act?

*

348

Abel drove Winnie, Louisa and Jason to Dover. On the way, husband and wife barely spoke, united perhaps in their grief for the loss of the baby.

'If I'd known, I would have thought twice about doin' the run,' she heard Jason mutter.

'You'd still have gone,' Louisa retorted sharply.

'It's a right airy day,' Abel commented as he flicked his whip across the horses' haunches, and Winnie guessed that he wasn't merely referring to the weather. 'How are you, Winnie? I'm sorry. I apologise for pryin'.'

'I'm worried about the prisoners,' she said, wanting to talk, 'and I'm upset because today I was supposed to be walking down the aisle at St George's.'

'Then I'm even sorrier. I should have remembered – I heard the vicar readin' the banns for the second and third time of askin'. It's a pity you didn't find your way out of the free trade before'and.'

'I hope you don't think me impertinent, but what about you? The rumour was that there was to be an imminent announcement of your engagement.'

'I don't know where you heard that one ...' He smiled wryly. 'Deal is a hotbed of meaningless gossip, and to be honest, I'm comin' to accept that I shall remain a bachelor, free to come and go as I please. Just to let you know, I don't hold any grudges, I wish you and Billy well.'

'Thank you.'

'I'll be waitin' with the horses when you come out of the courtroom, bringin' Billy with you.'

She forced a smile, wishing she could share his optimism, as they continued into Dover, joining a small procession of carts and carriages heading for the gaol. Having travelled along Gaol Lane and turned on to Market Square, Abel halted the carriage outside the main entrance where a group of traders were competing to sell fragments of what they claimed were materials from the Admiral's cape.

'I'll see you very soon,' he said, patting Jason's shoulder after he had helped them disembark. 'Look after the young ladies, cousin.'

Winnie glanced up at the façade, noticing the shackles on either side of the door, a warning to villains as to the fate that awaited them.

'Why are there so many people?' she whispered to Louisa as they waited in the slowly shuffling queue of men and women entering the building and making their way to the courtroom.

'Everyone wants to see the men who've been accused of smuggling the French prisoners across the Channel,' Louisa replied.

A soldier who'd been placed on guard to keep public order showed them towards some empty seats. Shortly after, the magistrates walked in and took their places at the Bench before the prison guards led the three prisoners to the dock. Gunner stood looking resigned alongside Smoker, who appeared hunched and defeated, while Billy glanced towards Winnie, finding her face in the crowd. He gave her a small smile and she blew him a kiss in return – she was past caring what anyone thought of her.

One of the magistrates – a Mr Roberts – read out the charges, emphasising that this was a preliminary hearing to assess the evidence against the men.

'Call the first witness: Mr Spottiswoode, apothecary of Deal.'

The apothecary stood and approached the Bench. Expensively dressed, with the trappings of ornate buckles on his shoes and a silver-topped cane, he came across as a gentleman whose word could be relied upon.

'You say in your statement here –' Mr Roberts tapped the piece of paper he was reading from '– that your suspicions were raised when the Misses Lennicker of Compass Cottage, Deal, where Mr Fleet is a lodger, called on your services several times in short succession, requesting medicines for the aforesaid Mr Fleet.'

'That is correct, sir,' the apothecary said.

'During that time, you observed this man on many an occasion, carrying out business around the town. You acknowledge that he has a wooden leg which causes him to limp, but you maintain that he certainly never was prostrate, confined to bed with the fever and sores that these young ladies described.'

'Much as it pains me to implicate members of the fairer sex in this matter, I am bound to tell the truth.'

'Tell us about your sighting of the Frenchman, Admiral Louis-René Perriquet.'

Mr Spottiswoode cleared his throat and polished his cane with his gloved hand as though he was enjoying his moment of fame. 'My suspicions having been roused, I called at the house with a tincture. I gave it to Miss Winnie Lennicker. At the time, I felt that she had something to hide, being keen to send me on my way as quickly as possible.'

'This is speculation,' Mr Roberts said. 'It is inadmissible. Do go on.'

'I took it upon myself to look through one of the windows. The curtains were pulled across, but there was enough of a gap to draw my eye towards a gentleman who was lying on a makeshift bed low down on the floor.'

'It isn't an offence to sleep in one's own home. Are you sure this gentleman wasn't one of the residents of the cottage?'

'I recognised his face from the poster on the board outside the Customs House.'

'What did you do after that?'

'I notified the authorities. However, I must express my regret at their tardiness in making a search of the house. I put myself out, carrying out these actions for the public good, not in anticipation of any reward.'

'Thank you, Mr Spottiswoode.'

The magistrate went on to cross-examine Constable Pocket who explained that he had arrested the accused with the assistance of the runners and militia, citing the fact that he had witnessed Billy firing a pistol. He had also noted that the prisoners' boots were wet from having waded through the sea.

'Your statement doesn't prove that Mr Fleet was involved in aiding and abetting the escape of the French prisoners across the Channel, but it does provide supporting evidence, building the case against him,' Mr Roberts said.

Winnie didn't like him – he didn't possess Reverend North's kindly manner.

'There is one more witness I wish to call,' he went on. 'Mr David Cloke, brother to one of the accused, also known as Hagister.'

Gunner's brother stepped up to the Bench, his expression stubbornly resolute. He had given a witness statement the day before, but having realised overnight that he had inadvertently incriminated his brother, he seemed keen to retract it.

'I can't tell you no more about it,' he insisted. 'I received a knock on the 'ead on my way 'ome from the tavern last night and I can't recall nothin' of what 'appened.'

Mr Roberts glared at him, but it wasn't enough to convince him to talk.

'This witness is dismissed as his apparent and rather convenient loss of memory means that he cannot be cross-examined.'

'I think they will get off,' Louisa whispered as Winnie crossed her fingers and toes.

While Mr Roberts consulted with his fellow magistrates, the crowd grew restive. Eventually, he banged down his gavel and called for silence.

'I find that there is a case to answer. The prisoners will be taken to the county gaol at Maidstone where they will be tried in front of a judge and jury.'

Winnie gasped. She wouldn't cry, though. She needed to be strong for Billy, and for Pamela. Although she was only fourteen months old, she would miss her beloved father in his absence.

'I don't understand,' Louisa said. 'There were at least forty people with wet boots on that beach and as for the quack, his evidence is circumstantial. The jury will let them off at the Assizes – they'll see the sense of it.'

Winnie stared towards the dock where the prisoners were being led away. Billy was struggling because he had lost his crutch, but he managed to glance over his shoulder and mouth, '*I love you*.' She couldn't say that he was innocent – they were all guilty of the crime – but she would never allow that they had made the wrong decision when it came to Pierre and the Admiral. Unlike Mr Roberts and Mr Spottiswoode, the smugglers had shown compassion towards their fellow men.

As she and Louisa met with Jason and made their way outside, Officer Chase appeared.

'That's justice,' he gloated. 'That more than makes up for the spyglass, Miss Lennicker.'

'Ignore him.' Louisa snatched her hand and led her past him. 'It's men like him who should be in the dock for oppressing people who are out to make an honest living.'

'I didn't get a chance to speak to Billy,' Winnie said, once they were on their way home. 'It isn't fair.'

'We could rally the batsmen together and storm the gaol,' Jason suggested.

'No,' Winnie said. 'I don't want anyone risking their liberty – or their necks – trying to break them out.'

'What about bribin' the guards? We have the means. Billy gave up his freedom for me. I owe him.'

'I can't have that either. The Lent Assizes aren't far away – let's wait for the judge and jury to tear the evidence apart.' In the meantime, she would carry on as best she could.

The Lent session of the Assizes came around quickly, the judge apparently keen to convict the county's murderers, felons and forgers by Easter. Winnie travelled to Maidstone with Louisa, Jason and Abel to attend the trial.

They found seats in the gallery alongside some society ladies who appeared to be enjoying a day out, commenting on this lady's hair and that gentleman's dress, and tittering behind their fans.

'Don't take any notice, Winnie,' Louisa whispered. 'And bite your tongue, or you'll be sent in front of the judge for contempt.'

'I'll try,' Winnie said through gritted teeth. Didn't these privileged women realise that they were spectators in a trial that could result in men being sent to the gallows?

The judge and court officials took their places before the guards led the prisoners one by one to the dock. It was the first time Winnie had seen Billy in two weeks – she had tried to arrange a visit, but her request had been turned down. Jason had surmised that his gaolers had been anxious to prevent Billy being sprung from captivity by the scheming Deal smugglers and they did this by refusing all visitors, no matter who they were.

Billy looked thinner, but well enough, she thought, staring at him, willing him to spot her. Suddenly, his expression brightened. She gave him a small wave and prayed that the trial would soon be over.

At the judge's bidding, the clerk began to read out the charges.

'I commit the prisoners – Mr William Fleet and Mr Joseph Edwards who also goes by the name of Smoker, and Mr Donald Cloke, commonly known as Gunner, before Lord Chief Justice Oldfield – upon an indictment of unlawfully aiding and abetting the escape of two French prisoners of war who had broken their parole in Alresford in the county of Hampshire, allowing them safe passage across the Channel. In addition, Mr William Fleet is charged with a count of using a firearm with intent to cause injury and loss of life.'

'How do you plead?' the clerk asked.

Billy, Smoker and Gunner stood behind the railings with their heads held high. 'Not guilty,' they said, one at a time.

'Let us have a conviction, your honour,' said the prosecuting lawyer who was representing the government. 'The number of acquittals is becoming a cause for alarm. It isn't right that judge and jury refuse to accept even the slightest doubt when it comes to settling on depriving a prisoner of his life or liberty.'

The judge, resplendent in his wig, black scarf, tippet and scarlet robe, looked down his nose and gave him short shrift. 'The witnesses will prove the case, and all the circumstances attached to it. You know very well that a prisoner cannot be convicted of a crime without incontrovertible proof.' With that, he went on to hear the evidence.

Jason had paid an attorney, a Mr Frobisher from Dover, to speak in the prisoners' defence. Mr Frobisher had made some enquiries and pored over the depositions submitted at the start of the trial.

'Your honour, is it possible that these three men, sadly lacking in education, are capable of carrying out the crimes of which they have been accused? There were other, well-connected gentlemen who had the means and intelligence to implement the alleged plan to aid the escape of the French prisoners. The accused are two erstwhile common fishermen and hovellers, and an impoverished sailor who has returned from serving on one of His Majesty's ships, his leg having been amputated after the bone was shattered by a musket ball.

'I find the evidence against them to be deficient. The case that has been built against them will tumble like a house of cards on closer scrutiny.' He paused for effect. 'The witness for the prosecution, Mr Spottiswoode, provides evidence of a link between Mr Fleet and a gentleman who resembles an artist's impression on a poster. As for the firearm, Mr Fleet did indeed fire it, but he fired it blank as a warning against the threat of attack, not being immediately able to identify the ominous figures approaching from the sandhills.

'Finally, evidence has been presented to show that the prisoners were discovered wearing wet boots. I believe that the entire population of the godforsaken town of Deal would hang on that point, their houses being built on the spit, exposed to wind and tide and prone to flooding.'

'Is that all, Mr Frobisher?' the judge said wearily.

'Yes, my lord.'

'Court is adjourned for luncheon.'

The trial resumed later, when the judge did his summing up and the foreman of the twelve good men and true stood to give their verdicts. Winnie gripped the rail at the front of the gallery as he spoke.

'We, the jury, find the accused, Mr Edwards, not guilty of all charges. We, the jury, find the accused, Mr Cloke, not guilty of all charges ...'

'How do you find the defendant, Mr Fleet?' the judge asked.

'We, the jury, find him guilty—'

'No,' Winnie yelped, her heart breaking. It wasn't long since she had been reunited with her beloved Billy, and now they were to be torn apart for a second time.

'For aiding the passage of the French prisoners across the Channel, and using a firearm, I sentence Mr Fleet to two years' imprisonment in the county gaol of Maidstone. You will also pay a fine of sixty pounds. Your ignorance and lack of judgement put our citizens in grave danger.'

How was Billy going to settle a fine of that magnitude? Winnie had some money in the box at home, but not sixty pounds. For now it was the least of her concerns though. She needed to see Billy, and to that end, she managed to pay one of the guards to let her speak to him before he was taken down, his hands cuffed.

'If I could step into your shoes, I would,' she said, hating the idea of him being locked away again.

He smiled weakly. 'I know you would, my love, but Pamela needs 'er ma.'

'I shall keep a candle burning for when you come home.'

'As soon as I'm freed, we'll be married. Winnie, don't be sad. I don't regret what I done – I owed it to Marlin. And please, don't feel guilty – we did the right thing.'

'I'll visit you when I can,' she said tearfully. 'I love you ...'

'I love you too,' he said, when the guard told them that their time was up.

Two years apart, she thought, watching in despair as he disappeared through a doorway leading into the bowels of the gaol. Pamela will have forgotten him by the time he's released.

Chapter Twenty-Four

A Change of Circumstance

Two days after Billy was imprisoned and the day before Easter, Winnie was walking along the beach with Louisa and Grace. Winnie held one of Pamela's hands and Grace held on to the other, helping her toddle along the shingle in the sunshine. When she began to protest because she wanted to linger and pick up shells and mermaid's purses, Winnie lifted her up.

'I'll prepare supper when we get home,' Grace said.

'There's no need to treat me any differently.' Winnie hugged a wriggling Pamela. 'I've decided that I mustn't waste the time that Billy's away, moping. Two years will fly by.'

'You're very brave,' Louisa said.

'I have no choice.'

'Jason's settled Billy's fine,' Louisa went on, 'so you don't need to worry about where the money's going to come from.'

'I don't know what to say ... thank you. I've been wondering how to pay it.'

'We're also going to give a proportion of the payment we receive for the guinea run to you and Billy.'

'It's kind of you to offer, but there's no need,' Winnie said.

'Jason wants to do it. He feels terribly guilty that Billy was arrested, not him.'

'I know, but he mustn't. We have to try to put this behind us and look to the future.'

'That's easier said than done.'

'But we will do it,' Winnie said firmly. As they turned the corner to remove themselves from the cold, blustery wind, she was surprised to find Middle Street bustling with people.

''Ave you 'eard the news?' said a stranger. 'Boney 'as given up the crowns of France and Italy.'

'What does it mean?' Grace asked, as a band of musicians approached, banging drums and playing their pipes and fiddles, a group of women dancing joyfully along behind them.

'The war is over. It's true – the Foreign Office 'as released a Gazetteer Extraordinary about it. Napoleon 'as abdicated and the French monarchy will be restored.'

Winnie had to pinch herself – she could hardly believe it. At one time, she would have been over the moon; now her relief that the fighting had ended was tinged with regret because it had come too late for Billy. The prisoners of war on both sides would be free to go home. There would be no need for elaborate schemes to enable their escape.

The church bells pealed and the vessels in the Downs fired shots to salute the end of the war and announce the beginning of several days and nights of celebration. There was dancing on the beach and the shopkeepers pooled their resources to put up extra lanterns along the alleyways to welcome the returning soldiers.

Although Louisa and Grace offered to mind Pamela so that Winnie could go out and take part, she preferred to stay at home.

*

By the beginning of May, the residents of Deal began to settle down and assess the impact of the change in their circumstances, bemoaning the potential loss of trade, especially for the farmers and market gardeners, the bootmakers, boatyard owners and smugglers. Jason continued hovelling with the *Whimbrel*, rueing the fact that there would be no more guinea runs.

Just as Winnie was starting to worry about how she was going to support herself and Pamela, the rewards for her ventures started to come in.

Firstly, Mr Cork paid her what he owed, sending his man to settle up. It was a tidy sum that she added to her money box under the mattress.

The following day, Mr Gambril paid her a visit.

'I am delighted to find you at home, Miss Lennicker. May I come in?'

She showed him into the parlour and offered him refreshment which he declined, saying that he had already called at the pot house.

'You have come for the book,' she said. 'Take a seat and I'll fetch it for you.'

She returned with the code book and handed it over to him.

'I don't suppose you'll tell me because it's classified information, but did you have any success with your enquiries?' she asked.

'As a master of intrigue, I set up some surveillance at Monsieur Boule's house and at Mundel Manor, and my agents have discovered notes sent between the Frenchman and Madame through other channels. Furthermore, they have overheard conversations that confirm Monsieur Boule's role in deceiving Sir Flinders, quite a feat considering that he's no gudgeon. Mr Cork considers himself a remarkably clever gentleman, willing to sell his soul to the highest bidder, but I haven't yet been able to prove him guilty of any misdemeanour. I'm afraid that he could be the one who gets away.

'I have news of a reward that is to be shared between us.' His lips curved into a smile. 'You see, I am an honest man, after all. I wonder if you have an account with a bank into which I can have the money paid? It is a generous sum, not the kind of amount that should be tucked under a mattress.'

She couldn't help blushing as she gave him the details, before showing him out.

'You may well be relieved to know that this will be our last encounter, Miss Lennicker,' he said. 'It's been a pleasure working with you.'

She smiled, but she couldn't bring herself to express a similar sentiment, even out of politeness.

The morning after Mr Gambril's visit, she received a letter. She opened it on the doorstep and began to read. The writing was pale and spidery, the date and address barely legible, but the rest of the content was clear.

Dear Mademoiselle Lennicker,

I am writing to let you know of the sad passing of my friend, the Admiral, two weeks after our arrival in France. I grieve not for him, but for his son and widow who miss his love and guidance greatly. I have never seen him so content as when he was reunited with his family for those remaining days that were all too brief. However, his joy made all our struggles worthwhile.

With the signing of the Treaty of Fontainebleau, I feel confident that I can return to England shortly to pay court to my dear Miss Meadows.

With deep gratitude for your kindness,
Pierre
Postscript: the funds have been transferred to the account in your name, held by Hulke etc. I trust that you will be able to make good use of the monies.

It wouldn't be much, she guessed, and assuming that it would be safer in her possession than with the bank, she decided that she would arrange to withdraw it from the account. To that end, she persuaded Louisa to accompany her again, feeling daunted by the idea of dealing with her finances by herself. When the manager told her how much money she had received, she could have swooned. This was proof of Pierre's claim that he was a wealthy man, a successful privateer and landowner.

'There must be a mistake,' she murmured.

'We never make mistakes. Everything is checked and double-checked. I assume that this is a bequest.'

'Yes, that's right.' It was easier to tell a white lie than try to explain how she came by it. 'Oh, I don't know what to do with it. It's too much.'

'As a banker and financier, I can assure you that one can never have too much money. If I may offer you some advice, I would recommend that you take a fixed sum to spend as you wish and invest the rest to provide you with a modest annual income.'

Thanking him, she said she would think about what he had said and make another appointment when she had decided what to do.

Winnie walked back through town with her sister.

'You are brown-deep,' Louisa said.

'I'm sorry. I have much on my mind.'

'Shall we stop by at Molly's to see Nancy and have a cup of tea? Grace won't mind, as long as we don't take too long.'

363

Winnie agreed, curious to know how Mr Gambril had left Mrs Stickles.

'Tea and apple cake are on the 'ouse,' Mrs Stickles said, greeting them as they arrived at her establishment.

'Ma's been in a very good mood since 'er gen'leman came callin',' Nancy said, looking through her veil across the counter. 'Sit down and I'll bring your order.'

''E isn't my gentleman as such,' Mrs Stickles said. ''E could 'ave been, if it wasn't for 'is situation. 'E travels for business and won't be comin' this way again. I'm referrin' to Mr Gambril.'

Winnie wondered why she wasn't more upset about the fact that he'd rejected her.

''E told me that I'll always 'ave a special place in 'is 'eart. And 'e gave me a book of poetry by John Keats, whoever 'e is, and a posy of flowers. I've borrered a press so I can preserve them for posterity.'

'Won't you miss him?' Winnie asked.

'I shall yearn for 'im, that's true, but I shan't shed no tears. Knowin' 'ow much regard 'e 'as for me is enow. I 'ave an 'appy life and I've realised that I don't want the bother of an 'usband under my feet.' She changed the subject. ''Ave you been able to see Billy?'

'Not yet. I'm still waiting for a response to my application to visit him next month.'

They talked of Pamela and of the changes being wrought in Deal by the end of the war, particularly Mrs Stickles's concerns for her business, before Winnie and Louisa walked home.

As they reached the front door, it flew open, and there, standing in front of them with a huge grin on his face, was Billy. With an unladylike scream of joy, Winnie threw herself at him. She wrapped her arms around his neck and leaned up to kiss him full on the lips before asking, 'What are you doing here?'

'I've been released early, somethin' to do with the end of 'ostilities. I've 'eard that Old Boney's reached Elba, 'avin' tried to poison 'imself and escaped an attempt on 'is life. 'E is indestructible, but 'is ambitions to become ruler of France are over.' Billy hugged and kissed her.

On hearing Louisa clear her throat, Winnie stepped aside to let her indoors.

'Thank you very much, lovebirds,' she said stiffly.

'There's no further punishment?' Winnie asked. 'They aren't going to grab you off the street and put you back in gaol?'

'There was some talk of sendin' me to the pillory, but it didn't go no further. I'm back for good, Winnie. We shall never be apart again.' He tipped his head to one side, his eyes twinkling. 'At least, not until death do us part, which reminds me that we were about to get wed, before we were rudely interrupted. I want us to set the date as soon as possible, if you're still of the same mind.'

'What do you think?' she teased and by the end of the day, they had arranged for Reverend North to officiate at their marriage on the second Wednesday in May, and Winnie had told Billy of their good fortune.

They were to have a small wedding at St George's with just her sisters, Jason and Nancy in attendance. Winnie wore her pink gown and white satin slippers, and Grace wove fresh flowers through her hair. Billy wore his Sunday best – a dark coat, the black shirt with the ruffles, and wide-legged trousers.

When they set off, the groom went ahead with Jason. Winnie and her sisters handed Pamela over to a delighted Mrs Witherall, before they followed behind the men.

Passing through the churchyard, Winnie paused at Terrier's grave which was marked with a stone inscribed with the words, *Here lies Alfred Roper whom Death by sudden call, has forced to leave the world and all. His wife and children, large and small, lament the accident which him did befall.*

'Come on, Winnie,' Grace called softly. 'Don't keep Billy waiting – he's waited long enough.'

They made their vows before Billy placed the ring that he'd bought for her before the guinea run on the fourth finger of her left hand. The vicar joined their right hands together and said, 'Those whom God hath joined together, let no man put asunder. Forasmuch as Billy and Winnie have consented together in holy wedlock ... I pronounce that they be man and wife together ...'

After the blessing and prayers, Winnie walked at her husband's side to the vestry where she sat down beside him and signed the register in her maiden name of Lennicker for the very last time.

'You haven't carried her over the threshold, Billy,' Jason pointed out when they returned to the cottage.

'Ah, I'm goin' to wait until we move into the marital home.'

'You haven't got one,' Louisa said lightly.

'Not yet, but my beautiful lady wife 'as arranged for us to view an 'ouse at two o'clock. One of Abel's grooms is goin' to drive us there and back.'

'Is it a long way away then?' Grace asked as she went into the kitchen to finish setting out the wedding breakfast of hot chocolate and huffkins, bloaters, ham and eggs, and wedding cake. 'Oh, I hope it isn't too far.'

'It's well situated in the hamlet of Westcliffe, four miles from Deal and Dover and not far from St Margaret's Bay,' Winnie said. 'That's all I can say until we've seen it.'

*

At a quarter past two, the carriage pulled up on a hill in front of a large house set back from a country road.

'Well I never,' Billy said, helping Winnie disembark. 'I thought you were goin' to settle for a cottage ... Are you sure about movin' so far away from your sisters?'

'I don't want to live in Deal,' Winnie told him. 'I want this to be a new beginning. As for the house, it is grander than I expected from the description: a gentleman's residence with gardens at the front and rear.'

'Can we afford a property like this? I wouldn't want you to be disappointed.'

'We have the funds – I've taken advice from the bank manager. I like the look of it. It looks solid, homely.'

'I 'ave another reservation. If we buy an 'ouse like this, people will talk about us be'ind our backs, saying that we're the kind of folk who think we're the bettermost, goin' around with our noses stuck up in the air.'

'It doesn't bother me.' Winnie took his arm. 'I know who I am. I don't need other people trying to tell me otherwise. Shall we go inside?'

The owner's agent, a servile lickspittle of a young man, showed them around, pointing out the galleried entrance hall, furnished drawing room and dining room with high ceilings and tall sash windows, and the kitchen and servants' quarters. A staircase dating from the time of Henry VIII rose to the first floor where there were five good-sized bedrooms. There was an attic and a cellar, and a secret passageway between the kitchen and hall.

'I'll give you some time to look around by yourselves,' the agent said.

'What are you thinking, Billy?' Winnie asked when he had gone, and they were looking around the dining room for a second time.

'That it's too good for the likes of us.'

'What do you mean by that? We are as deserving as anyone else, more so than some.' She was thinking of all the so-called honourable gentlemen who had allowed themselves to be drawn into the web of deceit connected with the spy ring, of Sir Flinders who'd let Monsieur Boule sham him because of his grasping need for recognition, and the conspirators who'd created the false announcement of Boney's death for their own selfish ends. 'Billy, you are a hero and you should be proud of it.'

'You're right, Mrs Fleet. You 'aven't done so badly yourself – you've served King and Country, restored the Admiral to 'is family, and … you saved my life. I tell you, if you 'adn't been firm with me, refusin' to 'elp me when I sank that low with the drink, I would never 'ave been forced to find the strength to change.

'Louisa would love this 'ouse for its 'idin' 'oles,' Billy went on with a chuckle. 'I like the place – I can see us livin' here. I can imagine Pamela slidin' down the banister of that staircase when she's older – under supervision, of course.'

'Billy, I hope you wouldn't encourage her.'

'As you know, I've l'arned my lesson. I wouldn't let any 'arm come to any of our children.'

'Any?' Winnie smiled. 'You are keen to have more?'

'Of course, if you're willin'.'

She slipped her arm through his as the agent came to find them.

'Have you any questions for me, Mr and Mrs Fleet?' he asked.

'I don't think so, thank you,' Winnie said.

Not being privy to the fact that Winnie had fallen in love with the house as soon as she'd set foot inside it, the agent went on to say that the owner would accept an offer if they wished to purchase the furniture as well.

'Then we will have it ... subject to the necessary contracts,' Winnie said. 'And we'll start a separate negotiation for the furnishings.'

'A wise decision. You won't regret it. Perhaps you would come to our office to make a start on the paperwork. I can recommend an attorney to draw up the legal documents. I'm available at eleven o'clock tomorrow morning, if that suits.'

'It suits us very well,' Winnie said, her cheeks aching from smiling.

'I can't believe we've just bought an 'ouse,' Billy grinned as they travelled back to Deal. 'We are goin' up in the world.'

She leaned against him, holding his hand, reminding herself not to forget where they had come from, no matter how far they rose.

Chapter Twenty-Five

Hearts of Gold

The purchase of the house at Westcliffe went through smoothly, and a few weeks later in the middle of June, Billy carried Winnie across the threshold. Keeping house, looking after Pamela and managing her charitable efforts was more time-consuming than Winnie had anticipated, her life growing even busier when on hearing from Mrs Stickles of Mr Jones's passing, she and Billy took on his two little girls, it being too late to save his son who had also perished in the poorhouse. To help her, she took on a cook and employed a gardener to work for them one day a sennight.

Summer brought long, sunny days when the dumbledores buzzed lazily from one fragrant bloom to another on the rose bushes in the borders. Early one August morning, Winnie could already feel the warmth in the air as she was dressing the girls – ten-year-old Daisy and seven-year-old Lily, and of course, Pamela.

'I don't like water very much,' Daisy said as Winnie gave her a flannel to wash her face, 'but the soap is nice.' She sniffed at the bar. 'Do you think the flutterbies will land on me because I smell like a flower?'

'I think it's quite likely,' Winnie said, hoping to encourage her to take care of her appearance. She recalled the state the two sisters had been in when she and Billy had collected them from the poorhouse. As the superintendent had introduced them, Winnie had bent down to speak to them, as she did with Pamela.

'What are your names?' she had asked softly.

'I'm Daisy Jones,' the older one had replied, clutching her sister's hand. 'This is Lily.'

Dressed in rags and shoes that had been stitched back together with string, they had looked cowed, dead behind the eyes. Both were blonde and blue-eyed, but their curls had been brown with grime. Daisy was a head taller than Lily, but neither were well grown, and Lily's legs were bowed like a sailor's. Lily had put her thumb in her mouth, at which the superintendent had promptly tapped her on the wrist.

Winnie had glared at him.

'That is a bad 'abit, and bad 'abits must be corrected,' he'd said roughly, as Daisy and Lily shrank away from him, and Winnie had made a solemn promise under her breath that she would never allow them to be cruelly treated again.

At home, Winnie had bathed them and combed the nits from their hair, fed them and introduced them to Pamela. At first, she and Billy had wondered if they'd made a terrible mistake because they were like feral kittens, afraid of their own shadows, skittish and unmannerly, but in time, they began to settle in and become part of the family.

The sight of Lily chasing the soap that Daisy had dropped across the floorboards, brought Winnie back to the task in hand.

'I'm sorry,' Daisy said, white-faced and cowering. 'I didn't mean to—'

'It's all right,' Winnie reassured her. 'Pop it back in the bowl, Lily. Thank you. Now, whose turn is it next?'

'Pamela's,' said Lily.

Winnie smiled to herself at Lily's wishful thinking, suspecting that the little girl lived in hope that by the time Winnie had battled through getting Daisy and Pamela washed, she might have forgotten about her altogether.

Once the three of them were ready, she delivered them to Cook with instructions to give them their breakfast in the kitchen. Having left them chattering together, she found Billy in the dining room.

He put down his newspaper and smiled.

''Ow are the littluns?' he said. 'I 'eard them messin' you about.'

'They are a challenge, but I wouldn't be without them,' she smiled back.

'Allow me to pour your tea. It's the least I can do,' he said when she hesitated. 'You 'ave a tougher time than me. Go on. Sit down.'

Thanking him, she took a seat beside him as he filled her cup and removed the strainer.

'I'm worn out already,' she said as he added milk to the tea and gave it a stir before serving her bacon, honey and huffkins, along with a kiss.

'I'm sorry I won't be 'ere to see Louisa and Grace,' Billy said as they ate. 'Give 'em my regards and tell 'em I'll be at 'ome next time they pay us a visit.'

'I'll make sure to remember. I'm looking forward to seeing them.'

'I never thought I'd say this, but I miss 'em.' He looked her in the eye. 'I even miss Louisa's naggin' at me.'

'Don't I nag you enough to make up for it then?' Winnie said archly.

'You wag your finger at me now and again, but you don't go on like your sister. Poor Jason.'

'There's nothing poor about Jason – he knows which side his bread's buttered.'

'You are 'appy 'ere?' Billy asked. 'It isn't what you're used to, bein' out of town.'

'I've never been happier – I love our home. I adore the peace and quiet, but most of all, I relish not being part of—' she stopped abruptly and glanced towards the door before going on in a low voice '– the free trade.' Winnie was certain that Cook knew exactly how she and Billy had obtained their fortune, but she didn't like to speak of it. The dangerous escapades crossing the Channel and exchanging despatches in Gravelines, the threat of arrest and hanging for carrying contraband, and the fear of being caught harbouring prisoners of war were in the past, but not forgotten. She still had Officer Chase's spyglass and the occasional nightmare to remind her of it.

'Talkin' of the free trade, 'said Billy, 'I've just been readin' about how the eighth and final conspirator accused of makin' the false announcement of Napoleon's death back in February 'as been arrested. You'll never guess who it was.'

'I have no idea,' Winnie said.

'Our friend, Mr Francis Cork.'

'I find that hard to believe. I quite liked him at first.' She recalled his kindness when she had arrived at Nomansland Farm without her boots and stockings, and almost frozen to the bone. 'Tell me more.'

''E must 'ave become consumed by greed,' Billy said. 'Didn't 'e get caught up in the debacle with Monsieur Boule?'

She nodded. 'They couldn't pin anything on Mr Cork in the end.'

'Well, 'e's 'ad 'is comeuppance now. I always thought of 'im as the *arbitry* sort, selfish and graspin'. I'll read it to you.' Billy picked up the newspaper from the table. '"'Avin' found the conspirators guilty, Mr Justice Le Blanc sentenced them at the Court of the King's Bench. Each man was to pay a fine to the King" – that's fair enow, seein' 'ow much money they made out of the deception. Some are to be pilloried, but the de Berenger chap, who turns out to be a French exile, and Mr Cork are to be imprisoned for –' Billy's voice went up an octave '– but twelve months. Where's the justice in that?'

'It is a lenient sentence,' Winnie agreed.

'It isn't right that they're let off lightly because of their status in society. If they 'ad been common people like us, they would 'ave been 'anged for defraudin' the Stock Exchange.'

'I think it will be enough to have consequences for Mr Cork,' Winnie said. 'He won't be acting as agent for the free traders of Deal in future, not after this. Times have changed. Not only has he wrecked his reputation for being an honest venturer, he has enraged our people by being seen to be treated differently by the courts.'

Billy took his watch from the pocket of his waistcoat.

'I'd better go,' he said, getting up and reaching for his crutch which he'd left leaning against the adjacent dining chair. 'I 'ave much to do today.'

'How are the plans for the workshop?' Winnie asked, following him into the hall and waiting for him to pick up his coat and hat.

'They're comin' along very well, but the alterations can't be done soon enow for me. I want to get started – that's one of the reasons for my trip into Deal today, to chase up Mr Chambers about the buildin' work. Even though the war with France is over, our soldiers and sailors continue to return 'ome, maimed in skirmishes and in battle. I can 'elp them, combinin' my understandin' of their sufferin', and the joy and satisfaction I find in workin' with wood.'

'I thought you'd always wanted to be a boatman like Jason,' Winnie smiled.

'The changin' tides of a man's fortunes can alter the way 'e feels and acts,' Billy said. 'Lookin' back, I can see 'ow selfish I was in many ways. Anyway, that's in the past. I'm goin' to work with Mr Price whose one of the bootmakers on Golden Street, to create false limbs – arms and legs, 'ands and feet. There are already some decent ones available with lockin' knees and jointed toes, but they're too expensive for the ordinary man in the street, let alone the impoverished invalid. I want to make them affordable and usable. They must be lightweight, resistant to wear and tear, and 'ard knocks. In short, Winnie, I'm very excited about the future. You could say that my plan 'as legs …' He grinned as he smoothed his untameable hair before putting on his hat, a round one that completed his outfit of navy tailcoat, white shirt, waistcoat, silk bandanna and pantaloons.

'You see, I can make light of it now,' he went on. 'I don't care if anyone calls me Pegleg – it don't matter. It's water off a duck's back. You do approve?'

'Of course I do.' His heart was set on his new project and she was confident that he would succeed. 'I'm very proud of you, Billy.'

''Ow do I look?' he asked, cocking his head.

'Exceedingly handsome, as always.'

Bidding him farewell with another kiss, she went to collect the girls from the kitchen and took them to the drawing room where she began to teach Lily and Daisy the alphabet while Pamela sat on the floor, playing with the puppy that Billy had found for them. It was a shaggy grey creature that had been abandoned in one of the alleyways in Deal. Bathed and brushed, and with a red ribbon in its hair, it had become the girls' constant companion and its presence had brought Daisy out of her shell. 'I don't like readin',' Daisy said. 'Pa says – *said* – there's no use in it.'

Winnie gave her an encouraging smile. 'I didn't think that knowing my letters would be of any use to me, but without reading, my life – and yours – might have turned out very differently. It was the means to an end that brought me great reward.'

'I don't understand it, though.' Daisy suddenly burst into tears. 'I don't know what it means. What is "a"? What is "b"?'

Winnie moved across to comfort her, letting her cry into her apron.

'There, there. We'll stop for today. Our visitors will be with us soon.' She looked out of the window towards the sea, catching sight of Louisa and Grace strolling up the path beside the church. 'In fact, they are here now.'

'How long will they be stayin', Ma?' Lily asked.

'They will want to be home before dark,' Winnie said, touched by the little girl's decision to call her 'mother'.

She took Daisy and Lily to meet her sisters, making sure they put on their felt hats with ribbons, and their coats over their blue and white linen dresses, before struggling to persuade Pamela, who was in short clothes and a pudding cap, to sit in the pram.

It was the happiest of reunions – she hadn't seen her sisters for over a month.

While Grace was looking after the girls in the kitchen with Cook, Louisa and Winnie sat in the drawing room talking over tea.

'I'd say that everything has come up roses for you and Billy,' Louisa said. 'I'm glad for you.'

'How about you and Jason?'

'Ah, my husband has sold the *Spindrift*. He's keeping the *Whimbrel* – he can't bear to part with her.'

'Is he planning to replace the galley punt then?' Winnie's brow tightened.

'No ...' A smile played on Louisa's features. 'Jason has decided that he's going to be a ten-shilling man. He's going over to the other side.'

'I don't understand.'

'He's applying for a post with the Revenue. I know – it's hard to believe that we're leaving the free trade, but times have changed. The war is over and there isn't the same money in smuggling goods as there used to be.'

'Where will the vicar obtain his communion wine and his medicinal brandy?' Winnie enquired. 'And what will you do to occupy yourself, Louisa?'

'Keep house, I suppose. We have plenty of money tucked away for a rainy day, investments that Jason has made over the last two or three years, and we own the cottage outright. I shall be forced to learn to cook for my husband. I won't find it dull – I have Grace at home for company.'

There was no mention of a child, Winnie noticed.

'How is Billy?'

'He's well, thank you. He's in town, meeting with an attorney to set up a fund to help the poorhouse children with their education, among other things, and ... don't mention this to Grace, but we're also putting some money into a trust for her. I used to think that money was the root of all evil, but it is the greatest gift when used wisely.'

'You both have hearts of gold. And Billy's become quite the gentleman – you'll be telling me he's risen to Lord Mayor next.' Louisa changed the subject. 'I'm sorry that it's over.'

'The war?'

'No, the three of us, the smuggler's daughters working together to make a living from the free trade. I won't miss the danger, but I'll miss the good times we had – stealing the rose leaves from the gardens at Mundel Manor to cut with the tea, long evenings letting down the cognac, and negotiating with the likes of Mr Gigg ...'

'Have you thought of moving out of the alley?' Winnie asked.

'We wouldn't do it because Mr and Mrs Witherall aren't well, and we can help them when they need us. I expect you are kept busy looking after Daisy and Lily as well as Pamela. How are they adapting?'

'They're making progress. As you know, when they first came here, they didn't laugh, or smile. Daisy seems more content and Lily has started calling me "Ma".' Winnie smiled. 'I'm pleased that they consider themselves part of the family, but I do everything I can to keep the memories of their mother and father alive – I often show them the bracelet and talk of Mr Jones. I know that some people think it better not to keep harping on about it, but I remember how I felt comforted when anyone enquired about Billy while he was missing.'

'On reflection, I've made many mistakes,' Louisa sighed.

'You should be proud of yourself – you're stronger than I am. As I've said before, I'll never forget how you looked after us after we lost Pa. If it hadn't been for you, I don't know where we'd be now.'

'Thank you, Winnie. I haven't always appreciated you as I should.'

'And I you, so we are even.' Winnie stood up. 'Come, my dear sister. Let's go and find Grace and the girls. As Billy would say, I 'ave a fair achin' tooth for a slice of cherry cake.'

*

378

Billy didn't return from his trip into town until dusk, long after Winnie's sisters had left Westcliffe. He doffed his hat and aimed it at the hook on the stand in the hall. It flew in a perfect arc, landing right on target, making Winnie laugh.

'Where are the girls?' he asked.

'Cook is telling them a story before I start getting them ready for bed, which means we have a few minutes to ourselves.' She took his hand and led him into the drawing room. They stood beside the fireplace looking at the beam above, where Billy had added their initials, carving them next to those of the previous owners of the house, who had left their mark in the dark wood. 'Billy, I've been thinking that perhaps next time we'll have a boy.' She was hardly able to suppress the excitement in her voice.

'What are you sayin'?'

'I'm with child.'

'Oh, Winnie.' He put his arm around her waist and pulled her close. 'Are you sure?'

'I've known for a while – I recognise the signs now. I didn't want to tempt fate by telling you too soon.'

'I thought you were growin' a little stouter.' He grinned as she gave him a playful shove.

'I don't care if it's a girl or a boy as long as it's 'ealthy,' he went on. 'Winnie, I love you. When times are bad, you're my port in a storm, and when they're good, you're the wind in my sails. Together, we can weather anythin'.'

'I love you too,' she said. 'Billy, I want you to know that you are – and always will be – my hero.'

Welcome to

Penny Street

where your favourite authors and stories live.

Meet casts of characters you'll never forget,
create memories you'll treasure forever,
and discover places that will stay with
you long after the last page.

Turn the page to step into the home of

EVIE GRACE

and discover more about

The Golden Maid

Dear Reader,

When I'd finished writing *The Lace Maiden*, the first in the series about the smuggler's daughters, I began searching for inspiration for the second, *The Golden Maid*.

While visiting Deal last year, I took a wander around the museum where among the exhibits, a guinea boat caught my eye. I'm not an expert in the history of shipping by any means – although I've had to learn a fair amount about the different kinds of vessels that my characters would have seen during the early years of the nineteenth century – and all I can say is that it was a very plain wooden boat without sails or decoration.

Its history though was far more fascinating than its appearance.

During the Napoleonic Wars when Winnie's story is set, the smugglers of Deal and East Kent would have rowed this type of boat across the Channel laden with gold, then returned carrying contraband from the French merchants in Gravelines. Some sources claim that the gold in the form of guineas was destined for Wellington's army while others say that it was to fund Napoleon's campaign. The smugglers also acted as go-betweens for British agents and spies, carrying despatches and any other information that they'd picked up from their travels.

On leaving the museum, I headed to Beach Street and walked along the seafront. Looking out to sea, I wondered what it would have been like to head for France in a rowing boat on a cold, blustery night, carrying thousands of pounds worth of gold, aware that the Revenue and privateers may well be lying in wait.

Gripped by this thought, I found an ice cream parlour where I sat and plotted an outline of *The Golden Maid* over a banana split, which meant that when I returned home, I was ready to start writing.

I hope you enjoy reading about how Winnie goes about righting her wrongs and come to love her as much as I did.

Evie x

Food for Thought

Sometimes readers ask me where my characters come from, and the more I think about that question, the more I realise that I don't really know. Take Winnie in *The Golden Maid*, for example. I had an idea that she should be quite different from her older sister, Louisa, whom I wrote about in *The Lace Maiden*, the first book in the series.

I gave her blonde hair to distinguish her from Louisa and made her shorter and stouter. As a picture of her began to build in my mind, I saw her in the kitchen at Compass Cottage, wearing an apron and stirring a pot over the fire. It wasn't a chore – she enjoyed cooking. She loved being at home, creating dishes for her family and making the most of the ingredients that they had at the time.

I used this aspect of Winnie's character throughout *The Golden Maid*, making the contrast between her desire to be at home living a simple life, and the circumstances that forced her into joining her family's dangerous escapades in smuggling gold, contraband and despatches.

Not only does Winnie cook for her family, she also prepares dishes suitable for invalids when she is involved in caring for a sick fugitive. When I was researching the recipes Winnie might have used, I came across Hannah Glasse's book, *The Art of Cookery Made Plain and Easy*, published in 1747. It became very popular because of the author's decision to use simple language that a servant or what she called 'the lower sort' would understand. It was still in use in the nineteenth century, so I gave Winnie access to a copy in *The Golden Maid*.

Winnie would have used local ingredients to make traditional dishes from Kent, such as Canterbury brawn, Whitstable oysters, Lambs tail pie and Folkestone pudding pie. She would also have had to preserve seasonal produce for the lean times, especially the winter months and early spring. For example, she would be responsible for dealing with the fish that her family brought back from their fishing trips in the waters around the Kent coast. There is a hang at the cottage where she soaks the herrings in brine before hanging them up by the gills and smoking them whole. This turns them into bloaters with a golden colour and gamey taste – they could be kept for a few days and served with bread or as a paste on toast.

The more I thought about Winnie, the more she revealed to me about her character. She's quiet, sensible and gentler in nature than her older sister. She will give her hard-earned money and belongings away to those in need, but the one item of food she would struggle to relinquish is her favourite, the Kentish huffkin.

This flat bread roll, about six inches across and an inch thick, is thought to have started out as food for the fruit pickers at harvest time. It's made from flour, yeast, water, salt and a little fat. When the dough has risen, the baker divides it into rolls and makes a dent in each one with their thumb. Once the rolls come out of the oven, they are wrapped in cloth while they cool to give them a soft crust. When they are ready to eat, they can be filled with pitted cherries, jam or something savoury like bacon. There is another story in *The Golden Maid* of how the huffkin acquired its traditional indentation, and its name.

Once I'd got to know Winnie a little better, I wrote her into various difficult situations and found that she was more than capable of standing up for herself.

I hope this has given you food for thought about how I dream up my characters. I think Winnie, with her compassion and fierce sense of right and wrong, is my favourite so far.

Happy reading,

Evie x

Turn the page for an exclusive extract from

EVIE GRACE

The Smuggler's Wife

Her heart led her to him, but will loyalty be enough to make her stay . . .

Coming 2021
Available to pre-order in paperback
and ebook now

CHAPTER ONE

A Breath of Fresh Air
Deal, June 1815

It was all very well Louisa warning her off – Grace knew beyond a doubt the reasons why. Her eldest sister had her best interests at heart, but she didn't know that she had a fancy for Isaiah so strong that she couldn't eat or sleep.

'Where are you going?' Louisa stepped across the hall, placing herself between Grace and the front door as she tied the laces on her boots.

'Back to the market before it closes – I forgot to buy the bread.' It wasn't a lie exactly – she had accidentally on purpose forgotten to pick up a loaf with the rest of the shopping.

'Haven't I told you before to take a list with you?'

On many an occasion, Grace wanted to say, but she managed to bite her tongue just in time.

'I don't feel so good, having been staring at the accounts all morning. Maybe a breath of fresh air will perk me up. Why don't I come with you?'

'You look well enough to me,' Grace said, standing up. Tall, slender and blue eyed, they were peas from the same pod, except that Louisa was five years older than Grace and an inch shorter, and her hair was a dark brown while Grace's was the colour of ebony.

'Where is your sympathy for your hardworking sister? Let me put my ledger away and fetch my bonnet. It's a lovely day. We can walk along the beach afterwards.'

'Are you sure you wouldn't prefer to go and have a lie down?' Grace suggested, but Louisa had made up her mind.

Her plot foiled, Grace reached for the willow basket on the shelf, at which a pair of green eyes peered over the top.

'Oh Kitty,' she smiled.

'What's that creature doing, lazing around in there when she's supposed to be earning her keep?' Louisa grumbled lightly.

'She's done her work for today – tell me when you last saw or heard a meaker?'

'Not for a while,' Louisa admitted.

'Mrs Witherall next door says she's overrun with them while we have none, proof of Kitty's prowess.'

'I'll suggest she gives her board and lodgings then – on a permanent basis.'

Grace's exclamation of protest sent the fluffy black cat leaping out of the basket onto the floor.

'How could you do that? I couldn't bear it.' Grace noticed the change in Louisa's expression. 'You are shamming me?'

'I am indeed. Although I was very annoyed when Isaiah pressed you into having her, she's turned out to be rather endearing.' Smiling, Louisa looked down to where Kitty was winding herself around her legs, then glanced back up. 'Hark. Do you hear that?'

Straining her ears, Grace listened for the faint medley of sound coming from the distance. Gradually it grew louder, and she began to distinguish the individual parts: the voice of the town crier; the steady beat of a drum; cheering and laughter; a piper's merry hornpipe; a troupe of fiddlers scraping their strings. The church bells pealed and the ships' bells clanged relentlessly from the roadstead.

'What is it? Has the world come to an end?' She pushed the front door open. Kitty dashed outside and shot back in again.

'Miss, miss, 'ave you 'eard the news?' One of a gaggle of shore boys who were half running, half walking along the alley stopped outside Compass Cottage. His face was as brown as a nut, his eyes alight with excitement.

'I can't say that I have, Cromwell,' Grace said, as Louisa leaned on her shoulder to listen to what he had to say.

'The Dooke of Wellin'ton and 'is men 'ave beaten Ol' Boney at Wa'erloo.'

'Is that the truth of it?' Grace touched her throat. She was seventeen – almost eighteen – and she couldn't recall a time when England hadn't been at war with France, when they hadn't lived in fear of Napoleon and his great army crossing the Channel and invading their shores. 'It isn't going to turn out the same as last time?' She had been bitterly disappointed to find out that the announcement of Napoleon's death which had been made back in February the previous year had been a hoax created to allow several so-called gentlemen to defraud the London Stock Market.

'Everybody's sayin' it's true and I think it 'as to be cos lightnin' don't strike twice. Major Percy of the fourteenth Light Dragoons carried the dispatches to Lord Liverpool and Prinny.' He was referring to the Prince Regent. 'Apparently, 'e was still wearin' 'is bloodstained clothes when 'e rode day and night from the battlefield to Ostend where 'e boarded the *Peruvian*. It weren't plain sailin' even then because there weren't no wind, so they 'ad to lower a gig and row the rest of the way.'

'What is the proof though?' Grace wanted to be sure.

'They 'ad two French Eagles in the boat with them, the standards what they captured in the fight.' Without waiting to see if he had managed to convince her, he punched the air and ran on.

'What do you think?' Grace said, turning to Louisa who was looking past her, watching an elderly couple struggling out of the cottage next door.

'I don't know. Mrs Witherall, have you heard that the war against the Frenchies is over?'

'We 'aven't 'eard nothing about it afore now.' Louisa's mother-in-law nodded towards her husband. 'Mr Witherall's been sufferin' from another nasty bout of gout and gravel which 'as kept us indoors.'

'Hush.' Mr Witherall frowned. His hair was silver, his eyes creased at the corners, and his complexion weathered by the elements. 'Nobody needs to know our business.'

Grace smiled to herself – everyone who lived on the spit knew about Mr Witherall's state of health. Seeing that Louisa would be distracted for a while, she took advantage and slipped away towards the beach. When she reached the street that ran along the top of the shore, she found herself swept into a milling throng of men, women and children, marvelling at the news they had wished for since Bonaparte had escaped from exile on Elba over one hundred days before.

'Let me 'elp you along, miss.' A bowlegged sailor, wearing a blue shirt, and wide trousers with stripes, who was swaggering along with his mate, offered her his arm.

'I can manage very well, thank you,' she said quickly.

'Excuse my friend for bein' so bold,' the sailor's mate said, doffing his tarpot hat.

'The excitement 'as gone to me 'ead.'

'The rum, yer mean. I think you've 'ad a drop too much.'

Amused, Grace squeezed her way through the crowds until she found her way blocked by a group of elbow-crookers who were standing outside the Rattling Cat, clashing their tankards together and spilling foaming ale as they toasted Wellington's victory. She recognised Lawless and Awful Doins, a pair of middle-aged smugglers who'd troubled her family in the past.

'Greetin's, Miss Lennicker,' Awful Doins said, grinning inanely and exposing a single grey tooth that didn't belong to him in the middle of his upper jaw.

'Let me pass,' she said sharply.

'I dunno about that.' Lawless who was dressed top to toe in black leaned in close, repulsing her with his foul breath. 'I think we should 'ave a chat about 'ow we can 'elp each other, you bein' party to certain information ...'

'If you think you can bribe me, you're wrong.' She glared at him. 'Step aside.'

'Oi, leave the young lady alone!' Her heart missed a beat as the landlord of the tavern and object of her affection, emerged from the open doorway. 'Do as I tell you, you pair o' lobcocks.' The men backed off as Isaiah walked across to her, his rough-coated black longdog at his heels. 'Pardon my language, Grace.' He stopped a few feet from her and grinned, revealing a fine set of teeth that were all his own. In his middle twenties, he was handsome in a rugged kind of way, his curly hair the colour of jet and his eyes deep brown. 'Aren't you goin' to thank me for rescuin' you?'

'I can stand up for myself.'

'I 'ave no doubt of that – you're very much like your sister.' He was referring to Louisa, not Winnie or her half-sister, Nancy, she thought, her brow tightening as she looked him up and down. 'What's wrong?'

'You look like a gentleman, not a tatterdemalion,' she said, recalling his usual state of undress, wearing torn clothing and no shoes.

'Only look like one? What a low opinion you 'ave of me.' He smoothed the lapels of his patterned waistcoat and tweaked his shirt's high-standing collar, leaving a smudge on the white linen.

'I didn't intend to cause offence. I'm sure you have some … gentlemanly qualities.'

'If you're goin' to dig yourself into an 'ole, make sure you dig it deep.' He chuckled. 'Just because I was born low don't mean I can't rise like cream to the top of the milk in society. I've 'ad a run of good luck recently, if you know what I mean, and I'm makin' the most of it. I'm 'avin' some building work done …' He nodded towards the tavern. 'The war's over for good – they won't let Old Boney come back a third time. Life's goin' to be better for all of us, you'll see.'

'How can you be certain?' she asked, unconvinced. 'When Bonaparte went into exile last year, the people who depended on the commerce of war began to struggle to make ends meet. It'll be worse now. With the soldiers gone and the barracks empty, who will buy the bootmakers' wares? Who will place orders at the boatyards? When the naval yard closes because there are no ships to provision, who will buy the market gardeners' fruit and veg?'

'Oh Grace, you're soundin' old beyond your years. You shouldn't listen to the doom-mongers and naysayers. New trades and businesses will rise from the ashes, ones we 'aven't thought of yet. People will come to Deal for commerce and seabathin' and I'm makin' sure I 'ave a piece of it. I'm aimin' to extend the kitchen and add several more lettin' rooms.' He changed the subject, apparently emboldened by the mood of the crowd. 'You're lookin' well.'

'Thank you.' It was merely an observation, not a compliment, she told herself as her cheeks grew hot.

'Come and join me. Bring your sisters and their menfolk. Let past arguments and strife be forgot,' he said earnestly.

'It's kind of you, but my sisters won't allow it. They don't approve of me talking to you.'

'I understand – there's bad blood between our families, and for good reason, but this is an inauspicious occasion—'

'I think you mean 'auspicious',' she cut in.

'Whatever it is, clever boots, it's a good time for makin' a fresh start. Bein' neighbours, livin' cheek by jowl, we should try bein' civil for a change.'

'Do I not speak civilly to you?' she said archly.

'Always,' he smiled. 'Although I do recall an occasion when you told me off – it was in no uncertain terms.'

It was strange how she could remember every word that had ever passed between her and Isaiah – at least, that was how she felt.

'You made a cruel joke, saying you would pelt Winnie when she was in …' She stopped abruptly, not wishing to be reminded of how her middle sister had ended up in the stocks after one of the Riding officers of the Revenue had arrested her for being in possession of a half anker of cognac. 'You upset Louisa when you gave me the kitten,' she said instead.

'Knowin' 'ow much you like animals, I thought it would make you 'appy.'

'It pleased me very much.'

'How is the dear little puss?'

'Kitty's an excellent mouser as you said she would be, and she's very affectionate.'

'I'm delighted to 'ear it.'

'I'd better run,' she said, taking her leave. 'Louisa will be wondering where I am.' She wished she hadn't said that – it made her sound dull when she wanted to appear as intriguing as he was dark and dangerous. 'I'm not under her thumb though. I offered to fetch a loaf of bread.'

'The last time I looked, the market was in that direction.' He pointed and quirked one eyebrow.

'I thought I'd go the long way.'

'Again? I saw you with your basket earlier.'

'It's a long story – I forgot to buy the bread the first time and Jason gets crabby when there's nothing to eat when he comes home.'

'Ah yes. Marlin's a ten shillin' man now.' Isaiah used Jason's nickname. 'Who'd 'ave thought it, eh? I can't believe 'e turned 'is coat like that.'

Grace wasn't sure why Jason and Louisa had given up smuggling French cognac and lace when they had made such a success of it. As a Deal boatman, the occupation that Jason had admitted to following was hovelling, which involved ferrying pilots and supplies such as anchors and cables back and forth to the ships in the Downs, and saving lives and property when a vessel was in trouble. For that purpose, he'd used his giant lugger, the *Whimbrel*, a boat built for speed and perfect for smuggling contraband.

However, the *Whimbrel* had been re-rigged as a cutter in the service of the King's Navy and renamed. Now Jason was a Revenue man, commander of the *Legacy*, prey turned predator.

'They say 'e made enow from the guinea boat to retire,' Isaiah commented.

'I don't think that was the reason.' It was true that her brother-in-law had made a small fortune from running gold across the Channel to fund Wellington's army – and possibly Bonaparte's too – in the past. The guinea runs were funded by wealthy investors and organised by an agent, a Mr Cork who had since suffered the ignominy of being convicted and imprisoned with his co-conspirators for the fraud that brought the false dawn of peace the previous spring. Grace's family were comfortably off and she didn't believe that Jason's decision had anything to do with money.

'Don't tell me 'e 'ad a sudden crisis of conscience.'

Grace noticed the spark of humour in Isaiah's eyes and the way he ran his hand through his dishevelled curls. His sideburns were long, and his chin was shadowed with stubble, and she was staring. Quickly, she glanced away, looking along the street where a band of musicians was marching towards them, escorted by a group of small children banging saucepans with spoons and blowing on whistles.

''E makes out that he's some kind of 'ero, but we all know 'e used to sail close to the wind. We were always runnin' up against each other, even when we were workin' on the same side: one gang against the other; your lot against the Rattlers.' A smile played on his lips. 'I'm what you might call a reformed character too, 'avin' decided to settle ashore. I've sold my share in the lugger …' she knew the one – the *Good Intent II* '–to a good friend o' mine to raise money for the improvements to the tavern. I'm 'er master no more.'

'I really should go,' she said even more reluctantly than before.

'You'll be back for the dancin' later? We'll be celebratin' on the beach till dawn.'

'Wild horses wouldn't keep me away – I love to dance. Now, I've wasted more than enough time talking to you – I have to run. I must find Louisa before she finds me.' Laughing and hitching up her skirts, Grace turned and hurried towards the corner where Beach Street met Cockle Swamp Alley. She hoped she hadn't offended him with her last remark. She hoped too that she hadn't attracted the attention of the gossips – they'd soon have her down as Isaiah's bit of muslin and then Louisa would find out, and she'd never hear the end of it.